HOW TO FIND LOVE WHEN YOU'RE WEIRD

A SWEET, GRUMPY/SUNSHINE ROM-COM

CAMILLA EVERGREEN

Reader Expectations

Heat Level: Fade-to-black, innuendos, oh boy the cursing (there are three fire fire hot hot curses, one donkey go neigh curse, and a couple extreme Norwegian curses in the epilogue), sensual description, mentions of sex
Notable Tropes: Guy falls first, grumpy/sunshine, neurodivergent leads, POTS rep, fake/practice dating, he so big; she so smol (not really, she's normal height), demi-sexual lead
Triggers: Alcohol, mentions of physical and emotional parental abuse, infantilism, depression, anxiety
Style: First person present, single POV
Stress Level: Low
Ending: HEA

Author's note:

I don't know Norwegian. I have not been to Norway. And I have never, not even once, been a viking.

Please understand that infantilism (in the sense of treating or perceiving someone as a child due to atypical behaviors) is a common issue between neurotypicals and atypicals. The situation that most strongly depicted this issue triggered me to tears, so. Yeah.

Copyright © 2023 by Camilla Evergreen

This book is licensed for your personal enjoyment only. This book is a work of fiction. No part of this publication may be reproduced, distributed, or transmitted in any form by any means, including photocopying, recording, or other electronic or mechanical methods, without the proper written permission of the publisher, except in the case of brief quotations embodied in critical reviews and certain other noncommercial uses permitted by copyright law.

If you are reading this book and did not purchase it from Amazon.com or receive a copy through Camilla Evergreen, Anne Stryker, or associates of Gossamer Wings & Ink Press, please report this to the author at annestrykerauthor@gmail.com.

Thank you for respecting the hard work that goes into publishing a book.

None of the characters in this book are actual people. Any resemblance to real individuals is coincidental. The mention of actual celebrities, songs, movies, or brands included in this book do not necessarily reflect the author's actual feelings or ideas about those individuals, creative works, or companies.

Edited by a Strange Little Squirrel
Cover Art by House of Orian Graphics

*For the atypicals and the unhinged.
Literally for anyone who humored letting me write a duck
POV into one of my books.*

❖

PROLOGUE

♥ Sometimes, love finds you.

I don't feel so good.

This was a terrible idea. And I knew it was before I agreed to it, but obviously my cognitive functions found themselves prematurely impaired. As in: I was not thinking clearly *before* the alcohol.

It'll be fun, they lied.

I really need to get better at picking up on lies.

I've never liked the ocean—that vast dark mass of water and grit—but here I sit (if my sprawl across this bar counter counts as sitting), afloat or adrift. My head swims, spinning. It's all so *wrong*. Yeah. That's the ultimate problem. I feel wrong, every inch of me. I'm not nauseous yet, but I know that's a side effect to expect. I hope my friends didn't lie when they said that part would happen tomorrow morning while I'm supposed to be safe at home.

I hope I can figure out how to get home.

This is awful.

I can't believe I did my research on alcohol, saw the warnings for myself, and *still* ended up agreeing to this.

No, wait. I can believe it. Because it happened. Solid facts—and especially ones I've experienced personally—are quite easy to *believe*. My mind is sloppy right now. If my mind were a kitchen, it would need to be cleaned.

A giggle starts in my chest at the image of a tiny kitchen inside my brain. Little cells rushing around, making thought dishes instead of food, talking about moths, screaming *order up* whenever any ideas are sent out.

Inexplicably, once my giggle mutates into a full laugh, tears slip down my cheeks. I sniffle, cave, and curl my arms around my head on the bar counter so they dry against my sleeve.

I didn't want this. Any of this. It's loud here. Crowded and empty at the same time now that my "friends" have left me. There's too much going on, and even though I'm securely by the wall, I can feel the movement of everyone packed into the booths and tables scattered across the midnight black tile. I like quiet, calm spaces in which I can control the sensory stimulation myself. I like familiar things.

Bar hopping for my birthday is all my least favorite things crammed into one.

I've come to this precipice of realization before—never half-laughing, half-sobbing in a bar though. It hurts each time I wake up with the irrefutable conclusion that, yet again, I've found myself surrounded by people who aren't actually my friends, who only want me around because I'm funny to laugh at, use, or trick. I had so hoped the people I thought I connected with in high school would be different than the ones I grew into because of who my mom and dad were friends with when I was born, than the ones I found in kindergarten, than the ones I found in middle school. Elementary was lonely. But I think I was happiest then.

Maybe it's time to stop trying, stop clinging, stop looking.

Friends are no longer required.

They only lead to disappointment.

Tears slip down my cheeks to rest in what I assume to be a tiny puddle on the bar counter. I'm glad this spot of the counter is clean. I'd be having a full meltdown right now if it were sticky.

I need to get home.

I'm not sure I can walk straight.

As long as the bartender isn't malicious, I'm probably safer here than I would be if I collapse on my way back to my apartment alone.

I should probably call my father to come pick me up.

The second my brain cells serve that winner of an idea a blast of icy shame pours across my limbs. Calling my father for help is the most logical thought I've had since I destroyed the efficiency of my frontal lobe, but waves of guilt refuse to let me act on it.

The process of calling my father is so simple—I learned a long time ago to break down every goal into manageable actions. It isn't *folding the laundry*. It's folding a pair of underwear. Easy. Simple. And now the fool that is the slab of meat in my skull has been convinced I must complete the entire task since I've already begun.

Calling my father means: I lift my head, or…turn it a bit. (Let's not get too crazy here.) I turn my head a bit, reach for my purse, and get out my phone. I unlock it. I tap the first contact in my address book. *Dad*. He will take things from there because I do not call people. If I've not texted, I am obviously in quite insidious peril.

He'll say, *Ellen? What's wrong?* I'll tell him I need a ride home from Temptations Lounge. It's that…*easy*. Except it isn't because nothing is ever that easy.

Historically, he'd be less disappointed in me than I am in myself. Historically, my parents' punishments for my misbehavior have paled in comparison to my own. I'm their baby, their only precious daughter.

I have the clear steps outlined in my brain. There would be little to no backlash. My father would get me home safe.

And yet, for some horrible reason, I can't begin.

Beginning is always the hardest step for anything. It's

what I tell aspiring authors whenever they contact me, wondering how to publish a book. *Just start writing.* I know it's hard. I know it's overwhelming. But every story begins with a line, which starts with a word, which is made up of letters.

Write that first letter.

The rest will come, and then however it does, your editor will (hopefully) be there to make sure it's good. To be honest, I don't normally work with people who don't know how to begin. Maybe I'm a hypocrite. Maybe I just know that if words aren't constantly and passionately spilling out of the people I work with, I'll get annoyed with them.

For my clients, at least, I make sure our energy matches.

This is not the case with my friends. And look at how that's turning out for me...

I wish there were a simple, statistical equation in which to calculate chance of survival at any given moment. If there were, I would probably not assume I am going to die in whatever spot I find my executive dysfunction dysfunctioning.

I can see the headlines now.

Ellen Little, last seen at Temptations Lounge, perished after having been abandoned by three "friends" on her twenty-first birthday. Witnesses claim she could have survived had she called her father, but her brain refused to allow such a thing to occur. As long as she could remember, her brain had been her greatest ally and strongest foe. The true enemies-to-lovers roller coaster none of us wish to stan is the struggle to love ourselves.

Pardon me if my own head has kept me at dagger point throughout my existence. It's not attractive when I can't get out of bed because my hair feels weird.

I really am going to die here.

"Hey," a deep, needlessly rough voice accompanies a heavy touch on my shoulder. The pressure is comforting, if unsettling. How big are this person's hands? And why are they touching me? I don't generally *do* touch, but the solidness of this isn't entirely terrible.

Either that or I'm simply too far gone to tense.

I mumble something as my internal narrative switches from *passed away due to inaction* into *murdered by someone with a really, really nice warm voice*. I shouldn't be thinking about his voice while I'm about to be murdered. It stands to reason such a thought is not conducive to survival.

"Are you supposed to be here?" the man asks.

Am I *supposed* to be here? Is anyone *supposed* to be anywhere? We are on a floating rock, charged with the ever difficult task of learning how to love one another after we forgot. We *are* supposed to be here, but not like *this*. Which is exactly my feelings concerning this moment. I murmur, "Yes. However, I would like to go home." My words are incorrect. They taste awful in my mouth, slopped together like pig food. The very cadence of them makes me cringe.

A gravelly sound that I think is a *hm* with such a low frequency only some animals can hear the full range of it flows over my body. The sound is as physical as touch, and it makes me shiver like I've done something illicit.

Oh wait. I have.

I'm never getting drunk again.

I'm never looking at alcohol again.

Alcohol is stupid. Well, no. It's an inanimate object. People who partake of alcohol are stupid. I am stupid.

"Can you stand?" the man with the wonderful voice asks.

"Inconclusive," I reply.

"Boss," someone, who I think is the bartender, addresses the man, "I carded her myself. She's just petite."

"She's just passed out," the *boss* growls, and I do mean *growls*. Yikes. I'm a stickler about getting the *growls* tag down to a minimum in my author's books. It's so overdone it's a cliché. Not only that, it's evolved into a joke. People don't growl and grumble and grunt around. Except, I guess, when they do.

My feelings concerning this new information are also inconclusive at this point in foggy-headed time.

"I've been keeping an eye on her," the bartender notes, lightly, and I recall that he was a young man maybe a few years older than me with a quiff of blond hair. I liked his hair. And his smile. He seemed nice and welcoming, and that made being here a little easier with everything else going on.

The man whose hand has yet to leave my shoulder sighs.

Blearily, I manage to lift my head and look at him.

Oh.

My.

My lips part as I look up, up, up. Forcing them closed, I swallow, shiver, stare. This *man* is a mountain, a wall, a giant. He's not *just* tall; he's massive. A white shirt stretches taut across his barrel chest, like his pectorals have it in a choke hold. If he flexes, it's going to shred just like in a cartoon. Tan tree-trunk arms *covered* in ink pour from the sleeves. Every bit of him is solid. He puts football players to shame. If he tackled *anyone*, they'd probably die.

My gaze finally reaches his face—or the severe mask covering his face, rather. He's horrifyingly handsome. Icy blue eyes so pale they seem otherworldly. Dark hair styled in a tapered fade. A caress of five o'clock shadow, even though it's well past five. Unmoved, he looks at me for the longest moment I have ever experienced.

"You're huge," I tell him.

A thick black brow jumps. "I'm aware," he rumbles.

"You're terrifying," I say, because even on a non-alcoholically-influenced day, I find myself without the barest speech filter. I think it; I say it. Anything less is dishonest, right? It's difficult to keep the things I shouldn't say inside my head because it's difficult to decide what those things are sometimes.

The boss draws his hand away from me, and I feel the loss of its weight more than I felt its presence. "I'm not so bad."

This is one of those moments when I'm not supposed to believe him, isn't it? I don't know why I want to.

Perhaps…it can be deduced…I am violently attracted to this man. That would be a first.

"Do you have a way to get home safely?" he asks, crouching into a rock in front of my bar stool. He's so big his head still nearly reaches my chest while my feet can't reach the floor.

Mr. Bartender wasn't wrong when he called me *petite*, but I'd not quite thought myself short until this moment. I am 5'6". This is an acceptable height. "How tall are you?" I ask.

"Six, seven."

I gasp and point at my chest. "Five, six—" I turn my finger to him. "—seven." Laughing, I smile.

He blinks, slowly, like a cat.

My smile vanishes, and I step off the stool. "Mouse. I need to get home. Mouse is probably worried." Unsteadily, I collide with the big rock of a man, and he braces his gigantic hands nearly *all* the way around my slender waist.

"Easy," he murmurs, and I realize there's a touch of something else off in his voice. It's faint, but he has an

English accent. At least here, in the sweet tea, biscuits and gravy south of northwest Georgia, it stands out beneath all the grit in his tone. I wonder when he moved south since his northern roots are clinging.

"I bet you call roundabouts rotaries."

His heavy brow furrows. "Perhaps I do."

I giggle.

He swallows, and his Adam's apple bobs, which makes me focus on his throat. His hands fit fully around my waist, but I don't know if mine would manage to circle his neck. Not that proper ladies think about wrapping their hands around people's necks.

Mom would be so disappointed. Or encouraging. I'm unsure.

"Does that amuse you?" he asks, seemingly unamused himself.

I open my mouth to reply, or ask if I can measure his neck with my hands, but what comes out is a muted, "I want to go home," and I'm not laughing or smiling anymore. Alcohol is dumb.

He drags one hand off my waist and catches a tear as he skates his index finger up my cheek. "I know, petal. Do you have a safe way home?"

Petal. That's so adorable. "I've never heard that before," I murmur.

"I've still not heard the answer to my question."

I cower. "I'm sorry. I didn't mean to upset you."

"I'm not upset." He wipes my other cheek. "I need to know if someone is coming to pick you up or if I need to call you a cab."

I don't have an answer. I know the right answer, but I can't figure out how to make it happen.

I look elsewhere, and the hum of the bustling space floods my head. It's a lot. A Lot. Squeezing my eyes shut, I clamp my hands to my ears. More tears splash down my cheeks. My clothes are too tight. Too warm. I hate this. I need to call my father. I need to tell this man that I need to call my father. Telling him will help me *do it*. But—

I turn weightless, and my heart leaps out of my chest. Eyes snapping open, I move my hands away from my ears and stare at the big man, who is now holding me.

"Whoa there, boss—" the bartender begins, but the boss grunts, "Shut up," as he turns. He weaves past full tables and takes me outside, into the Westville, Georgia spring night. The noise dulls once the door has closed behind us, and he sets me down on the sidewalk.

"Better?" he asks.

Absently, I nod, and I'm staring at him again. Do I weigh nothing to him? How much can he lift? Can he lift a car? I bet he can lift a car.

Realization hits me several moments after I've begun picturing him holding a Smart Car above his head, and I look down. I'm standing. Effectively. My feet are on the ground, and I can probably walk. Perfect! I don't live far. I'll walk home. I point down the sidewalk toward where I know the street veers out of downtown and into the gated community with my apartment. "Thank you. I can go home now."

His arms fold, and they really are dripping with ink. "Are you sure?"

I touch one painted forearm, and I might lean into him a bit more than I intend, but he's basically a building, so I don't think it matters. "I don't live far. Peach Plaza. Do you have any moths in here?"

"Any moths?" he asks, and his arms loosen slightly.

His tattoos are coils of snakes, but their bodies brim with scenery and pictures. Roses. Fire. Mountains. Nightscapes and galaxies. I trace one snake head to his wrist. Its open mouth and fangs seem fit to sink into the veins of his radial artery.

It takes me a long moment to realize the only reason I'm able to examine this part of him is because he's fully uncoiled his arms and is showing me.

That's kind of him.

Dragging my gaze up, I lock onto his very clear blue eyes. They're calmer than most eyes—a still lake rather than a raging sea. "I like moths. Have you ever held one before?"

"I've killed a couple."

I gasp.

His harsh expression softens. "Don't they eat clothes?"

"They do *not* eat clothes. Most moths don't even have mouths. Their entire purpose is to locate a mate. Only clothes moths, most commonly *Tineola bisselliella* in this area, cause any threat to fabric, and even then it isn't *the moths* but the larvae that do the damage. Refer back to: most moths don't eat." I gasp again and grip his arm as I stand on my tiptoes. "But you know what kind of moths *do* eat? Vampire moths!"

His brows jump, like I've shocked him, and there's something uniquely thrilling about having shocked a man his size.

I beam, positively glowing. "Vampire moths, or *Calyptra thalictri*, can feed on blood—even human blood. Now I know what you're thinking, and don't worry, they're only native in parts of Asia and Europe where they prefer fruit and animals to humans."

He stares at me, and it occurs to me that maybe I didn't know what he was thinking at all. Generally, when someone is told that a vampire *anything*—beyond that of the usual mosquitoes, ticks, and so forth—exists, irrational fear that it is coming for them occurs. In my experience, anyway.

Potentially, this giant man has no reason to fear something that only has an average two-inch wingspan.

I start to take a slight step back and give him his space in case I'm too close, but he follows, linking one giant hand behind my back and guiding me forward.

His low voice rumbles. "Are you a moth scientist?"

Due to his prompting, I start walking, and he falls into pace beside me, three of my steps equaling one of his. I let the cool, early spring air fill my lungs as I say, "No. I'm an editor."

"An editor?"

"Freelance, for independent authors."

He whistles. "And the knowing scientific names of moths thing is because…?"

A giggle bubbles up, and before I know it, I'm tucked against his side for support. So this is what *tipsy* feels like. I don't like it, but it is a bit better than it was ten minutes ago. At the very least, I don't think I'm going to die on a bar stool now. "I love moths, but I also love grammar. Words. Sentence flow. I'm the pickiest reader in the world, and so many tiny things just *bug* me, so when I stumbled into the knowledge there was a career to *fix* all the bad things while getting paid to read books, I went for it."

"You're past college age?" he asks, turning his entire body to let another couple pass us. Pressed to the side of a consignment store window, he catches my eye.

I smile up at him before we continue. "I'm twenty-one. It's my birthday." I don't know what *college* has to do with anything.

"Happy birthday."

I attempt a tiny curtsy, but he has to catch me before I plant face-first into the final block of downtown. For some reason, this makes me laugh. I could have gotten really hurt, but here I am, laughing. "Thank you. Thank you."

The tiniest sliver of a smile softens his full lips. "So. You're a moth enthusiast editor. And your birthday is March twenty-one."

"Yes. I like that quite a lot, don't you? March twenty-one. Three, two, one. Sometimes, I think the universe is much too kind with me." And other times, it isn't. But those are the kinds of depressing words we keep inside our heads so as to not bring others down.

"I take it you like numbers as well?" he asks.

I hum, letting my gaze trail up to the sky. Stars spill like glitter across the black expanse. "I like when numbers serve me. They're interesting, but their patterns don't quite fascinate me in the same way the complications of language do." I feel like starlight. Light and flying. "For instance, do you know why I said *do* instead of *does* after *language*?"

He puffs a breath, and I *think* maybe the sound was his laugh. "Let's assume I don't, petal."

"Subject-verb agreement. It's tricky for a lot of people in more complex sentences with phrases and clauses. *Complications* is the plural noun that connects to the verb *do*, not *language*. Language is just the object in a prepositional phrase. It's its own entity, unrelated to the rest of the line and unconnected to a verb since it modifies the noun *complications*. Removing it entirely doesn't change the fact you have a complete sentence."

"Though it would remove some clarity of context."

I bounce, tugging his shirt as he stops me before a crosswalk and presses the button to change the light. Cars whip by, and I'm glad he's still here because I don't know if I would have remembered how to cross this street safely on my own. "That's just the thing that makes it so *magical*! Words are everything we have. They let us communicate and relay ideas, form pictures, delineate emotion! Just two words or the very placement of a singular one changes the meaning and connotation of an entire line. They're wild, untamed beings that we harness—often poorly—in order to connect with those around us. Isn't that incredible?"

More breath puffs out of him. "You certainly make it seem incredible." He hunkers slightly down as the light turns yellow. "To be quite honest, I almost failed English three of my four high school years. I can't tell you the difference between a gerund and a gerbil."

My mouth falls open as he guides me across the street. Blinking rapidly, I stammer, "W-well, a gerbil is a rodent, and a gerund is a verbal." I don't know how I feel about the way *gerbil* and *verbal* rhyme.

"And a verbal is?" he queries.

"A form of a verb used as another part of speech."

Now I'm almost certain the corner of his mouth is tipping up. "You just have the definitions of grammatical terms at the ready?"

I don't think he's making fun of me, but then my record of awareness concerning when people are making fun of me is notoriously unreliable. Hesitant, I answer honestly, "Yes?"

"It's cute."

Something flutters in my chest, but I've no idea why. Tamping down the sensation—which I will determine as positive or negative at a later point in time—I ask, "Cute *endearing*, or cute *demeaning*?"

"Endearing."

Relief swarms cold into my cheeks before some measure of heat overwhelms it. I scrub fruitlessly at my face with my chilled fingers as we near the entrance to Peach Plaza. "Forgive me if this is a strange thing to ask. I'm not incredible at reading social interactions. Are…you flirting with me, or are you just being friendly?"

"It wouldn't exactly be appropriate for me to flirt with you while you're completely drunk and I'm just trying to get you home from my bar."

Right. Yes. Of course. That makes sense.

He clears his throat. "That said…it appears I am. Unintentionally."

Unintentionally flirting? That's a thing? I thought flirting ceased to be flirting unless it was intentional—see "women who are accused of leading men on when they are just being friendly" for reference. I'm confused. "You are or aren't?"

"Are. Against wiser judgment."

I stare up at the bottom of his chin. This is what I mean when I say people often poorly harness words in order to relay their feelings. He *is* flirting with me, but he doesn't want to be because it's not wise? He is in control of whether or not he does. If he believes it unwise—for any number of reasons that may trace back to the fact I have been rambling at him for the past ten minutes about niche topics nobody likes—he is not forced to flirt.

He tips his chin, glancing at me with those clear blue eyes. "Sorry," he says, putting some distance between us so I'm not nearly as tucked against his warm side. "I'm not trying to make you uncomfortable. I promise I'm only trying to get you home safely. Then you'll never have to see me again, unless you stop by the bar and ask for me."

I don't think I ever want to go to a bar again. I have no idea how my "friends" are managing to go to several tonight. It's awful. All I really wanted for my birthday was pudding. Because I don't know how to navigate the present conversation, I say, "Do you know what I wanted for my birthday?"

His gaze trails skyward. "A live vampire moth in which

to sic on your enemies?"

An excited bubble that shoves the previous confusion away ignites in my chest. He was listening to me talk about moths! He's listening to me! "That would be *incredible*. If underwhelming. Did I mention they're only a few inches long?"

"I might have missed that detail. An army of them, then. However many required to subdue a man."

I laugh some more and answer my question, "Pudding."

His eyes widen. "Are you calling me *pudding*?"

My already warm face burns a little hotter as I shake my head. "No. No, that's what I wanted. Pudding. Maybe five different kinds arranged in glass flutes that I can eat out of with a long silver spoon." We stop in front of the apartment complex gate, and I take a moment to remember my pin as I continue, almost wistfully. "Doesn't that sound terribly elegant?"

The gate eases open, and he guides me in, murmuring, "Terribly simple. How did you end up at Temptations instead?"

"My friends said it would be fun. Also, I didn't ask for the pudding. It's my secretest desire." *Secretest* isn't a word. The superlative is "most secret." How absolutely troubling. The alcohol has eroded my brain cells down to such a dreadful point.

His free fist closes, knuckles cracking. "You came with friends, and they left you there? You could have…" His jaw locks, and he gives his head a slight shake. Attention fixed dead ahead, he glares murder at the white siding of an apartment building.

"They aren't my friends anymore."

He grumbles, "Good."

I think I've upset him, which is hardly kind considering he walked me all the way home. "That's me." I point at my building, the quaint "H" settled snugly in the back of the development with pale purple siding that complements the pink and white azalea bushes. All over the grounds, early-to-late-flowering bushes keep a rotation of blooms from spring through fall.

I love the atmosphere here because it reminds me of home and my future cottage. I spent most of my teen years surrounding the cottage I'll inherit with a butterfly garden and creating a moth forest around it with fairy lights.

I miss my cottage.

Maybe I'll ask to go back once I'm done paying for this screw up.

The boss helps me up the steps and to my front door. My cat, Mouse, is close now. I bet he's lonely. No part of tonight was a good idea. I just wanted to have a nice birthday. That's it. One nice birthday.

"Thank you for bringing me home," I say as I pull away from him and stabilize myself at my front door. He's just about as large as my door, and I wonder if he'd have to turn sideways and duck to fit inside.

He hooks his thumbs in his pockets. "It's no problem. Take care you don't get sloshed again."

I laugh. "I don't plan to ever drink again, much less in this capacity, and I'm quite faithful to my plans."

Wiping a hand down his face, he murmurs, "You might want to drink some water and eat some bread before you go to sleep. It can help with a hangover."

"I do like bread."

The corner of his mouth tips, ever so slightly. "Yeah?"

"Except sour dough. Because it's gross."

"It does have an acquired flavor."

"The flavor is *sadness*."

He puffs, eyes warm. "If you say so."

"You like the stuff, don't you?"

His gaze trails off me. "Perhaps."

I fold my arms. "Even the smell is bad."

"I work around alcohol. Smells have long-since stopped bothering me."

My stomach turns over at the memory of forcing myself through every swallow. From this day on, I'm eschewing peer pressure. Nothing good comes of it. A sickening shudder trails up my spine.

He clears his throat, rubs his neck. "Well…have a good night."

"Yes, you too."

Turning, he marches away, and I reach into my purse to get my keys. The moment after I've unlocked the door, pounding footsteps thunder back up the wooden steps. "Sorry," he states once I've looked at him. "What's your name?"

I blink. "Ellen Little."

His mouth forms *Ellen* soundlessly, before a tiny smile rests across his lips. "Goodnight, Ellen."

My breath catches, and I want to ask for his name. I want to tell him he's beautiful and kind and I've never felt attracted to anyone like I think I might be attracted to him. I wonder if he can make sense of the way I'm feeling better than I can. I wonder if I'd just talk about more moths instead of wrapping my head around more important words…

No matter how badly conversation tightens my chest or how badly I'm dreading his absence, all I say is, "Goodnight."

CHAPTER 1

♥ In order to find love, we must all start looking.

(Almost) five years later

Speed dating. Statistically more effective than online dating with less creeps. Socially...more overwhelming. It's supposed to move fast, and I know that, but isn't it moving a little *too* fast? I don't know. Feels kind of like I have a fantasy audiobook on times three speed during the world building.

The pace of this event might be giving me hives. Or maybe the snack I ordered has MSG, which is causing a POTS flare up? Discreetly, while the man seated across from me at the chair-end of this half-booth, half-seat table talks about something I've forgotten to keep listening to, I settle my thumb against my wrist.

My heart's hammering.

But I *am* understandably anxious.

I can't stand playing the *which complication about me is causing my symptoms today?* game.

Ridiculous.

Meeting new people—even in a planned and quiet cafe setting like this—is exhausting on a good day. Today is a good day. I am actively following my *How to Find Love When You're Weird* book's suggestions on...how to find love when you're weird. Going to speed dating events was one of the most effective methods in order for a noob at love like me to begin figuring things out. I am, at the very least, discovering what traits interest me in a potential partner.

That is more than I have done in my twenty-five years of existence. Appearance aside, this man just reached for my potato chips—without asking—despite the fact they are neatly in a basket on my side of the table. Worse, he's still talking. He didn't take a breath as he popped the chip in his mouth.

I do not like people who chew with their mouths open, talk while they eat, or don't show any interest in what I might have to say. I know I can talk a lot, and I am trying to listen to other people more, but—

The bell rings, and I flinch, abhorring the sound. They just had to decide that the rotation noise would be grating. It couldn't be a muted gong. It had to be a piercing, clanging bell.

My partner, nicknamed *Flash* as seen on his name tag, stands, extends a hand and says, "Charmed," like he thinks he's smooth.

I am much too late to the understanding I'm supposed to shake his hand, and he scowls briefly at me before moving to the next table. Wincing, I shake off the interaction, jot down his nickname and a few of the reasons I'm not interested in my notebook, then look up to meet my next "date."

Tall. Receding hairline. Mustache. Nickname: Prof.

I glance over the list of potential questions we can ask and settle on, "What made you choose your nickname?"

Smiling, Prof leans an arm against the table, uncomfortably closing the distance between us. "I'm a professor."

A professor? I brighten some, shooing my pessimism. "What subject do you teach?" English? Please say English.

"Biology," he notes, and his gaze crawls down from my

face to my body in a way that makes me suspect his claiming to be a *professor* at all is part of a bit. Lifting his chin, he refers to my name tag, "Why 'Mouse'? Is it a testament to a shy character?"

I feel icky now. With intentional deadpan, I state, "No. It's the name of my cat. And he's particularly good at fending off vermin."

Prof's throat bobs before he glances elsewhere, flattens his mustache between two fingers, and grabs a chip without asking. At least he's chewing with his mouth closed?

Well, no, maybe this conversation is just completely over.

Lowering my attention to the list of questions and my notes, I catch up on details I missed writing down as I wait for the next round. All the women at the other tables are laughing and smiling and talking in their pretty dresses. I didn't feel comfortable wearing a nice dress to meet a bunch of strangers. I don't want my potential partner to only like me because I look pretty. Therefore, I'm in a t-shirt with a beige sweater zipped all the way up over it.

It's hot in here.

When the horrid bell rings again, I slip out of my sweater and reveal my shirt, which proudly relays my current feelings with an $E=MC^{scared}$ plastered across my chest. Instant regret hits me when "Pirate" slides into the chair in front of me and says, "Getting comfortable for me, sweetheart?"

"Our relationship has not evolved into endearments," I state, and…the heartbeat of the conversation takes its last thu-thump. Great. I've murdered another one. That's *five* people. Five. This isn't supposed to be frustrating. It's supposed to be fun.

Meeting new people has never been fun for me, though.

I only have fifteen more chances. I'm a fourth of the

way through. I am not here to waste time I could be reading or working on my favorite clients' latest books.

If this *mess* keeps me from editing a Blaire Featherstone or Lord Prince novel, *it is not worth it*. I have to figure out how to make it worth my while, and the only way I might be able to do that is if I start taking more initiative.

I glance around at the other women, and, psh, please… I've been mirroring behaviors all my life. This is simple. Just be myself intellectually while presenting more welcoming body language, right? I've got this.

My next partner enters the ring, and I smile, drawing my long red hair over my ear like a girl on the other side of the room does.

My new partner smiles back, adjusting dark-rimmed glasses. He's the first person so far who appears conventionally attractive, so that's something.

Don't mess this up, Ellen.

"Do you like moths?" I ask as my smiling brain short-circuits and forgets to check my *appropriate questions* list.

His smile tips toward surprise, then he sincerely contemplates my question. "Aren't moths pests?"

I spend the next four minutes explaining why they are not. When the bell jars me awake, I realize what I've done, and the man offers me a sheepish smile before he rotates.

Crap.

Swallowing hard, I mark down his nickname with a circle around it. Maybe I'll get a chance to apologize before we choose who we'd like to see again and I can attempt to remedy things on a real date.

I must be myself, or this whole process is worthless, but I also can't hog all the time. My questions should focus on points I find important, but not on my special interests lest I fall down the moth hole.

"Fox" sits down, and I maintain my bright exterior in an effort to at least do that part right. I ask, "Do you believe in dating for fun or dating for marriage?"

Fox's smile crashes and burns.

Next.

"What portion of household chores do you believe falls on the woman?" is my next important question.

What's-his-name quirks a brow, folds his arms, and leans back. "All of them. If I'm going to be working, my wife's going to be cooking."

Thu-thump. Beeeeep. But a good *thu-thump beeep*. Now I'm not wasting my time on this degenerate who probably makes two percent what I do. If that.

Next.

"How many children do you want?"

Next. Okay. That one's on me. I should not allude to such severe intimacy so early in a relationship. I know better.

"Do you like cats?"

Next. Who doesn't like cats?

"What's more important—emotion or function?"

Next. I didn't think that was a hard question, but he just sat there with his face screwed up, thinking about it the whole time.

"Do random facts fascinate you, and how often would you be willing to be informed of them throughout the day?"

Next. I don't think I can consider someone whose nose scrunches up at the idea of knowledge and suggests *a couple times a day, I guess* is an acceptable answer. I am obsessive. It is a personality trait intrinsic of my being. I want a partner capable of matching my energy. Anything less is useless.

By the time my smile feels plastic, I have exhausted my ideas on opening questions, and I haven't connected with anyone. The bell grates in my ears as I peer at the women lined up after me, circling the lobby of this cafe. Their new partners have barely sat down before some of them are holding out their hands and laughing their greetings. Am I missing a greeting? Am I not just supposed to start with a question?

That wasn't provided information.

This is discouraging.

Discouraging was the last thing I wanted this to be.

I need to find a partner sooner rather than later now that I'm running out of time. Why did I only start looking for a partner so close to the deadline Dad gave me last year? Executive dysfunction will be the death of me if procrastination doesn't get me first.

My new partner clears his throat, and I realize I've been completely ignoring him while attempting to dissect a clear pattern from the successful people ahead of me. Jerking my attention forward, I am met with chest.

Broad, broad chest. Eyes wide, I lift my gaze up the sheer expanse of this…behemoth, and my stomach knits into a terrified little ball.

He. Is. *Huge*.

My lips part, close, part again, and I have no idea what to say. I am looking for a lifelong partner, a husband. I know it's not the most important aspect of, well, anything, but physical intimacy is a part of the whole *romantic partnership* thing. So, maybe just maybe, whoever I end up with shouldn't have hands the size of my whole entire skull?

"Hi," he says, and a lump of fear tucks itself into my chest.

Like a little mouse, I squeak, "Hello." I glance at his name tag, and the rectangle of white on his black overcoat looks like a white-out strip on him. "Boss?"

His brows lift, and he throws a look down at his chest. "Ah. Yeah." He tugs on the lapel of his coat. It's a nice coat. A long coat. I'm fond of the aesthetic such a coat provides. If only it were on someone a little less...massive? "It's what my friends call me."

I know my heart rate is heading into troubling zones *now*, with or without the triggering assistance of POTS. "Are you a part of a mafia?" I ask.

His brows knit, a funny twinge taking over the icy blue of his eyes. Humor licks through his tone. "Um. No. Regrettably. That would be cool." He cocks his head slightly. "You...don't remember me at all, do you?"

Am I supposed to? My memory is either pretty good or pretty crap. Watch me tell you the scientific names of any moth you reference but also not, um, yours. I press my lips together and scan him. Big man. Big, *big* man. I don't think it would be possible to forget him. Maybe he's mistaking me for someone else. "I'm sorry."

A rumbling sound pours out of him, and since I know I am a highly critical person, I force myself to pick up on positives. Positive: this man's voice is a low caress of nice, good things. I think I could listen to the maple-warm sound tumble from his pursed lips forever.

He lifts a shoulder, which from my perspective looks like an absolute workout. "It's okay. You were absolutely pissed."

"I was...upset?"

"Drunk."

"Oh." I cross my ankles beneath the table, fidgeting. I've only ever been drunk once. It's not a nice memory. It's not a memory at all. But I guess this man existed inside it. "I—"

The bell jars, and I jolt, clenching my fists. Great. The one conversation that hasn't ended in flames, and—

"*Go around me*," Boss growls—actually growls—at the next man. Rolling his icy gaze back to me, he clamps his giant hands against the table and murmurs, "You were saying, petal?"

I was... Oh, right. I remember, but, man, *petal*. I love that. If only he weighed a hundred...*two* hundred pounds less. "I remember so little of the one time I got drunk that I made an appointment with my doctor to see whether or not I'd been drugged and raped."

Boss's eyes widen, and I bite my tongue, hearing what I've just said a moment too late.

People do not usually like topics of this nature. Also, what part of implying I determined whether or not my hymen was still intact qualifies as an acceptable not-even-first-date topic? Or, worse, what if he thinks I do actually remember him and am implying I thought he... Heat flares to my cheeks, and I rake my fingers into my hair, dropping my gaze off him. "S-sorry. I didn't mean... I..."

"*Am not incredible at reading social interactions.*" Everything about his expression softens, warms. He's beautiful, in a severe, "please don't touch me" way. "You told me."

Goodness. I cringe to know what all I told him. I can talk a lot when I'm sober and have some grip on what is and isn't okay to say thanks to a lifetime of learning all those details. Who knows what I went off about when I was drunk?

Well, probably moths. That's a safe bet, anyway.

Have you *seen* a giant silk moth up close? Have you *held* one? They are superior butterflies. In fact, butterflies are merely discount moths. My spirit animal is a moth, even though moths are a paraphyletic group of insects, not animals. And...now I'm ranting about moths in my own head. "I apologize for my forgotten behavior."

Boss shakes his head, clearing his throat again. "No, you behaved fine. Promise."

I want to believe him, but it's been a long day, and I'm overly anxious to a point it feels like I'm experiencing a POTS flare. Once, I trusted everything, so now I've learned to trust nothing. "Really. I'm sorry. I'm excitable at times, and I can only imagine what alcohol did to my nature. I haven't touched a drop since."

"That would explain why I haven't seen you around. Ah." He runs his fingers over the soft dark top of his hair. "I own the bar you visited. Temptations Lounge."

Absently, I nod. I still know of the place even if I don't remember a thing about what happened inside it. What a pity. He owns a bar. An alcohol palace. The bane of my existence for one night—and one garbage-awful morning—nearly five years ago. I don't think anything is more frightening than the idea of a man his size under the influence of alcohol. At the very least, all the other men I've seen tonight don't exactly seem capable of overpowering me.

I'm not weak, and I exercise when I remember in order to help manage my POTS, but I don't know if even the most trained martial artists could angle this man's weight against him. There is a reason wrestling occurs in weight classes.

"I'm sorry," he says without warning. "Am I making you uncomfortable?"

Quickly, I shake my head, because I don't think it's *him*, exactly? "You're just…so big."

He covers his face with one hand and deflates slightly. "Well. Yes. You mentioned that the first time. I'm 6'7"."

A tiny gasp escapes me. "I'm 5'6"."

Warmth sparkles in those icy blue eyes of his as he peers over the top of his fingers at me. "Five, six, seven."

I laugh. "*Exactly.*"

The bell screeches, stealing my joy again, but this time the people in charge are addressing the room.

Boss turns to face them, and it's truly daunting how dramatically he dwarfs the chair he's sitting in. It's toy furniture to him. I'm practically a doll by comparison.

As the coordinators direct everyone to where they will be organizing the conclusion of this event, I drop my attention to the eighteen names in my notes, not including Boss yet. No one really stood out in a positive way, but at least only a couple stood out in a garishly negative way? Let's look past hating cats and having slow answers... Maybe on an actual date, I can apologize for the awkwardness of this afternoon? I'll take a chance on anyone who isn't dangerous or stupid, and maybe they'll take a chance on me, too.

I am known to turn up my nose at a book after the first line if the flow isn't right. Passing fast judgment doesn't always work for people.

Okay. I have my list. I'm not being picky. This is a good enough start, and I can turn things around with more time to figure these people out.

Boss is still seated in front of me by the time I look up, and I startle. Because he's startling in every situation.

Eyeing me, he fixes the cuffs of his coat and finally rises from the chair. Wow. So that's what six seven looks like.

Scary.

Completely and utterly scary.

I slip out of my booth seat, abandoning my contaminated chips and watching him like he's about to pounce.

His gaze drops, sizing me up, but remarkably he only says, "I like your shirt."

"Thank you."

Nodding once, he releases me from the iron grip of his gaze, filtering into the group heading toward the event coordinators. Or, actually, he's more or less carving his way to the front. People part for him like they know obstructing his path would be to forfeit their lives.

I am not nearly so intimidating, so by the time I've reached the table in order to turn in my names, "Boss" is already gone.

Also, absolutely no one wanted "Mouse." Which is, you know…sad.

CHAPTER 2

♥ If at first you don't succeed, try try again.

It is unrealistic to assume that there is no one else like you in the world. Worse, such an assumption bridges on egotistical. However unique we are at our core, it stands to reason that there are others who share our interests, our ideas, our morals. While no one else will ever match exactly, with billions on this planet it is inevitable someone out there is *like* us.

A simile of us. An echo of whatever we are. Comparable. Akin.

My attention skims Melanie Richards' words, over and over. Even though I've read them a hundred times before, they are comforting after the disaster that was my first attempt at speed dating.

And then my second attempt…

And, most recently as of this afternoon…um…well… my fifth.

Discouraged due to the previous failures, I approached my fifth try with the intention of being myself but accepting everyone. Basically, I ran a science experiment, and the result is this: it's me. Hi. I'm the problem.

Even when I accept everyone, no one wants me. *Or* no one I've met *so far* wants me.

Chin up, Ellen.

Mouse purrs, curled in my lap. As a little pink hairless cat in a bunny onesie, he is the most precious thing on this planet, and if the crippling loneliness in my chest weren't

29

an ever-present feeling, if my parents hadn't put a "requirement" into my happily ever after, I'd be ready to settle down for a life with just us.

One weird human and one weird cat. Not that Mouse is weird, per se. He's just hairless. The concept isn't so odd that people don't understand he exists. But he does look like a newborn mouse who was shot with a growth ray, and that disturbs almost everyone who has ever met him.

Sighing, I flop *How to Find Love When You're Weird* closed and cuddle my baby. "You're my pinkie mouse, aren't you? Good boy. We don't *need* anyone else, right? I have you, and wonderful parents, and my amazing authors. Someone for cuddles, support, and appreciation."

Mouse coos, purring and snuggling.

Leaning back in my office chair, I wish it were actually true. Unfortunately, if I want to inherit my cottage, I need to have a serious partner by my twenty-sixth birthday. It's the small print my father added after seeing how I holed myself up here. Alone. Safe.

I look at my bookshelves stacked mostly with signed work from my authors. I've edited nearly everything in view. I have purpose and fulfillment. I'm independent. Stable. Secure. Each day is exactly like the last. My schedule is predictable and reliable. It's the perfect kind of life for me.

Even if it's lonely.

Even if, on an emotional level, I *do* want more.

I'm starting to hate the strings my father attached to the situation. Or maybe I'm starting to hate the parts of myself no one ever seems to want.

I know falling in love is a big change, and I haven't changed a thing about how I exist since I moved out of my parent's house so I could get Mouse. Or, rather, keep him. Let's just say I *got* him as an itty-bitty kitten because my father is allergic to cats. The parameters concerning "no cats" were unclear. I eliminated the reason I received every time I mentioned wanting a cat, but apparently my father's allergy was not the only issue behind my parents' house not being a fit location for a cat.

My love for the tiny creature overcame my irrational fear of turning everything in my life over. I owed it to Mouse to give him a good home. I committed to his existence when I got him. I don't make commitments lightly.

And maybe I felt a little guilty about my mistake.

I could have avoided this entire mess if I'd just moved out of my parents' manor and into my cottage a little further down the property back then. But, back then, the sensation I'd done something very wrong overwhelmed me, and I had to atone.

Is it really so much to ask for a *fragment* of the whirlwind romances I edit? And would it at all be possible to find it *before* my twenty-sixth birthday next month, when my father expects me to be seriously courting a man in order for me to inherit my portion of the Little estate?

My cottage in the woods tucked in the middle of my parents' several-hundred acre property has been my dream home forever because for as long as I can remember, Mom told me it was mine. It's the place I *should* be living right now, the place I can't live until I have met the terms.

The stupid tropey terms.

It's not that my father doesn't believe I can handle myself or he thinks I need a man in my life. He just knows me well enough to know that I'm sitting here in my little apartment all by myself because I'm bad at relationships and will very easily talk myself out of the effort.

I cut people off like it's an extreme sport.

And when I was twenty-one, I cut out the last of my

"real life" friends, leaving no one but my clients behind.

I am lonely.

I am doomed to stay lonely without a push.

A shame my executive dysfunction has made me nudge the deadline down to the final two months.

A shame I don't think anyone other than Dad and Mom *want* to love me.

Some studies show that humans can pick up on oddities in one another within thirty seconds of meeting them. These same studies also imply a strong connection between those oddities and disliking a person. People seek familiar things. It's why mirroring is a good tactic for getting a job. Subconsciously, someone will notice their own body language in you and like you better if you echo their performance.

People like people like them.

Problem with that is I've never found a person *like me*.

And, additionally, mirroring someone effectively requires a better perception than I've managed to acquire.

Huffing, I roll myself up to my computer and do a search for yet another speed dating event. "It's better than online dating," I mutter at myself. "Statistically, anyway. I'm not looking for catfish. I want to find a forever person to spend my life with."

Someone will like me for who I am, oddities and all.

Statistics says so.

❖

Statistics is a filthy liar.

Clearly, there was an outlier. Some goddess of a weird person successfully scooped up a thousand people, and all the normal weirdos like me were not even considered during the tests.

My soul has been sucked from my body. I am sad, dejected, $E=MC^{depressed}$.

Maybe I *should* make an online dating profile and put together a Leopard form in order to thin out my options. Not that my "friendship form" in high school went particularly well... Still I do already have my "romance form" drafted. I should edit it. Put it on a dating profile. Swipe right on *everyone*. Make whoever swipes right on me fill out my form.

Maybe my ideal person isn't the "type" to go to a social function. That seems entirely logical. I'm not exactly the "type" to enjoy a social function of this nature either. And, yet, I can't help but feel utterly outcast.

Eight is such a nice number—normally—not when it is the number of speed dating events I have managed to *utterly botch*.

"Come on," I mutter at myself as I slam my car door and lock my little luna-moth green Toyota Camry. "I'm not a bad person," I declare, for my own sake. Trotting up to the sidewalk, I ignore the open moving van in the space beside my car. Every last box is perfectly shut, labeled, and in lovely stacks, but the lovely stacks are not my focus. And I'm trying to stay focused. If I lose my focus, I'll fall into a depressive low and forfeit days to weeks of valuable time. "I want a lifelong partner. It shouldn't be against societal norm to mention that. Why would *anyone* want to walk into a relationship without clearly setting the boundaries?" Throwing my hair back, I fish in my purse for my keys and stomp up the wooden steps to my apartment. "I am *this* close to giving up and hiring a fake date. Who cares if I'm lonely after the agreement expires! I'll just *be lonely*!" So long as I'm *being lonely* in my little cottage, right? "RIGHT?" My head whips up once I reach the top of the steps, and I freeze, backtracking my thoughts a flight of stairs down...to the moving van beside my car.

The one I actively ignored.

Even though one of the boxes was labeled *astronomy*, and that's pretty cool.

Logically, it stands to reason that...I am no longer the sole occupant of the H building at Peach Plaza...

Tattoos. Snakes. Tall. Big. Sweating. On a still-chilled day in late February.

Boss is moving into the apartment across from me.

I swallow, hard, and take the smallest step back. But wait. I'm on stairs.

Crap.

Terror zips through my chest as my foot skids on the corner of the step and throws me airborne. A scream starts in my throat, choking before it can make sound. In a horrifying flash, the giant man is in front of me, on me, behind me, grabbing me. Clasping my wrist, Boss jerks my body into his. I hit his chest in a whirlwind that steals breath from my lungs. He smells like vanilla when I gasp.

He curses, clutching me with one massive hand and grabbing the rail with the other. The wooden beam creaks, groaning against his abuse, but he manages to plant his feet firm.

His chest heaves against my body, leaving me with just one question.

What in the world just happened?

Trembling, I brace my hands against his stomach, discovering the fact he's not pure hard muscle. Some of the heft to him is soft. Bulk. Big. Big and holding me. And maybe just saved me from falling head-first into concrete.

"Are you okay, Ellen?" he implores, tense.

He knows my name. I guess I told him that when I was drunk. Numbly, I nod. Then I recall what one is supposed to do when saved from potential injury and feasible death. "Thank you."

His breaths begin to level, and he unwinds one snake-painted arm from around me. "I'm sorry I startled you."

"You're a startling person," I say, because I'm in shock, and I have absolutely no filter when I'm in shock. Not that I tend to have one normally. But...yeah... I'm in shock, and he's beautiful, and I'm pressed against him, and he could break me in two with minimal effort.

His head shakes, then he combs my hair away from my face. The action is so mindlessly tender I don't know what to think about it. From the way he snaps his hand to his side and closes his fist, I don't think he understands what to think about it either. "Am I?" he asks.

Realizing I'm still leaning against him, I push off and find my feet. My being on the step up does little to bridge the distance between our faces. He is still egregiously tall, and it is still exceptionally overwhelming. "Yes."

"I don't mean to be."

"I'm uncertain whether or not it's something you can help. Genes. And all that."

"Ah, yes. Genes. The bane of my existence, yet also the reason for it."

My lips purse. "Well, they aren't really the *reason* for it."

Boss hums. "Byproduct of?"

I shake my head.

"Building block in?"

I think a moment. "That works. I suppose."

He puffs a breath that I think equates to a laugh. "Consider me edited."

My stomach ties at the thought. People hate when I correct their grammar in real life, which is why I'm going to say nothing about the error I just heard.

Boss releases the rail to fold his hand over his mouth and murmur, "Or would it be 'consider my words edited'? You didn't edit *me*. That's a..."

35

"Incorrect antecedent," I offer, potentially gaping at him.

"Right." He cocks a hip against the railing and folds his arms across his chest. He has got to be at least four hundred pounds of rippling muscle and sheer girth. I have a feeling he's being *casual* right now, but nothing he does can possibly look anything other than intimidating. The perma-frown creasing a line beneath his bottom lip doesn't help.

Not that I'm looking at his lips. Or finding them sensual. That would be a tiny bit insane.

"I've tried to be more aware of words since we met."

Heat blooms in my cheeks. "Oh no. Don't tell me I talked about words with you when we met."

A dark brow lifts. "You gave me an all-inclusive grammar lesson several times more comprehensible than the entirety of my educated career."

I cover my face with my hands.

A thread of humor lilts in his gruff voice. "It was adorable, and I assure you I thoroughly enjoyed it."

I whimper. "I'm so sorry. I do that."

His warm fingers touch my wrist, gently drawing one hand away from my face. "Hey." He angles his body to meet my eyes. "It's okay. I mean it. I learned a lot." Clearing his throat, he drops his hand. "I didn't know you still lived here, so I'm not moving in on account of trying to stalk you."

My brow furrows. "Of course not. It sounds like we met briefly five years ago. Why would you even consider me in your decision to move anywhere?" I blink, twist, look at the couch halfway shoved through the front door of the apartment across from mine. "You *are* moving in here?" I blurt.

First, we met five years ago—and I don't remember anything that happened. Then, we met again a couple weeks ago at that speed dating event. And *now* he's moving in across from me?

Those are coincidences befitting a romance novel if I ever saw them.

How…unsettling.

"I am." Carefully, he urges me up the final few steps, guides me clearly away from them, and returns to his doorway—where he moves the cream soft sofa into his living room without so much as straining to lift the furniture. Returning to the doorway, which he ducks under and exits at an angle, he says, "Rent's reasonable. The places are nice. It's near where I work." He rubs his neck. "I had no idea you still lived here."

His pretty eyes are very distracting when they flick to meet mine. My gaze startles off them, and by the time I've remembered how to communicate, he's saying, "Why exactly are you thinking about hiring a fake date?"

All the blood rushes out of my face, and it occurs to my body that I have been standing in shock stillness for several minutes now. A bout of lightheadedness sweeps over me, and I rock my weight from one leg to the other in order to get my stupid circulation going. Stupid POTS. I bet my legs have tinted purple beneath my yoga pants. "Well," I begin, and I just know the exterior stimuli and stress over the fact *he overheard me* is not helping the whole heart-beating-too-fast situation. "It's not really important."

"I'm not trying to pry, petal. Just concerned whenever I overhear a young woman yelling to herself about giving up and hiring male companionship, especially when it seems as though she should have no trouble finding it genuinely."

I stare at him. "This has happened to you multiple times?"

"Um." He blinks. "No."

Tensing, I pace to my doorway and fumble for my keys.

"I misunderstood your implications."

"My apologies. Allow me to be blunt—you're beautiful. I fail to understand why you would need to pay anyone for their company, and the motives of any man who would accept such an offer concern me."

My already-hammering heart thumps, and spots crawl over my vision, sending me to the ground in front of my door. I crouch there a moment, gasping shallow breaths through my mouth.

"Hey…" Boss curses, striding over to crouch next to me—massive. He lifts a finger toward the curtain of my hair, stops before touching it, and clenches his fist against his thigh. "Sorry. I'm not trying to be forward. Are you all right?"

"It's not you," I exhale. "I have post orthostatic tachycardia syndrome. If I stand still for too long, my heart beats too fast, and then my vision can get blurry or I get lightheaded. Some days are better than others, and today I'm already stressed. So…" I squeeze my eyes shut and try to ground myself. I don't want to worry him. Unfortunately, now traces of anxiety seem to be niggling their way in. If I don't get myself under control soon, I might pass out. And then what? "I just need a second. You can go back to what you were doing. I'll get inside and lie down for a little while. Then I'll be fine."

"Ellen—"

"Please. I don't want to cause any trouble. This is normal."

Graciously, he rises, and his heavy steps descend the stairs. They come back up what feels like moments later. "So sometimes you just can't stand anymore and black out?"

"Yes. Once, I couldn't see for several minutes, and my mother had to take me into a family bathroom where I lay on the floor against her purse until my vision came back."

He curses, and some stuff shuffles behind me. "That's literally terrifying, petal."

"I know how to better manage it now, so I don't have quite as severe flares."

His steps clomp away; he comes back. "So how do you manage it?"

"Water, salt, and exercise. Protein-rich snacks sometimes seem to help. It's not severe enough that I need medication."

Boss hums. "You like to exercise?"

"I'm more active than I look right now. Especially when I get excited for any of...various reasons."

"Would a *various reason* be seeing a moth?"

I cave a little deeper against my front door. "Did I talk to you about moths, too? While I was drunk."

"Yep." The thread of amusement in his voice is unmistakable. The recipe for the sound of his voice is as follows—rocks, polish (also known as the touch of a New English accent), humor. Tumbled together, it's something sultry. "Who knew the buggers were so interesting," he murmurs.

My attention perks at that, and I turn slightly to look at him. He goes clomping down the stairs, but he comes back, and I ask, "You like moths?"

"They're pretty cool. I didn't know some were so big." He sets a load of boxes down inside his apartment and looks at me. "Don't tell me *you* also like moths?"

I giggle. "Maybe a little."

"Shocking." The corner of his mouth softens.

"You're somewhat sarcastic, aren't you?"

"More often than I should be, according to my sisters."

I sit, leaning back against my door and folding my legs up. "You have sisters?"

"Two. The younger menace is about your age."

"How old are you?"

"Twenty-nine until summer."

That makes enough sense. The speed dating events I've been joining range from ages twenty to thirty. My brain trips into that topic, and I find myself asking, "Did you find anyone?"

His brow furrows, and he leans against his doorjamb, arms crossed. "Pardon?"

"At the speed dating thing? It was the first one I went to, around Valentine's Day."

Dragging his attention off me, he notes, "Ah." He wets his lips. "Uh. Well. No."

"You didn't like anyone?"

He continues looking off the balcony that faces out toward the parking lot. "The one girl I liked didn't put my name down."

Wow. I can't even imagine walking into a speed dating event with enough confidence to only put *one* person's name down. How can you even be so sure in four minutes? That's bonkers. "I'm sorry," I say, attempting to be polite and not mention anything that might allude to the potential I find him either arrogant or cocky. I don't. Confidence is attractive; however, mentioning that someone else comes off as confident can sometimes be misconstrued. And the last thing I want to do is offend my new, giant neighbor who spends a decent portion of his time around alcohol.

I could end up brutally murdered.

I shudder.

"You said *first one*," he murmurs, still watching the parking lot.

I glance that way in case there's something interesting going on out there. "Yes?"

"I take it you didn't find anyone either?"

Wincing, I clasp my hands together, and I don't know if he has a better vantage, but I don't see anything past the balcony worth focusing on. "We have the same problem. The guys I'm interested in getting to know better don't like me. I've tried eight times now."

He bristles, head whipping away from the lot. "*Eight times?* You've gone to eight different speed dating events since Valentine's Day weekend?"

Something heavy and big settles in my chest, making it a touch hard to breathe. Keeping my focus on the floor planks between us, I murmur, "I'm trying. I don't know what's so disagreeable about me."

"Nothing," he states, like it's an absolute fact. The stability in that one, harsh word drags my gaze up to his eyes. A muscle in his jaw jumps; an awkward twitch starts in his right eye. "You're not disagreeable at all."

That heavy thing in my chest eases, some. "Thank you. That's kind." I take a deep breath and rock my head back against my front door, staring at the ceiling between our apartments. "I know I'm not the easiest person to get along with. I talk a lot about things people don't care about. I'm extreme—in either direction. Some days, I can't stop moving. Others, I'll not have left my room until past midnight when I realize I've forgotten to do anything other than read on my phone. I'm a stickler for details. I'll throw tantrums if I get overwhelmed."

"That all sounds perfectly normal."

A forlorn smile tips my lips. "Thank you for saying so. Most of the world wouldn't agree."

"Most of the world is made up of selfish idiots who don't know basic human decency."

If he knew me better, I think he'd change his mind. At least that's been the consensus thus far. People are almost always more comforting and considerate when they haven't actually faced the problems directly. If it weren't so easy to be a third party, no one would play devil's advocate. Compassion and acceptance are simple when we aren't directly involved in the work of either.

"Why are you considering fake dating someone?" he asks again.

I grimace at him, intentionally. Screwing up my face, I look at him and hope he'll backpedal.

The stony mountain of a man does not oblige.

Jutting my lip, I cross my legs and fiddle with my shoelace aglet. "As of my twenty-fifth birthday, my parents want me to be in a serious relationship before allowing me to inherit a portion of their property. If I don't show up with a partner before my birthday next month, I don't get to move into my cottage until…well…you know. I get everything because of…yeah. I'm an only child, and stuff."

"I'm sorry," he grumbles. "What?"

I blurt, "If I don't find a serious partner before I turn twenty-six, I have to wait until my parents *die* before I can live in my cottage. And by that point I will be too emotionally wrecked to take care of anything. I—" My voice cracks.

Boss closes his eyes and swipes his hand in the air. "No, no. None of that. I mean *why in the world* are your parents requiring you to be in a relationship before you can own what will inevitably end up yours at one point or another anyway?"

"Oh." I manage a shaking breath. "I think because they know how I am, and they don't want me to end up alone because they know I don't want to end up alone, but also that my being alone is unavoidable without motivation. I only moved out at all because I got Mouse, my cat, and their house isn't suitable for a cat to live in."

"And they didn't want you to move into this cottage

property with your cat then either? You were younger than twenty-five when we met and I brought you home here."

I shift a bit, clear my throat. "Well...I, uh...I sometimes do this thing? Where, uh, I'll punish myself? I misunderstood why they didn't want me to get a cat, so when I got my cat, it felt like I'd done a bad thing, but it wasn't a bad thing, technically, or I've come to terms with the fact it wasn't a bad thing because I took care of it effectively, but in the moment when I felt like I'd done a bad thing, I had to fix it myself, so even though they hadn't yet made the rule about my inheriting the cottage and they were happy to help Mouse and me move in there, I ruined my opportunity to bypass this mess. Hindsight is twenty-twenty, they say."

One hand clamped to his mouth, Boss stares at me. After a long moment, he closes his eyes. "Could I... potentially...help you out?"

"Huh?"

He coughs, adjusting all that weight of his from one leg to the other. "Could *we* do the fake dating thing?"

My mouth falls open, and I don't know what to make of what I've just heard. He's offering to help me out by fake dating me? I lift my hands. "I was just rambling to myself. Fake dating is a book trope, for pretty much exactly a situation like this, and I was frustrated, and my mind is always on either moths or books, so that's what came out. I definitely don't want to trick my parents when they are trying to help me."

He drops his hand, and that massive chest of his fills with air. "I understand. Sorry if it was an uncomfortable offer. I was just thinking it might help me out a bit, too."

"What do you mean?"

He grumbles, "Well, I'm not really looking for a relationship right now, and the girl I kind of was interested in at the speed dating thing didn't pan out, so I'm back on my celibacy. Unfortunately, my family is full of meddling women. My little sister is the one who signed me up for the speed dating in the first place and told me I'd cause problems for the numbers if I didn't show. *Mamma* threw me into three blind dates last month with her friends' daughters. My eldest sister shoved me into her friend at our Christmas party, and then into *another* friend at our New Year's Eve party. I swear they coordinate these *romantic events* so I never get more than two weeks of peace at a time. Something about how I'm *almost thirty* and *need to find a wife.* I'm sick of it. Having an exchange where you can help me get the heat from my family off my back for a little while and where I could help you get your cottage sounds…convenient."

"That's awful," I state.

He grimaces, hands clamped to thick biceps. "Welcome to my life as the only male middle kid."

"Why would your sisters and mother do something like that to you against your will? It's one thing to encourage someone to do something they want to do but are having difficulties with and another to force them into situations that are uncomfortable for one or more parties." I splay my palm against my chest. "I'll help, if I can. I don't know how much your family might approve of me, but I'm willing to try if you are."

"What about your cottage and your parents?" he asks.

"I don't expect you to fake date me in front of them. I'll keep trying to find someone while we appease your family."

Boss rubs his twitching eye. "A month isn't really a lot of time to find a serious partner, is it?"

I shrug, undoing my shoelaces and tying them back in the shape of a moth. "It doesn't take long to fall in love, and if two people are honest with each other about their expectations, it shouldn't be too hard. I just have to find the right person."

"The right person," Boss echos, pressing his lips together. Shaking his head slightly, he asks, "So we're fake dating to placate my family for a bit? I'm assuming since you were the one who brought up the term, you understand the process better than I do?"

"Oh sure," I comment, getting to my feet now that my head has calmed down. I just need a couple glasses of water and some food now. Which means I need to stop sitting in front of my door and get into my apartment. Mouse probably misses me since I've been gone all afternoon. Getting my keys out, I say, "Why don't you come over for dinner tomorrow at six? We can discuss the parameters then."

"Sounds good."

The lock clicks, and I smile over my shoulder at Boss. "Any food allergies or dietary restrictions I should be aware of?"

His head shakes.

I don't know how to end the conversation, so I just smile a little wider and step inside my apartment.

Oh boy.

What have I just gotten myself into?

CHAPTER 3

> ♥ Fake dating is always an option in order to find love. Just make sure you have a clear set of rules that include *not* falling in love, so that, inevitably, you will.

Usually, I eat sandwiches. Sandwiches taste the same when you make them the same. Peanut butter always tastes like peanut butter. Jelly always tastes like jelly. Honey is honey. Deli meats and cheeses rarely deviate in texture or flavor. Iceberg lettuce is wonderfully reliable, not to mention crunchy.

Having sandwiches for breakfast, lunch, and dinner is normal for me—when I remember to eat so many meals. Breakfast PB&J. Lunch turkey and cheese. Dinner grilled cheese. Force some frozen mixed veggies onto the side at odd intervals and add a smoothie or two on occasion, and all the nutrient bases get covered well enough with very little backlash from my struggles with executive dysfunction.

Something tells me all my *usuals* aren't exactly proper meals for dignified company. Therefore, I make burrito casserole. With Fritos. Because adding Fritos provides an extra layer of enjoyment to what is basically a stack of tortillas, meat, refried beans, rice, sauce, and cheese. The *crunch* is a sensational texture variation. Crunches are always wonderful.

Scooping salsa, guacamole, and sour cream into a sectional serving dish, I finish up the last bit of prep work involved in burrito casserole—a la company. Burrito casserole "a la me" is as simple as the casserole and sour cream. Salsa is gross. Guacamole should be outlawed. I never bother chopping up lettuce when it's just me, but without the bowl of greenery, the meal lacks both color and the presence of something resembling a vegetable. Which is obviously incorrect for formal visitors.

And, yes, a giant tattooed alcoholic (unconfirmed) counts as *dignified company*.

In case it isn't obvious, I am doing my best to appear within the realm of someone resembling a mature adult with her life together. At the very least I am attempting to resemble someone who hasn't spent her whole afternoon restraining squeals because Arella and Lucien are *finally* breaking curses…in the book I'm editing.

Ugh. If I had a Lucien, I'd already be living in my cottage with Mouse. Is it so much to ask for someone to adore me? I'm not looking for *worship the ground I walk on* type stuff. Just heart-melting glances from across crowded ballrooms. A little flirting amidst sexually-charged sword fights.

I love me some sexually-charged sword fights… Like *oh no I'm totally going to stab you with my pointy stick, but I cannot be held accountable if we start kissing instead*.

Heh.

Enemies to lovers is absolutely bogus. I love it.

Smiling, I finish setting the table and tell Mouse to be good the second before the sound of a pounding fist sends him jetting toward his elaborate cat tree house in the corner. "It's okay, Mouse. It's just…" Huh. I don't actually know Boss's name. Wiping my hands on my apron, I open the front door and smile. "Hi, Boss, come on in."

Brows furrowing, he ducks under the arch and onto the slice of linoleum serving as my "foyer." All at once, I live in a dollhouse. Goodness gracious. He'd make Whole

Foods look small. "You don't have to call me 'boss'," he says, closing the door behind him.

I wait a moment for an alternative that doesn't come. Oh dear. I hope he hasn't already told me and I forgot. Taking the risk, I say, "I don't know your name."

He stills, dragging his gaze away from my living room and to me. "It's Hayes. Hayes Sallow."

"Hayes," I murmur. It's a softer name than I expected, but I like the sound. His full name flows well together, too. I grin. "Nice to meet you, Hayes Sallow."

The hint of a smile crosses his lips. "Nice to formally meet you as well, Ellen Little."

A momentary shock zips through me because apparently I told him my full name five years ago when I was drunk, and *apparently* he bothered to remember it. That's impressive. And a little insane. I would never put a momentary interaction like walking someone home when they're drunk into the important memory section of my brain. It would enter and leave on the same breath.

Head full of moth facts. Sorry. Busy labeling the parts of a compound sentence. Try again later.

Hayes, Hayes, Hayes. Fit into the important memory section, dang it, or I sense we'll have a problem. People get offended pretty easily when you forget their name.

"Something smells good," Hayes notes, shredding through my kitchen in two steps and reaching my itty-bitty dining table. He fixes his attention way, way down on the document I threw together yesterday and arches a brow. "Fake Dating Guidelines?"

My oven timer goes off, so I pull my casserole out and set it on the table. Whaddaya know? When Hayes isn't in my peripheral, my table returns to normal size. He's like a walking optical illusion on perspective. Quite cool. Changing my entire world back into itty-bittiness, I face him. "I took the liberty of outlining every important point I could think of in a cohesive location that we can use for reference in order to most efficiently reach an amiable conclusion where your family is concerned."

He sits heavily in my dining room chair, and the wood groans beneath him. "Huh."

I watch his gaze trace over the first page in front of him a moment before I remember we need a drink and I need to turn the oven off. Or check that I turned the oven off.

After everything's settled and I'm in my chair, he rests an elbow against the table and scratches his cheek. "No falling in love?"

Said in his rumbly, deep voice, this entire thing sounds like a big joke. But it isn't like *I* was the one who seriously pressed forward with wanting to fake date. That was all him. And there's some comfort in the fact something *weird* isn't my fault. "It's a trope expectation to include that rule within the agreement," I clarify. "I don't foresee us having any difficulties with it, though."

Hayes looks at me.

My heart thuds, and it occurs to me we are the only two people in this building at the moment. Not only that, I don't know this man very well, and now I'm discussing a *fake romantic relationship* with him. No matter how beautiful, his girth alone frightens me.

What am I doing?

To drag my mind off sudden bursts of fear, I reach for the burrito casserole serving spoon. "I hope I made enough, and that you like it. It's a recipe that I made up." I deliver several heaping spoonfuls to his plate. "You can add lettuce and any of the sauce toppings. Um…please use the designated spoons for each. I only like sour cream because the others are disgusting." I bite my tongue to keep myself from saying anything else that might imply I believe him to have disgusting tastes.

While I'm serving myself a normal person portion, Hayes moves his plate near the sauces and scoops massive amounts of salsa on top. "You got salsa and guacamole special for me?"

"I understand they are staples for this sort of meal. It's only right to provide them for a guest." Regardless of the fact one tastes like slime and the other like pond scum.

I do not dictate the palate of my guests.

He just about empties the entire section of salsa onto his food, and the squishy red chunks wash down over his heap of casserole. I'm still staring at the revolting mess when he sets his plate back down in front of him and lifts his fork. "You're very considerate."

I get the sour cream, putting a modest pile apart from my casserole on my plate, so it won't get warm, and so I can control exactly how much I want in each bite. Like a sane person. You know, a sane person who doesn't invite giant strangers into her home where no one but a scared kitty might hear her scream… "It's general knowledge."

"Isn't 'don't walk in on one another in various states of undress' general knowledge as well?"

"You would be *shocked* how often that manages to occur wherever this trope is involved. For some reason, men wind up shirtless *constantly*. And then the women stare in order to describe even ridge and plane for *several* uncomfortable paragraphs." Shaking my head, I lift my knife and cut a bite of casserole free before dabbing a touch of sour cream on top. "Whenever I see a shirtless man out and about on a walk or something, I look away. If it's impolite to stare at a shirtless woman, it is impolite to stare at a shirtless man. Double standards upset me." They over-complicate already complicated rules. Why can't *one thing* be the *right thing* in all situations?

Ridiculous.

Hayes delivers a heaping bite to his mouth with a baby fork while he watches me, eyeing me more intently than feels appropriate. I have no idea why. I have to double check and make sure I didn't accidentally give him a salad fork. Or an oyster fork for crying out loud. Usual dinner cutlery is outrageously tiny in his massive hand.

I do not believe I have made enough food.

I do not believe I *own* enough food.

Finishing his bite before opening his mouth, Hayes says, "Are you actually concerned that any of the questionable things you have written down here are going to happen against your will?"

"Questionable?" I ask. I put down purely logical situations that tend to take place once one crosses the line between reality and *rom-com* reality. The second you say "okay" to fake dating, or hanging out with your brother's best friend, or working on a project with your grumpy boss, or even looking twice at an attractive neighbor, you better be on the lookout.

Oh dear. I just remembered this man is my neighbor. He's objectively attractive. Quite attractive, honestly. Probably the most attractive man I have ever seen. And I have more than looked twice—I have made him dinner.

I'm in rom-com danger whether he abides by the information I've so graciously outlined for him or not.

"According to this—" He drags his finger down my list. "—we are at great risk of emotional and physical injury should we proceed. It makes me think I've asked a great deal more of you than I thought."

"Well, what did *you* think fake dating entailed?" I ask, perhaps harsher than intended.

"The next time one of my sisters or my *mamma* tells me about a great idea on how to fend off my 'crippling loneliness,' as they call it, I tell them I have a girlfriend. When they doubt me, I send them a picture we've prepared and taken together. Then they'll probably invite us to dinner or something. We go. They see you aren't an AI-generated image. I'm spared from their antics for at least a couple months. The end."

I bark a laugh. "Oh no. No, no, *no*. That's the *beginning*."

He taps the pages. "Petal, some of this reads like sexual assault. Are people actually kissing other people on account of peer pressure? That isn't at all what I intended to imply when I asked for your help here. I don't want you to kiss me unless you want to kiss me. I assumed we'd spend a little time together, get to know each other, so when my family does invite you over, we aren't complete strangers. I'm not interested in…" Grumbling, he narrows his eyes on the page, and mutters, "Invading your personal space while your modesty is compromised, ending up locked together in a confined space without warning, kissing you for show in front of anyone, winding up in any precarious close-physical-contact situations due to sudden bouts of inexplicable clumsiness—"

I interject, "Technically, that one already happened when you caught me on the stairs yesterday."

Hayes's head whips up, his eyes hitting mine with enough force to shoot a hole through my chest. "There was nothing indecent about that. You were falling. I caught you."

My face heats, and I focus on my food. "This stuff is not *indecent*."

"Yes, it is. Without your express consent, all of it is indecent. If you're actually worried about any of these things, I'll feel like I'm taking advantage of you, and that is the *last* thing I want to do."

Blinking rapidly, I attempt to sort through what's going on. He's upset. We're alone. I don't understand. I don't know what to say. I've offended him, but I don't know why. These things are just par for the course. I'm warning him so we can take precautions and be prepared. I don't like surprises. Why do people get mad when I attempt to make life make more sense?

Fake dating stuff *almost always* blows up at the end of the "agreement." We need to be prepared for when someone "finds out" nothing was real around the time one or both of us are starting to believe everything is.

Not that *that* part is going to happen.

While attractive, Hayes's size alone terrifies me. Tack on the whole *owns a bar* part, and on moral logic alone, this can't go anywhere unless he gets rid of his entire career.

I'm not stupid enough to think love conquers concrete things like physical incompatibility and my aversion to people who imbibe alcohol.

Alcohol is stupid. People who *enjoy* it are stupid.

I'm not being judgmental.

I *might* be a little judgmental…

But I'm not wrong!

Who in their right mind *enjoys* splitting headaches and vomiting or feeling adrift in their own body?

Stupid people.

Or crazy people.

Or dangerous people with penchants for chaos.

I…wonder which category Hayes falls into.

Gruff, he murmurs, "Petal, I don't want to take advantage of you. If I've pressured you into agreeing to something far more disturbing than I thought, you can tell me."

"It's not disturbing. You just don't understand the

context."

"Is the context a felony?" He shoves a big bite of burrito casserole in his big mouth.

I frown, slicing an elegant bite and topping it with dainty precision. "Not usually."

Hayes half-swallows, half-coughs. Covering his mouth, he reaches all the way across the table, gets the juice, and pours himself a glass. Once he's downed the entire thing in three gulps, he sputters, "Not *usually*?"

"Sometimes it is! Sometimes people fake a whole marriage to trick the government!" I state.

His wide eyes stare. His lips part and close.

I narrow my eyes. "You know what? We're going to do this."

"Pardon?"

"We are *going to do this*." I stab my finger down against the table. "You're going to see that I'm not being weird and it's not disturbing. I guarantee at *least* ten things on my list take place."

"So I'll only be doing, what, twenty years in prison for sexual assault, harassment, or—"

"Ha ha ha," I laugh dryly. "See? Look at us, joking about the evident tropey aspect already. Point eighteen, unless I'm mistaken."

That right eye of his twitches after his gaze cuts to my list.

I fill my glass and take a sip, then I blurt, "I find you terrifying, Hayes, but that's no reason for me not to try and help you. We are going to do this. Strange things are going to start happening. You'll see I'm being perfectly reasonable. And then? Then when nearly every last rule and guideline I've put down ends up overturned thanks to mysterious forces, you'll stop ridiculing me."

"Every last one?" he asks, that warm, low voice of his

brushing over my frazzled nerves.

I clear my throat. "*Nearly* every last one. Stories can only cram so much into standard-appropriate word counts. *I* don't make the rules."

"You just write them down in unsettling detail?"

"It is *not* unsettling." I lean toward his bulk, agitated, heated, uncertain why something in my chest won't stop tingling. "Do not make this an enemies to lovers, boss."

"I thought we agreed you could call me *Hayes*, pudding."

I blink. My brain breaks. My mouth opens and closes. Why in the world did he just call me *pudding*? I love pudding. But *why*?

"Also…" Before I've recovered, he's settling his chin against his fist and leaning toward me, putting our faces mere inches apart. "What was that about *to lovers*?"

"Nothing," I breathe.

"If you say so." He hums. "So you find me terrifying. What is it about me that scares you? The tattoos? Snakes are cute."

He's not wrong, but what? He has to *ask*? "You're *massive*."

"I wouldn't hurt a moth." Humor siphoning through his crystal gaze, he adds, "Now that I know most won't eat my clothes, anyway. I've converted fully to team catch-and-release."

I think he's playing with me. Teasing me, rather. I'm used to being teased. It's been the constant dynamic between me and anyone I've considered a friend for my entire life. However, I don't think the teasing has ever settled quite so low and warm in my stomach, right near the place I assume moths might take flight if I find myself in love.

"Appearances can be deceiving, pudding," he offers.

"Why are you calling me *pudding* all of a sudden?"

He arches a thick brow. "Because we're 'dating' now, and that's the endearment I've chosen."

"But…petal."

"Is not a romantic endearment. I call my little sister *petal*, too."

I pale. "I remind you of your little sister?" And we're about to fake date? I might be an only child, but even I know that's uncomfortable.

He puffs a breath and returns to eating his food. "Absolutely not. I call her petal because she likes plants and it miffs her because of how poorly it fits. She's 6'1" and wears three-inch heels." Shifting, he pulls his phone out of his back pocket and begins going through photos. Once he's found what he's looking for, he nudges his phone toward me. "She's anything but delicate like you."

Did he just call me *delicate*?

Is that a compliment or something I should be concerned about?

Delicate things are easily snapped in half, after all.

Warily, I drop my attention to the image of a woman with half her head shaved. The other half is poison green, short, and spiked. She's throwing the ASL sign for love while her tongue sticks out to display a piercing. I like her baggy shirt. I don't know what the single word on it means, though.

Is the font just weird, or is that not English?

"See?" Hayes notes. "You don't remind me of my sister at all."

"I like her shirt," I say, for lack of anything better to comment on. Our styles are vastly different. She's outstandingly cool. She looks like the kind of person who would bully me for existing in the same space as her. Is Hayes's entire family made up of incredible and terrifying people?

He glances at the image, then he says a word that is absolutely not English in an accent that is not New English. Catching my eye, he clears his throat and murmurs, "It's a band."

"From…"

"Norway."

My eyes widen. "Are *you* from Norway?"

Touches of humor lighten his very blue eyes, and he says, "*Ja*."

"But you speak British," I blurt, foolishly. I know better. He speaks *English* with a slight *British* accent. I wince at myself, pull back mentally, and say, "No. No, you know what I mean. I'm not ignorant. I don't call the English language *American* over here. I promise."

"I believe you," he offers, still somewhat amused. Returning to his food, he scoops some extra salsa onto his next bite. "*Mamma*'s from Norway. *Far* was from England. We grew up in the north of Norway, but we visited his family throughout our childhood, so we learned English from the Brits. We moved here after he died in a freak goating accident fifteen years ago."

My mouth falls open. A…what? A *freak goating accident*? I don't know what to say to that. I… "My condolences," I exhale the second I remember the semi-appropriate, if tired, response.

Hayes chews and swallows his next bite. "I'm joking. It wasn't a freak goating accident."

I blink, unaware that people were allowed to joke about the death of their parents. I don't have a singular clue what to say that won't come out exceedingly harsh. Death isn't a joke. And especially not the death of someone who took care of you and raised you. That's disrespectful.

He clears his throat. "It's easier to joke about him not

being around at all than it is to say he moved us all over here fifteen years ago so he could cheat on my *mamma* in person while he groomed me to take over his bar. He ran off with the other woman once I'd turned twenty-one."

Oh.

Wow.

In *that* case, it's totally okay to joke that his father died in a freak goating accident. I stab my food. "I can't stand it when people break their vows. Words are sacred."

"I thought it when we met before, but you have quite a fae-like appreciation for words, pudding."

My heart leaps, and I stare at him the moment after I've shoved my angry bite in my mouth. I forget I'm chewing and sputter through my food, "You're familiar wit—" Covering my mouth, I swallow. "I'm so sorry. I didn't mean to speak with my mouth full."

"It's all right." He seems entirely unconcerned. "Yes, I know some mythology. I don't avidly *believe* in any of it, but I grew up in an atmosphere of people who do. Norse mythology is pretty popular throughout the world. Nisse and elves and what have you. *Mamma* still puts out gifts for Julenisse on Christmas Eve, and my sisters take every opportunity to convince children that if Santa Claus were real, he'd prefer porridge to cookies." He gestures vaguely back toward my living room. "I noticed fantasy on your bookshelves…so…"

I've scooted toward him, eyes wide, entranced. Cultural differences in holiday celebration and fairy tales have always fascinated me. There was a time when I hunted down every last version of Cinderella that I could find. It's magical to pick apart the realism hidden in how an environment mutates a story.

Mythology might not be real, but the elements that twist a culture's perception of the same thing are.

Those variations say, "We are different, but we are still flesh and blood. Even the strangest among us can find harmony in the cores of what we are."

The corner of Hayes's mouth softens. "So you're very much interested in folktales as well as moths?"

Clearing my throat, I contain myself. "Well, they're *not* moths."

"No. I suppose fantasy pales to the reality of moths. To think there are colorful, winged creatures with fuzzy bodies that let you hold them without much protest. A nisse would never."

I bite my cheeks, tell myself to calm down. *Normal* people mention topics in passing without the intention of discussing them in exaggerated depth. I'm pretending to be *normal* with this giant man.

Finishing his first plate, Hayes reaches for the serving spoon. "I found a cecropia last spring. It was as big as my hand."

Something inside me—like my willpower—cracks. "Did you take pictures?" I grab his phone off the table and hold it toward him. "Was it a male or a female? Do you know? Hyalophora cecropia are the largest moths native to North America. Their caterpillars are huge, too, but once they become adults, they don't *eat*. They don't have mouths!"

"Most moths don't," he comments, gently taking his phone from my fingers. Unlocking it again, he scrolls, showing me a picture of him outside at night with a cecropia moth on his head. It's literally sitting in his hair like an accessory.

I gasp, grab his phone, zoom in, and vibrate. "It's a girl!" A spark bursts inside my chest, and I grin. Shooting out of my chair, I plant myself beside him, careful not to touch him as I show him the moth's antennae. "If this were a boy, they'd be thinner. Also—" I swipe down to the plump abdomen. "—the girls are chunkier, so they can hold over a hundred eggs." Pushing a straying strand of hair over my ear, I beam. "Did you know that? Cecropia moths lay over a *hundred* eggs."

He looks at the picture, a thick brow arched, and I tense.

Crap.

I stammer, "I-I mean, it's just…"

"Cool," he interjects, stonily interested—I think. "It's just cool." His eyes meet mine, and an eclipse of moths take flight in my stomach. He murmurs, "It is cool, but we got off topic."

Cautiously, I set his phone down and ease myself back into my chair. "I do that sometimes. I'm sorry."

"I don't mind."

People normally do.

I wet my lips. "It's just sometimes something will make me think of something else, and then sometimes I just have to say it. I try not to all the time, but…"

"I don't mind," he repeats.

My head shakes. "It's not good, and I shouldn't do it. I need to be more respectful of others. I always find a way to talk about moths or grammar, no matter what the conversation is about to start with. It's rude."

He locks his phone. "It's not."

"It *is*."

"It's not," he repeats, gruff, and I think I'm upsetting him with my apology now.

I have no idea how any prolonged interaction between us is going to work. Agreeing to help him with his family is only going to make things worse. We won't so much as make it to the "third-act" break-up drama. This whole thing is going to collapse on top of us well before then.

"A conversation is supposed to be like this meal," he says.

My already muddled mind blanks as I register his words. "What?"

He nudges the casserole dish toward me with a bare hand, like it isn't still hot. "The conversation." He points at my sectioned dish, which still has a heaping helping of guacamole, some sour cream, and hardly any salsa. "What we each add to it." Referencing his plate, he shrugs. "I put some salsa on mine in the form of bringing up folklore. You put some sour cream on yours in the form of moth facts. It's only rude if I force you to add salsa to yours or if I refuse to eat with you because you add sour cream."

Lips parted, I watch the giant man as he reaches for thirds. Awkward, I say, "Some people can't stand the smell of sauerkraut and refuse to eat in the same room with it." And when it comes to conversations, I've learned that *I'm* the sauerkraut.

"Can you stand the smell of salsa?" he asks.

"Yes," I murmur. I wouldn't have bought it if I couldn't.

"I can handle your sour cream, too." Thoughtfully, he chews another massive bite and watches me. "The only thing anyone should be sorry about right now is the fact you've only managed to find people who can't. I promise I'm not one of them."

I used to trust everyone when they said things like that. Now, I wait a bit longer for the facts to reveal themselves.

Letting my gaze drift down, I catch sight of the fake dating document beside him before I lift another bite of casserole daintily topped with sour cream to my mouth. I'm a little scared what might happen if I dare to believe him.

I don't know why, but I don't think I'll be able to recover from getting close to this one. Something about him. It's…different.

Softly, he rumbles, "Are you comfortable with this, honestly? I have absolutely no intention of taking advantage of the situation or putting us in precarious positions that might frighten you."

"They'll happen whether you intend for them to or not," I say. "That's why we need to be prepared."

"Prepared? Prepared to *not*—" He looks at the list. "—run through an airport for any reason? *How?* How would security not immediately tackle someone running through an airport to the ground?"

Hayes is a *lot* of man to tackle. But okay. Sure. Keep doubting.

He references the paper. "And marching band serenades are banned? I'll really have to put in the effort to avoid that one. Breaking out in spontaneous song is among my top-ten favorite pastimes."

I sigh. "Don't worry about it. If you're just going to assume it's crazy, I'll handle everything."

His bushy brow rises again, then he shrugs those massive shoulders and finishes yet another plate. "So long as you don't mind, I'll leave making sure we aren't stranded in a place with only one room, one bed, and my t-shirt for pajamas up to you, Miss Editor. You're an incredible cook, by the way."

"I can only make three proper meals including this one. Everything else is sandwiches."

"I like sandwiches."

"They are versatile. If someone doesn't like sandwiches, they just haven't found the right one yet. The same concept applies to books."

Humming, he adds, "And people."

Huh.

And people.

What a whimsical thought. It's almost a theme. Or a

point that spurs along character development.
How…troubling.

CHAPTER 4

♥ It can take time to warm up to the idea of love.
___

Hayes: My number.

I add Hayes's number to my contacts and glance down at where he's taking up my entire living room floor. Breaking the salmon filet I gave him into tiny pieces, he creates a trail from where Mouse is hiding in the cat tree to the sofa where I'm sitting. Once he's done, he relaxes back against the seat cushion with the remainder of the filet dangling loosely from his fingers at his side. He looks up at me.

My heart jerks, and I hope he doesn't realize I've been watching him intently ever since I finished putting his number in my phone.

He's like a black hole, swallowing up everything in the vicinity, pulling everyone toward his massive gravitational force. I'm not even an asteroid. I'm a speck of space dust. Hurtling.

"So…" he murmurs, and my stomach knots with the understanding I suggested we relocate to my living room because we finished all the food, and—in my experience—reconvening in the parlor is the proper next step of having company over.

Now that he's finished his plot to bribe my cat out of his hiding place, I fear I don't actually know what happens next.

When my parents have company over, they talk about boring business or life things while I sit and listen until I zone out. I don't know what to talk about now. Have we covered everything important concerning pretending to be a couple so his family will leave him alone?

If I'm about to get invested in this scenario, will I have any time at all to find someone genuinely interested in dating me so I can inherit my cottage?

Should I talk to my parents and promise I'll keep trying even if they let me move into the home I've always wanted? In fake dating situations, the parents usually find out. For drama. What will I do if that's one of the points that gets checked off?

I've been silent too long. Worse, I've been staring at him the entire time. Eyes locked.

My lips part, but I still don't have any idea what I'm supposed to say, what the right thing to say is. Awkward silence has been my near-constant companion throughout most of my social interactions. It's not supposed to be this difficult to navigate conversations.

"I promise I don't bite," he murmurs at long last.

"I didn't... Sorry." I force my attention down to my laced fingers. The room changed, like it was supposed to, but now I have to "read it" all over again. And without food to distract me, the weight of this agreement is settling on my shoulders. "I'm trying to sort out my thoughts, make sure I haven't missed anything."

"Take all the time you need. I have a feeling your cat is going to take a minute to warm up to me, too." He relaxes, sighing, and Mouse's glowing green eyes peer cautiously at the first little offering.

"Mouse is shy," I note. "He's very friendly once he gets to know you though."

"Or when he's talking about moths?"

"He can't ta..." My face reddens, and I exhale. "Very funny."

Hayes puffs a breath, settles his head back on the seat cushion, and closes his eyes.

Calm silence unweighted with expectation fills the atmosphere, and Mouse peeks his nose out in order to steal the first bite of fish. Uncanny comfort nestles in where my anxieties are suspiciously vacating.

Come on, Ellen. You've spent the past few weeks meeting new people with unprecedented vigor. What's the problem now? I'm the one trying to help him. If I mess up and he doesn't want my help anymore, I'll have less to worry about while I try to find love before the twenty-first of next month.

Or something.

Why does my brain put so much weight on all rejection, even when it comes from people I shouldn't care about?

Sometimes I wish I were a sociopath.

To not care for connection or be harmed by its absence sounds almost freeing.

Mouse locates the next piece, and Hayes hasn't moved a muscle. His soft breaths stretch his chest and test the fabric of his shirt.

He's incredibly attractive.

Will his family believe that someone like him belongs with someone like me?

I'm not unattractive, objectively, but I've never given my physical appearance much thought. When it comes to how I present myself, I've put more weight on actions. No one picks what they look like, and no one else struggles like I do. Therefore, whatever it is that I do wrong must be within a human's control.

Appearance isn't the issue, logically. But, logically, wouldn't it be one now?

"Are we a believable couple?" I ask.

"Believable?" he murmurs, his low tone barely above a

whisper.

"Do I compare to other girls you've dated?"

He grunts. "Haven't dated anyone. Seemed like too much trouble while I was in school. Then *Far* messed up my perception of relationships around the time I was thinking about careers and families. He ripped up any of my own plans as far as a career could be concerned and made the idea of starting a family somewhat…" Breath leaves him; he doesn't open his eyes. "…I don't know. Unstable."

That information is awfully intimate. I'm surprised. Normally I'm the one oversharing like that. It's almost comforting to be on the other end for once. "I guess your mother and your sisters have noticed your aversion and are trying to help?"

He mutters, "Something like that."

"But it's not really helpful."

"Not at all."

Because forcing someone into anything never "fixes" them. Things like relationships have to happen naturally. Forcing anything about them, I know, only leads to disappointment. At some point or another, the mask cracks. The truth comes out. Bad things happen.

Welcome to the seventy-five percent mark of fake dating stories…

This is probably not the best idea, all things considered. Since I don't foresee us falling in love with each other, there's nothing to smooth over that nasty moment when everything comes undone and lies reach the light. I don't know enough about his family to assume they'll take this whole mess as a wake up call and realize Hayes is willing to do something insane with a basic stranger in order to get them off his back.

They'll either meet him where he is and understand, or

they'll get upset.

Given the fact they've not stopped their incessant matchmaking thus far, and Hayes seems strong enough to grumble at them to stop, I'm assuming they've already ignored him on numerous occasions and will get upset.

"Is this even a good idea?" I ask.

"Are you having second thoughts?"

I am past second thoughts. I've had several hundred thoughts between when this was mentioned yesterday and tonight. Like, excuse me, I made an entire outline of my thoughts. "I just don't see how it helps you long-term."

"I'll take it helping me for a month. One month where I don't wake up to three hundred texts guilting me into a blind date is all I'm asking for." Hayes remains steady and still, so Mouse creeps forward to the next bribe. "If it makes you uncomfortable at all, I'll completely understand and drop it."

It's strange. I can't remember the last time I felt comfortable with anyone, but now that he's still, I think I'm warming up to his presence just like Mouse is. There's calm in him, regardless of his career choices, and I guess as long as I don't see him with the products associated with his career, I don't mind the atmosphere he gives off. "I just don't want to make things worse for you."

"What about for you?" His lips thin as his brows lower. "I'm interrupting your time to find someone and get your cottage."

"Honestly? I don't think I understand how to relationship. I've read several self-help books, and I've even found one that seems to precisely outline my situation, but I've not so much as managed to achieve a real first date. Maybe pretending to be in a relationship will help me figure something out. Reality has been wholly disappointing. Fake dating with a side of 'date practice' seems like the next viable option in figuring out what I'm doing wrong."

"A subtrope? Will you have to alter your list?"

I hum, letting the tension in my muscles ease as I lean back into the couch, stare at the popcorn ceiling. "Maybe. It does add another layer of…" I notice blue eyes glimmering with something akin to mischief before I get fully through my thought. Deflating, I ask, "Are you teasing me?"

"Yes. You're adorable."

I bite my cheek. "I don't think you're supposed to say that to a woman. It's demeaning. I think."

"You *think* it's demeaning?"

"I feel like I've read about it being demeaning or unwelcome, yes."

"How do you feel about it?"

I feel like I don't mind being regarded as someone worthy of adoration, so long as it's intended as a compliment. Sometimes semantics and connotations only achieve dissonance and agitation without ever considering intentions. Intentions are important. Our society seems to forget that in favor of offense sometimes.

Nowadays, even normal people have too many rules to keep track of.

"I don't mind," I offer, focusing on Mouse.

My cat is so close to taking a chance on the chunk of fish in Hayes's hand now.

I don't know why exactly it feels like I'm being lured in closer as well.

"I'm happy to help you practice dating. I don't know if my heart will be able to take another five-page document outlining horrors, though."

Considering there's an aspect of "date practice" that leans into "intimacy practice," yeah… I'll spare us both the discomfort of outlining *that*.

Mouse reaches the chunk between Hayes's fingers and begins licking.

Very subtly, Hayes glances at my cat. "Is that a bunny costume?"

"Mouse doesn't have any fur, so he has many costumes that I change regularly after his weekly baths."

Hayes puffs a breath. "Cute. We should plan a date."

My thoughts stumble to keep up with the fact he didn't pause before changing topics. Planning a date seems perfectly logical. And tacking *dating practice* onto this whole thing actually helps me out a ton, too. I'm feeling better about this situation already. All I have to figure out now is how to subvert the inevitable rom-com plot points as they arise.

I thumb through fake dating first date disasters, reminding myself that *at least* I won't have to worry about any random paparazzi since Hayes is not a celebrity. Unless he's a *secret* celebrity. Secret identities is a thing that can blindside the main character in a rom-com. Our "fake dating" is already official. Next thing I know, he'll be the prince of Norway. "Is Norway a monarchy?" I ask.

"Kind of? It's a constitutional monarchy where the king's power is largely symbolic." He watches Mouse steal the fish and run back to the cat tree before he faces me. "What does the government of Norway have to do with us planning a date?"

"Nothing," I squeak. "Hopefully. You can never know these days how many tropes you'll end up bombarded with. You know?"

"Let's assume I don't know."

I shift, wringing my fingers. "The more the merrier. People like what's familiar. It's easier to sell feelings that are prematurely understood, so you cram as many as you can fit—"

"—into the standard-appropriate word count," he drones, shaking his head slightly. Rising, he pins me with a look that simply must be the grump's equivalent of *tender*.

Oh dear.

He's definitely a grumpy.

Am I a sunshine?

I might be, at least when I'm talking about moths. See? The major tropes are rolling in. I must remain vigilant.

Combing his fingers through his hair, he looks *way* down at me. "If you're comfortable with it, why don't you come over Sunday after breakfast? I'll take you somewhere I think you'll like."

"*After breakfast?*" I ask.

"Around ten?"

"Exactly ten?"

"Do you like absolutes without surprises?" he asks.

I press my lips together and adjust my tone so it doesn't bite when I say, "I gave you a five-page outline of what we can expect going forward. Of *course* I like absolutes without surprises."

"Come by at ten. Wear comfortable and weather-appropriate clothes—walking shoes. I looked into POTS, so I'll bring the peanut butter crackers if you'll bring your favorite water bottle. We're going to the zoo. We'll eat there. Then if you're up for it, we'll go stargazing in my favorite spot after sunset."

I gasp. "Stargazing?"

"Yep."

"The *zoo*?"

He nods.

That sounds amazing. But... "If it's a bad POTS day, salty crackers and water might not cut it..."

"Then the zoo has wheelchairs. I've got you, pudding. You prepare for trope disasters. I'll manage the more

71

realistic ones."

I fold my arms. "For the last time, my 'trope disasters' are not unrealistic."

"Uh-huh."

"You'll see."

"So long as you're not uncomfortable, I hope so."

I don't know what that means.

He stretches, somehow getting taller, then he yawns. "I should probably head to Temptations and check on Vince."

I know this one. That's a goodbye cue.

I rise, standing as tall as possible in front of him. "It's been lovely having you. You should come by again sometime."

"For sandwiches, maybe?" he asks.

My rehearsed farewell lines shrivel up on the tip of my tongue. "I'd love that!"

"Then it's a plan. See you Sunday, pudding." With a nod, he turns a look toward the cat tree, says, "Bye, Mouse," and strides out of my apartment in three steps.

The second the door shuts I realize I'm kind of fake/practice dating a giant man who is about to check on his bar.

Nifty.

I'm not frightened that this will get out of hand at *all*.

I just hope the rom-com gods know I am not cut out for the stress of rehabilitating an alcoholic. I was built for the meet cutes, not the bar fights. Besides, you can't actually *change* anyone, and I will not perpetrate a speculation that you can.

It's a bad message.

Disgraceful.

CHAPTER 5

♥ If he's asking to take the "fake" out of the first date, maybe don't overlook that?

Nine fifty-five, I'm standing outside Hayes's front door and tapping my morning reflections into a self-care app on my phone. The more words I type in a harried frenzy of *I'm about to go on a date, kind of*, the more money I get in order to buy little things from the store.

I am a simple creature.

Give me a tiny virtual animal to take care of, and I'll remember to drink water.

Now if only the tiny virtual animal were a *moth*, it might just cure my brain completely. Anxiety? Who's she? I'm busy deep breathing in order to get my tiny virtual moth a tiny virtual *hat*. His antennae are cold. Depression? What's that? I'm spending ten minutes in sunlight meditating on which new floof color my moth needs to have.

I'm the simple one. The world's what's complicated.

At nine fifty-six, I startle, whipping my attention up as the door swings open.

"Thought so," Hayes grumbles, folding his arms. The long sleeves of his v-neck shirt outline every muscle of his arms, and I'm surprised he found something casual that fit the length.

"Thought so?" I echo.

"You'd rather die than be late, so you're early, standing outside and waiting on the agreed-upon time because it's rude to intrude prior to that. Despite the fact you live three seconds from my door. Despite the fact you're allergic to *standing*."

"I am *not* allergic to standing." I shift my weight. "It's just not entirely advised sometimes." It's not like it's a hot day. Heat makes it worse. Showers can be evil. I'm perfectly *fineee*.

He mumbles, "Uh-huh." His gaze drops to the pale green backpack at my feet. "What's that?"

"Emergency gear."

His eyes narrow. "Emergency…gear?"

I put my phone in my sweater pocket and pluck up my backpack. "Don't you worry about it."

As though he almost trusts me, he shrugs and sets the presence of my backpack aside. Patting his pockets, he does a *keys, phone, wallet* check before grabbing a fresh box of peanut butter crackers off the table beside his door and stepping out with me. "Ready to go?" he asks, locking up.

I sure hope so. Giving my best smile, I nod.

❖

I am a tiny toy person.

Hayes drives a GMC Canyon, which is a GIANT truck. Four doors. Massive bed. So much leg room I'm surprised mine aren't dangling. He fits snugly in the driver seat, and primitive parts of my brain can't help but take note of the way he carefully maneuvers the beast on the highway.

Other girls I've known go on eternally about a guy's butt.

I find safe driving sexy. Or maybe my anxiety does.

TBD.

He's a good driver, safe, cautious. Being in vehicles normally gives me a great deal of anxiety—one of the many reasons I am desperate to go home to my cottage on the outskirts of the city rather than stay in the heart of it—but I haven't reached for the "oh crap" handle even once since climbing in here.

And, yes, I do mean *climb*.

Had to pull myself in like a wee toddler.

Hayes catches me staring out of the corner of his eye, and my heart lurches, so I hug my backpack against my chest and tell my heart to calm down. I'm seated. It shouldn't be pounding so fast. It's always so charming to play *what condition is making me feel* off *today.* POTS? Anxiety? Allergic reaction to MSG, which triggers the POTS, which triggers the anxiety? Something else I just haven't discovered yet?

Hormones?

If it's nothing else, it's usually hormones. Screw hormones.

"What animal are you most looking forward to seeing?" he asks.

"I want to feed the giraffes."

His brow lowers, heavy above his eyes. "You can feed the giraffes?"

"Of course you can feed the giraffes. Have you never fed a giraffe before?"

He changes lanes. "I've never been to the zoo before."

My mouth falls open.

"What?" he asks.

"You've never been to the zoo before? Why not?"

He lifts a shoulder. "It's not something you do alone, and no one else I know would be particularly interested. My sisters prefer concerts or shopping or arboretums. *Mamma* would rather go to a restaurant. And the guys at Temptations…would really rather hang out at Temptations."

My nose scrunches. "Animals are cool. Better than

beer."

"Agree." Single-handling the wheel, he rubs his neck. "I'm glad to finally have someone to go with."

Something light as cotton candy and just as fragile puffs in my chest. I inflate with the feeling and beam. "Oh sure. I love doing new things. I just… Sometimes they're difficult to navigate, or loud, and I need accommodations or someone familiar with me in order to make them comfortable…so…" The cotton candy meets water and vanishes as my voice trickles into silence. I'm high maintenance. Maybe that's the problem. Maybe all the guys I've met speed dating know I'm high maintenance when they meet me so they bail before they have to handle any problems.

"I'm familiar?" he asks.

I straighten, clutching my backpack tighter. "Uh…" We've met several times now. We've had dinner together. He coaxed Mouse out of hiding for a few seconds. Right now, he's more familiar to me than anyone else I know in person outside of my parents. The bar is quite low, however. "…sure?"

He makes a low *hm* sound. "If you start feeling tired, please don't hesitate to let me know. I can and will carry you."

The comment hits me between the brows and leaves me gaping. First of all, what? Is that the sweetest thing anyone has ever said to me concerning my, honestly mild, case of POTS? And second of all, should I be concerned that he knows he is capable of carrying me with such little effort? Because I'm stumped, I ask, "Is that a normal thing to offer?"

His big shoulders lift and fall. "Does it matter?"

"Huh?"

"Who cares what's 'normal'? We're going to have fun

today. If having fun means carrying you to the nearest wheelchair, so be it. You think anyone's going to confront me on the matter?"

I scan him from the top of his head near the ash gray ceiling down his long legs. Dang. The seat is all the way back, isn't it? And he could still drive with his knees. Yeah, no one is going to oppose him. I don't think anyone *can*. "What if someone thinks I'm being kidnapped?"

"How do you think I'm going to be carrying you?"

"Like a sack of potatoes."

He puffs air out his nose. "Absolutely not. You're a princess. A moth princess. You deserve equivalent respect."

My cheeks flare red, and unacceptable levels of attraction go charging through my limbic system, overriding my frontal lobe, maybe turning it off like a light switch.

Moth princess.

I'm a moth princess.

Hayes merges off the highway while my brain creates fantasy worlds ruled by beautiful fluffy moth princesses. I'm going to have to drop this hint off with Blaire. She must write me a moth princess book.

"Do you tell all the girls your family makes you go out with that they're moth princesses?" I blurt.

"Shockingly, no. I don't think I've ever been half so unhinged." His thumb taps against the wheel as he follows signs toward Westville Zoo. Murmuring lowly, he notes, "I wonder if I'll ever recover."

I don't think I'm going to. It's the most perfect compliment in the world. Forcing myself to look out the window, I regulate my breaths in an effort to calm down. Moth princess. An adorable moth princess. I don't think I have ever wanted to be perceived as anything else.

Despite my protests, after we park and head up to the

gate entrance, Hayes pays for my ticket. Sternly he hands me the slip of paper and says, "I invited you, so I pay. That's the correct procedure."

I find myself utterly incapable of arguing with that sentiment. I may have been peeved had he said something stupid about how he's the *man* and the *man* should pay for dates, but he didn't. A correct procedure isn't a double standard. That means if I invite him somewhere, I'll have the opportunity to pay. And that is perfectly fair.

Even though I haven't been in over a decade, I love the zoo. At this time of year it's just about perfect. It's not too hot, so my body is holding up well. The animals are more active in cooler weather, but it's not prime zoo-going time like in the spring or fall, so it's not nearly as crowded as it could be.

It's basically a perfect date.

Once lunch time hits, we settle into a booth at my favorite childhood zoo restaurant. Tucked into a food plaza overflowing with gardens, outdoor tables, and the occasional gift shop, Bison Burgers does not serve actual bison. What they do sell is soft-swirl ice cream as big as my head. Also, grilled cheese. I'm picky about my burgers. I'm less picky about my grilled cheese.

Hayes doesn't seem to be a picky eater at all if the *three* massive burgers on his side of the table are any indication. Every last one of them is complete with a side order of overflowing fries, too.

Exactly how many calories does he need to survive?

And why am I suspicious that the answer is *all of them*?

"So you used to come here when you were a kid?" he asks, placing a single fry on my plate beside the other half of my grilled cheese and my yet unopened bag of chips.

I nod, munching into the buttery, flaky, three-cheese masterpiece that is my grilled cheese sandwich. "I like soft and sweet things, so the first time I saw one of the ginormous ice cream cones, I fixated on it. We hunted it down, and this became our go-to place to eat at the zoo ever since."

Glancing toward the ice cream machine behind the ordering counter, Hayes hums and takes a massive bite out of his sandwich. It makes sense why he got three. Even though they are kind of huge, his mouth makes them a four-bite ordeal. Wiping a speck of mustard off his lip, he licks his thumb.

I don't like mustard.

But at the sight of whatever it is he just did, my brain does silly things.

Silly *rom-com* things.

Heart-pounding, mind-wandering rom-com things.

I have never wanted to kiss anyone in my entire life.

I kind of want to kiss Hayes.

How foolish.

I pick up his fry offering and control myself.

A mouth that shreds through a double cheese burger with all the fixings in four bites is not the kind I want on mine, thanks. Let's just keep that information in the forefront of my thoughts. I am not edible. I am a delicate moth princess.

Biting down my smile, I try not to get all giddy—again—at the memory of him calling me a *moth princess*. I'm having an amazing time. Perhaps the best time I've had since I moved away from home. I can't let my tendency to get over-energetic due to the smallest things ruin this. Hayes is obviously the calm, cool, and collected type. Our personalities don't mesh, and I don't want to inconvenience him by clashing with his energy.

"You're vibrating, pudding," he comments, slipping another fry onto my plate. "What are you thinking about?"

Kissing you.

I choke that immediate response down and beat it with a stick, chirping, "Nothing. I'm not vibrating." I might be. I totally am. I'm ecstatic. I fed a *giraffe* this morning. Their tongues are so long. They look like fried plantain. I love them. "I'm just…happy. I don't know. I haven't done anything this fun for a long time."

"Neither have I," he offers.

I laugh. "You said you had a Christmas *and* New Year's party with your family." A family that puts out porridge for fairy creatures. What's not amazing and fun about that?

"Parties during which I ended up shoved into two people who remind me of my sisters…the second one right at midnight…" he snarls, reaches for the ketchup bottle, and creates a red mountain in place of where his first burger once lived.

It's gone now. Completely gone. I swear I've only blinked twice, officer.

Disgust curls his lip, but I only tilt my head. Catching my eye, he sighs. "It's a 'thing' to kiss the person you're closest to at midnight on New Year's."

"*Oh*," I blurt. Right. I knew that. I wince and mute a shudder at the idea of having that expectation thrust upon me. "That must have been awkward."

"To say the least. I wasn't expecting Liv's friend to smash her mouth into mine at a moment's notice. If she asked, I didn't hear her, and it was not at all a pleasant experience. Liv's my older sister, and she's a bit more tame than Marit. Her friend…clearly not so much."

Genuinely, I think I would vomit. From the stress of having no idea what I'm supposed to do in such a situation alone, I would hurl. "I'm so sorry," I whisper.

He lifts a shoulder and scoots me another fry before scooping an uncanny amount of ketchup onto a cluster of about five and shoveling them into his mouth. He finishes chewing before muttering, "Needless to say, I really appreciate your willingness to help get me some peace."

My revolt settles, and my chest warms. "I'm happy I can help."

"I do wish I could help you out more, too. I really don't love the idea of you rushing into a relationship just because those are the terms your parents have set forth. I have a feeling they intended for you to start looking earlier than you have."

I take my fries and munch, refusing to look at Hayes's dredging stare. He's judging me. I can feel it. And I *know* my parents didn't intend for me to procrastinate what is easily one of the most important decisions in my life. But excuse me if they underestimated the severity of my executive dysfunction.

Sometimes, it's impossible to act without enough perceived reward. And even with one, it can still take some severe arguing to get from point A to point B. Every day can be a battle. And a lot of times I lose.

"I'm not trying to criticize you," Hayes mumbles. Reaching for his Cheerwine, he takes a sip that downs about a fourth of the glass. He rolls the straw between his fingers. "I'm just suggesting that maybe, for your well being and your parents' ultimate intentions, we let you practice date me through your birthday, meet your parents together, and get your cottage. You've only got a little over four weeks between now and then. Let's say we practice for half that. Is two weeks enough time in any stretch of the imagination for a guy to be ready to meet your parents, and, more than that, to be approved by them?"

Probably not.

I shake my head slightly and let the hum around us drown into my thoughts as I watch a spare few couples outside the window meander past a central fountain topped with a roaring lion. Why is it always lions? Why couldn't it be a giraffe?

Hayes clears his throat while I'm still trying to parse through my thoughts, the situation, the ultimate end goal. The best course of action.

Life's just like editing a book, except plot holes can't exist, yet we all manage to fall in pits anyway.

"If you don't want to lie to them, we don't have to. We're already going through the motions of dating. We could just…date."

"No." I manage a breath and drop my focus into taking a bite out of my grilled cheese. "That's okay. I'm only interested in dating in order to marry, so it wouldn't work out. It's kind of you to offer, though. I do appreciate it, and you're right. It's going to be difficult to find someone in the time I have left before my birthday. I think I'm going to talk to my parents and see if I can extend the deadline by a few months. They should understand. Then I'll have time for you to tell me what I'm doing that turns people off."

He scoops more fries into his mouth, and his gaze burns into me for long moments. I pour all my energy into eating and attempting not to look nervous. He asks, "Would your parents have a problem with me? I can wear long sleeves whenever we meet."

My brow furrows, and I look at the long sleeves he's currently wearing. Oh. "The tattoos?"

He nods.

I laugh. "No, I don't think they care about stuff like that. They're not uptight like most people in their position."

He lifts a brow. "Then…what part doesn't work out? You couldn't see us getting married if we continue to enjoy one another's company?"

My smile feels plastic on my face, and I don't know

how to answer. I'm intimidated. He frightens me. I'm inexplicably attracted to him, but people far less terrifying have hurt me too many times for me to ever trust my impressions of people ever again. I don't think I'd be able to pull off pretending that I want to have a serious relationship with Hayes in front of my parents. I might enjoy his company as a person and find him attractive, but it's an attraction that I barely understand and wouldn't know how to act upon without picturing how it could all go wrong.

There's simply no way I could ever be enough for him when I've never been enough for people half so overwhelming.

Being his average girlfriend to get him some peace from his family is different, especially since his family doesn't know me. My family will pick up that I'm being weirder than normal. I don't like his career, and that's one of the first things parents bring up concerning their children's significant others. They know how I feel about alcohol, especially since guilt pressured me into telling them everything after my twenty-first birthday. They barely chastised me. They said it was *normal* to go out for drinks when you turn twenty-one. They were more upset that my friends didn't help me get home safe, but they were glad that I'd clearly been lucid enough to find my way back on my own.

They know I don't have the same opinion as them when it comes to anything serious like relationships or alcohol or drugs.

I am extreme in my emotions and worldviews.

Bad things are bad. No semicolon. *Period.* And serious things are serious, not meant to be taken lightly. I commit and go all-in.

I can't do that with Hayes.

I'm still scared that all the peaceful, quiet pieces of him end up overturned whenever he drinks. I hope I never have to see it. So long as I don't see it, I may not have to think that it exists.

The bottom line is: I don't trust anything anymore.

There's no way my parents would believe we're together. Not even with rom-com magic. Never in a million years.

Surprising me, Hayes lowers his attention to his next burger and softly asks, "Is whatever doesn't work out anything I can help?"

Even if he could, it wouldn't be fair to him. It's devastating for me every time someone makes me feel wrong for being who I am. Just because Hayes isn't right for me doesn't mean he's not perfect for someone else, and I refuse to make him feel less. "I don't think so," I say, carefully. "I'm sorry."

His head shakes. "You don't have to apologize." He takes a big bite, chews. His Adam's apple bobs. "I'm sorry if it seems like I'm pressuring you."

"No, not at all. You're trying to help me. I appreciate it. A lot. Really." I take a deep breath. "All I need to know is what I'm doing wrong when it comes to dating, though. I can figure the rest out from there."

Hayes provides me with a waning glance, a sigh, and another fry. "If you say so, pudding."

CHAPTER 6

♥ Strange things happen when you start to fall in love.

Hayes's right eye twitches, forehead pressed against the locked door, one giant fist crushing the knob. I half expect the metal to deform beneath his grip. Instead, it just rattles as he shakes it. "*How?*" he growls at the slab in front of him.

In case you're as lost as Hayes is looking—despite my flipping outline warning him of situations like this—we are locked in the space between the reptile exhibits in the dimly-lit emporium of cold-blooded creatures.

How? you ask?

Rom-com magic.

Or, well, actually someone left the door open. I assumed it wasn't supposed to be open. I went to close it. Another visitor nearly rammed into me when they came laughing around the corner, and Hayes swept me away from collision. Promptly inside. And the door closed. Then locked.

So, basically, rom-com magic.

It figures the knob needs a key from both sides. Normally, isn't the inner side easily unlocked without one?

No, no, no.

We're *fake dating*. Getting locked in a cubby space between giant snakes and tiny frogs is absolutely on the table.

Smug, I smirk at Hayes. "And you doubted we'd end up locked in a closet."

"Ellen, is this really the time to be gloating? There was only one other group of people in here. We don't know when someone will find us. And if we make a ton of noise, it'll disrupt the reptiles. That's rude. This is their home."

I agree with everything he's just said, and I appreciate the fact consideration for the animals makes it on his list as well.

He rakes his fingers through his hair. "Maybe the door was open for a reason. Maybe someone is coming back soon."

"Are you claustrophobic?" I ask, finding a frog stuck to the inner glass of one tank. It's very cute. I like him.

"No," Hayes snips, tensing when I move toward him. "What are you…"

His breath catches as I squeeze myself past him and crouch to look at the lock. I hum, dropping my backpack onto the stained cement beneath me.

"Ellen…" he exhales my name, and I look up. Face white, he's pressed to the wall right next to me, my head just barely reaching his trunk-like thighs.

"There's not a lot of space on this side. Could you stand over there?" I nod at the other end of the small room.

He glances that way, and a swallow moves his throat. He doesn't budge.

A laugh bubbles out of me. "You are totally claustrophobic." Flipping open my bag, I down a gulp of water from my bottle before I shuffle through my emergency equipment.

"I am *not*," he growls.

"Then move deeper into the cramped room, Hayes. Away from the door."

He does not. His big chest fills with air, and he folds his arms. "What are you doing?"

Presently? Finding him adorable. To think a giant guy

like him would be scared of small spaces when his very existence in most rooms creates them. "Getting us out of here."

Uneasily, he begins rolling up his sleeves, revealing all the inked patterns and coiling snakes beneath. "How?"

I pull out a lock-picking kit.

Hayes swears. "What? Why…"

"I told you I'd take care of the rom-com stuff."

"Why in the—" Curse. "—do you know how to lock pick?"

"I went through a phase." It was several years ago, but I think I still know the way it feels to get the pins and tumblers in the right places. If I don't, I know brute-forcing is an option that works at the detriment of the lock. Worst case scenario, I'll pay to replace it.

"A phase?" Hayes echoes, baffled.

"Sure. A client wrote a spy story, and I got interested in the details. I pride myself in fact checking whenever possible." It takes me a moment to remember how one manages to be a super secret spy, then it's almost too effortless. The lock clicks, and I open the door. "Ta da."

Hayes stares at me, right eye twitching.

It occurs to me that perhaps I have not displayed normal human behavior, and my smile falls. Shoving the kit back in my bag, I say, "For the record, I've never done this in front of a potential boyfriend, so it can't be the reason I can't find one. I've not even mentioned it during speed dating."

He keeps staring.

His eyes pierce me like knives.

Swinging my backpack on like a security blanket, I try to stand tall, breathe deep.

He swipes a hand down his face, cupping his mouth, and I slip out of the way when he exits, like a bullet train.

Once out, he relaxes. Slightly. And I close the door behind us, both of us safely outside.

"That's the problem," he says finally.

"What's the problem?"

He turns toward me, still a little twitchy in his right eye. "Clearly, you're not playing to your strengths. *Knows how to lock pick* should be one of the first things you mention when you meet a potential suitor."

So they can stare at me like he is? I don't think so.

Folding my arms, I mutter, "You're being sarcastic, aren't you?"

"I'm attempting to wrap my mind around getting stuck in the feeding room of a reptile exhibit and you calmly pulling a lock-picking set out of your bag like you knew it would happen. Worse, I can't wrap my head around playing a significant role in causing it to happen."

I throw my hands in the air. "*Hayes*, I *gave* you an outline! Characters in rom-coms are always getting stuck in places together. It's called *forced proximity*. Ever heard of it?" Crap. He probably hasn't, and now my tone might be a little too rough.

"*We aren't characters*," he bellows.

I tense, and my stomach tightens. I'm ninety percent sure my tone wasn't *that* rough.

Stiffening, he takes a step back and clenches his fist. Voice softening, he says, "Sorry. I'm sorry. It's just... This is real life, Ellen. Sometimes relationships go to crap, and there's no magical force at work behind the scenes. Sometimes you fall in love, and it hits you like a juggernaut. You have the best night of your life, but things change, and there's nothing you can do. It doesn't work out, and there's no ultimate plot on your side to make things better. In real life, second chances are bad ideas because we naturally give people we love all the chances in the world, so when things do end? They should stay ended. Forced proximity is uncomfortable. Grand gestures are awkward and harassment and, let's be honest, expensive. Real life, a real relationship, takes work and effort and learning to communicate when you want to be anything but vulnerable in front of the one person capable of destroying you." He takes a shallow breath. "This…was weird."

Those three simple words cut me to the core of my being, and I drop my gaze to my shoes. They're a nice pair of shoes. Or they were. Once. They're worn almost entirely through now, because I've used them for five years, because change is awful. I like familiar things. Patterns make me feel safe. It's why I draw comfort from stories, tropes, and archetypes.

I know the rules at a glance. The same isn't always the case in *real life*. But sometimes? Sometimes we forget that no fiction exists without a firm foundation in reality.

Melanie Richards put that into words. And it makes too much sense to ignore.

"Just because it's weird," I whisper, forcing myself to meet his eyes, "doesn't mean it's bad."

"Getting locked in a closet isn't bad?"

"Not when you have the tools you need, no. It's an experience. A story. Something you can share later and laugh about." I rock my weight from one leg to the other. I think this is a panic attack more so than a POTS attack. I'm uncomfortable. It's too hot in my sweater. That's a panic attack. I don't know what I'm supposed to do with the information, though. I don't have a way home. I don't want to offend Hayes by prematurely ending our "date." My voice tremors. "I'm sorry you're claustrophobic, and this freaked you out, but it's not a big deal. I'm prepared."

"I'm not claustrophobic," he exhales.

I frown. "You're freaking out."

"I—" His eyes close. "I *might* be the tiniest bit claustrophobic."

"Do you need to sit down for a moment?" I ask.

"Do you?" He cuts his fingers through his hair. "You're doing the rocking thing." He whispers a curse, and his eyes snap open, sudden realization spearing through his stature. He strides toward me, and my already-hammering heart lurches. Without a moment's notice, he sweeps me up into his arms—moth princess style. "You're doing the rocking thing," he echoes, looking at me, so close. "I've got you. I'm sorry. I don't…small spaces. It's not very manly. But…"

"Being manly is stupid," I offer, meekly. And if we're going to judge *manliness*, this boy is having a panic attack of his own…while carrying me like I weigh nothing. So. I think even by societal toxic masculinity terms, he's well and fine and good.

"What do you need?" he asks, tone pinched with nerves.

"I'm fine." And well and good. I think our faces are closer than when we're standing in front of each other. Yikes.

Whatever I do, I can't look at his lips. Just don't. With all the rom-com magic around, glancing down means consenting to a kiss. Man, the stuff we let romance novels teach sometimes.

Consent is *only* an enthusiastic, spoken *yes*. Not a glance during a sexually-tense moment.

N-not that this is a sexually tense moment.

Just…eyes on his eyes, Ellen. Eyes on his eyes.

"I don't want you blacking out on me," he grumbles. Turning, he finds the exit and plows outside. Moments later, he's setting me on a bench, sitting down beside me, and patting his lap. "Here. You can put your backpack down and…"

I witness the exact moment he realizes that *lap pillow* was on my outline—for just a time as this. Why would a character even have a medical emergency if not in order to lap pillow? Seated and—honestly—amused, I start coming down from the tension spike. Slipping out of my backpack, I set it on his lap and lie back, staring up at the canopy of trees above us. "This makes three."

"No." His brusque tone washes over me, and the chaotic emotions sweeping through it are comfortingly apparent. "Three?"

"Four actually, I think." I lift my hand, counting on my fingers. "Lap pillow, locked in a confined space together, rescued from danger, princess carry."

His lips soundlessly form the words *princess carry*, then he winces. "I…forgot about that one."

"Should have gone with the sack of potatoes like I mentioned before you overloaded my frontal lobe by comparing me to a moth princess."

Breath leaves him, and he combs my red hair away from my cheek. His touch tickles around my ear, and my lungs hitch halfway through drawing in air.

Clenching a fist against my chest, I say, "Miscommunication bothers me."

His eyes close, exasperated, and he murmurs, "Miscommunication is a daily part of life. Marit asks me if her dress makes her look fat. I say *what dress?* She doesn't talk to me until she asks if I want to take her and Liv out for tacos. I didn't mean anything rude, but that doesn't matter." Grumbling, he mutters, "I'm sorry if my definition of a dress involves a skirt that at least pretends to reach the thighs." He shakes his head. "People miscommunicate in nearly every conversation. It's impossible to know exactly what someone means when every word comes laced with thoughts we can't begin to assume. Miscommunication's irritating and bothersome, but it's realistic."

"And maybe that's the most bothersome part, but, Hayes, that's not what I'm trying to say."

His fingertip traces my ear again, and I shudder. He murmurs, "Then I guess we just miscommunicated, pudding. What are you trying to say?"

"Do you hate me?"

His eyes widen. "Absolutely not."

"Then you hate how I translate things into book terms? You hate that I'm right about the rom-com stuff?"

His mouth opens and closes. He mutters a word I don't understand, and I think it might be a Norwegian curse. Rough as rocks, he grumbles, "Pudding, I don't hate a single thing about you. I just recognize that the situations you've outlined are unnerving, and I don't feel right being a part of some of them. You deserve more respect. I, especially, owe you more respect."

Every muscle in my body relaxes. "You're very respectful."

"I try, but often I'm weaker than I should be," he mutters. His gaze locks on his hand, then he closes his eyes and pulls his fingers away from my skin. "Are you familiar with the concept between nurture or nature?"

"Vaguely."

He rests back against the bench and tips his attention toward the sky, staring past overhanging branches at the slices of blue. "I want to do right by the women in my life the way my *mamma* and sisters have taught me, but I'm constantly worried that the nature my *far* bred into me is going to show up and turn me into someone who…breaks things. Hurts people. Takes advantage of them. And…is just selfish. When presented with temptation, I fail to do the right things just like him. You…" He clears his throat. "The situations you've described are full of temptations. And I don't want to break anything or hurt you if…or when they come about."

I lift my hand to his face, cup the stubble that's already darkening his jaw, and draw his attention back down to me. "You aren't your father. And as long as you don't want to be, you won't become him. He made conscious choices that defined his life and character. You make conscious choices that define yours, and if you want to be better than him, that's what you'll become." Pulling my gaze away, I let out a soft breath. "Trust me. It's a lot harder than you think to copy someone else. Even when you're making a conscious effort, you mess it up. I can't imagine doing it by mistake."

His fingers close around my hand, delicate and gentle yet firm even as they dwarf, completely swallowing. The corner of his mouth brushes my palm as he murmurs, "You don't need to copy anyone else. You're fine just the way you are."

"Even with my book tropes?"

His gaze cuts sidelong. "Clearly, there's scientific evidence at play. We just haven't found the logical correlation yet."

"Magic."

"No, not magic," he grumbles.

"Of course it's magic."

He scowls at me.

"When you take a risk on something new or scary, it's magic. Maybe not the kind that says nisse and elves are real, but when the hardest thing in the world to do is believe in something weird, belief in itself becomes… magic."

His head tilts so that the puff of breath leaving his nose runs over my wrist. "You really are a little fairy creature, pudding."

"Moth princess," I correct.

"That's what I said."

"Do you think that's why no one wants to be in a relationship with me? They can tell I'm a little too… fluffy?"

"Are you joking?"

I lift a shoulder. "Not really. Maybe I'm not realistic enough for people."

Rolling his eyes, Hayes combs his fingers through my hair and hunkers down to press a kiss against my forehead. "Or maybe you're too real for them, and it's terrifying."

"I don't…" My entire body heats, overwhelmed by the gentle touch of his lips against my skin. I don't know what I'm trying to say. I don't understand. But exactly *what* I don't understand isn't something I know how to explain. I don't understand what he's trying to say. I don't understand how his lips are this gentle. I don't understand why he's kissed my forehead.

I gave no indication that should have prompted such a thing.

Was "forehead kisses" on my list?

I don't think so.

They would fit on my list, but I didn't add them because I didn't think something entirely within his control would happen, outside of trip-and-fall sort of accidents. I was wrong. I suppose rom-com magic disintegrates logic along with spurring uncanny situations.

He draws back. "You feeling better?"

I force myself not to touch my forehead when he releases my hand. I might be flushed. Or this might be the heart-beating-too-fast thing.

Man, I sure do *love* playing symptom roulette…

"Yeah," I squeak. "You?"

"More or less." Sighing, he says, "No more closets,

okay?"

"It normally doesn't happen more than once in a story."

His jaw locks. "*Normally?*"

I clear my throat. "Have you ever read or watched a rom-com?"

"Briefly. Against my will." With finality, he mutters, "Sisters."

Ah yes. Sisters. I wish I had sisters growing up. They sound kind of awesome. "Rom-coms are chaos. Unfortunately, I cannot accurately dictate everything we might have to expect going forward." I wet my lips. "If it's more trouble than it's worth now that you believe me, I'll understand."

He watches my mouth a long moment before blinking, sighing, looking away. "Keep the lock-picking set on you."

"Of course."

"And, Ellen?"

I tilt my head before I start to sit up. "Yes?"

"At about which point do I need to worry that the fake part has turned real for you, but you aren't telling me, because drama?"

I laugh, and I'm definitely flushing now. Against better judgment, I finish sitting up while my heart pounds worse. "Don't worry. I'll just tell you. Forced drama gives me a headache."

His tongue roams his cheek a moment before he nods. "'Kay. Cool."

'Kay. Cool.

I wonder if that has any deeper meanings I'm not picking up on.

It wouldn't be a first.

CHAPTER 7

♥ Can you have a "sick day" chapter if you aren't sick?

Call your parents, Ellen.

The thought slips into my brain for what must be the eightieth time this morning.

My gaze slants toward the clock in the corner of my phone screen, and I wince. Okay, maybe it's the tenth time *this afternoon*. I wonder if I'll manage to crawl out of bed before I'm hitting my fiftieth time *this evening*.

I have to call my parents and ask for an extension on this "relationship deadline." If, for some reason, they decline, I need to make a plan on how to move forward, but I'm frozen. Completely frozen. I've done nothing but look at cat videos on Leopard, listen to "Never Enough" by Velette (otherwise known as Colette Hart singing with her husband, Velspar), and wonder if I need to take a shower when I get up or if I can skip it. Again.

I haven't done anything since I went to the zoo with Hayes. Two days ago. And while I know that whole event exhausted me to a point we cut things short and skipped going stargazing, I also know I can't blame this slump on it.

I had a great time.

Since Mouse is curled peacefully against my back instead of meowing at my face, his food and water dispensers have yet to run dry. That's not to say *I* shouldn't probably (really, definitely) eat something more than the protein bars I keep in my beside table. My nightstand is a disaster of empty water bottles and wrappers. I have only left the space beneath my covers in order to go to the bathroom. Which is approximately ten feet in front of me.

Mouse needs his weekly bath soon.

I need to shower.

I probably should wash my sheets.

Eat a real meal.

I hate getting stuck like this...but hating it doesn't make it better. Hating it just makes it harder to escape the spiral.

Forcing myself out of the Grand Time Suck that is social media, I go to my self-care app. The only boxes I've been checking since I started my unexpected hibernation have been "drink water" and "work emails."

Eat a healthy meal—daily task, protein bars don't count —glares at me. Along with *shower*.

This probably won't last another two days, because according to my future tasks calendar, that is when Mouse needs his bath. And if anything is sure to force me out of this mental freeze, it's Mouse.

At this point, Mouse takes care of me more than I take care of him.

Sighing, I close my eyes as though I'm not at risk of falling asleep and losing whatever remains of this day. Since I don't open my eyes again, it's clear I enjoy living on the edge. That's the only thing you can expect from Ellen Little—she likes to live dangerously.

My phone buzzes mere moments before I've passed out, and my groggy heart lunges. The only people who contact me are my parents.

It's time.

Wide awake, I sit up and answer. "Hello?" my voice rasps, so I clear the lingering sleep from my tone and hope Mom or Dad didn't hear it. They know me well enough to know what my being groggy at this time means. And showing such irresponsibility wouldn't bode well for my request.

The silence that flows through the line is piercing. Then it's gravelly. And I realize I've made a grave error.

"I'm sorry. Did I wake you?"

Hayes.

My heart thumps, and I suck in a breath. Answering my phone for my parents is one thing—I've known them my entire life, they've known me, we understand how to communicate in this format. Answering the phone for someone I barely know?

I haven't had to navigate this treachery for some time.

"I…uh…" Do normal people take naps in the afternoon, around lunch time? No, wait. I wasn't asleep. Or I don't think I was. I might have been. My heart's racing. "I don't think so."

More silence I have no clues on how to interpret, then: "You don't…think I woke you?"

"I may have fallen asleep, but I'm uncertain."

A rumbling *Ah* siphons through the line. "I've been there," he comments, cordial, like he actually understands, and my nerves settle some at the notion.

Silence.

Am I supposed to say something?

I clear my throat again. "So…what's up?"

"I showed my family the picture."

The picture. The one we took of us together at the zoo. Specifically for the purpose of him proving I exist when his family tried to set him up again. In the picture, we're standing together in front of the chimpanzee cage, and I'm distracted by the fact one of the monkeys is hanging off the netting and staring directly at me.

It was very unnerving. My smile was all wobbly because of it. But Hayes said he liked it.

"As expected, Marit accused me of manufacturing the picture using an AI."

My nose scrunches. Okay. I know the picture isn't the greatest, but do I look as creepy as those AI-generated images?

I hope not.

A female chirps Norwegian in the background, and my eyes go massive when Hayes's tone turns more curt than I've ever heard it. He rambles Norwegian back. Heaving a sigh once the background noise has turned into giggles, he says, "Sorry about that."

Oh my word. He's within range of his family *right now.*

Suddenly, this already awkward phone call feels like an awkward phone call with an audience. My face heats, and I slip out of bed in order to pace in front of my dresser, tapping my thigh with my free hand.

"Anyway…" He sighs again, the weight of the world on his shoulders. "I know it's an odd request, and there's no obligation, but would you mind…" he mutters.

A heavily accented woman's voice shouts, "Speak up, *lillebror*!"

Hayes outright huffs before gritting, "Would you mind sending me a photo?"

A…photo.

I freeze in front of my dresser and look at the vanity mirror. I am in my pj's, which is a worn t-shirt I've used for over ten years. No bottoms. Just holey underwear. But that's not the worst part. No. My hair is dripping with oil. My face shines—pallid, disgusting.

At the sight, it hits me through the chest that I feel *absolutely gross*. Worse. I'm lightheaded because I haven't eaten much of anything for several days.

Skin crawling, I melt onto the floor in an effort to at least not pass out.

I have to shower before I try to do anything else. But if I get in a hot shower right now, my vision is going to spot. I have to eat first. But there's no way I'm going to be able to cook when I feel like this. I've really gone and messed myself up now. I—

"Ellen?" Hayes murmurs. Then he curses in Norwegian.

His sister's voice is closer now, and she rambles something I don't understand before, "Just FaceTime her!"

My stomach turns over.

"She doesn't have an iPhone!" Hayes growls.

I do. I do have an iPhone, but I bite my tongue before I blurt the correction, because it's a bad idea to admit. I definitely cannot FaceTime someone right now.

The person I'm assuming is Marit snaps, "She does so. Your texts are blue. *Text*, rather. Don't tell me *my* big brother prefers phone calls for once?"

They argue in Norwegian for several minutes, and when Hayes talks to me again, he sounds livid. "You know what? Never mind. My stupid sister will get over it."

An older woman's voice crackles through the line in Norwegian, and Hayes's tone tames even as he demands, "*What?* She's being stupid. I can't say she's being stupid?"

The older woman's voice bites, and someone else— who I assume is Liv—starts laughing. It's a lot of noise, all at once, from a place I can't see, and partially in a language I don't understand.

Tense, I whisper, "I'm sorry..."

Hayes roars, "Liv, Marit, will you *be quiet*?" The noise hushes, with only the occasional giggle remaining, and— delicately—Hayes murmurs, "I'm sorry, Ellen. Forget this ever happened. Please."

I can't shake the feeling I've caused a problem. It congests in my chest, and I curl my legs up so I can press my forehead to my knees. Weakly, I whisper, "No. It's okay. I'm sorry. It's just... I..." Haven't showered. Am in my pj's in the middle of a work day. Am a little lightheaded. Don't like phone calls. "It's a bad time."

"A bad time?" Concern laces beneath the harsh, brusque, British-tinged words. "Is everything okay?"

"No..." The dam breaks. "I've been stuck in bed since Sunday surviving off protein bars and cat hugs. My water bottle reserves are about to run out, and I'm in week-old pajamas with greasy hair, so I can't send you a photo. And I'm sorry. I would if I could. But it would be indecent right now."

Moments pass. And I remember that when people ask if *everything's okay* they expect a *of course, and you?* not the truth. Biting my tongue, I clench my jaw and wait for judgment, awkwardness, this silence to stretch until I figure out how to either break the discomfort or freak out and hang up.

Freaking out and hanging up would look pretty good if I didn't live across a short wood deck from him.

This definitely would go on my list of *reasons I can't find a stable relationship*, but I've never exactly done this to a potential partner before. Just friends. And, honestly, their reactions should have been hints to inform me that I should *never be honest about how I am ever again.*

Hayes says something in Norwegian, and his mother replies, "Of course" and "Foolish" and "Go, go" breaking up words in the other language.

"Thanks, *Mamma*," Hayes says gently before quipping something at his sisters, then there's a lot of movement, kitchen noises, Norwegian comments, half-English replies. Finally, a soft, "Ellen?" draws me back to the fact I'm not just a bystander listening in on an unseen scenario.

"Yes?" I whisper.

"Give me thirty minutes, pudding? Okay?" It's the sweetest his voice has ever sounded, all deep and kind… and assertive. But.

Wait.

No.

What did he just say?

Thirty minutes?

Thirty minutes until *what*?

Have I missed something important?

Ultimately confused and a little frightened, I squeak the only thing I can think, "Okay."

He hangs up.

❖

I have just *barely* survived my shower—through sheer force of will and mostly sitting on the floor of the tub—when someone pounds on my door. Hair up in a towel and a discount moth bathrobe on, I ease my way out of my room.

My head's swimming.

My skin is red.

Purple tints my legs, splotchy.

Showers shouldn't be ordeals, but such was the trade off for knowing how to use a comma.

I don't make the rules.

The person at my door knocks, loud, and I wince, reaching the peephole.

Hayes's giant body passes in front of the door, back again. Plastic shopping bags and a canvas bag weigh down one arm. He swipes his hand over his face. "Ellen?" he calls, that deep voice of his booming.

I blink, swallow, and open the door.

Hayes towers. His frantic gaze pins my eyes, then my bathrobe, then my eyes again.

I look down and notice that the soft butterflies swirling

across the white fabric barely reach my knees. If I flush any harder on top of shower lag, I am going to pass out, so I close my arms around myself, keeping the front of my robe perfectly secure, and watch Hayes pale.

He takes a step back. Lifting the bags, he whispers, "I…" His gaze scans me again, and he looks decidedly elsewhere. "I brought medicine. Food from *Mamma* and Liv. Cold packs. A stuffed animal."

A…stuffed animal? My head tilts, and my towel's balance winds up compromised.

The wet thing flops off my head, freeing the damp red strands of my hair in a stringy mess over my shoulder.

Hayes's gaze cuts toward me, off again. A hard swallow moves through his throat.

His eyes close when I bend to get the towel, and you know what isn't a good idea when you're lightheaded? Getting something off the floor. Needless to say, I do not make it back up as I cave into a vision-spotting crouch with a whimper.

Sheer panic melts into every last fiber of Hayes's being. "Ellen," he breathes, right in front of me, hunkered down, hands hovering near. He curses. "Are you okay? What can I do?"

"Why are you here?" I whisper.

"Why…?" he grunts. "You're sick. You live alone. You said you hadn't been able to get out of bed. You were almost out of water. You were only eating *protein bars*." The growl in those last words makes it seem like he has a personal vendetta against protein bars.

Well. At least things are starting to make sense now. Great. We did a miscommunication. Again. Marvelous. Love that for me.

"Given what happened the last time we were together, I'm…" Breath leaves him; he sucks it back in. "I'm worried that if I step into your flat while you're only in a bathrobe, *somehow* one of the really, really, *really* troubling points on your outline will end up checked."

What in the world is he talking about now? For the last time, my outline wasn't troubling. It's a rom-com. A sweet rom-com, more likely than not. This isn't a dark romance. Our tropes aren't *billionaire mafia boss* meets *virgin good girl*. Not even one chili pepper.

I'll start with the problem I at least understand… "I'm not sick."

"Yo—" Hayes's voice drifts, fizzling away. "What?"

I'm embarrassed. I hate this. "I'm not sick. Sometimes…I just don't take care of myself very well. I have an app to help with it where I take care of a little bird when I complete my tasks, but it's not a little moth, so sometimes it's ineffective. And I'll get stuck doing nothing in bed for days." My vision is finally settling some, so I look up in time to find Hayes staring at me like I've just told him I murder kittens on my off time.

A giant breath fills his lungs, and I expect only bad things to happen next. Instead, his eyes close, he collects himself and mutters a curse followed by an apology. Shifting his weight, he reaches into one of his grocery bags, pulls out a giraffe stuffed animal, and hands it to me. "Here," he grates. "I'm going to pick you up now."

As elated as one can be on the verge of passing out, I take the soft, spotted friend before his words register. In fact, they don't register until I'm squeaking in his arms, staring at the stubble on his chin, and being carted into my living room. He sets me on the couch, hooks his finger in a straying lock of my damp hair, and pins it back over my ear. Seated, I hug my giraffe and blankly look up at him.

What is going on?

Why does this person think it's okay to just pick people

up and relocate them?

My eyes narrow, and I suspect *rom-com magic*. In rom-coms, *for some reason*, the guys are always these body builders with a tendency to toss the female lead around as though she weighs nothing. Drop a touch of fantasy into the mix, and the freaks of nature will do it *with mortal wounds*. Nope. I'm not even surprised Hayes thinks it's okay. This is perfectly normal. Since we're fake dating.

We invited the rom-com magic in. Now we must reap the consequences.

Hayes shuffles through his bags, pulls out a bottle of electrolyte water and sets it firmly in my hands. "Hydrate."

I look between the bottle and Hayes for a long moment, reading the big *0* on the label. Zero sugar added. Fake sugar makes me anxious. I don't know how to say that. I'm not even sure how to separate the fake sugar anxiety from the *what is going on?* anxiety.

He thought I was sick and prepped an entire sick day chapter.

No one has ever cared this much about me apart from my parents.

Rom-com magic is insane. Is it actually brain damage? Are we going to be okay?

"What's wrong?" he asks when I haven't moved.

I squeeze my giraffe. "N-nothing." Drinking the water he brought me is the polite thing to do. Except then I'll die. I'll get cancer and die.

Hayes crouches, cupping my chin in his big hand. Yet again it's baffling how gentle he's capable of being amidst these threads of assertion that leave me feeling a tiny bit… tingly.

Definitely brain damage.

I need medical help.

He murmurs, "You can tell me anything, pudding. If

I'm making you uncomfortable, I'll fix you a plate of food and leave you in peace. I just want to make sure you're okay before I go. I'm sorry if that's aggressive of me."

The eclipse in my stomach swells, fluttering wings reaching into my chest. My lashes flit, and I jerk my attention off his eyes. In this moment, I don't know why— either rom-com magic or my still somewhat light head, probably—but I feel like I really can tell him anything. It's been a long time since I've accepted people at their word. It took many years to realize other people's words didn't match mine.

Most don't say what they mean, and the rest don't mean what they say.

"I don't like fake sugar. I read this study about how it causes cancer years ago, and it's given me anxiety ever since." I swallow, whisper, "I'm sorry."

His gaze falls to the bottle in my hands, and he slips it free of my fingers, pulling his firm touch away from my chin as he turns the label around. "I think this is just added vitamins and minerals, no sugar or sugar alternatives period? If you don't want it, I understand, and I'll keep the fake sugar thing in mind. I also prefer real stuff."

It doesn't have either?

Oh.

Now I feel stupid...

Squeezing my eyes shut, I try to gather my thoughts. It takes longer than I'm proud of, but I finally say, "I'll drink it. Thank you."

He nods, returning the bottle to my hands, and I diligently open the cap as he steps around the couch. Plastic bags rustle as he sets things up in my kitchen. "*Mamma* made fresh bread for breakfast this morning. I brought goat cheese to go with it. Do you like goat cheese?"

"Yes."

He nods, pulling container after container out of the canvas bag. Arching a brow at a jar, he mutters, "One of my sisters decided you needed pickled eggs. Probably Marit. She's crazy."

"That sounds disgusting," I say before I can think twice. His sisters helped pack food for me. Because they all thought I was sick. That's the sweetest thing anyone has done for me. Ever. I've never had a friend who put in half that much energy.

Hayes lifts a shoulder. "They're all right. Just an odd addition. Do you like stew?"

I bite my cheek. "Depends?"

He continues unpacking like I'm not a picky ingrate.

And I appreciate that.

"On?" he asks.

"I don't really like the grainy texture of over-boiled potatoes. They have to be mashed. Or fried. Or baked."

He lifts a container. "We have fried potatoes. I am in possession of pretty much my mother's entire fridge of leftovers. Or, potentially, just her entire fridge period. May I use your stove?"

Dumbly, I nod, and he turns his back to me as he sets about preparing the food. I sip my water and watch him hunt around for the right pans and utensils. He spares no energy, going so far as to slather a slice of fresh bread in goat cheese and broil it until the top has browned.

Eternally dumbstruck, I stare at the plate of food he delivers to me and let the warm scent rise into my body.

He doesn't wait for me to take a bite before he's heading back to my kitchen and starting on the dishes. "Do you want to try a pickled egg?" he asks once I'm lost in the heaven that is homemade bread and toasted goat cheese. I have located a new fixation. This is joy.

"Hm?" I ask as cheese melts on my tongue to the tune

of warm, soft crunches. It's divine.

"Do you want to try a pickled egg? They're sweet with a kick. Like salt and vinegar potato chips. I don't think the texture's weird if you like normal boiled eggs."

I do like normal boiled eggs. And some part of me wants to prove I'm not a picky eater. "I'll…try it."

The sink water stops flowing, and Hayes returns to the living room with a little dish harboring one egg. It smells… bold. Similar to how sauerkraut smells bold. I don't actually mind sauerkraut though. I take the little glass bowl and lift my fork. I take a bite.

It is strange.

Sweeter than expected.

"Like it?" Hayes asks.

"It's weird."

"Want another?"

"Yes, please."

The corner of Hayes's infinitely-downturn mouth softens as he takes the bowl. "You're—" He curses. "—adorable, Ellen."

My stomach erupts, and heat crawls up my neck. "What did I do?"

Head shaking, he returns to the kitchen and gets me another egg. "I don't know. It's not something you *do*. It's something you are." Once he's given me my second egg, he goes back to the dishes. Water runs beneath his deep voice. "Are you feeling better?"

"I wasn't sick."

"Not traditionally, but I think being in bed for the past few days counts." Eyes lowered on the suds, he clears his throat. "Did…something happen?"

I fix my attention on my food, stab my second egg. "Not really. I just need to call my parents. And I don't want to. So I froze up. It happens sometimes." Emotional lows.

Standstills. I try not to think of it as proof I still have *depression*. I don't lie in bed and think everyone hates me, so I would be better off dead anymore. I've pretty much gotten rid of *everyone* in my life, and I'm happier guarding my energy now than I was while fighting for relationships that just made me tired. "It's normal for me."

"It's executive dysfunction."

I blink and freeze, an inch away from biting into my second egg. I look back at Hayes. "Yeah. How'd you…"

He lifts the wooden spoon he used to heat the potatoes. "Sometimes there just aren't enough spoons to go around. I get it."

I get it. If he knows about spoon theory, I think he actually does *get it*.

A lump tightens in my throat, and I put my back to him as I bite into my weird egg. It's difficult to swallow, but I manage. "I do my best with the spoons I have."

"No, you do better than your best because everything is ten times harder."

"Not everything."

"Select important or fundamental things. Like feeding yourself. Or getting out of bed."

Wincing, I murmur, "I'm very sorry for inconveniencing you."

"You haven't."

"But…"

"I was looking for an excuse to see you. Hence why my sisters pressured me into the embarrassing phone call."

Something electric zips down my spine.

He turns the water off and moves to my love seat, turning it into a child's chair. Clasping his hands together between his knees, he looks down at his thumbs. "I don't know how to say this correctly."

He's discovered what's wrong with my approach to

dating. If it has anything to do with today, that just seems obvious. Who would want to deal with someone who crashes at a moment's notice? Who in the world wants to deal with a person whose spoon fairy occasionally doesn't give them *any*?

Prepared to be hurt, I nibble on what's left of my toast and watch him.

"You don't have to be so tense around me."

My thoughts freeze. I wasn't expecting that. "Huh?"

"Talk about whatever you want. Do whatever you want. Don't feel like you have to apologize so much. You're not a burden or an inconvenience or a bother. I like being around you. I don't mind making accommodations so you can be more comfortable. I don't even mind coming by and cooking for you when you can't bring yourself to do it on your own. Friends take care of friends."

Stilling, I watch him with my lips parted in awe. "We're…friends?"

His gaze lifts, glaring. "Either that or enemies, right? Those are the options for *to lovers*, aren't they?"

"Well, there's also strangers to lovers, and the variations on friends and enemies—childhood, brother's, rival… Each comes with a different set of expectations, emotion, and relationship dynamic." I brighten, gasping. "Right now, I like idiots to lovers."

"Idiots to lovers?" he echoes.

I nod. "The characters are too stupid to see they're hopelessly in love with each other. The chaotic energy is marvelous."

Hayes stares at me. His right eye twitches, so he lifts a hand to rub it. "Hm," he rumbles. "Well, if it's okay with you, I think I'd prefer friends over idiots."

I haven't had a real friend for…ever. I may never have had a real friend. Definitely not someone willing to come by with food and help me out of a funk. My chest tightens, and I look at my now-empty plate. "I'm worried that I'm not a very good friend. I've never been able to maintain any kind of relationship for very long."

Roughly, he grates, "And I am entirely doubtful that's your fault, pudding. You're not hard to get along with."

"I'm not?"

He lifts his chin, pointing it at the giraffe I'm still hugging in the crook of my arm. "That was five dollars. You haven't let go of it. You're painfully polite, and you're exceptionally easy to please. If someone pays attention for five seconds, they'll realize how wonderful you are. And they'll probably learn something about moths or semicolons, too."

"Semicolons only have two functions. Most people think they do more. But they don't…"

The corner of Hayes's mouth actually pulls upward in response to my dazed comment. It's not quite a smile. But it might just be the most beautiful thing I've ever seen. Dryly, he says, "See? What'd I tell you?"

That I'm wonderful.

And it's the first time I've ever heard that from a human being that I'm not related to.

It's the hardest thing in the world to believe.

"I would very much like to be friends," I say at long last.

Hayes nods once. "I'm glad. As your friend, I'm here for you. I'm only one call, or text, or stone-throw away. So don't hesitate to knock on my door. If you ask, I'll come."

I spent so long existing in impulse and getting hurt that now I hesitate before I do anything.

I'm scared.

But something is different here. I know that much even if I can't identify it. Something is different here, and it's weird…but it's not bad.

CHAPTER 8

> ♥ "Touch her and perish" should raise red flags in real life. Right?

Temptations Lounge.

I told myself I'd never step foot back in this place or any place similar to it, but then I started fake dating the boss…and he asked me to meet him at work between literally seven in the evening to two in the morning once I was feeling up to it. After all his help this afternoon concerning my whole crash, it seemed only right to oblige.

Besides, we're kind of friends now?

And friends respect other friends' choices. Even if the other friends' choices are stupid, dangerous, or wrong. You cannot address the stupid, dangerous wrongness unless you're *best friends*. Attempting to before that point leads to unsavory situations.

Honestly, this is a distraction from calling my parents. My parents keep odd hours and can sometimes be up most of the night, so no time is a solace from the guilt of not calling them. If they're having a party, they'll stay up extremely late. My parents are pretty wild.

I hope Hayes doesn't get wild.

Do bar owners drink while on the clock?

I hope not.

I really don't like this…

Slipping into the dimmed space, I regulate my breaths in an effort to maintain my composure. It's like walking back into a nightmare I had a long time ago. I dislike this.

The smell. The people. The low lights obscuring uncomfortable interactions tucked into neat rows of circular booths.

The bartender throws me a smile, his friendly green eyes welcoming as he cleans a glass. It's a very proper *bartender* thing, and the familiarity of the action helps ease my nerves the smallest bit. I dodge past tables and locate the bar stool in the very corner of the room, by the wall.

"You favor that spot," the bartender says.

My brows rise.

He tosses his towel over his shoulder and reaches across the counter, offering me his hand. "Vince. You were sloshed last time we met and just about passed out in that seat until Boss took you home."

Oh... Letting a tight breath free, I clasp his hand and shake even though I don't know what to say.

Thankfully, he says, "I'll get him," like he knows exactly why I'm here and what's going on between his boss and me.

The Boss and Me.

That would be a fun book title.

It would take after the renowned *The Prince and Me.*

Thank goodness Hayes hasn't yet turned out to be a secret prince of Norway. What in the world are so many royal people doing at American colleges anyway? Sighing, I glance over the wall of liquors plastered behind the bar. It's a very clean place, all things considered, and while the burn of alcohol does somewhat saturate my senses, it's at least not as fetid as my muggy morning-after memories would lead me to believe.

Hayes keeps his place comfortable and tidy.

I appreciate that.

Now if only he served purely juice.

"Hey, sweetheart," a man's half-slurring voice whispers

near my ear, sending an unwelcome shudder down my spine. Grimacing, I turn to find a tall, thin man slipping into the seat next to me with a beer bottle. "Come here often?" he asks.

Judging by the beer belly pushing at his shirt, I'm assuming *he* does and would therefore know whether or not *I* do.

He throws back a gulp of beer, eyeing me as he swallows. "Shy?" he asks, and the putrid scent of his breath curdles my stomach.

"Anti-social," I correct.

He barks a stinking laugh. "That's a new one. Playing hard to get?"

I think he's attempting to flirt with me.

Wow.

I'm offended.

I spend weeks actively searching for a romantic partner to no avail, and now a drunk man is coming onto me. Am I only desirable through the filter of mental impairment? Rude. Rude, rude, rude. Scowling, I focus on the counter in front of me and lace my fingers.

"Hey," the drunk prompts, his slurred tone adopting an edge. "Hey, I'm still talking to you." He grips my shoulder, forcefully turns me to face him, and mutters an insult. "Are you ignoring me?"

"Yes, but you're making it difficult."

A slimy smile curls his thin lips, then it dies, morphing into a wince. His fingers snap open, off me, and I witness the giant hand shackled around his wrist, dragging his touch away.

Looking way, way up, I find Hayes. Blue eyes hard and coal-dark, he growls, "Look at her again, and I break your arm. Talk to her again, and I break your leg. *Touch* her again, and someone will have to scrape you off the floor.

Am I clear?"

The man curses, tugging futilely to get his arm back. When Hayes finally lets him go, his hand whips back into his jaw, and he sputters several more colorful words as he fumbles off the stool.

Once he's retreated fully, Hayes sighs and takes the now-vacated stool beside me. "You okay?"

Am I okay…?

Hayes just pulled a *touch her and die*.

I've witnessed a *touch her and die*. On my behalf. That's literally the best thing in the entire world. I can't believe this. That was so cool. Okay. A touch morbid. But this isn't a *fantasy*, and it's *probably* not a dark romance. I mean, my giraffe, Spotz (with a Z), does happen to be sticking out of my purse right this very second. Not very dark romance genre of me.

Hayes's gaze locates Spotz's neck peeking out of my bag and arches a brow.

"He was lonely at home," I defend.

The low rumble of a *hm* escapes Hayes, and the corners of his mouth only soften. "I'm glad you like him."

"His name is Spotz. With a Z. Because he's very cool. Thank you for him."

"I'm only sorry he doesn't have a fried plantain tongue."

My cheeks heat because I *may* have absolutely gone on for a while about how giraffe tongues remind me of fried plantain. Hayes's biggest comment during my spiel was that he has never had fried plantain. I'll have to get the recipe from my mother. "He's perfect just the way he is."

"Just like his *mamma*."

More moths in my chest. I clear my throat and play with the tuft of brown hair on Spotz's head. "So…why did you want me to meet you here?"

Hayes grunts. "I thought it would be a good idea to follow up these past few days and get you out of the house. Break the cycle up a bit. Reboot. Turn the brain processor off and on again."

I laugh.

"Also, if you're up for it, we weren't able to go stargazing before. I'd love to take you tonight."

Stargazing might be just the thing I need to help "reboot." With the downward spiral broken, I'll be able to call my parents in the morning and get everything sorted. It's the perfect plan. "You're allowed to leave work?"

His eyes roll toward Vince. "My team is fairly self-sufficient. I'm basically a mascot at this point."

Vince snorts, and his brows wiggle. "You kids go have fun. Want anything on the house?"

Hayes's eyes roll again, this time toward me. "Want anything?"

I shake my head.

"Nachos, fries, onion rings?" Hayes prompts, and my eyes widen.

I look at Vince. "You have that stuff?"

Vince bites down a smile that turns his face funny. His eyes cut to Hayes. "You were right."

"Shut up. She wants snacks."

"Got it, boss."

As Vince preps the food, I watch Hayes for several long moments. He reaches over the counter, grabs a glass and a spout attached to a long tube. Filling the glass with something faintly amber and bubbling, he asks, "What?"

Wary of whatever drink he's making, I cross and uncross my ankles. "What were you right about?"

"Very little." He slides the cup toward me, and it stops right before I can even attempt to catch it. Before I understand anything, he preps another drink for himself and downs a gulp.

Every muscle in my body tenses. "Are we not driving to go stargazing?" I don't know how well he'd fit in my car, but he gave me the same stuff, so it's unsettling to assume he's okay with not only drinking but also *drinking and driving*. Even alcoholics generally agree that's a bad idea.

He takes another more languid sip and cocks his head. "Ah." Humor glistens in his eyes. "It's ginger ale, pudding. It's a soda gun. We've got water, Sprite, ginger ale, and beer on tap."

Oh. I don't know fancy bar things. This is only my second time inside one…

But, so far, things are going more smoothly than they were the first time. When Vince sets a to-go bag of snacks down in front of us, I admit that things are going *significantly* better than they did the first time. Those friends of mine sucked if they didn't even *mention* the fact I could get nachos here. What in the world did I ever do to them?

Huffing, I look Vince dead in his kind green eyes and ask, "What was Hayes right about?"

Vince's blond brows jump, and he runs his fingers through the swooping tuft of hair atop his head. It's like Spotz's. I appreciate that. His bright eyes flick toward Hayes, who appears to be glaring murder, then he laughs. "I'd tell you. I just don't make a habit of risking my life on weekdays. Mind stopping back on the weekend? Specifically when I'm not scheduled to work?"

I hate not being in on a joke, especially only to find out later that I'm the butt of it.

Hayes throws back the rest of his ginger ale, grabs the snack bag, and stands, sighing heavily. "I may have rambled about you, pudding."

"What?"

He nudges me onto my feet and sets the soda in my hands. "I *may*," he grumbles, "have mentioned how you're adorable and get excited over the simplest things."

I blink, shivering when Hayes's hand plants against my back and guides me securely past tables with inebriated patrons. "And…that's a bad thing?" I ask.

"Absolutely not."

I startle, dig my heels, and freeze as I notice a *no drinks past this point* sign on the tinted glass door. "I'm taking a glass."

Hayes puffs air out his nose. "I own the glass. It's fine. Let's go stargazing, *cutie*."

My cheeks heat. He should provide me with two to three business days of warning before he gives me new nicknames.

CHAPTER 9

♥ In love, you can never prepare for everything.
___

There are eighty-eight constellations, and Hayes knows them all.

From the moment we left Temptations, piled into his truck, and headed toward where my parents live in the countryside of Westville, Georgia, he's been talking about space. And I've been enraptured to the point I didn't say a word when he pulled off the two-lane side road, parked in the grass under a canopy of trees, and started carting blankets, equipment, our snacks, and a cooler through the brush. To a wide open field. That my parents own.

It's a coincidence, and no one can easily tell that this swathe of cleared land several acres displaced from the main house belongs to anyone specifically. The "no trespassing" signs are at the head of the property and near the connecting roads. Not dropped on random trees off the side streets.

Weird.

This is weird.

Very, very weird.

At least I'm not actually trespassing? Dead ahead through an opposing wall of trees, a horse trail leads from the stables to this area. I warmed my pony in this space, galloping her in circles once both of us were old enough.

It's nostalgic to see this field garbed in moonlight.

I can't believe I never thought to set up a picnic here before.

I can hardly believe I'm having one right now.

"There," Hayes says, eyes twinkling just like the stars above as he moves from the viewfinder and makes room for me to scoot my blanket-bundled self up to the telescope. "That's Gemini."

I look through and see…sky. Stars. Some are brighter than others, sure, but that's a sky if I ever saw one. Yep. "Ooh," I note, politely, but I fear it sounds robotic.

The brusque chuckle that rumbles out of Hayes ignites a spark at the end of my every nerve, and I look over at him just in case he's smiling in a way that might reveal his teeth —an expression I'm slightly desperate to see.

Unfortunately, he's not.

But his lips are gently curved, the warmth in his eyes blazing like a campfire.

Next time we do this we need a campfire.

Huh. Strange. Normally my social excursions leave me feeling so depleted I never want to do them again, but right now I already know I don't want these moments to end. And if they must end, I want them to repeat.

Hayes is dangerous.

For too many reasons.

If I didn't have my wits about me…what would I convince myself is okay when it comes to him?

Pulling a napkin away from beside our snack containers, he clicks open a pen and sketches a weird box with a couple tails, highlighting three larger dots in the image. He taps two of them in turn. "The twins, Castor and Pollux. Pollux is more golden, and Castor is white."

"They're fraternal?" I ask, looking at the sketch.

He puffs a breath. "Yeah. I guess so. There's an entire mythological story about them, and I guess now you know why I have some interest in folktales."

Peering through the lens again, I can now make out the

shape, the twins, and I laugh. "That's so cool."

"Isn't it?"

"What got you interested in the stars if stars got you interested in mythology?"

His softened mouth hardens, and he clears his throat, pouring his attention down at the napkin. "I...don't want to say."

"Why not?"

"It's stupid."

"I try not to judge stupid things harshly in front of people." Which is why I haven't put any thought or attention into the fact there's a cooler with unidentified alcoholic drinks inside holding down one corner of our picnic blanket.

Beer is stupid.

Very stupid.

And I can come off harsh without meaning to, so it's better to pretend it's not even there.

Hayes closes his eyes, lets out a sigh. "*Barbie in Swan Lake*."

I wait for more clarifying information. It doesn't come. "I don't understand."

His eyes snap open. "Have you not seen it?"

Pressing my lips together, I hum. "I was a strange child who didn't enjoy age-appropriate entertainment. I spent most of my time in the library."

Hayes's eyes narrow, skeptical. "There are movies at libraries."

Not my parents' library, which is what I'm referring to. I poorly regulated my emotions in public places as a child, even libraries. The silence put me on edge, made me itch or have panic attacks. Therefore, my parents built me one. And I didn't want the pictures.

No.

I wanted the words.

I sit patiently until Hayes swipes a hand over his face and shakes his head. "Liv's always been interested in media from different countries. She's got wanderlust and goes *somewhere* just about every summer. Something about it being too hot here is her excuse. Anyway…she found the movie at one point, and there was this bonus feature thing on the DVD where…uh…Barbie told you stuff about stars. When…" His voice trickles away, and he shakes his head, passing me the napkin with another scrawled constellation on it before he nudges past me and repositions the scope.

"When?" I prompt.

His eyes catch on mine before they close. Sitting back, he leans across the blanket and opens *the* cooler.

The cooler I have been ignoring.

My stomach tightens until he pulls out a cherry coke. "When *Far* found out, he went on a tirade about how boys shouldn't do girl stuff. Liv got in trouble for letting me play with her DVD. I misunderstood what the *girl stuff* was at that point because I was just a kid growing up with two sisters and an absentee father. I never knew the rules with him. I thought he hated the stars. Which made me love them more. I snuck astronomy books around like drugs and kept learning everything I could. It wasn't just the stars for long. I fell in love with space. The vastness. The mystery." Pressing the soda to his lips, he lifts his free hand to the heavens, fingers wide, and takes a sip. "It's perfectly silent up there. Calm and void. Speckled all throughout with raging balls of gas, icy spears hurtling in vacuum, and supernovas that become black holes, which swallow light itself. It's powerful, and incredible, and when you think about it for too long, all the problems you might be facing turn into dust." His attention lowers, finds me.

My breath catches, and I press my lips together as my

cheeks heat. "If your father hadn't left you in charge of the bar, then you wanted to be an astronaut?"

His lips quirk up in one corner as air huffs out of his nose. "Absolutely not. First of all, confined space in order to reach deadly space. Second of all, I barely scraped through high school. Any scientific job requires a field of basic knowledge that I don't want to stuff in my brain for the sake of vomiting it out onto standardized tests. I don't need to feel like the dumbest person in the room just because algebra doesn't make any sense."

"It makes sense."

"No, it doesn't."

"The parts that don't we're still working on figuring out and solving."

"It literally involves irrational numbers. I prefer to stay rational, thanks. Who knows what they'll come up with next in their fruitless effort to sound intelligent when one plus one starts equaling three? Invisible numbers?"

"Imaginary. They're called imaginary numbers."

Hayes takes another sip, reaches for me, and combs his fingers through my long hair before murmuring into his can, "It's like you don't hear yourself, pudding. *Imaginary* numbers make sense to you?"

They made enough sense that I survived AP Calc in high school. But they don't *always* make sense, I guess. That is why we have unsolvable problems and cash rewards for figuring them out. Life's the unsolvable problem for me. Most of the time numbers, words, conceptual or imaginary things make more sense.

They are whatever you make them. You don't have to search for the hidden meanings. You assemble math problems and words in order to create the solutions you desire. They're simpler than people. Everything that isn't *people* is simpler.

Hayes's fingers slip out of my hair, and he leans back, continuing to drink his cherry coke as he looks up at the sky. "If I'm honest, pudding, I'm bitter. That's it. *Far* left me with something I don't want, but it lets me take care of myself and my family. If he hadn't, I don't think I would have made it through college. I don't want to be a scientist. I just like collecting the information, pouring it out on anyone who will listen. The things I like are just hobbies unless I wrap my mind around a whole other realm of stuff I don't care about. It's frustrating when your brain niches down on a topic you can't really utilize in the grand scheme of survival."

I frown. "Don't be stupid."

His brows lift, and he looks at me.

I wince. Oops. That was harsh. "Sorry. I mean. You *aren't* stupid just because you have trouble keeping up with all the useless things people pretend we have to know and understand in order to be well-rounded. You've mastered something incredible, and it's a shame that you undermine that because you don't compare to people who know a bunch of other random stuff along with a fraction of what you do."

"A jack of all trades is a master of none, but oftentimes better than a master of one."

My body erupts with heat, and I stammer, "O-okay. I absolutely love that you know the full saying…but the very fact our society has trimmed it down to just the first half means there's merit to mastery. I didn't go to college. You know? I didn't go for similar reasons. I didn't want to waste time or money on things I didn't care about, and I knew everything about what I did care about already because it's the only thing I can think about most of the time. You want to know what one of my clients is doing right now?"

"Sleeping?" Hayes jokes, and I bite my lip to mute my smile as I shove him.

He doesn't budge.

Rock of a man.

"I didn't mean right this second, although he probably isn't. I don't think he sleeps." My eyes roll, and I crawl my bundled self over to the cooler in case there's another cherry soda. There is. It's all cherry soda. No alcohol at all. "He's going through the process in order to turn his series into a TV show. His characters and world are so widely popular that there's merch at our mall." I very carefully pop the can open, flinching at the sound anyway. Taking a sip, I face Hayes. "If you don't see a place for you, make one. There are always options, and sometimes we forget that our minds are more elastic than solid. Some of the lies we've been taught become walls we have to break through. When you're brilliant, you figure out the path that takes you to your happiness eventually. It doesn't have to be traditional or expected. Approach your ideal life honestly, and I promise you'll find what you're looking for."

Hayes finishes the last of his can then tosses it into the grass beside our blanket. "I'll pick that up when we leave. Promise."

I startle slightly at the shift of conversation. "Oka—"

He closes his hand around mine.

My heart skips.

Looking in my eyes, Hayes watches me take another sip of my soda until I'm too embarrassed to continue. I don't know what's happening, but I'm electric. Confusion has never been so enticing, or so safe.

"I want to believe you," he says at last. "I'd love to believe that you find good things so long as you're looking for them sincerely. One thing makes me doubt it, though."

"What?" I whisper.

His hand is warm, gentle. Steady. His lids lower as he glances at our joined fingers, then he murmurs, "I wasn't looking for you…and you might just be the best thing that's ever happened to me."

My heart thuds. He… I… What? Is this… Is this dating practice stuff? *Now?* Don't tell me he's trying to pull some of the attention off our serious conversation because he's scared to keep talking about making career changes.

He kisses my knuckles.

My brain turns off.

Restarts.

Begs for more.

Without reason or sense, I want to be closer to him. I want to touch him and trace him and ask him what he means, why he's doing this. They're cloudy, irrational thoughts—honed in on the fact I have never found anyone this hopelessly attractive before him. But…

Minthe barks.

At the sound of my family's guard dog, I blink awake, coming out of the daze.

Hayes swears in Norwegian.

I turn, looking up the roll of hill that leads into the patch of trees that obscures the groundskeeper's house, where Minthe lives with Mr. Jerome. Her glowing yellow eyes streak across the moonlit grass.

Dropping my hand, Hayes jolts to his feet, creating a barricade between me and the German Shepard. In other words, Hayes has just thrown himself between me and a dog I've known since she was a puppy, a dog trained to defend me against threats. My stomach lurches as Minthe crouches into a growling, snarling mess, ready to attack on cue.

A flashlight beam spears the woods as I manage to untangle myself from the blankets. Hayes continues cursing beneath his breath, existing as the mountain between the German Shepard and me.

Once on my feet, I state, "Minthe, no. *Down*."

Minthe's flattened ears perk before she drops at the command.

The stark instant of silence tips toward suspense. Achingly slow, Hayes turns, faces me, finds my eyes. Unacceptably fast, Mr. Jerome arrives on the scene with his flashlight. Heaving breaths, he wipes at his brow with the back of his hand and flashes the light over me, burning my eyes for an unpleasant moment. The light moves to Hayes, and when my gaze refocuses, the rotund man is staring with his mouth wide open as he continues to blind my friend.

Drawing his fingers through the wisps of gray hair atop his head, Mr. Jerome says, "Miss Little…what a late surprise. And…with such…unusual company."

Hayes squints, one tattooed arm thrown over his face, and I suppose this is unusual company for me to keep. I have no idea how I'm going to explain this to anyone.

Before I can so much as try to sort out my thoughts, my father's golf cart streaks down the forest path that leads all the way to the manor at the head of the property. My mother half-stands in the passenger-side seat, her elegant gossamer nightgown flailing like a wraith behind her. She peers ahead beneath the plateau of her hand and gasps. "Ellen!"

"Ellen?" Dad asks, hitting the brakes two yards from us.

Mr. Jerome sniffs. "Sorry, sir. I didn't mean to get you up so late without real concern."

Dad waves a hand as he steps down in his bathrobe and a pair of slippers. Very hesitantly, he scans Hayes, murmuring, "Not a problem at all…"

The longer Dad surveys Hayes, the worse my heart

does that beating-too-fast thing. I'm out here in the middle of the night, clearly on a date that involves blankets. It's ultimately indecent. I should probably be in trouble. But… these are my parents. So. There is a reason why I adapted a tendency to punish myself worse than they ever have.

To them, I can do no wrong, and that's wrong, so I handle justice myself.

My cheeks flush as Mom glides off the cart and sizes Hayes up.

My toes are cold.

I should have kept my socks and sneakers on.

I just didn't want to get the blanket dirty.

For several long moments, my tiny family takes in the giant among us, then—as a collective—Mr. Jerome, Dad, and Mom look at me. Dad tosses a thumb at Hayes and raises his brows before miming *huge* in the form of putting his palms together in front of his chest then drawing them vastly apart.

I know he's massive. Thanks.

Hayes snaps out of the shock before I do and throws his giant hand forward in front of my father. "Hayes Sallow. Sir."

My father's gaze travels the full, twisting length of snakes up his arm before he completes the gesture, shaking firmly. "Luther Little. And my wife…"

Graceful and already composed, Mom brushes back her brilliant red waves and extends her hand as though she's awaiting a kiss. "Elaina. It's so nice to meet you. I'm terribly sorry that we've interrupted."

Awkwardly, Hayes attempts to take her hand, shakes it once, and transforms fully into stone at my side after letting go.

Calling my parents to ask for an extension was one thing. Now I have to explain that I'm fake dating someone in an effort to practice dating so I can discover why I can't seem to attain even one real first date? Dad will get upset and go on about how there's *absolutely nothing the matter with me*, and *if people can't see that, it's their loss.*

In my life, a lot of people have "lost." Shame it feels like mostly me...

Hayes clears his throat, coughs, and rakes his fingers through his hair. "We...weren't...really doing anything. Just...stars." He references the telescope. "We were looking at the stars."

Mom just about melts, setting a hand against her chest. The billowing sleeve of her robe cascades, making her look so much like an angel it hurts that I didn't inherit a speck of her grace. "How *enchanting*." She shivers without warning, and Dad's focus rests completely on her.

"Are you cold, my love?" he murmurs.

"Slightly, dear." Her lips form a tiny smile. "Why don't we all have some hot chocolate to warm up and chat for a moment, then it's terribly late. Is there anything you need to get back to the city for, Ellen?"

Yes, as a matter of fact. My sanity. I left it there.

I should have known better than to leave the most important thing *ever* off my rom-com preparation outline...

In romantic comedies, nothing ever goes to plan.

CHAPTER 10

♥ The best, and most romantic, confessions happen within three feet of a bidet.

I'm still gripping my cherry coke by the time we make it up to my parents' mansion. Cresting at the top of the property, the large building swallows everything in my vision, and I try to take it in through a stranger's eyes. The brick driveway. The dove fountain centerpiece. The high towers at the four corners. The balconies framing select windows on either side of the massive double front doors—which rest at the head of a staircase.

Dad parks the golf cart at the base of the stairs, and the entire vehicle shifts when Hayes bends his body out of the backseat. From the front seat, Mom shoots me back a wide-eyed look that I have no idea how to respond to.

Possibly because I have no idea what the emotion behind it is.

It's either shock, awe, and joy at the fact I've found an incredibly beautiful boyfriend. Or terror highlighting worry.

I clasp my chilled fingers around the soda can in my lap and try to remain calm.

I don't know what to do or what to say.

I need a second to gather my thoughts, create the script, explore the responses and counter responses. I don't want to blubber on like an idiot who can't do anything right and has discovered an insane solution to a troubling problem. I want to make my parents proud of the person I've grown into on my own. I want to be the daughter who edits for celebrities—not the mess who can't get a real date.

"Ellen?" Hayes's low murmur draws me out of my thoughts after my parents have ascended the stairs to open the door. I look up from my seat to find him standing beside me, bracing his hold on the roof of the cart.

Goodness.

He mustn't actually be leaning against this vehicle. If he were, it would pull into his gravity without question. I'm pretty sure he could dead lift it.

Who knows what's going through his head right now?

My jaw locks, painfully tight.

He lowers himself into a crouch. Voice almost too deep to make words out, he asks, "Are you royalty?"

That question short-circuits my thoughts, and my brow furrows. "What?"

"Your parents live in a castle. Are you *actually* a moth princess?"

Heat floods my cheeks, and no.

No.

You can't be serious.

No. Way.

I refuse to accept it. I *refuse*.

Don't tell me *I'm* the secret princess in this story?? I will not allow that. That's *insane*. I was joking about him being a prince! I was hopefully joking. Okay, I was genuinely a little on my guard. Guys don't just immigrate from other countries and *not* rule them in rom-coms. It's against the rules, or something.

I realize I'm staring at Hayes with my mouth open right around the time my tongue goes dry. Forcing myself to close my mouth, I swallow, whisper, "I don't think so."

"Hm." His brow arches, and he seems to be the skeptical one now.

I don't blame him. It isn't like I told him my family is

rich. It's not information that goes over well in front of the people who don't intrinsically know.

He murmurs, "Is this one of those rom-com coincidences? I've been coming out here to that field for years, and no dogs named after nymphs have *ever* interrupted me." His gaze slants off me. "I didn't even know it was private property."

I cower when his attention hits me directly again, and I know what he's thinking now: I should have told him the second I realized where we were.

In my defense, I hiss, "You were talking about the sky."

"What?" he grumbles.

"I would have told you, but you were talking about the sky, and it was so interesting, and I didn't want to interrupt you." I bite my tongue. Now it sounds like I'm blaming him for this mess. That's not what I'm trying to do at all. Flustered, I stammer, "I'm sorry. I should have told you. It's just that…you were so eager and—" I don't know what I'm saying or what I'm trying to say.

Hayes cups my cheek, and the action is too natural, too comforting. It settles my nerves and confusion with very little effort. His thumb swipes, and my hammering heart settles. "Can you show me where the toilet is?" he asks, and that seems a touch off topic, but it's not like bathroom visits can be planned.

Here I am, panic rambling, when he has to go to the bathroom.

"Of course," I murmur.

"Come on, you two," Mom titters from the top of the steps. "Let us have a few minutes of your attention."

"Hayes has to go to the bathroom," I call, stepping off the cart when he rises and steps back. "I'm going to show him where it is then meet you in the kitchen."

"Marvelous, honey."

Dad swings the front door open after putting in the code and declares, "Show him to the *nice* bathroom, with the bidet."

My cheeks flush as I make it up the stairs. "Dad, for the last time, no one cares about the bidet."

At my side, Hayes mutes his exhale laugh with a cough and scrubs the back of his hand against his mouth.

Dad steps aside to allow us in and says, "Let the *company* decide that. Who are we to keep a fine gentleman from choice and freewill?"

Ready to turn into an embarrassed puddle, I whimper, "This way, Hayes," and wander through the expansive foyer to the spiraling staircase etched with bronze. We head up, cresting the second floor to the low sound of Hayes's whistle. He frees a soft curse as he examines the cherub wallpaper flitting up to the crown molding.

It all seems so pretentious now that I've been living in my city apartment for so many years. Well, rather, it was always a little more pretentious than I cared to think about. That's why I preferred my cottage to this entire…palace. I'm easily overwhelmed, and getting lost in your own house is somewhat overwhelming.

Finally reaching the *good bathroom*, I motion to let Hayes in, but he grabs my hand and tugs me inside with him. The door closes behind me, and my heart lurches. It's not the same as a confined space. Not even close. It's a full bathroom with a separate chamber for the toilet and a gold-plated jacuzzi working as the centerpiece. Four massive mirrors hang at key locations, which open the room up even more, but *still* any space feels confined when Hayes is in it, particularly when he's inches away from you.

I swallow, hard, and look in his eyes, wondering if he realizes that he's got his hands plastered to the door on either side of my head.

Wall pining wasn't on my list. Again, I thought I'd be safe from the things fully within his control.

Ha, ha. I have been a sweet summer child…

"You okay?" he asks.

I sense the possibility his needing to go to the bathroom was an excuse to have a secret meeting. Gasping, I cover my mouth with my free hand—because, yes, I'm still clutching my soda for dear bubbly life. "You're brilliant," I whisper.

He arches a brow.

I throw back a burning sip and let it calm me some before I slide to the floor. I'm not going to stand here and wait for my legs to change color, after all. Hayes follows me to the floor, resting his arms on his bent knees, and I let the moment's quiet facilitate my raging thoughts.

"I don't know what to do," I say. "I couldn't bring myself to call them. It's obvious what they think we are. I'm embarrassed to tell them the truth, but I don't want to lie to them."

"We don't have to lie to them. In every way that matters, we're dating right now."

"Problem," I note, "if *we're* dating, I don't get an extension on my cottage. And then what will they think when I find someone who wants to marry me and start a family and all that, and he isn't you?"

Hayes's jaw locks, and his body stills. When he finally moves again, it's to let a breath out his parted lips. He swallows, inhales. "Ellen…"

"I know relationships aren't always predictable, but still. It feels wrong. And I get *very* wound up when things feel wrong."

Hayes clenches a fist, eyelids half lowered over his bright blue gaze. "We'll just say we're casual right now. Once you're done practice dating me, we'll break up, you can tell them we have, and then you can ask for a little more time or something. Will that work? At least then, we're not 'fake' dating, you're clearly trying to meet their requirements, and there's no complete lying. Just partial truths."

Partial truths are lies. But if I don't want to blurt the entire truth, it's all I have. "I'm bad at keeping secrets, and they'll see I'm acting weird with you because we're not like a lovey-dovey couple or whatever."

"What secrets?" he mumbles. "I like you. I'm not your type, but you're sweet enough to give me a chance. I'm waiting, breathlessly, for you to warm up to me." He curls a finger beneath my chin. "No secrets here." His gaze lowers to my lips, and a shock zips through my heart when his thumb swipes a caress across them.

For a breathtaking moment, I believe what he's saying. "Hayes…"

"Hm?"

I bite my cheek, take a shaking breath. "Do you…want to kiss me?" According to all my romance book knowledge, he's completed the steps that convey interest in doing such a thing, even if I can't imagine why. He's gentle and doesn't take advantage of people. But maybe, just maybe, he finds me attractive in the same way I find him attractive? And I'm not at all intimidating enough to make him second guess that?

His eyes close, and I fear I've made a mistake when he pulls his hand away. Harsh, he murmurs, "Yeah." Inexplicably, he rises after providing that life-altering information. Looking down at me, he lets his tongue roam in his cheek for a long moment. "I told you I don't have much experience when it comes to dating or women, pudding. You're beautiful, and I'd love to kiss you. But I want to be better than my *far*, and there's no way in hell the first kiss you remember happening between us occurs on the floor in your parents' bathroom." Pinching the bridge of his nose, he lets something that almost looks like the ghost of a smile touch his firm mouth. "I'm more likely to use the bidet. And that's not happening."

Some mix of nerves and giddy mess spill out of me as a laugh. "Wow." I wish I hadn't left Spotz in his truck. He's probably cold. Worse, I need an emotional support giraffe right now. I clutch my soda to my chest, caving the metal inward with my grip. "I've never been kissed before," I say.

He stills. Dropping his hands to the pockets of his jeans, he links his thumbs in the fabric and taps his fingers against his thighs. Rough, he murmurs, "Really?"

"I've never met anyone who made me feel comfortable enough to want to be…intimate. I guess. It doesn't even cross my mind. Hasn't even. For anyone. Not even actors or celebrities." I don't know what I'm saying, or why I'm confessing. Because he's the first person who has made me wonder? Because it feels like I have to fight and remember my good reasons *not* to just…kiss him? "Sorry. That's probably not appropriate to say. I'm flustered. No one in their right mind has ever expressed wanting…me."

His hand clenches into a fist before he lets it loosen and holds it out for me. "People are stupid as rocks, Ellen."

I don't hesitate to take his hand, and he pulls me to my feet, closer than expected, looking way up at him, barely an inch away.

Rom-com magic.

You can't just be helped to your feet. Nope. Gotta be practically on top of the love interest who assists you. If your breaths don't catch, were you even helped up?

Hayes takes a polite step back and releases my hand. "So the story is: I love you, and you're giving me a chance, even though I'm nothing like what you expected for a partner."

"Like, not love, otherwise it's a lie."

He drops his face level with mine. "You sure about that?"

My skin flushes. "Hayes, don't tease me right now. I'm already very flattered and overwhelmed."

"Flattered? You said you were flustered."

"Women are complicated. I can be both."

His lips soften, then he moves to press the most delicate kiss ever against my cheek. It's soft as a moth's wing beat, and it melts my insides into pudding. "I'll say my truth, you say yours. Sound good?"

It sounds like he just confessed to me.

But that's insane, isn't it?

I open my mouth to ask what he means, if he can clarify, but he slips past me, to the door, and murmurs, "Your parents are going to think we're being indecent up here if we don't head down. For similar reasons, you might want to stop blushing."

I cast a look in the giant mirror over the sink and straighten my spine. "It's not my fault!" I blurt as I stumble after him, pressing my cold soda can to my face in a futile effort to calm down.

"I take full responsibility."

"Don't sound so pleased," I snap.

"But, *Ellen*." The way he says my name sends a shock wave down to my toes. "I *am* pleased."

A laugh explodes out of my chest when he looks over his shoulder at me, brows dipped, a pout on his lips. It's the silliest face I've ever seen him make. And it's hopelessly endearing.

When he offers me his hand, nothing feels more natural than taking it, and we head downstairs. Together. Like an almost-couple.

CHAPTER 11

♥ If you want to find love when you're weird, let yourself be weird.

"So—" Mom scoots forward at the large kitchen table, her hands wrapped around a mug of hot chocolate topped with giant rainbow-shaped marshmallows. Her eyes glimmer as though it isn't nearly midnight. "—how did you two meet?"

Hayes pulls his attention away from the floor-to-ceiling window, which displays a moth garden of trees framing the pool, and looks at Mom, then at his own mug with rainbow marshmallows, then at me.

Our eyes lock, and I tighten my grip around the warmth of my pale green mug. Biting my cheek, I peer down at my drink. "You remember my twenty-first birthday?"

Dad clenches a fist against the table and takes a drag of his hot chocolate as though it's a beer. Wiping his mouth, he mutters, "Unfortunately."

More refined, Mom lets her bottom lip jut, regal. "I never did like those awful, awful girls."

I trace the rim of my mug with a fingertip. "Hayes is the reason I got home safely."

Shock washes across my father's face, then both him and my mother stare directly at Hayes.

"*Really?*" Mom scoots ever closer to the table, practically draping herself across it. "You've known our Ellen *that* long?"

"And you, young lady." Dad gives me a half-pointed, half-wounded look. "You didn't tell us?"

Hayes touches my shoulder, his giant hand heavy and comforting. "She didn't remember anything. And, until recently, I thought she…regretted our meeting."

"Oh?" Mom asks.

Hayes nods. "I own the bar she was at, and I asked her to come see me again, but she never did. So I cut my losses."

He…what? Is he embellishing a story to make this whole situation more believable? I hope it still comes off as believable now that my parents know he owns a bar. I don't know what I'll do if they question anything. I'm terrible at keeping secrets, and the whole truth might come spilling out.

"We met again a few weeks ago," Hayes concludes and takes a sip of his hot chocolate before grunting a *huh* at the colorful mush of foamy sugar.

My parents' attention sweeps toward me, so I tense, offering a meager, "I went to a speed dating thing. For Valentine's Day. He was there."

Mom covers her mouth, eyes wide, expression… *interesting* in a way I can't decode.. "And Hayes remembered you from that one night nearly five years ago?"

"Of course he would," Dad declares, throwing a hand out toward me. "Just look at our Ellen. How could anyone possibly forget our sweet girl?"

Hayes slurps his hot chocolate, watching me out of the corner of his eye, and I don't know how to feel about the fact it's easier to read his sarcasm than it is to track my mother's emotions in this moment.

My cheeks heat. "Dad, please."

Dad huffs. "Am I wrong?"

"No, sir. Ellen is entirely unforgettable," Hayes comments, clearly amused.

Mom reaches for my hand, her smile slight. "She's quite the character."

I shift in my seat, uncomfortable, like I'm looking in on a conversation about me instead of sitting right through it. All this focus makes me itchy.

Dad hums, pondering. "If you two only reconnected a few weeks ago, that means this is a fairly new relationship. Why did you bring him home so soon, Ellen?"

It's my turn to slurp my hot chocolate and eye Hayes.

He stares back, holding my gaze until the itchiness turns into flutters, like we're about to share an inside joke. "Honestly, I didn't know that field was private property. I've used it before to go stargazing without consequence."

A laugh bubbles out of my mother. "My, what a wonderful coincidence."

"It's like you two were meant to be," Dad confirms.

I shrink a little further into my seat.

Mom and Dad chat with Hayes about fate and destiny and other whimsical words I'm certain he doesn't particularly want to hear until we've finished our hot chocolate. When my parents ask if we'd like to stay the night, Hayes is the one who says I need to get back home. To Mouse. And that's the truest statement to have come about in the past hour.

Reluctant, Dad takes us back to the field on the golf cart and helps us transfer everything from the back of it to Hayes's backseat. Once he finally bids us goodbye, I melt into the front seat—exhausted. They didn't give a single opening for either of us to mention the potential temporary nature of this relationship. It took all my energy just trying to keep up with the conversation.

I don't know what I'm supposed to do. Maybe it's enough that they know this relationship is new? Maybe that in itself will make when it "doesn't work out" later make sense? Relationships don't work out all the time.

The instability of them is probably why I've avoided them for so long. I want the connection… I just… I don't know if it exists.

I'm tired.

I'm so tired.

"You okay?" Hayes asks as he settles into the driver seat and begins warming up the truck. "Seat belt."

Wearily, I tug the belt into place and look at him. "I'm so sorry. I should have just told you my family lives here."

He shrugs, like it's no big deal. "It was unexpected. But I don't mind. I've never seen that kind of luxury before, but I've also never seen marshmallows with that much food coloring."

"Really?"

"There were tiny clouds. I was quite impressed."

"You can get those at any Whole Foods."

"I've never been to a Whole Foods before in my life."

I blink at him. "Normal people shop at Whole Foods." Softly, I add, "Don't they?"

Hayes braces an elbow against the wheel and watches me a long moment before cursing. "You're adorable."

As he pulls his seat belt on, I huff and sag in my chair. "That's starting to feel patronizing."

"Not my intention. I mean it in a sense of you are absolutely and incomprehensibly precious."

Precious.

I cut a glance his way in a futile attempt to learn whether or not he's teasing me, being sarcastic. As he eases out of the grass and onto the street, I decide it doesn't matter. I've been teased before. No one has ever done it in a way that makes me feel like more instead of less. Calm silence carries us to the stop sign at the end of the road.

"Thank you."

"For what, pudding?"

Taking me stargazing. Meeting my parents. Knowing what I need before I understand it myself. Being my friend. Really, truly, honestly *being my friend*. "Everything?"

"Everything," he repeats, mulling the word over as he turns right. "I've not done much."

"How can you say that?"

"Because it's true."

"You packed a picnic blanket and comforters along with a telescope and drinks for tonight."

"That stuff's always in my truck."

My mouth gapes. "Seriously?"

He exhales a puff. "No."

I cross my arms and huff. "I'm being serious."

"You often are."

Fixing my gaze out the window, I watch the quiet countryside roll by on our way toward the interstate that leads into the city. "Is that part of my problem?"

"Your problem?"

"You haven't given me any information about why I can't seem to find a guy interested in me. Maybe I'm too serious? It's just…*a lot* to interact with people, and if I don't take things seriously, it's harder to make sure I don't offend anyone."

"I'm not easily offended. Go ahead. Try to."

I blink. Turning slowly, I look at the mountain of a man. "You might be big, Hayes, but you still have emotions. Everyone can be offended."

"I didn't say I couldn't. I said it'd be difficult. Give it a shot."

"I don't want you to hate me."

"Unlikely that you'll ever be able to manage making me hate you."

Those words settle deep in my chest, warm and gooey

and safe and wonderful. "I don't offend people on purpose. Most of the time, I don't know what's offensive until I've made a mistake and the entire tone of the conversation changes. I just say what I'm thinking."

"In that case, tell me what you think of me. You said I was terrifying once. Still think that?"

My chest tightens, and I whisper, "Wait, was that offensive? It seems kind of obvious. You're huge and tattooed and don't smile."

"I'm smiling on the inside whenever I'm with you."

My skin hums, buzzing with warmth, and I remember something I'm almost certain is offensive. "I don't like your career. It's stupid."

"Feeling's mutual."

"No. I mean it. Alcohol is dumb and dangerous, and I wish you weren't around it. I'm scared of what a guy as big as you might do when you're drunk."

His brows rise. "You think I'd hurt you?"

"I don't know. All I know is that I lost an entire night to the stuff. And I've read about mean drunks, angry drunks. I can't possibly know what alcohol does to you."

He rocks his jaw. "You wanna find out?"

I'm shaking my head before I can even register the words. "Absolutely not."

"Then I guess I won't start drinking."

My mouth opens, ready to protest further, but his words compute seconds later. "What?"

"It smells awful. Why would I drink it?"

"You…"

"Besides, *Far* loved the stuff, so that's all the more reason for me to avoid it. I've seen what it does to people more times than I can count, and I've been on the receiving end of drunk fists more often than I want to admit. Not everyone turns into an endearing little moth rambler." His eyes roll as he shifts lanes to get around a semi. Lip curled, he adds, "Unfortunately."

Just to make sure I'm understanding things, I ask, "You don't drink?"

"Not alcohol."

"You run a bar."

"Against my will, as we've established."

I stare at him.

He catches my eye. "Am I still scary, or was that all you were worried about?"

"Well, you're still built like a tank," I blurt.

He barks a laugh, a wry quirk to the corner of his mouth. "Yet another thing my father cursed me with. Genes."

I giggle. "You're funny."

"Oh no. You've figured out how to offend me—with compliments." Head shaking, he sighs. "Pudding, I mean it when I say people are stupid. They've got you so worked up about figuring out how to navigate them, they don't realize that you're a blessing. It's always the truth with you. I don't have to worry about hidden meanings or manipulation. I can relax. To somewhat answer your question: I don't think you're too serious; I think you're too tense."

Too tense.

Is that all?

"I have social anxiety. The tension is a package deal, but I can try to do better about managing it."

Hayes hums. "You try too hard."

"What do you mean?"

"You're fine just the way you are. Try less."

My history with people would suggest otherwise. I tangle my fingers together. "I don't know about that."

"At least with me then? I am your practice, so might as

well, right?"

My tone is clipped when I say, "I can't just turn years of conditioning off. I've spent my entire life trying my best."

"Didn't say it would be easy to unmask. But, for what it's worth, I think you should. Wanna know why?"

Skeptical, I say, "Sure?"

"Because you're adorable."

I groan, slouching into giggles. "I walked into that one."

"You sure did, cutie."

Sighing, I relax against the headrest and watch him for long, quiet moments. Everything I've always known suggests I need to be wary. But the fragile, hopeful pieces of myself that I thought were gone suggest that, maybe, this time I'll be okay.

CHAPTER 12

> ♥ Falling in love comes with complex emotions and undefined steps. This can cause anxiety.

It's March. Which means my birthday is in twenty-one days. Three weeks. Three weeks, and I haven't asked for more time in order to inherit my cottage, the only information I have concerning how to get a significant other is "be *more* of yourself," and Blaire's writing me my moth princess book.

At least one good thing is happening?

We were chatting about her last book when I casually slipped in how cute it would be if she based her next set of fairies around lepidoptera, particularly moths, and *there's a possibility* I've mentioned that I like moths before, because she said, *That sounds like fun! I'll have it done in time for your birthday!*

Which, of course, means I'll get it in five days, and she's probably planning to *publish* it on my birthday.

Blaire Featherstone is insane. All she does is write. I don't even think she takes a break to eat most days.

Speaking of which…

Pulling my brain out of work and words and putting commas in the right places because Lord Prince doesn't understand the difference between an essential and a non-essential clause…I discover it's five in the evening. Mouse is on my lap—a pleasant surprise—and I may not have eaten yet.

I can't destroy my body again after a recent slump. I

should really clean my room, too. I don't want to know where Mouse has put all the protein bar wrappers I never took care of.

First things first, I need food.

Second thing to consider…I do not want to make food.

Thirdly, only one thing is remotely appetizing to me right now.

And it's mall pizza. Mall pizza, of all things. I want a giant slice of mall pizza.

I hate going to loud places by myself. I didn't plan this either. I don't even go shopping for groceries without giving myself advance notice.

Attention, Ellen. We shall be venturing into the unknown—which is actually quite known, and calm, because it's Whole Foods—at precisely this date and time. Is twelve business days of notice sufficient?

No?

Does the threat of starvation change that?

Yes?

Good. Glad to hear it.

My general distaste and avoidance of people is potentially why I have never "naturally" located a partner through meet cute. Turns out, you need to interact with people in order to meet them. This information brings me exceptional amounts of distress.

What a scam.

Heh.

What day is it?

Where in the world is my phone?

Picking Mouse up, I go on the Great Phone Hunt of… whatever year it is. It seems I don't know that either. But it's fine. Adding a specific year to a book is rarely advised on account of the fact it dates the content. Not that my life is a book. If it were, my author has some explaining to do considering the fact I ordered my happily ever after package when I was six, and it's taking its sweet time showing up.

Once my thoughts are done being bitter and sarcastic, I locate my phone tucked between the still-dirty comforter and sheet of my bed. I don't know how many weeks it's been since I last washed my bedding.

Usually, I'm a vaguely responsible adult.

I've just caught myself in the aftermath of a bad time.

I have messages?

Blinking down at my notifications, I unlock my phone and begin reading.

Hayes: Hey, pudding. Want to do something later?

Hayes: Involving food, maybe?

Hayes: My treat.

Hayes: Obviously.

Hayes: I'm not trying to spam you, I promise, so I'm not going to press send anymore. I want to make sure you're taking care of yourself and eating properly, so even though we just saw each other last night, I might nag you over the next few days. Drink water. Have breakfast. Stay beautiful. All that good stuff. Let me know about lunch.

Hayes: Or dinner.

Hayes: I don't want to be a creep and come over there just because I know where you live (insert disturbing laughter, /joke), but if I don't hear anything by tomorrow night, I'm knocking on your door. This is a warning.

A laugh spills from my lips, and I cover my mouth before I realize I'm crying.

I'm actually crying.

Tears splash against my hand when I close my eyes, and it takes several gasping breaths for me to get myself under control. Melting onto the foot of my bed, I swallow, wipe my eyes, and read the texts over again.

They're punctuated. Proper. Polite. Funny and caring.

I have never met someone as kind as Hayes before in my life.

Until him, I had friends who didn't even have auto-capitalization on, despite knowing it made it more difficult for me to understand the tone of their messages. Whenever I asked for clarification on whether or not something was sarcasm, they wouldn't tell me. Or they'd laugh and say *you can't tell?*

No. I can't always tell. It's *text*. And in case you didn't know, it's not a book. I can't check the tag or the action associated with what you're saying. There's highly limited contextual clues. It wouldn't hurt to shoot me a /sarcasm, would it? Or, at the very least, clarify without belittling.

Some of them would "k" me just for fun. Just because they knew I knew it meant someone was upset, and I wouldn't know what I'd done.

People are mean.

So unnecessarily mean.

It takes me several minutes to decide on the message I want to send in order to be perfectly clear, but at last I turn:

Ellen: Oops. I lost my phone in my bed and have been in my office falling in love with fictional people all day. I didn't mean to ignore you, or make you worry, or cause you to threaten knocking on my door (truly terrifying, /joke). If it's too late, I understand, and I don't know if you're working or not. I'm not actually sure what day it is. I forgot to check. Oh. My phone says it's Wednesday. I like Wednesdays. Want to get pizza at the mall?

Into:

Ellen: I'm so sorry. I've been working all day, and I lost my phone in the other room. Thank you so much for checking on me. It means a lot. Sorry I missed the opportunity to spend time together today. Really. Offering was very kind.

Commending myself on being normal, I intend to set my phone down and see if I can convince myself there's something worth eating in my kitchen, but my fingers don't leave the box before it's buzzing in my hand.

Hayes: What missed opportunity?

Hayes: I'm three seconds from you.

Hayes: And it's only five.

Hayes: I'm spamming again. Sorry about that. All I'm saying is: if you haven't eaten yet, neither have I. Let's find food.

I stare at the messages for a while, damp lashes fluttering. Wiping more tears from my eyes, I reply:

Ellen: I don't mind spam. That's how I prefer to text, too. Do you not have work tonight?

Hayes: I own work. And I haven't gone in yet tonight.

Hayes: What about you? Do you still have work?

Hayes: I can pick up whatever you feel like eating and bring it by if you need to focus on finishing up for deadlines or something.

Hayes: I don't know what editors do.

Hayes: You do have deadlines, right? Or is your job dictating those to your subjects (authors) like a sovereign (moth princess)?

I laugh, and my heart pounds.

Ellen: I don't think you want me to go off on that tangent.

Hayes: Untrue. I would love for you to go off on that tangent. But in between bites of food.

Hayes: Want me to come by so we can plot our dinner in person? I don't think I'm going to get what you want to eat out of you unless I'm intimidating you with my presence (/non-threatening).

Ellen: I'm feeling threatened /joke.

Hayes: I've been told I'm a pretty scary guy.

Ellen: Even though your snakes are so cute.

Hayes: They really are. I'm glad someone appreciates me.

Hayes: Non-threatening ding dong.

Ellen: Is that your way of saying you're outside?

Hayes: My sister has recently said I knock like the cops are coming to arrest murderers. So, yes.

Laughing, I put my phone down and head to my foyer. Once I've opened the front door, Hayes slips his phone into his pocket, and his expression softens. "Hey, pudding."

"Hi." *Hi*. It's the only word my mouth can manage when what I want to say is *no one has ever been this nice to me*, and *you're wonderful*, and *I'm already scared of losing you*, and *please don't let me ruin this*.

"Have you eaten today?" he asks.

Pressing my lips together, I shake my head.

"Water?"

I nod. "Some. I keep bottles by my desk."

"Are there roughly forty empty bottles littered around in your office and your bedroom?"

I shift my weight from one leg to the other and fiddle with my fingers. "How do you know all this stuff?" I keep my *company areas* spotless. No one should suspect there's so much dirty laundry on my bedroom floor you can't see the carpet anymore.

His big shoulders lift and drop. "Kindred spirits recognize each other."

I tilt my head.

He offers me his hand. "You need food. Where am I taking you?"

I need… "My purse. I need my keys." Absently, I turn, leaving the front door open.

Kindred spirits recognize each other.

I like the way that sounds. I like the way that feels. I may like Hayes.

Freezing as that thought hits me, I stare at Spotz's glass brown eyes poking out of my purse.

I might like Hayes.

How?

How do I like him?

As a friend? As more?

"Ellen?" he calls from the front door, and I tense, straightening up with my purse like I've been caught with my illicit thoughts.

"Yes! Sorry! I'm wading through an ocean of plastic bottles! Spotz is drowning. Oh no! Spotz!" What? What did I just say? "I'm joking!" Sweeping back my hair, I press my fingers to the pulse in my neck.

Crap. Crapppp. Am I having a panic attack? A POTS attack? Am I just hungry?

"I know you're not really joking, and it's only because I don't know if it's socially acceptable or not to offer to help you clean up that I'm staying firmly outside your flat…"

Turning sharply on my heel, I throw my purse strap over my head and wade out of my room, heading back toward Hayes. "When isn't it socially acceptable to help save a baby giraffe?"

"Potentially when that baby giraffe might be drowning in a young woman's underwear alongside her protein bar wrappers."

My face explodes with heat. Goodness gracious. Hayes makes perfectly valid and logical and underrated points.

Hayes steps back from the door to let me out, then pauses. "Will Mouse be okay for a couple hours? I don't know when his dinner time is."

"He has a big dispenser, and I filled it yesterday. You'll have to come over some more so he can get used to you." I don't know where my thoughts are going or why I'm saying them aloud. Biting my lip, I lock my door and try to regulate my breaths. I might pass out. There's a big chance I pass out before I even get downstairs. What if I pass out on the stairs?

Ellen Little. Last seen attempting to figure out *feelings*. Obviously a poor decision on her part. Died by falling down the stairs.

"I'd love to," Hayes says, and a shudder goes up my legs.

Maybe I should have grabbed a coat.

Or maybe my legs are going numb.

When we've both survived climbing down the stairs, during which Hayes said nothing about the way I was grabbing the railing like a little old lady, he opens his truck door for me and asks, "Food?"

At least this is a question I know the answer to. Climbing in, I say, "Whatever you want is—"

"I've had a real craving for whatever you want lately." He leans against the side of the vehicle, getting comfortable and blocking the doorway.

There's no "backslash non-threatening," so I can only assume this is threatening.

Oh dear.

He can't possibly know what I want, so he can't possibly know that it's what he's been wanting lately. I don't think he can read minds, even if he has accurately described my bedroom as though he's seen it personally.

"I'm saying you're picking where we're going to eat, pudding."

Oh. That makes more sense. "Sorry. I'm high-strung tonight. I think."

"Couldn't tell."

Blinking rapidly, I ask, "...sarcasm?"

He nods.

I'm glad he's not lying to me. It's nice to not be lied to even if I'm not thrilled my panic is front-and-center. "I picked where we ate at the zoo. And then you brought me food when you thought I was sick. And then you let me have all the snacks I wanted for stargazing." I hug my purse —and Spotz—against my chest. "Honestly, Hayes, this friendship is starting to feel one-sided in my favor, and I'm not used to that at all, and I don't want to put you in the positions I've known all too well."

The corner of his mouth tips. "Cutie."

"*Hayes.*"

Puffing a laugh, he steps back and closes me inside the truck.

I wait for him to climb, or *step*, into the driver seat before I fix my scowl on him. "I don't want to take advantage of you. If I decide where we eat, I want to pay."

"Absolutely not."

A screech takes up residence in my chest, but I refuse to let it free. "I thought the rules stated—"

"I invited you to pick a place. I still invited you. So I still pay. But also even if you invite me somewhere, I don't think those particular rules should apply where I'm concerned."

"And why not?"

He fixes me with a skeptical glare. "I am five American football players in a trench coat."

The image hits me between the eyes, and the accuracy of the statement makes a laugh explode out of me. I clap my hand to my mouth, puttering into giggles. Throughout the entire ordeal, Hayes only watches me, warm, the barest hint of a smile on his lips. It's so beautiful it chokes sense. "That's not fair for you at all."

"I'm a successful business owner. I can pay to keep

myself fed."

"*I'm* a successful business owner. I can feed forty-five percent of a football team."

His eyes close. "Is that accurate math?"

"What do you think?" I sniff, sticking my nose in the air.

Hayes whispers a curse, shaking his head as he runs his fingers through his hair. "You know what, Ellen?"

"Hm?"

"*You* terrify me." Sticking the keys in the ignition, he starts his truck up. "You have until I pull out of the complex to tell me where we're eating, or I'm stopping at every restaurant I see and ordering one of everything on the menu until the bed of my truck turns into a road-safety hazard."

My eyes widen.

He backs out of the parking space beside my car and cuts a glance at me. "Backward slash, *not* joke."

I'm not gutsy enough to try him, so right before we reach the gate, I cave, "Pizza. Mall pizza."

"I—" He curses. "—love mall pizza. Mall food, in general, actually. I fear you're going to see a disturbing side of me." He switches to the correct lane after we exit the gate. "But now we have a problem."

My nerves tighten. "What?"

"There's a bookstore at the mall." Sighing, he merges onto the highway. "I'll have to take you."

"Oh, no. You don't ha—"

"Nope. I gotta."

"Really, I don't want to cause any trouble."

"Ellen." He stops at a light and looks at me. "We're having dinner and going to the bookstore. Third date. Let's see what rom-com mischief we run into this time."

Sucking in a breath, I whisper, "I don't have my

emergency backpack."

The ease in Hayes's expression falters, and he shifts into the wrong lane after the light changes. Next thing I know, he's pulling a U-turn while mumbling, "We're going back for it," under his breath.

Yet again, he's read my mind.

CHAPTER 13

♥ Oh dear. Here's the start of that character growth you alluded to.

"Can I take a picture of you?" Hayes asks, on the other side of the Great Wall of Food between us. He got something from absolutely every restaurant in this food court. A clatter of evening patrons surrounds us, and I'd feel a little more guilty about being at a table for six if Hayes's body didn't fill out the whole side across from me.

Tilting my head, I merrily chew my spinach and feta pizza, happier than anyone else in the whole world. Even though it's loud. Or perhaps *because* it's loud. All around me is an overwhelming nightmare, but I'm sitting here with the pizza I wanted and doing just fine in spite of the noise.

Little life wins.

It doesn't take all that much to make me happy.

Hayes lifts the phone I couldn't see him holding beyond the mountain of throw-away containers. "Liv's texting. She wanted to stop by the bar and drop off something she baked, but I told her I'm not there. That descended into something about how I don't have a life, so what could I possibly be doing, and if I'm in the hospital again, I better tell someone this time…"

I blink and swallow. "I'm sorry. What?"

He grunts. "Sometimes people have knives."

Excuse me?

"So sometimes I get stabbed. And sometimes stab wounds need stitches. And sometimes I have to go to the hospital because drunk people don't have the best aim." He watches me, calm, then he seems to remember something. He murmurs a very serious, "Yes, I do have a nasty scar. No, you can't see it right now. It's inappropriate to show you in public," as though I'm about to threaten to remove his shirt.

Excuse me?

I think I'm still smiling, but *what?* People have just *stabbed him* before? And he's acting like *that's normal?* Wetting my lips and making a valiant effort to match Hayes's nonchalance, I move back to a topic that doesn't threaten to break my brain and say, "Sure. You can take a picture. Proving you actually do boyfriend stuff with your girlfriend is part of the point, right?"

"Yep." He takes a picture without even asking me to pose, and he's putting his phone down before I can ask to see it.

Welp. That doesn't make me anxious in every possible way.

Hayes drags a mouthful of Chinese noodles out of a to-go box with a plastic fork that would look small even in my hand. In his, it's hilarious. Dollhouse cutlery. I dwell on the silliness while I continue to eat in order to keep my mind off what his sister might think of me. I hope I wasn't blinking. I hope my clothes are okay. I didn't really prepare for a *date*, not that I wore anything special the other times we've been together. Is that a problem? Maybe I don't look like I put effort into my appearance, and that makes me seem uncommitted?

"Hayes?"

He looks up from his noodles. "You're welcome to anything of mine that you'd like. I don't know how you'll survive off one little slice of pizza."

Right. One little slice of pizza the size of my head. I'm

going to starve to death. My eyes roll. "You're so sweet. That's not what I was going to ask though. I was just wondering...since we're at the mall..." It feels awkward to suggest he help me clothes shop, and I'm almost certain guys hate clothes shopping. Yikes. That's right. Guys *hate* clothes shopping. I can't ask him about proper date attire, much less to help me find any. That wouldn't be kind.

"If there's a store you want to go to beyond Barnes and Noble, we've got until this place shuts down, so don't hesitate to ask."

He really is sweet. Sickly sweet. Pure melted and condensed sucrose. I bet he gives people high blood sugar just from looking at them.

My mind wrestles for an alternative to what I was going to say. Video game store? Does Hayes even like video games? Will he be suspicious when I know nothing about them?

Sighing, Hayes plucks an onion ring from one of his containers and holds it out for me. "Forget what other people have taught you, pudding. You're safe to speak your mind with me. I promise."

Setting the rest of my pizza down on my plate, I take the onion ring in both hands, like I've just been handed an award or a certificate, then I nibble the breading.

Hayes rests an elbow against the table and leans his cheek against his fist. "Hamster."

I blink. "What?"

"Nothing. Absolutely nothing." He reaches to the other end of the table and grabs a takeout of fried chicken. "What were you saying before?"

I bite into the ring in order to give myself an extra minute to think. The truth has failed me before, but maybe it'll be fine with Hayes. Hayes is different than anyone I've ever met before. "I haven't wanted to 'dress up' for my speed dates because I haven't wanted people to only like me for my appearance, but now I'm wondering if it's just made me look lazy and if my thought process was flawed. As a guy, what do you think?"

"Guys don't care about clothes."

Oh. Right.

"There's only two types of clothes to a guy." Hayes lifts a finger. "On." He lifts another. "Off."

Blush crawls up my throat, and I clap my hand to my mouth, hissing past my fingers, "*Hayes*."

"I'm just being honest."

"You mean to tell me guys don't notice when a girl dresses up nice *at all*? That's a little rude to your entire gender, isn't it?"

His gaze roams off me, drifting, and he pulls meat off bone. "I don't think I've given it much thought. Personally, I liked the shirt you wore to the speed dating thing. Didn't even cross my mind that you weren't 'dressed up'." He takes a sharp breath, then he hunkers, dropping his attention directly to his food like a squirrel.

"What?" I demand.

"Nothing." He munches.

"*What?*"

He reaches for a honey mustard package, opens it, and dumps it over another piece of chicken. "*Nothing.*"

"You don't want to help me?" I snap.

His eyes flick up, hard. "I don't want to make you uncomfortable."

Baffled, I stare at him. "Just tell me. If you expect me to be more honest and open and *myself* with you, I need that in return."

He glares, but for the first time in…*ever*…I'm not concerned. I don't think his glaring or being upset is going to haunt me. I don't think it's a precursor to my getting hurt or being rejected. He huffs. "I just remembered the only time I've ever given more than two seconds of thought to what someone was wearing."

Finishing my onion ring, I wipe my hands on a napkin then thread my fingers together in my lap. "Yes. Good. This sounds like it'll be valuable information for me. Proceed."

His expression wanes, and his lips pinch. He exhales a curse, then looks just left of my face. "The butterfly bathrobe."

I blink.

"I can still remember how soft it was. Like, do you realize how cute you are, or are you completely oblivious? Follow up question, did you actually mean to open the door in your bathrobe? Because I've never seen you in anything more revealing than long pants and a baggy t-shirt." Closing his eyes, he mutters, "I grew up with sisters. I'm pretty immune to noticing anything about a woman's body. 'Oh wow, is Marit walking around in her underwear again? That doesn't make me uncomfortable *at all*.' But that bathrobe…" Air puffs out of him, and he shakes his head. "Sorry."

"Hayes, I can't wear my *bathrobe* out on dates."

His right eye twitches, and he finally looks at me again. "Yeah, I wouldn't recommend that. The heterosexual male population wouldn't be able to handle it." He wets his lips, mumbling, "*Although*, that is one way to take down the patriarchy."

I laugh, then I stop and frown. "No, I'm being serious right now."

"You're being adorable. Per usual." Hayes yawns, reaches for one of his three drinks, and downs a quarter of the cup. "It's not your personality. It's not your clothes. It's not *you*."

"Then *what* is it?" I implore.

"The *other* people." He sets his cup down, and the ice rocks together.

Voices, laughter, movement. Noise surrounds me. Strollers and sizzles and sloshes and shoes against sticky tile floors. My head shakes. "It can't be every other person I've ever tried to interact with. At one point or another, I have to accept that I'm the common denominator."

"Don't bring math into this, pudding." Hayes stacks his empty containers up on one side of the table, clearing away some of the wall between us. Once he's done, he grabs a napkin, wipes his hands, then picks up his phone. "Liv says I'm a terrible boyfriend."

The topic change gives me whiplash, but I'm nothing if not trained to be versatile when it comes to the unpredictable nature of human communication. "Why?"

"Because her response to the picture I sent is, and I quote, *Would you like a little more girlfriend with your meal?*" Hayes's eyes go wide, and he rakes in a breath, tensing up to his full height. A curse spills out of him. "Crap. No. She was being inappropriate. I'm very sorry." In another instant, Hayes has his phone to his ear and is barking Norwegian at his sister, who I can hear faintly laughing on the other end of the line.

I've missed the joke completely. But I have a feeling I don't want to know.

Siblings must be fun. Like built-in friends who *have* to be there for you. Even when they say stuff that makes you call them and yell at them. I don't think I'd have been half as lonely with a brother or sister.

After a few moments, the tension in Hayes's words dies down. I finish my pizza, reluctant to admit that he was right and I'm still hungry. He's still got food left, and he said I could have some…so…

I steal a dumpling and a spring roll, pray neither has

MSG, and bite into the crispy one first.

The second my mouth is full, Hayes holds his phone out for me. "Liv wants to talk to you."

A stone drops into my gut. "Am I in trouble?" I whisper, covering my spring-roll-filled pie hole.

"No."

Well. That's good to know anyway?

Swallowing, I force myself to take his phone and bring it to my ear. "H-hello?"

"*Heisann!*" Liv chirps, her accent thick even after she stops speaking Norwegian. "I'm glad to see you've recovered from your illness."

Do I confess that it was a misunderstanding? Thank them for the pickled eggs? What if Marit was the one who put them in my care bag, and Liv didn't see her do it?

Thankfully, she doesn't wait for a response. "Your future sisters-in-law are going to a party this Saturday. It starts at seven, but we'll meet up around five, or three, to get ready. You know how it is."

I don't. Also, five *or* three? There's a two hour difference between those times. Which is it?

"You in?"

I stare at the spring roll in my hand, frozen. My lips part, but no sound comes out.

"*Hallo?*"

"Uh…" I haven't been invited to a party in ages. And I have never enjoyed one. If I go with Hayes's sisters, I won't have my car in case it's too much for me to handle. I'll need to plan an escape route.

"Ellen," Hayes says, safe deep vibrations in my name. All he does next is dip his chin in a brief nod.

"S-sure," I stammer, finding breath again.

Liv exclaims something positive in Norwegian, then rambles off how she'll text Hayes the details.

Details. Details are what I like to have before committing to anything.

Once Liv hangs up, I pass Hayes back his phone and whisper, "I don't remember how to do parties. I don't know how to dance. I don't drink." Shock pierces through my chest, and I fix a look on Hayes. "*Drugs*. I absolutely do *not* do drugs."

Amusement flickers across Hayes's face. "If my sisters are doing drugs, *Mamma* will skin them alive. You don't believe me when I say you aren't a problem? Fine. You're going to spend time with my sisters and realize for yourself that you've just been around the wrong people." He pops his other spring roll entirely in his mouth, chews, and swallows. "Also, I figured it out while you were on the phone."

"Figured what out?" I dare to ask.

"You want to go clothes shopping."

My head shakes. "No, that's all right. I don't want to cause—"

"I'm curious."

My brow furrows. "About…what?"

"About whether or not The Butterfly Bathrobe Phenomenon is a true phenomenon, or if it can be replicated easily by my seeing you in something that isn't some t-shirt, sweater, pants combination." His eyes narrow. "We're going clothes shopping. For science."

Well…science is pretty cool. And I probably need something nice to wear to the party with his sisters. It's a logical course of action that will allow me to avoid figuring out how to get party clothes by myself between now and the weekend.

Hesitant, I give in. For science.

CHAPTER 14

♥ *She made an OUTLINE.*

Hayes curses when I step out of the fitting room wearing the outfit he specifically picked for me—otherwise known as an elegant forest green dress complete with waterfall skirt, lace trim, and off-the-shoulder sleeves. I loved it before the exact second he saw me. And cursed.

And closed his eyes.

And pressed his fist to his mouth.

Half-frantic, I look at myself to make sure I've not screwed something up. Leave it to me to fail at putting a dress on. The skirt's not stuck in my underwear. It is absolutely right-side out. Maybe the peeky hole below the high neckline is too immodest? Either that or the fact my bra straps are showing?

It's an off-the-shoulder dress.

He had to know they'd be showing.

Unless he expected me to take my bra off?

That's indecent. How dare he?

Dragging a breath into his lungs, Hayes opens his eyes. "Freckles."

I stare at him.

He drops his hand to his side. "How much is that? You need it."

"You like it?" I ask.

"I love it. Is it comfortable? Is the fabric or seams weird at all?"

I smooth my hands down the shorter front of the skirt,

take stock of any seams I can feel. Exactly zero. Wonderful. "It's fine." My brow furrows. "Why'd you say freckles?"

He lifts a finger, pointing at one shoulder. "Secret freckles."

Secret...

I laugh. "I'm a redhead. I *have* freckles, Hayes." Pointing at my cheeks, I step up to him. "See?"

His throat bobs. "No. You clearly have never been outside." His brow furrows, and he cups my chin, squinting. "Wait. I see one. Three. Holy—" He curses. "You're hiding them all. How are the ones on your shoulders more defined?"

"I sunburned my shoulders last summer. I was better about protecting my face."

"Huh," he mumbles, caressing his thumb against my cheek, over the only prominent freckle I know I have. "You keep getting cuter. Is that allowed?"

"I haven't been arrested yet."

"Probably because you don't go outside. The authorities haven't been able to track you." His hand slips from my skin, and I instantly miss the warmth.

I think that means I like him.

But I'm also standing right in front of him with my head all the way back just to meet his eyes...hence the *stuff* that people *do* when they *like* each other is nowhere near my thoughts. For fear of bodily harm.

Can you like someone and not be interested in *things and stuff* all the time? I've never really looked at anyone and wanted to do anything. Hayes is the first person I've ever even wanted to kiss.

Because of silly rom-com magic.

Obviously.

Taking a step back, I clear my throat and drop my attention to my socks. "You think I should get it?"

"Either you get it or I get it for you. You've got a birthday coming up, don't you? I think so. Yeah, that's a great excuse. Either you get it or happy birthday."

"Incorrigible," I murmur. "I can buy my own clothes, and I don't need anything for my birthday. You met my parents. They're probably planning to get me a country."

"I can absolutely see that. Which one are you hoping for?"

"Venezuela!" I dip back into the dressing room to put my clothes back on.

Hayes calls, "On account of which moth?"

"I am *not* that predictable."

"Yes, you are."

Biting back my smile, I shout, "The Venezuelan Poodle Moth! It's only been photographed *once*, and we know next to nothing about it, but it's so fluffy and cute, and I want to find it, so if I *owned* Venezuela, I could take the necessary measures in order to ensure the safety of its habitat all while I live in a little rain forest hut and wait for it to come visit me." Now back in my original clothes, I push out of the dressing room and stop short when I find Hayes leaning against the wall exit, covering his face, and…potentially… shaking from silent laughter. "What?" I demand.

His head shakes. He keeps trembling.

Slinging the dress over my shoulder, I grasp Hayes's inked arm and tug. "*What?*"

He obliges to drop his hand away from his face just far enough for me to see his lips twisted into a smile below glittering eyes. "*Jeg elsker deg.*"

My brow furrows. "Yai eske die?"

His face warms a touch, unless I'm mistaken. He murmurs, "Too close." Taking my hand, he draws my fingers up to his lips, kisses, and turns, pulling me along with him. "Do you want to look at more clothes, or go to the bookstore?"

"Bookstore, please. If you think this dress is okay for the party. I don't know anything about it. But I'm assuming you're more familiar with the places your sisters go?" Maybe *he* can help me know what to expect.

"This dress gets nowhere within twenty feet of my sisters." Hayes weaves us past clothing racks to the main walkway, then guides me toward the cashier near the exit into the rest of the mall.

"Why not?" I ask.

"Liv's chaotic domestic. She'll break it."

"I don't know what that means."

"You'll find out when you come over Saturday. They'll take care of everything, so just wear whatever's comfortable. And remember I'm only a text away if you need anything at all."

That is somewhat comforting.

Dropping my attention off his broad back, I locate his hand around mine.

Big. Warm. Gentle.

I wonder if I feel as delicate as glass to him when he touches me. I wonder if that's why he's so cautious. I wonder if the one person who seems like he can break me without a thought is the only one who won't.

Maybe I'm wrong about liking him…or maybe people like me grow into *liking* in the same way normal people grow into shoes.

❖

Quick and tense, Hayes's breaths come deep in the darkness. Curses fall from his lips in rapid succession, and I knew it was a bad idea. I *knew* it, but logic dictated I was being crazy.

Foolish.

Logic has no power here—not in rom-com world.

I knew better. I KNEW BETTER. This *exact* situation was delineated on my outline as a point beneath "getting stuck in confined spaces." Avoid closets and elevators, I typed, like a loon.

Who's crazy now?

We're stuck in the elevator that leads up to where we parked in the garage.

Hayes noted that I was looking tired after charging full-gusto through the entirety of Barnes and Noble four times on the cusp of closing. He said he didn't want me passing out on the stairs. I said I was fine and he didn't have to carry me. He said taking the elevator would be a compromise.

In the moment of my grand error, it seemed a logical solution.

"Hold on," I whisper, again and again, because while I may not know how to rectify this situation in its entirety, I do have a flashlight in my backpack. I find it and accidentally blind myself when I turn it on. It's a mega-duty light, with strobe, just in case random creeps started coming onto me and I needed to defend myself. It happens in rom-coms so the guys—especially cool and collected grumps—can show they care. And it never happened to me even once before…

Yesterday. At the bar.

Huh.

To think Hayes played out the proper male lead role then. Good thing, too, since I forgot my backpack.

After my eyes relax from being shocked, I turn to find Hayes pressed in the corner, staring blankly at the ground in front of his feet. He's shaking. His breaths tremor through his chest.

I wet my lips. Crap. He's not got *a little* claustrophobia. He's got it bad.

His blue eyes flash toward me, helpless, and he croaks, "Can you call?"

I look toward the panel with the phone, but that's not going to work since we didn't just *stop*. The power cut. And if I know this situation—and…well…okay…science—I'm not going to have reception in this box inside a cement parking garage. Just because I want to do whatever I can, however, I check my cell. Unfortunately, I'm right.

Not a single bar.

Sometimes I hate being right.

Hayes puts it all together before I can figure out a way to tell him. Cursing, he shifts his language to Norwegian as he caves in on himself, sliding to the floor.

I follow him down, place my backpack beside us, and set my flashlight to point at the ceiling. "Hey," I whisper, bringing my hand up to comb through his hair. "Eyes on me, big guy. It's okay."

"We're stuck in an elevator," he bites out.

"The power's out," I say.

He gives me a look that I *think* translates to *that is worse*.

"The first place to check when the power goes out are the elevators, Hayes. Everyone else has phone lights and can push open the doors. No one else needs help, so we're top priority."

He wipes his hands on his jeans. "How long will it take?"

I…don't have any conceivable idea. I've never been stuck in an elevator before. I've only read about it. And, in stories, the situation is resolved after it moves along the plot.

His eyes close. "You don't know."

I bite my lip. "My experience is limited and fictional."

He curses, and the hard word slices into my chest. I

know this is my fault. I knew better. It's only because he was trying to be nice because my stupid body is stupid that this was even a suggestion. I don't know what to do. He curses again, this time the word is hoarse. "I'm so sorry, Ellen."

"No, no. It's my fault. I'm sorry."

His head shakes. "This is pathetic. *I'm* sorry. We're not in danger. I shouldn't be freaking out like this. I'm not a child. I may not know when we can get out, but I've not been maliciously trapped here. Everything is *fine*."

"I freak out sometimes when I'm not in danger either. It's okay. You're okay. We're okay. Everything *is* fine."

Reaching up, he grips my wrist, presses my palm into his cheek. Even his fingers are trembling. His touch has never been this solid before, but it's not painful even when I don't think he can control himself.

I scoot a bit closer to him, kneeling between his spread thighs. "It's okay," I repeat softly, framing his other cheek with my hand. A stupid thought enters my stupid brain, and I wince.

"What?" He exhales the word.

I shake my head. "No. Trust me. You don't want to hear it right now."

His voice rumbles. "If you have a rom-com magic solution to this rom-com magic disaster, I'm a converted member of the rom-com chaos religion. *What?*"

I lower my forehead against his chest and whisper, "This sort of stuff only happens in order to progress the plot, meaning it has to serve a purpose. We're a fake dating couple, which means our relationship is central to the plot."

His fingers tense, going still for a second. "Is the elevator peer pressuring us to kiss?"

I whip my head up, face red. "What? *No*. What the... That would be a really creative twist, actually. I've seen *kissing to fool the family* and *kissing to fool the paparazzi*, but *kissing to fool the elevator*?" A laugh explodes out of me. "Wow. The author would have to be absolutely *mental* to pu—"

Hayes presses his lips to mine, and I lose all the air in my lungs.

It takes an instant.

A singular second.

Literally.

His lips brush mine for half the span of a thought, and the lights turn back on. The metal box continues its ascent, and the doors open behind me.

Hayes sweeps me, our bags, even my flashlight up into his arms and *charges* out. Cradled in his embrace, I remain still as he drops against the wall beside the up-and-down arrow panel. Heaving breaths fill him; muttered curses leave his…lips. Blankly, he stares at the concrete past my body, then he goes ghost white. His blue eyes flick to me, and he spits a louder curse. His head shakes. "No, no, no…" Carefully, he lets me down, sliding my body against his, across every muscle and softer plane. I don't have the strength to pull away from him. I don't know what to say.

I'm barely breathing.

Hardly thinking.

My hands rest against his chest while I look up into his eyes, mouth going dry because my lips are parted, and I don't know how to close them.

It actually worked.

I was only going to suggest we share our deepest secrets in order to "advance" our relationship, but this little "event" achieves something, too. I'm not sure I want to identify what it is. I'm very close to overwhelmed, so my brain is turning a lot of things off as a coping mechanism.

I am perfectly calm. Eerily so.

"That's crazy," I whisper.

"That wasn't a real kiss," he says. "It was just a peck. I'm sorry. I wasn't thinking. I was panicking. I *am* panicking. I'm sorry."

"Hey," I murmur, letting my hands trace up to his cheeks. I'm outside my body, numb, resting my weight fully against his big body, letting him keep me stable. The world is wonderful and strange and full of so much magicless magic. Weirdness. So many times I've hated being a part of it, but at least for this moment? Nothing is wrong. "You're all right. It's all right."

"It's not. I did something unforgivable. Selfish. I promised myself I wouldn't. I promised myself I'd treat you better. I—"

I step up on my tiptoes, pull his face forward, and touch my mouth to his. It's another not-kiss, but the very fact I don't mind is huge for me. I've never felt this comfortable with another person that I'm not related to before. Never. My own audacity is shocking. "Sit down."

Hayes's brow furrows, but he does as I've asked, slowly easing his way down onto the cold concrete floor. He relinquishes my books, dress, and backpack beside him, bracing my waist as I sit on him. His thighs are entire chairs, and I take the right one. Reaching in my purse, I pull out my phone and rest against his chest as I tap into my self-care app.

It's pastel.

Bright and bubbly.

We are greeted immediately by a screen that asks how we're feeling today on a five-face scale ranging from frowns to smiles.

"Ellen..." My name rumbles in Hayes's chest, which happens to be pressed against my back.

"Hm?"

"What is going on?"

"I don't know what you're talking about." I hold my phone up. "Choose a face."

He lifts his hand around me, and it hovers before he taps the neutral emoji in the center. My phone cheeps at him as the app opens up on the little bird I take care of. His body flinches around mine, and he grumbles, "Is this even real life?"

"Hush." I go directly to the breathing exercises and select one for panic.

"Ellen…"

I breathe in with the image of a filling circle and hold on cue. While holding my breath, I meet Hayes's eyes, and although the right one twitches, on the next inhale, his chest inflates.

We finish the minute-long exercise; my bird congratulates us.

Hayes drops his forehead against my shoulder and mutters, "Very masculine of me."

"I think so. Do you want to dress her for the evening?"

"Obviously," he mutters in my ear, then he takes my phone in his left hand and curls completely around me to tap the outfit icon. Crossing his legs, he keeps me perfectly in the cocoon of him, and it's safe here in his warmth. "I hope you didn't spend real money on all five thousand of these outfits."

"You get store money when you take care of yourself."

He grunts. "Clearly there are no penalties for when you don't."

My mouth falls open. "I've never been more insulted in my life."

Hayes nuzzles against my shoulder, and his breaths fan across my neck as he puts my bird in all pink. Like a very manly man.

I think he has a secret "thing" for adorable stuff.

"Are you feeling better?" I ask him once he seems content enough to give me back my phone.

"I'm sorry," he murmurs. "Really. I can't apologize enough."

"That doesn't answer my question."

Closing his eyes, he says, "I am up and not crying…so I guess I'm feeling better. Apart from the self-loathing. Thank you."

"You said you wanted to kiss me yesterday."

"Preferably not on *any* floors. And preferably with consent as well. You know? That's a pretty important detail." He pulls in a deep breath. "Why aren't you more worked up about this? I just *kissed* you without any warning."

"I thought you said it wasn't a real kiss. And I did the same back to you."

He blushes.

Red crawls up his neck to fill his cheeks, and he covers his mouth. He mumbles something I can't make out behind his hand.

"What was that?" I ask.

"You're right. You did. I feel violated."

Tensing, I whisper, "S-sarcasm?"

Completely bashful, he glances at me out of the corner of his eye, then he looks elsewhere. "Yeah."

Oh my word.

He's adorable.

I'm glad he's joking, too. I never want to *violate* anyone. I don't even like the way the word sounds.

Biting my lip, I smile. "I don't feel violated either. I'm perfectly calm. I had a good dinner. I have new books. Everything is great."

"You are so easy to take care of. It's insane." He taps

me in the forehead, inexplicably. "Be. Pickier."

My lashes flutter rapidly as my smile drifts away. I've been picky and spoiled my whole life. No one has ever told me to be pickier. "Why?"

"I don't know. Because you deserve nice things?"

"I had a pony growing up. I think I'm good in the 'nice things' department."

"Holy—" He curses. "You aren't serious."

"I am. Butterscotch."

"You did not name a horse Butterscotch."

"I *did*, and she was a pony."

Cursing again, Hayes finally seems relaxed enough to *almost* smile as he helps me to my feet. "I am deeply grateful to have not offended Your Majesty, Princess of Moths, with the brush of my peasant lips."

I refuse to look at his "peasant" lips or think about how soft and gentle they were even amid panic. The last thing I need right now is to spiral.

"If I'm a princess, the proper title is 'Your Highness', 'Your Royal Highness' if I'm the heir apparent. And I probably should be considering I'm an only child."

Hayes frees a long exhale, whispering something that sounds suspiciously close to what he said in Norwegian at the dressing room earlier. Grabbing up our bags, he starts toward the truck, and I trot after him.

"What does that mean?" I ask.

He casts a look over his shoulder and says, "Everything."

CHAPTER 15

♥ When in doubt, cheese.

Hayes: It's a slumber party.

Hayes: They told me not to tell you, but that's stupid, so here's every last detail I have managed to attain.

Hayes: It's a slumber party with their other friend Haley, or Hallie, or something like that. It's at that friend's flat—I have looked up the location online, and it is in a minimal crime area about ten minutes from us, so if anything happens, I'll be there in five. There's going to be a lot of cheese. I don't understand why this information was accessible. After learning that you are just barely younger than Marit, my sisters have a grand scheme to spoil you, which is why they want you to come over at three unaware of the fact you had to bring stuff for overnight. I will be home. They have expressed an intent to banish me once you arrive, but I'm difficult to move.

Hayes: What else…

I stare at my phone as more typing dots appear, and I have to say I'm glad Hayes knows better than to listen to his sisters' request. If I'm staying the night anywhere, I kind of need to account for Mouse. A four-person party seems almost manageable. A four-person party with copious amounts of cheese feels like it could almost be… fun.

Mouse—freshly bathed for this week and in his sweet little bear costume—snuggles up against me while I sit on my kitchen floor, listening to the hum of the fridge and feeling its vibration against my back.

Combined with Mouse's purrs, it's a sensory haven, and it's helping with the anxiety that says I'm going to a sleepover tomorrow.

I've never left Mouse alone for a full night before. Whenever I go to visit my parents for overnight, he comes with me. He takes a while to warm up to people, but he doesn't have any problems in the car. I made sure of that when he was a kitten. I bullied him constantly, so he wouldn't cause problems as an adult.

"Isn't that right?" I whisper at him, nuzzling his little paw without consequence. "Your feeties are mine, and you never ever scratch anyone, 'cause you're just a lil baby."

My phone buzzes, so I look, but it's not from Hayes.

It's from me.

I've just sent audio.

My stomach falls out, and I die.

Ever so breathlessly, I tap the play button.

"Your feeties ar—"

I lock my phone and screech on the inside.

The screen lights up, and I flinch.

Hayes: Are you trying to kill me with cuteness?

Hayes: Every time I think I'm safe, you find some other way to obliterate my sanity.

Hayes: Also, hi, Mouse. Who I assume is present.

Hayes: Hope, rather.

Hayes: I'm fond of my feeties, and I don't want to part with them if that message was for me. I might scratch if anyone tries to take them away.

Letting my phone slip from my fingers and onto the floor, I curl over Mouse, who doesn't even protest, and whimper.

My phone buzzes on the floor, and I dare to look at it.

Hayes: Will Mouse be all right with you gone?

I look at Mouse's pink, wrinkly face, and I miss him already, so I think the real question is will *I* be all right while I'm gone?

Ellen: I've never left him alone for this long before. He gets lonely.

Hayes: I can pick you up before everyone goes to bed tomorrow night and bring you back home if you'd like? Or he can come stay with me? Uncertain if he'd like that.

Ellen: It would be better if you stayed with him.

I blink at the text after I've sent it, and then no amount of fridge-hum therapy can take the anxiety spike out of my chest. I just invited Hayes to come stay in my apartment. That can't be normal human behavior. I'm almost certain that's inappropriate.

Hayes: I can do that.

I choke on my saliva, grip my phone in both hands, and stare. He doesn't mind? He doesn't care? He's actually going to do it?

I need to clean.

I get to my feet so fast my head tumbles over and my vision darkens, but I'm so used to it, I barely pause. My sight returns once I've stepped into the living room, and I plow for my bedroom.

The sheets come off my bed first, joining the pile of laundry on my floor. I'm going to have to do all of it. Fold it. Put it away. There's no way I want an overflowing hamper when he comes over. Bottles and wrappers are *everywhere*. I'll have to clean the trash out of my office, too.

My phone buzzes.

Hayes: Do you have any questions? My sisters are crazy, but I'm pretty much positive they'll take good care of you. I know that doesn't really make the experience anything familiar or innately comfortable, but at least know they aren't going to be like the kind of friends who abandon you drunk on your birthday.

Hayes: That's a really low bar.

Hayes: But…yeah.

Put that way, it is an obscenely low bar. What have my friend choices been up until this point in my life?

Ellen: If they're even half as sweet as you, I think I'll survive.

It's shocking how much I believe that when the most mundane situations can sometimes convince me I'm not going to make it. Example…I chance a look at my bedroom and swallow…I might not live through this deep clean.

❖

"*No,* all of you, *back*," Hayes roars after I ring the doorbell to his family's cute suburban house. It's about twenty minutes away from where we live, tucked neatly into a neighborhood with trim lawns and pastel siding. The two-car driveway loops down from the double garage to the cul-de-sac, and thankfully there was room for me to park on the street. I didn't want to block anyone in, and I hate having to move my car. Especially when people are watching.

I nearly flunked backing up when I got my license. I'm still shocked the person allowed my nine-point turn.

A pair of bright blue eyes peek at me through the blinds covering the window next to the door a single second before they're dragged away and the slats shudder back into place.

Hayes growls, "I *mean* it. Give her some space. *Go. All* of you." His voice softens, a touch. "Even you, *Mamma.* Please."

At long last, the door swings open, and Hayes's body fills the archway almost entirely. Beyond him, three women peek around a corner that appears to lead into a kitchen.

Wide smiles plaster across clearly-related faces, and the eldest woman—Hayes's mother—whispers something in Norwegian that makes her girls giggle like they're teenagers instead of grown adults.

Hayes whips around, facing them with a scowl, and they jerk out of sight. With a sigh, he looks back at me and moves to let me in. "Welcome."

"Thank you."

He closes the door behind me, and I give myself a moment to look over the cluttered living room, assess where I am. Every surface overflows with stuff, even the couches that face a small flat screen TV. Knickknacks and paintings. Blown glass and Christmas ornaments. Cloths in a hundred different shades pile high over every seat. A sewing machine sits on a desk in the corner, and as far as I can tell, the area surrounding it is the only space that's clean.

"It's like a museum," I say.

"Is that what we're calling this mess?" Hayes asks.

His mother barks something at him in Norwegian, emerging from the kitchen with her arms braced at her robust hips.

"*Mamma*, I asked if we could speak in English while Ellen's here."

Arching a brow in a very familiar *Hayes* way, the woman tosses her hand at her son and speaks with a thick accent, "You want me to chastise you in front of your girl in a language she understands?"

Hayes shifts his weight. "Not particularly."

With a deciding nod, she rambles in Norwegian for a moment, sniffs, then smiles at me. Spreading her arms wide, she closes me into a tight hug that I'm uncertain how to return when I'm holding my overnight bag, so I don't. Once she pulls back, she cups my cheeks and looks down at me. "It's so nice to finally meet you, Ellen."

"You as well," I offer, distracted when Hayes's sisters emerge to stand, grinning, behind their mother.

It takes me a long moment of overwhelm to realize…I have entered a world of giants. Among them, Hayes's mother is the shortest, but she's still a good head taller than me. Marit looks exactly like the photo Hayes showed me before, except her hair is now a dark purple instead of the acid green. She's got a pair of platform boots on—which bring her close to Hayes's height with a more slender disposition—and the strap buckles go all the way up to her thighs. Liv's attire is significantly more tame: a soft pink dress with a white apron stretched around her ample figure. Pulled back in a ponytail, her hair matches her mother's dark blond, but…

Um.

Are people allowed to be this *big*?

Softly, I echo a numb, "It's very nice to meet you," as I take a tiny step back.

Liv sets a hand against her chest, and her pearly pink nails meld flawlessly with the style of her adorable dress. His sisters are fashion icons. I love them. I want to be them. I can't exactly *not* look up to them.

Liv murmurs a gentle Norwegian expletive, then says, "*Lillebror* tattled."

"I *know*," Marit says, her American accent clearer than Hayes's. She folds her arms and eyes my bag. "You've come *prepared*. The audacity."

I clutch my overnight bag against my chest, and I don't know what to say. I think I might start hyperventilating. I don't know how to act like a person or a good girlfriend, and the weight of the trouble I'll cause if these people hate me is suddenly hitting me full force. "I…" My voice cracks.

Hayes sweeps his arm around my shoulders without a moment's notice. Brusquely, he takes me down a hall and into a cramped bedroom. It's vacant, clean, harboring only a double twin bed and a glass desk. Slightly forceful, he sits me on the navy comforter, and it occurs to me…I'm in his room. Or what was his room before he moved out. It's so… small for him. And did he *ever* fit comfortably on this bed?

"Scandalous, big bro," Marit teases from the doorway, and I half expect Hayes to slam the door shut in her face. Instead he just rolls his eyes at his little sister and shoos her.

Graciously, she dips away.

Crouching in front of me, Hayes deflates, bracing his arms on his knees. "They're excited to bully me. I promise that's all it is. I've never brought a girl home before, so their enthusiasm exceeds acceptable levels."

"Your family is very tall."

The corner of his mouth lifts. "Yeah, we are a bit on the big side. I'm not going anywhere until you're comfortable, so take all the time you need. I'll even go to the party with you if you want. I like cheese just as well as most people."

A weak laugh escapes me. "Is there actually going to be a ton of cheese?"

"Liv's been making mozzarella to go on a warm loaf of *Mamma*'s bread all morning."

My frail smile disappears. "*Fresh* cheese?"

"I told you she was chaotic domestic. She gets some of it from *Mamma*, but most of it is just 'cause she's crazy."

My nerves settle, bit by bit. "This room is too small for you."

Hayes glances around. "A bit, yeah."

"Did that ever…bother you?"

He clasps his hands together. "Sometimes. I kept the door open, and the window didn't have blinds while I was living here."

I look at the window now, complete with blinds and a navy set of curtains pulled to either side. The view looks out on a fenced-in yard, and closing it would shrink this space significantly. I can't imagine being his size with his phobia living in this little room or sleeping on this little bed. "I like how our apartments have an open floor plan," I offer. "My cottage is open like that, too. It's cozy, but not confined. Big windows and comfy window seats. I think you'd fit nicely." What am I saying?

Hayes graces me with a tiny, warm smile. "I'd love to see it sometime."

"I'd love to show you."

"*Hayes*, you're hogging our little sister!" Marit yells from the other room.

Hayes drops his smile and rolls his eyes again. With a sigh, he rises. "You good?"

Absently, I do a physical assessment. My heart's slowed down. My nerves are calmer. I'm not sweating inexplicably. My clothes are no longer too confining. I think I'm okay again, so I nod.

He gives me his hand. "My sisters really like you already, okay? So just ignore any comments about how you're joining the family and we're getting married."

I blink, taking his hand. "What?"

"They want to keep you, which is an emotion I understand, but they aren't burdened by anxiety on account of being a large man, so they don't have filters and probably intend to embarrass me however possible." Hayes helps me to my feet.

I am utterly confused as to what he is trying to tell me.

"They have no decorum, but you can tell them if they're making you uncomfortable. They will stop, so long as you aren't their brother. I genuinely think they hate me sometimes."

"I doubt that," I say, because it's the only thing I understand. I don't know how anyone could hate Hayes. He's so sweet. Even I know I like him. I'm just trying to decipher whether my "like" runs toward *friend* or *romantic partner*.

The fact I don't think I'd mind kissing him again has me skeptical for sure.

His hand is very firm and warm. I don't know that I want to let go.

His attention flicks from my eyes to our hands, then every part of him settles. He bends, touching a kiss to my cheek. "Be yourself. Talk about moths. Eat cheese."

I think I should get that in the style of a *Live, Laugh, Love* poster. Words to live by. The secret to happiness.

Without reason, I hug him, soak in his strength, and pull away before he can return the gesture—if he would return such a gesture. Smiling, I salute him at the door. "I'm off to see how cheese is made. Thank you for sharing your family with me. When in doubt, I'll spew moth facts. Yes. That's good. Natural human behavior. Okay. Bye." Marching, I escape down the hall and find his sisters in the kitchen.

They beam, put me in a frilly pink apron that looks handmade, and teach me how to finish making mozzarella cheese.

If they notice, they say nothing about the fact my face is completely red.

CHAPTER 16

> ♥ Relationships are hard. Even platonic ones.

Despite the fact I came prepared and brought my own clothes, Liv and Marit refused to let me leave the house without first shuffling through an exorbitant amount of clothing. In every single size imaginable. Apparently, there are thrift stores where entire bags of clothes are only five dollars, and Liv takes her shopping very seriously.

She's the seamstress. The baker. The cook.

Marit prefers music, painting, anything that has the potential to get wild or messy.

She plays five different instruments, and Liv can alter a dress while waiting for cheese to finish up.

I wish I were as cool as them.

I wish I hadn't told Hayes I was fine, gave him my key, and reminded him where Mouse's snacks are before the *great dress up event*. Marit painted my lips with a touch of gloss and braided my hair into an elaborate crown while Liv was altering an elegant gown for me. Sitting in the passenger seat of Liv's SUV right now, I feel like a proper moth princess in all this flowing green, and I wish I could have seen Hayes's reaction when I left Marit's room.

Do I look silly? Is this appropriate attire for a slumber party? I'm glad Liv's in a pale pink gown of her own since Marit's baggy black shirt and dark torn-up jeans directly contrast.

"You're pretty quiet, Ellen," Liv notes as she turns down a road lined with apartment complexes.

Massive gated communities and neighborhood signs close in around us as I murmur, "Am I?" It's nothing I haven't heard before. It's always *you're too quiet* or *you never shut up.* The first comes before I'm comfortable, and the second when it's too late for me to cleanly cut my emotions out of the relationship. I haven't done *girl friends* for so long.

Marit scoots forward from the backseat to poke her head above the armrest between Liv and I. "Introverts are like corpse flowers. It takes them years to bloom, but it's super cool when they do."

Liv's nose scrunches. "Don't compare Ellen to a stinky, poisonous flower."

"Why shouldn't I compare her to a *beautiful* flower with a strong musk that attracts *exactly* what it desires and poisons whatever doesn't deserve it?" She scoots closer, blue eyes bright on me now. "It's a flower the size of a person, Ellen, and it has this fleshy texture that's warm and pulses like a heartbeat. Isn't that awesome?"

It sounds like the kind of monstrous plant Blaire might write into one of her fairy worlds, except it's real, and that is incredibly awesome. Offering a small smile, I nod.

Marit grins, flashing white teeth. "I thought you'd think so. *Be the corpse flower* in a world full of mundane roses, Ellen. Don't let anyone tell you it's wrong. The people who matter will wait for those precious hours when you bloom, and they'll think it's the coolest thing ever. The people who don't matter will be too busy plugging their noses to appreciate anything."

Be the corpse flower in a world full of roses.

What a statement.

We arrive at *Paisley's* apartment, and I repeat her name over and over in my head after Marit and Liv introduce me. It seems I'm not the only one who has issues remembering names. How weird that Hayes remembered my full name after a twenty minute walk five years ago.

I wonder if Mouse is going to warm up to Hayes at all tonight. Should I check in with him? He should have made it there by now.

"You're quiet," Haley—no—*Paisley* says, dragging me out of my thoughts to discover that somehow we're all seated in her living room now. I'm uncertain how I transitioned from greetings to her couch, but sometimes stuff like that blurs. The menu sequence for an animated movie repeats on the TV screen, looking awesome and fairy tale, but that's not what I'm supposed to be focusing on at the moment.

I'm overwhelmed, by three people, and I don't have Hayes here to sweep me away so I can decompress.

Likely, I'm dissociating something fierce. Am I smiling? Shouldn't I be remembering to smile?

Before I figure out the right move, Marit swipes a kernel out of the popcorn bowl between us and throws it across the room to where Liv and Paisley are sitting, sending it bouncing off Paisley's forehead. "She's a *corpse flower*, you ingrate. Let her open when she's ready."

Paisley snorts, her mouth splitting in a lopsided grin that displays a gap between her two front teeth. She brushes the popcorn off her light blue gown, and it occurs to me that Marit is the odd one out. Not me. That's…interesting.

"I absolutely understand every word you just said." Paisley nods, decided, before tossing her curly brown hair back and shifting the subject. "We look like if the Power Puff Girls were princesses."

"What's that make Marit?" Liv asks, reaching for the elaborate cheese board on the coffee table in front of us. She grabs a cube of cheddar and pops it in her mouth. "The evil monkey?"

"I resent our relation deeply, sister." Marit rolls her eyes. Brightening, she swipes a cube of swiss, and conversation about a show I've never seen flows easily while I try to pay attention, try to work up the courage to reach for a snack, try to stay grounded.

I don't want to cause problems. I don't want to offend anyone. I don't want Hayes's sisters or their friend to hate me. So I smile, nod, mimic the body language Paisley displays to the best of my abilities, and itch to check in with Hayes, or figure out an opening in the rambling conversation where I can ask where the bathroom is. Not because I have to go. Just because I need a break from monitoring my face and actions.

I'm scared.

I don't want to mess up.

This is a lot.

Too much.

What if I let it slip that Hayes and I aren't actually a couple? What if they can tell when I say the wrong thing?

Paisley's hazel eyes flick toward me, and I make sure my smile is in place even as tension fills every single one of my muscles. "Okay," she says, and I wait.

Nothing more comes.

Marit and Liv glance at one another.

"Okay?" Liv asks, graciously. Now I don't have to.

Paisley sighs, gets more cheese that I want, and braces her forearm against her knee. She looks more like a mafia boss than a princess like that. The light from the TV glints across her dark skin as though it's coming from a dangling bulb in an interrogation room, and I shrink under the scrutiny even though she's the shortest one here. "Hayes Freaking Sallow," she declares slowly, leaving each word weighted.

I only blink, but both Marit and Liv gasp.

"*Paisley, no!*" Marit throws her arms around me, tugging my face into her chest and squeezing me tight. "This is our precious, innocent future sister, and you will not jeopardize that or frighten her."

Paisley's lips curl, feline and impish. "You're telling me you aren't *at all* curious about the secrets your brother's first girlfriend might possess?"

A beat passes. Then another.

Then everyone is looking at me, waiting, and I have no idea what's going on. "W-what?" I ask.

"What do you mean *what*?" Paisley's white teeth catch pale, colorful TV light, and the cheerful background music spilling on loop doesn't fit the sudden dread rising in my chest.

I'm beginning to understand.

This is about to become an *event*. I must somehow prove that I am actually seriously dating Hayes. I have no idea how to do that. Is this really going to take a turn toward the climax when everyone finds out?

"How did it happen?" Paisley points a piece of cheese at me.

I carefully ask, "How did what happen?"

Liv presses her lips together, shifting her gaze between Paisley and I.

Marit releases me in order to grab my shoulders, then she shakes me. "How in the world did you end up with *our brother*? AKA the social disaster of the century. AKA I'm allergic to romance, girls, and intimacy. AKA Mr. Not Interested."

"He…hasn't told you?" I ask, wide-eyed.

Liv sighs, suddenly sullen. She rests against the cushions, throwing her arm over the back of the couch in utter despair. "Hayes doesn't talk about anything important."

Paisley, also seemingly dejected, lets her lip curl as she huffs. "That man's primary language is grunts."

"Raised brows." Marit joins the solemn display, releasing me fully in order to slouch and drag her leg up against her chest.

"Grumbles," Liv adds.

"*Hm*," Paisley utters, deeply reminiscent of that sound Hayes does, in fact, make rather often.

"Communication is a basic *no*." Marit scoffs, shaking her head. "We don't know anything about him or his life anymore. Haven't heard anything of real substance since he moved out. We could barely scrape information out of him while he lived with us, but now? Now only Mum can get close."

Liv's eyes roll. "You know how we discovered he was *moving out*, Ellen?"

I shake my head, clasping my hands in my lap in an effort to be proper and not add to the clear distress surrounding me.

Marit deepens her voice. "*I found an apartment closer to Temptations. I completed the paperwork yesterday. Honestly, I need a place where I can cry myself to sleep without bothering anyone. So.*"

My brows rise.

"Exactly!" Marit points at me. "He was packed and gone the next day. No explanation about the foreboding line either. Maybe something happened that destroyed his world. Maybe he was joking. Sometimes you can't tell."

That's...true.

Delirious laughter spills out of Liv, and she lays her hand across her face, murmuring a Norwegian curse before saying, "Care to know how we found out about you?"

I suppose so? "How?"

Paisley's laughter is less depressed as she blurts, "He

sent them a group text. Show her!"

Liv shuffles through the puffing fabric of her skirt and digs her phone out of a hidden pocket. She swipes across the screen, then she shows me the text.

It is prefaced by a picture of me with a giraffe looking over my shoulder for more food. Its tongue flails, and I'm beaming, holding a bundle of leaves in my hands and sticking my tongue out as far as it can go.

Hayes: Gf obtained, plz stop setting me up as I have found my wife. Thx

I blink at the shorthand, at the image, at the whole thing. I don't know what to say. I have a feeling the whole *wife* part is sarcasm, because we have not talked about including any mention of marriage in this farce.

That's a different aspect of this trope.

It would have come with an entirely different outline.

Also, he *had* to send this picture? What happened to the monkey one? Well, I guess the monkey one isn't actually better though…

Finally finding my voice, I say, "Oh."

"*Oh?*" Paisley slaps her hand down against the couch. "*OH?* That's all you have to say for yourself? No. I won't allow it. What mystical powers of seduction do you possess, Ellen? This man once, casually, considered joining a monastery. At a family dinner."

Liv groans, melting into the couch. "Ugh. I remember that. You were over so I could get the finishing touches on your prom dress, and my *lillebror*—" A wild laugh spills out of her. "—says, 'I've been thinking about becoming a monk.' Without. Context!"

"Mum smacked him, and they argued throughout the next hour," Marit adds. "But the only thing that really stopped him was the fact he didn't know if he fit in a position of 'religious enlightenment'."

"I remember him grumbling something about how he wished there were sincere celibate societies he could join that didn't feel like extreme religions or cults." Paisley snorts.

Liv and Marit deflate.

"Despite this, you've been eager to pair him off with someone?" I ask, and my tone might be a touch more scathing than intended.

"He's lonely," Marit notes.

I frown. "Has he expressed this to you?"

"Not in so many words, but his only friends are his staff and his family, and, like we said, he doesn't really talk much." Liv sets a hand against her chest, graceful, regal. "We were trying to help him."

"Unsolicited help isn't helpful."

Marit sighs. "Okay, we were teasing him a bit, too. We are his sisters. That's our legal primary career description."

"It's unkind, and it's troubled him."

"He never said so, and he never exactly refused to do any of the stuff we planned for him." Liv scoots forward to cut into the ball of mozzarella and spread it across a slice of bread.

As she takes a bite, I clench my fists. "He's too sweet to stand anyone up, and you already said he doesn't communicate much about important things like telling you he doesn't want to do something. Teasing someone directly is one thing, but holding him in front of someone else is just…just *cruel*."

Paisley barks a laugh and raises her hand. "I can confirm Ellen's right."

Liv bumps into her. "*Sureee*."

"What?" Paisley sticks her nose in the air. "Subjecting anyone to that man's mouth is cruelty."

My stomach drops into my feet, and I blurt, "What?"

Paisley dives for her own slice of mozzarella bread. "He's an *awful* kisser."

"He didn't want to kiss you on New Year's, and we absolutely didn't tell you to *attack* him," Marit defends. "But also, ew, ew, ew. We are not going to talk about *that* stuff where it concerns *our brother.*"

Paisley's feline grin spreads, fully Cheshire. "I took my chance. I regret it. Sorry, but your brother is kind of hot, and a girl can dream."

Paisley is the *friend of Liv's* who kissed Hayes *against his will* on New Year's. A mix of emotions I can't identify collide in my head, chest, stomach, and this was a bad idea. A very bad idea. I don't know what I was thinking, trying to do the *friends* thing again. Harsh words stick to my tongue, but I know better than to directly let them free. They aren't attempts to inform Hayes's sisters of the trouble they may be unaware of. *Everyone* should know that sexual assault isn't okay.

To say anything about it is nothing more than pushing blame in an effort to make someone accountable. It won't resolve anything. And people don't like being blamed or made accountable.

Is staying quiet morally acceptable? Does it make it seem like I approve of what I'm hearing?

Am I even *right* in labeling it as what it was?

The social expectation of a midnight kiss on New Year's surely doesn't absolve an assault crime, right? But does it lessen the charge since the offender may not understand the gravity of the situation? Is a social expectation "consent" to some people?

How did she even reach his face?

She's shorter than me!

"I think I broke her," Paisley murmurs. "It was just a peck, promise. A very uncomfortable peck."

"How could you…"

Her head cocks. "Hm?"

"How could you do something like that? Hayes might be gruff, but he has feelings, and it's horrible that you've all been playing with them, worse that you've convinced yourselves you're *helping*." My heart's stampeding. I can barely breathe, and my voice is shaking. "He doesn't need or want your help. He's perfectly capable of taking care of himself."

"We know that," Marit says, and she's not smiling.

No one is smiling anymore.

My heart lurches up into my throat.

Liv looks at the rest of her bread like it's the most interesting thing in the world. "Hayes takes care of everyone, Ellen. He's been taking care of all of us his entire life, shielding us from *Far*, acting as the real man of the house, being *Mamma*'s emotional support."

"He does everything for everyone else, and he accepts nothing in return from any of us. We want him to have someone he lets take care of him, too." Marit lifts a shoulder, and although she's significantly less bulky than Hayes, the action is familiarly his. Her gaze cuts sharply toward Paisley. "He's easy to take advantage of."

Paisley's eyes go wide. "I did *not* mean to take advantage of him! As far as I could tell, I gave him plenty of flirty hints."

Marit slaps the couch. "He doesn't understand *flirty hints*, Paisley! And now you've broken Ellen, someone who *clearly* cares about him as much as we do and—therefore—*must* be assimilated into our girl group so we can *all* plan the wedding together." Marit crushes me against her again, huffing. "Think about what you've done."

"I do! Every night as I'm trying to fall asleep. I promise the *disaster* that was New Year's nestles right next to me ripping my jeans at dodge ball in the fourth grade." Her eyes go dark, distant, and she stares blankly over the tops of our heads. "I can still hear the laughter. Haunting me."

Half-muffled, I ask, "You thought Hayes wanted to kiss you?"

She blinks back to the moment. "I'm not in the habit of forcing my kisses on people. Not even really, very incredibly hot people."

Liv gags and finishes her bread before making another slice.

"He leaned down and everything. In hindsight, I think he was just trying to hear me when I asked if we could kiss." She jerks a thumb toward Liv. "This freaky family breathes from an entirely different atmosphere than us. Sound travels different in the exosphere. It was like kissing marble."

"Wow. Okay. You've jumped quite a few spheres there." Marit deadpans. "And thanks to Hayes, I know every last one in order. So. Yeah. Ya rude."

"Excuse me. I know the spheres as well, and I selected the correct one." Paisley flutters her dark lashes. "How you three didn't break your mother is one of the world's greatest mysteries."

Marit releases me and points. "*Rude, rude, rude!*"

Paisley sticks her tongue out.

Liv passes the bread slice she just made to me, and I gasp, taking it with no small amount of awe. My irritation, anger, and unrest all fall away, partly because I'm gathering that the assault was somehow *accidental* social misconduct (something I understand well), and partly because this fresh cheese on fresh bread from the Sallow kitchen is the most beautiful thing I have ever seen. "Thank you," I murmur and indulge in a reverent bite.

Liv smiles sweetly. "You really are adorable."

Marit snorts. "It's the only thing outside of astronomy and space that Hayes can't seem to stop talking about."

Liv groans, mumbling something off in Norwegian before saying, "He was being absolutely insufferable when he came over for brunch a few weeks ago and *Mamma* asked about you. *Isn't she cute? Look how cute she is. Have you ever seen anyone more adorable?*"

"The number of candid zoo photos was creepy," Marit drones, tossing a handful of popcorn in her mouth. "He's obsessed."

"But he's also *impossible.*" Liv sighs, shaking her head. "We asked when he was seeing you next, and he shrugged." She imitates his tone. "*I don't know.*" She drops his tone. "Except not the actual words. Like the mumbled cousins of the actual words. He has this amazing, life-altering date with this amazing life-altering girl, and *he doesn't even know when he's seeing her next?*"

To be fair, we live two seconds apart.

Do his sisters not know that?

I keep munching my bread and wonder exactly what information Hayes has been providing while over-selling our "relationship" with more gusto than I have ever witnessed from any fake dating story in my life. Like, goodness, a public kiss normally cuts it. End scene. Roll credits.

Marit smirks. "So I told him I didn't believe him and he probably got all the pictures mass-produced from an AI robot."

"An ultimately effective plot, although we did then have to sit through about ten minutes of him berating us on the immoral implications of condoning the use of art bots." Liv sighs.

Fondly, Marit crosses her arms and mimics, "*You're an artist. Why are you joking about this?*" She snickers.

"Because my portrait eyes don't ever come out looking demonic, thanks. They may not always match, but they probably won't steal your soul, and I think that's important."

"Nightmare fuel," Paisley mutters. In a burst of energy, she pops up and swipes the remote off the coffee table. "Let's start the movie! Afterward, we'll plot the downfall of art theft bots around a bonfire on the front lawn until the neighbors call the cops. Until then, cheese."

CHAPTER 17

> ♥ Finding love from someone else begins after finding love for ourselves.

Crazy cartoon movies take a lot of tension out of attempting to fit in. Crazy cartoon fantasy movies where the main characters look like butterfly people make me wonder what I've been doing with my life.

Forbidden romance. Enemies to lovers. Music.

It's flawless.

It's my new favorite movie.

I love it.

In a world where I've grown used to *girls' movie night* meaning *over-sexualized chick flicks*, this is more than refreshing. Not only that, earlier when I was stressed and misunderstanding, they didn't get mad at me. I can't believe it took my lagging brain nearly an entire movie to realize, but now that it has, I think I understand something else, too.

This wasn't a mistake.

I'm having a good time.

I am having a good time with girls my age.

"You expect me to believe they fell in love in less than a night?" Marit asks as the final scene turns inexplicably kaleidoscopic. Potentially, it's in reference to the fact the collective noun for a group of butterflies is "kaleidoscope"? Or, potentially, this movie was created by someone on drugs. Either way, it's a masterpiece, and I must secure a copy for myself.

"They're bug people. That's probably half their lifespan," Liv says.

"Butterflies normally live for several weeks to several months, so *half* is a bit exaggerated," I comment.

"They're *fairies*, so they probably live forever," Paisley states, well-informed.

When the characters kiss, I gasp, covering my mouth with both hands.

"*Ewww.* What the heck. Is that allowed?" Marit throws an unpopped kernel of popcorn from the bottom of our empty bowl at the screen. "I thought this movie was rated E for everyone."

"Grow up! It's rated PG, and we have Liv here to parent us." Indignant, Paisley sniffs and turns toward Liv. "Mama Liv, please provide insight for us, your sweet baby children."

Regally, Liv says, "When a mommy butterfly and a daddy…what is he even?"

"Technically, she's a fairy and he's a goblin," I inform.

Liv makes a brief considering sound then continues, "When a mommy fairy and a daddy goblin love each other very much, they get high on LSD, sing a duet together, and touch faces in front of their entire combined kingdoms."

"Does this movie have a sequel? I need answers." Marit scrambles to reach the DVD case where it's resting on a now-decimated snack table.

Excitement sparks through my chest at the very idea of a sequel, and I reach for my purse. If this movie does have a sequel, that would be the best thing ever. Otherwise, I'm going to end up rewatching just it every day for a month. Patting Spotz on the head, I pull out my phone, intending to do a search for potential sequels when I discover messages Hayes sent about thirty minutes ago.

Hayes: Best friends.

The second message is a picture of Hayes in my living room with Mouse on his shoulder, and it's the cutest thing in the world. I must save it and cherish it forever.

Hayes: I hope you're having a good time and they haven't made things too awkward for you.

Hayes: Mouse misses you.

Hayes: And so do I.

"Whatcha smilin' at?" Paisley chirps, and I jump out of my skin to find her hovering above me with a stack of empty food platters.

Her eyes gleam, so I tuck my phone against my chest. "Nothing." I cough, clearing my throat a bit. Logically, boyfriends check in with their girlfriends while they're out with their sisters, maybe? With that thought in my head, I say, "It's just Hayes."

A collective gasp—which has nothing to do with the exceedingly strange post-credit scene—goes through the room. Marit crowds over my shoulder while Paisley's curls nearly fall into my face as she leans down.

"What's he saying?" Liv asks, all at once at the edge of her couch cushion, blue eyes sparkling with interest.

"Tell him we're being perfect angels," Marit says. "So much so, he should treat us to tacos tomorrow."

"He just sent me a picture to show that my cat's warmed up to him." I provide the photo evidence. Like a girlfriend might. I think. This is an interesting kind of "dating practice," and my teacher appears to be curled up on my couch with my cat, looking very cozy.

"Gah," Paisley exclaims before straightening and marching into the kitchen. "I can't. He's too beautiful, and I'd be jealous. If he were a better kisser."

"We aren't bringing up the kissing thing again!" Marit throws a kernel into the kitchen.

Paisley drops the empty platters off on the counter with

some force. "Marit, if you throw one more thing, you're cleaning my apartment."

"Someone probably should!" Marit calls, and I don't know what she's talking about. Aside from the clutter we've brought, this place is immaculate.

Oddly enough, the prickle of nerves that inspires me to figure out every single detail I don't understand tamed at some point between the first difficult conversation and the fairy/goblin romance. These people prefer a fairy/goblin animated movie over tired clichés and drama.

I appreciate that.

And it makes me feel like I'm not the only weird one.

Ellen: I'm having a good time. It was a little bumpy at first, but I think I'm figuring out how to socialize again.

Ellen: It's been a while.

Ellen: Ha ha.

I hope that doesn't make me sound pathetic. If it does, I can't tell from his response.

Hayes: Did you forget to talk about moths at first?

Hayes: I'm glad you overcame that if so.

Hayes: The absence of moths in a conversation would make it a little bumpy.

A stupid little smile rises to my face, and I'm almost oblivious to the fact Marit's shamelessly looking over my shoulder. Almost.

Ellen: Marit is spying on our conversation.

Hayes: Hi, Marit. You're being rude.

Marit scoffs. "I'm not being rude. He's interrupting girl's night."

"You know he loves with his whole being. He's probably having girlfriend withdrawals." Liv gathers up trash, and a random popcorn kernel that somehow ended up by the TV. She brings it all into the kitchen before adding, "I still don't know how he survived some summers in

Norway."

That piques my interest. "Why?"

"We lived in the north," Marit answers, tapping to enlarge an image Hayes sends of Mouse in a duckling outfit. Seems he found Mouse's clothes. "Some days the sun only set for maybe four hours. And some nights space boy stayed outside the entire time, soaking in the darkness."

"We used to tease that his love of the night was why he was the only one of us who came out with dark hair." Liv smiles, but there's a touch of something else in the expression.

I don't understand until Marit mutters, "Dad had *other* reasons he liked to mention for why Hayes looked different, usually whenever Hayes failed to live up to his unnatural expectations. What an idiot. He knows *Mum* was never the one who cheated."

"He's still our parent, Marit. Be respectful."

"He's our sperm donor, and he lost all my respect the first time he…" Her eyes flick off a short video of Mouse wiggling in his duckling costume and catch mine. "Never mind. Your cat is adorable."

"He's a wrinkly baby."

Marit grins. "He definitely is."

"His name is Mouse."

"Heh. Because it's ironic?"

My head tilts. "Because he looks like a baby mouse." I've literally never realized the irony. Wow. All this time I've just been thinking in the context that he looks like a pinkie mouse. Imagine if he were an outdoor cat and hunted mice. His poor victims would be so confused as to why a giant offspring has it in for them.

Hayes: I took those before I left for work, and I'll have to get back to breaking up fights and ordering chips or whatever else it is I do here in a moment. I wanted you to know that we're buds now, so he won't be hiding in a corner shivering all night.

Hayes: Side note: it only took half the box of kitty crack to achieve this level of trust.

Marit whistles while I'm contemplating my reply, and she bounces off the couch. "Liv, Hayes writes to his girlfriend in complete sentences. With periods. And commas. He just used a colon. Can you believe it? He knows what a colon is. It's crazy."

"There's no way. Hayes doesn't even know what capitalization is for."

There's a potential I told him while I was drunk.

Shaking that thought out of my head, I reply.

Ellen: Thank you for keeping him company and befriending him.

Ellen: I'm sorry that he's a bit of a handful.

Hayes: It's no trouble.

Hayes: I guess only opening up under the influence of drugs or alcohol is a genetic trait passed from mother to child.

My face burns red, and I'm glad Marit has stopped looking over my shoulder.

Ellen: I'm never touching another drop again.

Hayes: Probably for the best.

Hayes: I bet drunk tropes are bad for my sanity.

They really, really would be. It's a miracle I didn't kiss him that night. I have no idea why I'm thinking about that all of a sudden. Potentially tonight the topic of kissing has come up more times than entirely reasonable. And potentially my soul still hasn't recovered from being at the mall with him, in the elevator.

It wasn't an awful kiss. It wasn't a real kiss.

It was soft and warm and brief, laced in frantic energy.

Definitely makes a girl curious about what the real thing might be like.

Hayes: I'm glad you're having a good time. I'll see you tomorrow.

Ellen: Okay. See you then.

To sign off, he sends me a gif of a moth, so I send him one of a galaxy.

Periodically throughout the rest of the night and until I've giggled myself to sleep, we send pictures back and forth of the things one another loves. It's a constant reminder that I'm not alone or too weird for him, that I'm not a bother or a burden.

And with his sisters and their friend laughing and talking with me, including me, not getting upset or frustrated with me even when I know I can come off harsh, it finally feels like I've found a place where I belong.

I don't want to lose it.

Is it too predictable if I say I'm done pretending, and I want this—*all* of this—to be real?

CHAPTER 18

♥ It's not the end until the weirdos fall in *love*. "Like" is, obviously, different.

Is this…a trope?

If it is, I can't think of a concise wording for it…

It's noon, and I've just finished having lunch with Hayes's (amazing, stunning, the best ever) family, driven home, and found him asleep on my bed, under my cat. Mouse purrs, sprawled across his very nice broad chest, content. Hayes's breaths lift and lower Mouse, threatening the threads of his shirt with every slight move. He's lying dead-center in the middle of my bed, on top of the comforter, one of my pillows tucked beneath his head.

I swallow, and I know I did just walk up the stairs from my car with a practical ballgown thrown over my shoulder, but my heart's overreacting. The dress Liv let me keep wasn't *that* heavy before I tossed it over the couch, and…I exercise. Because stamina. Very important for those of us with heart-beating-too-fast syndrome.

I have never seen a man other than my father in anything even resembling pajamas before. This feels indecent.

Very indecent.

I should not be looking.

If *I* were asleep in my pajamas, Hayes wouldn't be looking at *me*. 'Twould be improper.

With that thought, I make an about-face and erase the image of his black t-shirt and black plaid pants fighting for life against the sheer girth of him from my mind. I don't think they make an XL number high enough to contain all that Nordic muscle. Clamping a hand to my mouth, I consider the fact I might be objectifying my neighbor. Not just my neighbor.

My friend.

My pet sitter.

My fake boyfriend.

Objectification is icky, but now that I've done it, I don't want to pretend I haven't.

That would be even ickier.

It has crossed my mind that Thor Odinson is asleep on my bed right now. I own up to this disgraceful fact. I am very deeply sorry.

Now…

What in the world am I supposed to do?

How does one awaken a Nordic god? Why is a Nordic god asleep past noon? He *did* send his last gif at three in the morning. That potentially has something to do with the reason he's still asleep. Great. Now I know *why* this has happened.

I still lack all points of reference that might assist me on knowing how to deal with it. Sleeping people in stories… sleeping people in stories…

Sleeping Beauty.

Wow. Okay. No. Calm down. That story is violently concerning.

I also doubt he's choking on an apple, so Snow White's not going to help me either.

"Pudding…?" Groggily, my nickname drifts from behind me, snaking up my spine. It's physical. Harrowing.

I have been caught in an illicit act, and I have no literary guidance. Melanie Richards outlined nothing of this sort within *How to Find Love When You're Weird*, and why am I even thinking about that right now? Thinking about *that* implies I believe I'm meant to find love with *Hayes*. And...I'm not aiming for that, even if we're fake dating and all the other tropes are lining up and he doesn't actually drink and I'm getting over the whole *he so big, I so smol* thing.

Because I'm not small.

I'm above average even.

He is just freakishly large. Weirdly large. Weird. Like me. And it's the most comforting thing in the entire world.

Squeezing my eyes shut, I manage a weak, "Yes?"

"What are you doing?" he mumbles.

With a coo, Mouse awakens and bounces to me, rubbing his head against my ankles. I pick him up for emotional support as I force out my reply, "Behaving myself."

Threads of amusement weave into Hayes's tired voice. "What?"

A breath shivers through my lungs. "I was unaware you were asleep when I entered the room, and I didn't know how to properly wake you." Mouse rubs into my chin, precious, purring.

"With a kiss," Hayes informs.

I suck in a sharp breath and face him.

Humor lilts about in his eyes as he rests back on his elbows, watching me. Tousled dark hair. A dusting of shadow across his jaw. He's hopelessly masculine, and on my bed.

My face explodes crimson.

Of course he's on my bed.

I told him he could sleep here. I informed him that I changed the sheets for him. I slept on the couch the night before because I accidentally changed the sheets too early. I asked him for a favor. He *graciously* obliged, and now I'm

—I'm *admiring* him? I am an awful, awful person.

"I'm joking," he murmurs, tone rough with sleep, exhilarating, seductive.

"I know," I blurt in order to cut my thoughts off. They are intrusive. The same nasty things that occasionally suggest I walk out into traffic or jump off my balcony. They are unreliable.

His head dips toward his chest at a slight angle. "Are you all right? Did everything go smoothly this morning?"

This morning was amazing. We woke late, exchanged numbers, made plans to *do this again in a few weeks*, then returned to his house in time for his mother to have lunch waiting.

He must know he's breathtaking. He must see that my face is blistering. He must think this is funny.

"Don't tease me," I say as Mouse wriggles in my arms. He escapes my hold and bolts out the door.

Traitor.

Now I have no idea where to put my hands. Or my eyes. Or my body.

Confusion ripples across Hayes's face. "I finished teasing you with my crack about kissing me awake, pudding." Drawing himself upright, he stretches.

Oh.

Sweet heavens.

His muscl—

No, bad. Cease and desist.

I squeeze my eyes shut, cover my blazing face with my hands, and attempt logical thought.

I'm hyped up on a fantasy romance movie and being told that this man loves me, wants to marry me. Why on earth did he have to be *that* dramatic? I get that he's sarcastic, but that's extreme. People are misunderstanding. I've fallen in love with his family, with being *little sister*.

I've wanted sisters forever. I want his family.

And I can't forget the slight touch of his mouth on mine. The nearness and comfort that followed, that felt so mindlessly natural. Gentle, inexplicable forehead kisses that I'm no longer certain I can live without...

Hayes's fingers brush my wrists, achingly careful, but I jolt, tensing into stone, knowing his unexpected touch will linger with me for days.

Softly, he murmurs, "Pudding?"

A breath trembles into my lungs. Out.

"I love your family," I exhale.

"They're all right." His words are blunt, but tenderness highlights each. He applies a slight pressure, intending to coax my hands away from my face, but I don't budge, and he doesn't force.

"I've never felt this...*normal*. We talked all night, Hayes. We laughed and joked, and when I misunderstood, got confused, *even upset*, they didn't tell me I was wrong or crazy or overreacting." My voice breaks like I'm on the verge of tears, but I don't think I am. I might even be mad, mad that I've never found these kinds of people before. "No one gave me odd looks that I couldn't decode. Even when we were all half-drunk and delirious from staying up so late, nothing changed. I never felt that strange neglect I always have to brush off as my imagination."

"You're not wrong or crazy, and no one can measure what is or isn't an overreaction," Hayes mutters, fingers skimming down to my elbows in two scalding trails. "Some people let differences offend them. Others know better than to think they're a threat."

Sucking in a tight breath, I finally lower my hands and look at him. "Your sisters say you're bad at communicating, but you're very well-spoken with me."

His gaze skitters away. "They're...my sisters. It's hard

to explain. It feels like the important stuff has already been passed through our DNA, our overlapping history. It's pretty pointless to say much out loud."

"You use text slang with them, but not with me."

"I also send them pictures of frogs in top hats. They're my sisters. And you're…not. So." His touch slips away from one of my arms, and he rubs his neck. "Why are we comparing the way I treat them and the way I treat you?"

Because it's different, and I'm wondering if there's a chance. Because my head is full of a lot of different, overwhelming things right now, and I don't know how to get it all out in pretty, collected ways unless I write a very long email.

Because I think I like you more than I thought and in a way I've never liked anyone before.

Everything about you, Hayes, is right in ways I don't understand, right down to the company you keep and the people you share in order to prove that—somehow—I'm not all of the things I've been led to believe.

I want to stay like this.

I want to keep feeling the way you help me feel.

And, maybe, just a little bit, I want the right to improper glances when my mind strays to the fact you are the most beautiful person I have ever seen.

It's my turn to drop my gaze to my feet. Clenching my fists at my sides, I think I've been upright for too long. However, given this conversation, who can really tell the reason behind the stampede in my chest? "I…think…" My stomach hurts; I'm dying. I'm beginning to think that *maybe* drama for the sake of drama isn't why characters in stories have trouble at this point. Maybe struggling with these emotions is realism seeping between the lines, and people don't read in order for reality to be thrown in their faces, so that's why it's annoying.

Everyone is so brave when they aren't faced with the problem themselves.

It's easy not to be an idiot when the full impact of a situation's stress isn't weighing down every brain cell.

"You think...?" he asks.

"Ilikeyou." The words leave my mouth like a bullet to the chest, and my vision blurs immediately after. My head tips, light, and my knees buckle. My descent to the floor is not graceful, but thanks to the fact Hayes is still holding my arm it's not disastrous. Could have been worse. All things considered...could have been worse.

Crouching in front of me, past a collage of blots similar to a Rorschach test that I fear cannot assist me in defining my current psychological state, Hayes murmurs, "Ellen... hey...are you all right? What did you say? Do you need something? Is this a POTS attack?" He cups my face in his warm hand, and I let my eyes close as he lays me back against the carpet.

Universe, why?

He didn't understand me.

I swear.

Rom-com magic sucks sometimes.

Rom-com magic, in its coarsest form, dictates two simple things: whenever two characters are about to kiss, they will be interrupted (unless it's the last chapter or episode or final twenty minutes—well, depending on heat levels), and no romantic moments may transpire seamlessly. Do people even understand the stark irony of a rom-com? In a romantic comedy, first and foremost, the romance is a joke.

As if anyone in their right mind has the audacity for grand gestures. Sometimes I don't even have the audacity to get out of bed.

I want to repeat myself and spite the rom-com gods'

intervention, but now I feel foolish. I'm on the floor. Because I walked upstairs and stood around for longer than ten minutes.

Why would Hayes want a girl like me? His sisters want someone who can take care of him.

And I can barely take care of myself sometimes.

Weirdness aside, from a physical standpoint, I'm a burden.

"Ellen…" His voice whispers with concern, and friendship really is the better option here, for both of us.

Opening my eyes, I stare up at the popcorn ceiling, waiting for my vision to clear, my heart rate to settle. Fun times. Love this for me.

Hayes curses, gathers me up, and brings me to the bed. It's warm from the heat of his body, and it smells like… whey protein powder. Vanilla. A broken laugh escapes me, and I want to cry. I'm angry. This is infuriating.

"I make good money," I say, gripping a fist to my forehead. "I'm not useless. I've overdone it. That's all. I've survived for years by myself. I've taken care of Mouse, too. I've bathed him. Every week. For years. I haven't skipped a single time."

Hayes looks down at me, his heavy brow furrowed. Slowly, he says, "…yeah."

I bite my lip because I don't know what he's thinking, and I hate it. Right now, I want every thought. Every last one. I want him to say everything in his head, give me information, truth, something to rely on. "What are you thinking?"

"That you nearly fainted and now you're rambling things without any context, which makes me heavily debate whether or not I should call 911."

My eyes widen.

Very softly, he says, "Are you *sure* your POTS isn't a

severe case? This seems kind of…severe."

"I don't even lose consciousness."

"The bar shouldn't be that low, right?"

Heck if I know. I find his eyes, but they're too bright and kind and *much*, so I look at his mouth. Shockingly, that doesn't improve my mental state. My cheeks flush deeper, if it's possible, and I attempt to regulate my breathing. "There's context."

"What's your full name and date of birth?"

My entire being levels, deadpans. I drone, "I don't have a concussion."

Hayes's lips pinch. "Why aren't we taught more protocols in school? All I have to offer right now is asking you whether you smell burnt toast—"

"There's actually no solid evidence that smelling burnt toast indicates a stroke."

"—or telling you to stop, drop, and roll."

"…I'm not on fire." Unless we're counting my face. But, oddly enough, this conversation is soothing in a weird way. Weird, weirder, weirdest. Hayes should decide if our weirdness matches or not. That's not a decision that makes sense to keep in my hands alone. I already know that he finds me, on some level, attractive. We get along well.

I'll not make his decisions for him. If I'm too much, he'll tell me. It's not like I haven't faced rejection before. I'm used to it.

"I am not useless," I repeat.

"I know that," he says.

"I like you."

Silence.

My chest tightens with every moment that passes, and it grows progressively harder to inhale. He's staring, and his eyes burn into my flesh, melting it straight off the bone. I might throw up. "I-I can probably learn how to cook more than three meals, and I could compete in cleaning competitions, if threatened with company. I don't think any one person in a relationship should have to deal with everything, especially if both parties work, so I'll do my best to pull my weight. I don't know cars or home repair, but I do make enough to hire professionals as necessary."

"Ellen," he grits my name out, and I wince.

"S-sorry. I told myself it was a bad idea to tell you, and *trust me* I've read so many friends-to-lovers romances. I have seen absolutely every variation of 'I don't want to ruin our friendship' out there. But ruin isn't what deeper emotions bring. I don't think so anyway. I care about you more than I thought. How could that ruin anything…right? I don't know. I don't know about this stuff. I just know I like you. A lot. And I'd like to like you more. If that's okay. If it isn't, I understand. I—"

"*Ellen.*"

I choke on my words and stuff them down in my gut.

His fingers graze my cheek. Harsh, he asks, "You like me…romantically?"

Taking a breath shouldn't use up all my energy, but it does. "I think so. Yes. Sorry if that makes you uncomfortable. Although it shouldn't. I was perfectly cordial when you told me you wouldn't mind kissing me, so…"

Quiet moments pass, drawn out long enough that I dare a look at him.

My heart hits my rib cage.

Predatory is the only word I can use to describe the way he's watching me, and it shocks straight through my tendons and sinew. He's still stroking my cheek, but every motion is more…calculating.

I don't believe I've ever been more attracted to or more afraid of anyone before in my life. These next moments are going to hurt. I've overestimated someone again, no doubt. He'll tell me we can't be friends anymore. I'll lose everything. Again. And I'm almost positive it would be ridiculous for him to move away on account of this, so I've just booked my foreseeable future with awkward meetings as I pray for something like a second chance to end up in my storyline.

Hayes kisses my nose.

My spiraling thoughts hesitate.

He hisses a curse, touching his forehead to mine. Still-minty breath fans across my lips when he speaks. "I like you, too, Ellen. I was devastated when you didn't put my name down. I didn't know what I could have possibly done wrong in less than ten minutes when we got along so well while you were drunk. I thought maybe you remembered something from that night that you hated. The chance that I hurt you or made you despise me…was terrifying. Whatever I did, I'm sorry."

A loading screen occupies my mind for a handful of moments, then I say, "I'm sorry. What? When I didn't put your name down where?"

He winces, drawing back a few inches. "I… At the speed dating thing. You were the girl I liked. But you didn't put my name down. When we started talking about 'fake dating', I thought maybe it would give me a chance to fix however I messed up if we got to know each other again. My family is insane, but I wouldn't ever sincerely try to trick them. I have no doubts that they mean well in their own way and would stop if I managed to speak up about my apprehensions."

My lips part, but no sound comes out.

His jaw locks. "Did I…just ruin everything?"

Numbly, I shake my head. "You…" My lashes flutter as I try to understand, figure out a place to grasp, which part to respond to. He's liked me? Since the speed dating event? What did I do that made him like me? At least I know why I didn't put his name down. "You're really big, and I'm easily overwhelmed. I'm also very used to people getting upset with me, and I didn't think I'd survive your anger. You...scared me."

He sighs, and his jaw locks. A fragile curse leaves him. "I should have known. I scared you the first time, too."

"When I was drunk?"

He nods, attention elsewhere. "I told you then I wasn't so bad. I guess it takes a minute longer to convince you of that when you aren't pissed."

"I'm sorry. I was trusting once, and it kept hurting me...so...I stopped. I grew to be more cautious and guarded."

"I won't ever hurt you. I promise. You're tougher than you look, in so many ways, pudding." He skates his index finger around a lock of my hair and draws it to his lips, holding my gaze. "You can handle me."

My soul abandons my body as a rush of prickling heat floods across my skin, raising every hair from the top of my head to the tips of my toes. I squeak, "I'm very new to a real relationship. Please go easy on me."

He arches a brow. "Cutie, I think you know more than I do."

"Huh?"

He clears his throat. "I, uh... I was attempting to locate some fine literature in order to edify myself while staying in your humble abode, and I may have discovered a bookshelf containing numerous signed tomes thanking you as the editor."

Those are just books, and books are a little different than experiencing things in real life. "I don't understand."

He presses his lips together for a long moment. He

opens his mouth. He shuts it. Opens it again. "I'll go easy on you. If I must."

"I'd appreciate it."

Resting an elbow on the side of my bed, he cradles his chin in his hand. "If we're real dating now, does that mean I no longer have to fear getting locked in closets with you? Or any of that other stuff? I lie awake at night in terror thinking about it all."

I take a moment and consider his words. Removing the main trope *does* make me suspicious that rom-com magic will leave us alone, *but* the real question is *are we at a resolution?* Have I, through entering into a real relationship with Hayes, completed a character arc of some sort? *Or* are there still gaping plot points left unresolved? "I'd be wary until the conclusion concerning my parents and my cottage. When tropes end up tired and overdone, they become clichés, so authors are getting more creative in how they utilize what they're given in order to avoid predictable conclusions—despite the fact romance is an utterly predictable genre at its core."

Hayes mumbles, "You mean the fake dating couples normally fake date to the end of the books and only have this climactic 'I don't want it to be *fake* anymore' at the *very* end?"

"I mean. Yes? Toss a third-act break in there somewhere, too." I gasp. "We haven't broken up. Not once."

He grumbles, "Because that sounds stupid. I like you. I'm not going to break up with you, and if you try to break up with me for a reason that can inevitably be resolved within the last thirty pages of a book, I'll just stare at you until you're intimidated out of the foolishness."

He is *quite* intimidating. Especially when he's scruffy. He must shave three times a day. I can't believe he grew so much fuzz overnight. Irrationally focused on his scruff, I say, "I like to resolve issues. Canceling communication or not working through a misunderstanding is problematic. Always makes me wonder if such a relationship is truly sustainable long-term."

"Starts on a lie. Crumbles under pressure. Whips back together because of an elaborate and unrealistic display." He grunts. "Yeah, that sounds pretty garbage."

I shiver. "I really like you, Hayes."

He whispers a curse, the tiniest smile crossing his lips. "I really like you, too, Ellen."

I lift my pinkie. "No third-act breaks?"

He lifts his massive hand, linking his pinkie with mine. "No third-, fourth-, fifth-, or eighth-act breaks. When I like something, I don't let go." He clears his throat. "Non-threateningly…of course."

I giggle. "Stars, space, and Ellen."

His smile breaks in a little deeper, a little brighter, and he pulls my hand to his mouth, kissing. "Grammar, moths, and Hayes."

CHAPTER 19

♥ Please normalize relationship agreements. Please.

I have a boyfriend. I don't exactly know how to have a real boyfriend. It's different than doing a favor for him, helping get his family off his back, expecting him to "summon" my assistance as necessary. Or, well, it's *probably* different.

I do not actually know how to reach out to people or initiate social interaction.

Example: I have wanted to message the group chat Liv, Marit, and Paisley set up for us every day since I got back from the slumber party. I have not done this. Because I do not know how to make conversation without any clear goal in mind. Not only that, people can feel vastly different in text than in person. My brain struggles with correlating the differences and reacting to one side with the memory of the other.

I'm grateful Hayes feels the same both on and offline.

This by no means makes me brave enough to say *hey, boyfriend, may we engage in a relationship activity at your nearest convenience?*

It's Wednesday now. Two weeks till my birthday. Three days since I last saw him, even though he lives right outside my front door. I sincerely and truly do not go outside, do I? No wonder my freckles are secret.

This can't be healthy.

With a sigh, I send an email to a client along with the attached draft of their copy-edited book. Putting together information about the overall subjects that need improvement comes easier to me than sending a two-sentence text to someone whose lips have briefly touched mine.

That's real dumb.

I need proper guidelines for clarity of existence and peace of mind.

A pebble of dread hardens in my gut as my mind drifts toward the document I drafted once upon a time. My romance form. The extensive test I compiled with the intention of avoiding unnecessary hurt from a romantic partner who lacked the essential qualities I'm looking for in a lifelong companion.

People didn't react well to my friendship form in high school, but clearly I never should have foregone it in favor of picking my own friends without any basis. Picking friends all willy-nilly results in abandonment at bars.

Hayes is an adult. Also, he's oddly accepting of my "quirks." I'm certain presenting my boyfriend with a multi-page document questioning him on topics I find important as well as his expectations for me in this relationship won't present even a singular issue.

It's just *smart*.

Why drag a relationship out until our emotions are too invested? If something is going to be an issue in the future, it's better to discover that now. Also, having clear information on how *not* to make him despise me would be lovely.

This is excellent.

Nothing can go wrong.

❖

Ellen: When can you come over?
Hayes: Now. Later. Whenever you want me to.
Ellen: I have made egg salad sandwiches, and I'd like to discuss something over dinner.

Hayes: I'm outside.

Because I hate the awkwardness when people tell me to *just come on in*, I finish setting the table and head to the front door.

Seeing his hulking body shouldn't feel like breathing for the first time in ten minutes. But it does.

It very much does.

"Come on in," I say, and he ducks beneath the arch.

"Is everything…good?" he asks once I've shut the door.

"Hm?"

"You said we have to discuss something. Feels ominous. 'We need to talk' vibes."

"Oh! No. Everything's fine. Sorry. I didn't realize any comment concerning communication translated so readily into the dread of 'we need to talk'." I'll have to update my social rule book. But…if that's the case…how do I ask to initiate conversation without causing stress?

Emojis?

Potentially emojis.

A breath flows out of him, and some tension in his broad shoulders eases. "I thought maybe I messed up again."

"How?"

"We haven't talked since Sunday. And I didn't want to come on too strong. So I figured it better to wait for you to reach out."

I brighten. "I'm glad it seems we're both struggling with similar things. I have the solution. And sandwiches." Referencing the dining room, I usher him to the table where I've set an overflowing platter of sandwiches in the center alongside a pitcher of fresh lemonade. Next to each of our smaller plates is The Document, a pencil, and an eraser. I scoot into my chair while Hayes looms over his, looking down at the pages in front of him.

My heart rate spikes, memories of rejection and ridicule igniting in my head.

He'll laugh at me. Well, no. Probably not. Hayes doesn't really laugh at much of anything, and he's too kind for that even if my solution is stupid.

He'll say this isn't how relationships work. Then he'll tell me why.

I wouldn't like him if he felt easy to lose. Being with his sisters and Paisley solidified the fact I am tired of relationships that easily crack. I want something stronger now. I need something stronger now. I deserve something stronger now.

Pulling out his chair, he takes a seat, and I take that as my cue to speak up. "If there's anything I've missed that you want to share answers to, I left space in the back, and I can print off more lined pages."

"Okay." He reaches for the pencil and a sandwich. Taking a bite, he starts writing.

Biting my lip, I grab my own sandwich and pencil, practically humming with elation. Everything is going to make sense soon. Moreover, this is the farthest I've gotten when it comes to my relationship forms.

Usually, they end up snatched out of my hands, torn up, or in the trash.

He's through his fourth sandwich and on the fourth page by the time I'm starting my second sandwich and nearly done. When he starts the fifth page, he chokes and drops his sandwich into his plate in order to grab the lemonade. Pouring himself a tall glass, he downs it, scrubbing the back of his hand over his mouth.

"Are you okay?" I ask.

His eyes snap to me, his cheeks tinted red. "Uh. Sure. I guess...I just wasn't expecting...PG-13 content."

That's an adorable way to refer to the intimacy section.

"It's important to outline sexual expectations in a romantic relationship. Any five minute internet search will tell you that."

"You've included...kinks."

"Of course." I stare at him.

He swallows, hard. "And...you've listed some."

"As examples in case you're unfamiliar with the term. They are not a depiction of my preferences." My brow furrows. "I don't understand what's confusing you. Depending on your answers, it could be an obvious deal-breaker. For instance, I don't like pain. If we're incompatible in our intimate interests, it's important to know that as soon as possible. I think. Romantic relationships inevitably must be satisfactory in both emotional and physical ways." I swore this was common sense.

His right eye twitches. "You sincerely terrify me, Ellen."

I laugh. "Why?"

"I don't think I can explain it..." he mumbles, running his fingers through his hair. Blowing out a breath, he puts his pencil back to paper and leaves the disarray of his sandwich in his plate. I know he hasn't eaten enough yet. He mustn't want to get his hands dirty, so after I'm finished with my questions, I get him a fork.

He looks up from the last page at the utensil, then at me. "Oh. Thanks." He slips it from my fingers and rests it against his plate. "Sorry. I got...distracted. I like your egg salad. I also like that you understand how much I eat."

"I'd be a bad girlfriend if I let you go hungry."

"I thought you were against gender roles."

"Feeding someone isn't a gender role; refer back to you paying for my food at the zoo and the mall." I smooth my pages, gathering them up in order and tapping them against the table to align them. "Feeding someone is a love language."

The corner of his mouth softens, and he murmurs, "Should I go back to that question? I put down 'quality time' but if I need to change it to 'eating' for accuracy's sake, I will."

Warmth spreads from my chest out along my limbs. "Silly. Are you done?"

He nods. "I don't think I have anything to add. You're unsurprisingly thorough."

"I think that's in my editing bio." I hand him my papers, and he hands me his. "Let's scan for deal-breakers first, okay?"

He takes a deep breath. "I wasn't aware I was being graded."

"It's only logical that we consider matters of conflict we can't work past before we get in too deep."

That low *hm* rumbles in his chest as he rests his cheek against his hand and begins reading.

The first thing I notice when I look at his papers is that his handwriting is distinct and neat. Smaller than I expected. The second thing I notice is that a great number of his answers center on me.

When and how often are you comfortable with me contacting you? *Whenever you want and however often you feel like.*

What level of intimacy do you expect before marriage? *Whatever you're comfortable with.*

What character traits are most important to you in a partner? *Grammar knowledge and moth facts. Adorableness.*

How many children do you want? *However many you do.*

Is this concerning?

"Do you not know how many children you want?" I ask.

His eyes stop scanning my answers for a moment, and he shrugs. "I've never given it much thought. I guess the fear I'll parent like my *far* has kept me from bothering to consider it. I've wanted a family before. I've just not been brave enough to put that desire in any solid or attainable terms."

That's reasonable. "Are you sure you don't mind me contacting you a lot at potentially weird hours?"

"Text me. Call me. Come over. Do you want a key so you can just let yourself in?"

"That's not going to be overwhelming?"

"You don't overwhelm me."

My chest flutters.

Those simple words feel like some I've been waiting my whole life for.

Pushing my hair away from my face, I look back down and continue reading. As far as I can tell, even with so many answers fixed in my favor, he's given each question serious thought. He's sincere. Committed. Open to working on a relationship. Interested in conflict resolution as well as creating a protocol to follow in case an argument gets too heated.

On paper, I'd marry him tomorrow. He embodies everything I'm looking for, and nothing I'm not. Like a foot kink. Which, you know, is nice. Rather, he put down *healthy kink*. And I'm fairly well-read when it comes to Blaire Featherstone heat levels, but I have never heard of a *healthy* kink before in my life. It can't mean he's ableist because he knows I have POTS. I have to ask. I have to. "What's a healthy kink?"

"Hm?" he grunts. "Oh. That's when you drink enough water and eat good meals multiple times a day and make a point of looking at the sun at least once a week for something resembling a prolonged period of time." He turns over a page, muttering, "It's incredibly seductive. I'll hardly know what to do with myself."

I bark a laugh. "You're hilarious."

He continues reading lines, murmuring, "I am not joking. I care about your well-being." His brow arches. "What's a..." He presses his lips together, and there's no *tint* now. His face is completely red.

He's on page five.

"What's a what?" I ask.

"I don't know if I'll be able to handle an answer. I'll look it up later." He swipes a hand over his mouth. His fingers tremble. His eyes close. "You are...very thorough."

"Honesty is important to the foundation of a good relationship."

"Sure is," he murmurs into his fingers. "You're sure you're comfortable with all of this? You asked me to take it easy on you, but it feels like you're not going to take it easy on me."

"I was recovering from a panic or POTS or who-knows-what attack. My answers today are based off the fact I remembered that I love when characters kiss during thunderstorms. I would like something passionate." Crossing my ankles, I add, "Please."

The hand covering his mouth moves over his eyes, and he stays like that for a moment. Finally, he says, "Yeah. I can..." He clears some roughness from his voice. "I can manage that."

"Thank you."

We go over more details, adjust some answers, talk about a future together, plot our conflict resolution protocol, and eat egg salad sandwiches until hours have passed like minutes. With every comment and consideration, I want him. With every dry joke or sarcastic line, I want him. With every look, every slight touch, I'm more certain about him than I ever have been about anyone. At a fundamental level, I think he gets me.

And I *know* that feeling isn't always safe or factual, but I also know that it's never felt like *this*. Not once. This time, I'm not overlooking hints of warning because I am so desperately lonely and starved for connection. This time, I'm approaching a relationship after I've taught myself to be happy alone.

This time, being with him is better than being alone.

CHAPTER 20

♥ Love is meant to be comfortable and safe. Passion does not equate to stress.

"Well, if it isn't Ellen." Vince grins at me over the bar counter as he fills a glass with an amber liquid. "In her usual spot, too."

I smile. "It feels the safest."

Vince hums, sniffs, rolls the short glass across the counter to a man at the other end of the bar like we're in a choreographed movie or something, and braces his hands in front of him. "Debatable. You're at the wrong end if your goal is safety."

I look at the other side of the polished counter, which ends after veering into the center of the bar and has tables surrounding it. It's nearer the bathrooms over there and cuts off abruptly to make room for booths behind it. This side, first of all, has a wall. Walls are secure. Even if you can get cornered against them, at least you don't have to worry about someone approaching from within them. Second of all, I now know that this is where the soda gun is.

Vince cocks his head toward the decidedly more-incorporated and rowdy part of Temptations Lounge. "Boss's office is on that side. He'd be able to see you."

My cheeks heat, and I push a lock of hair over my ear. Resting my purse in my lap, I pet Spotz's tuft with my thumb. "Is…he in his office right now?"

"Yep. I'd tell him you're here, but he might kill me."

"What? Why?" I startle off the stool. "Am I not

supposed to be here tonight?"

Vince laughs. "Oh, no. You're fine. It's the fact he's wallowing through mid-month budgeting and ordering. He gets grumpy when he has to do math, but he's a bit too controlling to hire out a manager. We're a small, thriving business, which basically means he does a lot of the work himself. Like a neurotic mobster."

Maybe I have come at a bad time?

I missed him. And we outlined yesterday that we don't consider one another an intrusion. So I worked up the courage and went on an evening walk. I've been slacking on exercising lately, but I'll need to reinstate a routine even with Hayes in my life. Maybe we can coordinate time to exercise together? A man who looks like him and smells distinctly like protein powder is very serious about exercising.

And a girl like me only does it so she won't fall over in Whole Foods while getting eggs.

I probably wouldn't be able to keep up, but—again— that's on him to decide. Open and honest relationships are safe ones. Passion shouldn't stem from discomfort or confusion. Anxiety. Worry. Anger.

It has other places to originate.

"You can go to his office, if you want?" Vince chuckles. "He's completely wrapped around your little finger. I bet it'd be a relief for his girlfriend to interrupt him right now."

"I wouldn't want to interrupt him while he's busy."

Vince's smile tugs into a smirk. "Doll, the way he talks about you, I think he begs for your interruptions."

The way he… "What does he say about me?"

Vince shrugs, lifting his chin as another patron flags him over. "What do men usually say when they're in love?"

I have absolutely no idea. I'm not a man. I've never been in love.

But Hayes has less-than-subtly dropped the L-word before. Per chance…when anyone's in love, do they just kind of…say it? To whoever they feel they can, or however they can manage? Love's probably the most overwhelming emotion I can think of.

I bet it spills out at the seams.

Vince has already moved to the other end of the counter by the time I manage to sort out my thoughts enough to slip through the mass of drunk, laughing people and toward an *employees only* office door. We promised to be honest and direct with one another just yesterday, and he said nothing about *love* then. I won't make an assumption until he tells me.

Even though he waited to tell me he liked me until I told him first.

My hand hovers in front of the door, beside a panel of one-way tinted glass I bet he can see through even if I can't.

If he's being polite and waiting until I catch up to tell me such feelings, I'll appreciate that courtesy. After all, right now, I don't think I'd even know what to say in response.

I knock as loud as I dare to make sure I'm heard over the voices and music. It's not club-level noise, but it's definitely a lot.

"Is someone dying?" Hayes growls.

Unaware if I'm supposed to yell back the answer or what, I stand perfectly still.

He swears.

Then pounding footsteps reach the door, and he looms in the entryway half a moment before drawing me in and kicking the door shut behind us. "Sorry. I thought you were…" He wets his lips. "Literally anyone else."

That's sweet. He's sweet.

The low lights of his office draw out the overall vibe of Temptations, from the mahogany-dark wood of his desk and the surrounding bookcases to the burgundy carpeting. It's neat. It smells like cherries and vanilla. Not alcohol.

Hayes's fingers flinch around my hand, as though he's just now realizing how he tugged me inside. When he starts to pull away, I hold tight. "I hope I'm not intruding. I'm told that you're very busy right now. With your favorite thing."

Using his free hand, he sweeps back his hair and melts, just a touch. Warmth suffuses into his eyes and lips. "Sarcasm makes you particularly adorable, pudding."

"Is 'adorable' the only compliment you know?"

He kisses my forehead. "Have I overused the word, Miss Editor? Going to throw a thesaurus at me?"

I giggle. "I've missed you today."

He sighs, tugging me along with him to his industrial-sized desk. It's his size. So is the chair. Sweeping me up, he sets me in the clean space beside his computer, then he falls into the dark leather seat. "I've been fighting for my life. You're very much a distraction. So I've locked my phone up in the bottom drawer to keep from texting you constantly for relief."

I tense. "I didn't mean to waste your productive efforts."

"I'm glad you have." His brow furrows, and he crosses his painted arms before his chest. "No. Actually, you haven't wasted any effort. I needed a break before I started my own bar fight. I'm glad you're here. I'm glad you felt comfortable enough to come to me." Eyes hot in the dim lights of his office, he watches me, reclining in his chair. "This is what I want. You to be comfortable with me."

A shiver trails down my spine. "I'm trying. It's hard to be comfortable with people. I've learned not to be."

He nods, like I'm making sense of everything in the world. "I know, pudding. It's not just a matter of being comfortable with someone at this point. It's a matter of remembering what it's like to be comfortable with yourself, too, isn't it?"

Exactly. Exactly that. And it's so bright when put into words that it almost makes me want to cry. To stop myself, I bite my cheek and nod.

Hayes unravels his arms, scoots his chair closer, takes my hand, and bends a kiss to my fingertips. His touch treasures, and I'm hypnotized by the shape of it, the way his dark lashes fall against his cheeks. He's precise and gentle in a way that suggests he's plotted every movement. His lips fall against each of my knuckles; his breath heats my wrist. He skims the inside of my palm with his nose, and my breaths shorten.

He kisses, and I jerk away, clutching my hand to my chest. Every cell in me tingles.

Slow, he lifts his head and finds my eyes.

My back straightens. "S-sorry. I…" Words fail.

Words fail.

Everything in my head catches on the tip of my tongue, and I can't form sentences, thought. It's hot in my chest, on my skin, but the hair along my arms has stuck on end, in a constant shiver. My heart's pounding. My breaths are erratic.

This is the most intimate I've ever been with someone.

It's overwhelming. Complicated. Unfamiliar and unplanned.

It feels like falling and floating and flying.

Hayes holds out his hand, patient, intimidating, just as threatening as the first time I remember meeting him, but the things I fear most now aren't in him. They're in myself.

Hesitant, I slip my fingers against his palm.

"Good girl," he murmurs, and I jerk away again, blushing in hues of deep, blooming crimson.

He barks a laugh and leans back. "Well. That's not fair."

"Y-y-you…"

His eyes glimmer. His lips hook up in the corner, smug. "I did my research. I said I'd look it up. 'Praise kink' is words of affirmation on crack, right? It's fairly vanilla, apparently. I honestly don't know what I learned, but I gather that the way you enjoy intimacy is as easy as saying I appreciate you. And I can do that. Gladly." His gaze scans me, slow, intentional. "You are adorable." Sighing, he rolls more toward his computer than me. He wakes up the screen and hunkers, muttering, "I'm actually in a sour mood, and I shouldn't be teasing you in order to feel better. I'm sorry, cutie." Rubbing his eyes, he deflates. "I hate this stuff."

"This stuff" is a spreadsheet. Full of numbers. Neat rows. Whether he hates it or not, if he set it up, he's clearly committed to working through the stuff he hates. He would have done fine at college…

I would not have.

If I hate something, I burn it. And the very frustration of focusing my energy on things not immediately relevant to the career I wanted *while paying thousands for it* would have angered me regardless of whether I understood what I was learning or not.

"What are you doing?" I ask.

"Projections. Temptations' clientele is consistently expanding, so I'm predicting what I need to order for this next week and running the numbers to see that margins are being met. The company I order from just shifted their prices, so I need to determine whether I have to adapt to that change, so on and so forth…" His eye twitches, and he rubs it. "I'd rather tell you you're pretty and watch you blush."

My heart skips, and I rely on Spotz for support, hugging my purse and him in my lap. "You saw that I didn't want to go past kissing until after marriage, didn't you?"

"I did."

"And you know that…teasing me in this aspect is…" Absolutely overwhelming. Enchanting. Makes me want to fall into his arms and beg for more ways he'll make me feel —at the core of myself—somehow…wanted. "…inappropriate."

Hayes clears his throat and types something into a row. A slew of other numbers shift, and my goodness. His spreadsheet is set up with equations and everything. "Maybe."

"*Maybe?*" I squeak.

"Some people think kissing is inappropriate. You'd be surprised."

I would not be surprised. I read. I know a great many things. In fact, I don't *just* read books. I read articles. Reviews. I have seen a very wide span of information on a great number of topics from a great deal of people with a vast array of thought processes. I am aware that some people find kissing inappropriate—I am, in milder terms, one of them.

Real kissing is very intimate.

I do not take it lightly, because it can lead to mistakes regardless of predetermined plans. In the heat of a moment, it can feel like forever anyway.

In the heat of a moment, it's easy to forget that I've felt many *forevers* that were lies.

"If it makes you uncomfortable, I'll wait," he says.

"You'll…wait?"

"Until we're married."

My eyes widen, and I stare at him, numbly aware that numbers on his screen are shifting as he references different material and inputs values.

His blue eyes cut toward me, and his fingers freeze, hovering over the keypad.

Long, shivering moments pass.

Then he frowns, and on him it's a severe scowl. "We both said that we date with the intention to marry, Ellen. Why do you look so shocked?"

Because this isn't a sarcastic text to his family. Because no one has ever been the one to look at me and say *forever*. Because I'm always the one trying to puzzle that solidity out of them. Because he's saying that he's going to abide by my wishes, accommodate my feelings. Instead of brushing my beliefs and wants aside or reasoning that *if we're doing this with an end goal of marriage anyway, it doesn't matter*, he's telling me my pace is fine.

It's been so long since I've allowed myself to invest in another person. When I invest in anything, it's dramatic. It's not just correcting grammar and commenting on places to improve—doing my job. It's leaving thousands of fangirl moments strewn across pages and sending novellas of developmental information.

It's adoring. It bridges on obsessive.

It's hard to enjoy things partway. Why would anyone not want to live as fully as possible?

Hayes touches my hand, lifting it away from my purse. Pressing a kiss to my fingers, he says, "You are beautiful. Every last inch of you. My dreams revolve around your eyes, and the shade of your hair consumes my fantasies. You're bright as liquid sunlight given human form. Your smile haunts me when I can't find it and soothes my soul when it appears. Anyone with half a functioning brain cell would be delighted to marry you. Forgive me if I'm so bold as to assume I fall among those with such bare minimum intellect."

I curse.

Hayes startles, his blue gaze jolting up to mine.

I throw my free hand over my mouth.

A touch of humor sparkles through his eyes. "Did you just…"

My lashes beat, and I don't know where to look, so I squeeze my eyes shut. It's worse than leaving them open, I realize, as the darkness allows me to focus on the way he's tracing each of my fingers, playing with my hand. There's something starkly amused in the demeanor of his touch.

He puffs a breath. "Is my bad behavior rubbing off on you? Will it be difficult to get your father's blessing when I'm teaching you to curse?"

"Hayes…"

He rises; his heat closes in, cages, and he kisses my hand, surrounding me in the sensation of his warmth. "It's a crime that you've not lived your life showered by adoration, Ellen."

"I have."

"Your parents don't count. Anyone can see that they adore you, and anyone on this planet with a decent parent knows that parental affection doesn't measure up to that of someone who isn't *supposed* to love you."

There's that *love* word again. Teasing me. Taunting me. He's right. I am desperate for a love that isn't built-in or expected. I'm desperate to be chosen.

"I'm overwhelmed," I breathe.

He releases my hand, and the leather of his chair creaks when he sits back down. He doesn't say or do anything for either several long moments or several short minutes, I can't be sure.

Tension eases from my muscles, a bit at a time, and when I open my eyes, Hayes isn't even looking at me. He's sitting perfectly still, fingers locked atop his abdomen, eyes closed.

Effortless and unquestioning. No push-back or argument. He's quiet as the ocean far from the shore, a mass of power without anything to crash into. An ebb. A flow. A constant so safe in theory, so necessary.

So frighteningly unknown.

I slip off his desk, and his eyes open a crack, watch me a moment, close again.

Breath fills him. "I'm sorry. I'm still taking my irritations out on you. I meant it when I said I'd rather tell you you're pretty and watch you blush. I'm going too far."

I'm almost positive that *taking irritations out on someone* has never been so gentle. His spirit is so quiet, even when he's frustrated with things he doesn't want to do. I want more. I want to know everything. "Can I play with your numbers?"

His brows rise before he opens his eyes. "You want me to teach you how to navigate hell?"

"I already know how to do that."

His head tilts.

"I'd like you to show me how to do your numbers, so you aren't irritated anymore."

He glances at the monitor and straightens, shaking the mouse so the screen wakes up again. "That's one way to get me to stop bullying you, I suppose."

It's hardly bullying. This isn't even the teasing I'm familiar with that makes me feel small. Hayes makes me feel as large and menacing as him, someone stronger, worthier.

He grunts. "I should probably get you a chair. Unless you want to sit in my lap."

Before he can stand, I scoot forward and seat myself on the broad expanse of his thighs. Lifting the strap of my purse over my head, I set it and Spotz on the desk. Then I face Hayes.

My heart jolts.

He is near, and he is awed. "I…" he breathes the word as though he doesn't know what comes after.

"I wanted to," I say.

His throat bobs when he swallows. Roughly, he draws in a breath, then he scoots forward, leaning around me, encasing me in his arms, his scent, his heat.

Safe.

With tormented, strained words, he shows me what he's doing, how he's filing information, what margins he strives to maintain, what products sell most effectively, which prices he's debating raising. His left hand finds a home at my hip, and it lives there, his thumb mindlessly stroking my sweater as he navigates the information using the mouse.

I learn a lot.

But my favorite lessons are the ones he's not putting into words.

CHAPTER 21

> ♥ History repeats itself if you weight long enough. No, that's not a typo. This chapter includes exercise.

"This is nostalgic," Hayes murmurs as we trail along the sidewalks back home. His gaze remains largely fixed on our joined hands, and I suspect it's because that part is new, but then he says, "Except you were closer the first time."

"Really?"

"Couldn't drag yourself away from me." Humor sparks in his moonlit eyes. "Because you would have fallen flat on your pissed face."

"Pissed" as in blackout drunk.

Sighing, I shake my head. "The shame of that night is never going to go away, is it?"

Hayes tucks me a little closer as we pass someone. "Your actions that night weren't shameful."

"I bet I could hardly remember my name."

"No, you remembered it quite well and provided it almost clearly."

Almost clearly. I pout as we come to a stop at the intersection.

Hayes cups my cheek, running a thumb over my jutted lip. "What a cute expression."

My chest does itty bitty somersaults. "Hayes, behave yourself."

"It's difficult when I've had you in my lap all night." He presses, gently parting my lips. "For hours. Constantly."

The light changes, and I yank him forward, dragging

him along behind me like he's not three times my size. "I thought we solved your irritations when we finished putting together the order."

"We did," he mumbles.

"So why are you still coming onto me?"

Air puffs out of him. "Is that what I'm doing? I thought I was spoiling you as thanks for rescuing me." His throat clears, a distinctly low sound. "Coming onto you would… look very different."

I shove the curiosity that appears way into the abyss as I turn down the road our apartments are on.

Cars rush by, and Hayes swaps hands, settling me away from the traffic side. He is consideration. Silent, deadly kindness. It makes my flesh warm even as a cool breeze fans across my cheeks. I'll be in my sweater for another few weeks. Hayes has been transitioned to short sleeve t-shirts since what seems like the start of the month.

The rom-com urge to describe his biceps attempts to compel me every time I notice them. Like wow. Big.

"Do you eat after you get home from work, even though it's this late?" I ask.

"I have a snack, exercise to decompress, then have a protein shake. It helps with muscle synthesis while sleeping and can lead to better rest."

My mouth falls open. "Really?"

"Apparently." He glances at himself and mumbles, "I wouldn't exactly be surprised."

Nope. Neither would I.

"May I join you?" I ask, because our relationship discussion yesterday dictates that we can express whatever we want from one another without fear of backlash in the event a request isn't okay.

"Trying to get buff, pudding?" he asks, lips quirked up in one corner.

"Always."

We make it back to our apartments, and I get winded on my way up the stairs like I haven't just survived the walk from the bar without complication. Hayes says nothing about it as he unlocks his front door and leads me into his apartment.

It's...masculine.

That's my first impression, and when I notice as much, I wonder what I expected.

There's a couch in his living room, bordering the space between it and where the kitchen pours into the dining room, just like in my apartment. There's no TV, but a barbell rests on the floor beneath where one would go. It's loaded, and if I had to guess...three hundred pounds. The carpet indents beneath it. Although that's not entirely a feat, considering a set of massive dumbbells appearing around fifty pounds do the same beside what look like twenty pounders.

The carpet's not hard to indent.

"Sorry about the mess," he comments. "Have a seat while I get our pre-workout."

"What's pre-workout?"

He lumbers into the kitchen, making the fridge look small. He doesn't fit in this apartment. But I guess after seeing the bedroom at his house, it's a significant upgrade. "Usually? It's a supplement with caffeine and other stimulants to assist in energy and muscle growth."

"And not usually?"

He pulls a stack of containers out of the fridge, setting them on the counter. "It's my after-work snack."

I stare at the *snack*, which appears to be an assortment of raw veggies, fruit, and boiled eggs.

He divides some of the contents up into two bowls as he talks. "I work out to burn stress, so I'm not really interested in hyping my system up on more stuff to burn. I'm also not interested in lifting four hundred pounds on an empty stomach." He grabs a bottle of ranch dressing out of the fridge, stuffs a fork in each bowl, and enters the living room. He hands me the cereal bowl while taking the serving bowl for himself. "If you want more of anything, just let me know. I boil about fifty eggs at a time, and there's plenty more fruits and veggies."

I take the offering and look down at the assortment. Grapes and broccoli and carrots and blueberries and orange pieces. "You just...put it all together like this?"

"Yeah." He sits beside me, scoots some of his food over, and squeezes the dressing into the bowl.

My anxiety spikes when he hands me the bottle, and while I do take it, I do not move to mimic the crime he just committed. A shudder goes through me when he lifts a fork that contains broccoli, ranch, and a blueberry.

I close my eyes so I don't have to see him eat it.

Tender humor taints his voice. "Pudding, do I need to get you a sectioned dish?"

"I-if it's not too much trouble…"

I feel him take my bowl before he kisses my forehead. He rumbles, "You're never trouble. Sorry. I wasn't thinking."

My eyes open in time to watch him dump my food into his bowl. Moments later, he provides me with a dish that has everything separated out into three acceptable portions. With the plate, he hands me a small bowl filled with ranch, then he returns to his place and continues eating his abomination like he just trusts every fruit and veggie.

It takes us the same amount of time to get through our food despite the different portions because I'm checking every grape and blueberry, quarantining anything with spots, pinching any brown bits off my broccoli, and…

probably coming off like a complete brat.

"Your trust issues run deep," Hayes comments the moment I realize I'm being incredibly rude.

"It's not…" I tense. "I trust that you've given me good food. It's just that… Aren't you bothered when you bite into something expecting one thing and get another? Like when your blueberry is mushy instead of firm, or sour instead of sweet, and then what about when your carrots are slimy or your broccoli tastes too *green*? The different tastes sometimes come with different looks, so it's easier to understand what I'm getting into when I check, and…and I don't like spots." Weakly, I say, "What if the spot is there because a bug climbed inside?"

"Protein."

My face morphs into horror.

Hayes barks a laugh. "Sorry." His body shakes, hunkering, and he covers his face, cursing amidst his laughter. "That was cruel. I'm so sorry." More swears, and he pulls in deep breaths. "Why—how—are you so precious?"

"I'm not trying to be cute or quirky. Or rude. I promise."

"You are the least rude person I know, and the fact you aren't trying makes it all the more adorable." He lifts a finger and skims it across my forehead along the lines of my hair, tucking the strands more firmly behind my ear. "You're not picky. You're precise. You care about quality and texture. And you're allowed to reject what doesn't meet your standards." His teeth bare, and the grin is wolfish. "All the better for whatever does. You might make me arrogant if I continue to be worth your time."

My heart pounds with renewed fierceness after nearly giving up on the stairs, and I jerk my attention away from how terribly beautiful this man is. "We're going to exercise?"

"Yup." He takes my plate and bowl, trucking everything back into the kitchen. Once he's put the containers back in the fridge and dumped the dirty dishes in the sink, he stretches. "Normally, I exercise with earbuds."

"I don't mean to intrude on your routine. We can play your usual music still."

He eyes me, amused. "It would scare you. It's Norwegian death metal. It scares me sometimes. Most of it's not even words. Just kind of like…screaming?" He sniffs, striding toward his equipment and pulling on a pair of fingerless gloves with pads. "Get me under four hundred pounds for ten consecutive reps and five consecutive sets, and it's the equivalent of what my soul is saying. The screaming helps keep it in my body."

"It?" I whisper.

"My soul." He rubs his neck. "Sorry, was that an unclear antecedent?"

I flutter at his talking grammar to me. I take a breath. "Maybe no screaming."

"I'll try to avoid it, the screaming, for your sake." He sets up two itty bitty weights, boasting an alarming total of five pounds each, hands them to me, and lifts his twenty pounders with the same amount of effort before settling on the floor in front of where I'm still seated on his couch. "I'd let you use my fifties, but without gloves, they'd hurt."

"Yes, that's the only reason I need to use these ones. Certainly not because my arms would snap."

His lips pull up in one corner. "Exactly. You could probably lift me if you just had gloves."

"Easily," I confirm. "Just not while standing."

"Because of the POTS."

I nod. "Yes."

He references the weights. "How many curls?"

I make a show of testing their paltry weight. "Oh, maybe five hundred."

Hayes's brows rise.

"Just to start with, of course."

"Of course." The way he's looking at me…it might just be everything. "Why don't I start with fifty and do ten sets while you reach for the thousands?"

I reel back slightly. "Wait. Are we still joking? You're going to lift those things fifty times? For ten sets?"

"I might have to now."

"Please don't show off on my account. It's very obvious you are quite…well-endowed." My face heats, and I add a quick, "Not that I've noticed in any particular detail."

He begins aimlessly curling the weights in tandem. "Because that would be indecent?"

"Wouldn't it?"

If he weren't completing perfect reps, I think he'd shrug. Instead, he lifts his brows and tilts his head briefly. "Naw. You're my girlfriend."

Because I think it might help, I mimic his actions with my little weights. "Yes, girlfriend. Not wife."

"Working on it."

Breath catches in my throat, but I'm exercising, so I push myself to maintain even inhales and exhales. I am not going to go into detail about each of his flexing muscles. I don't care that this is a fitting moment for comments about things like straining forearms. It's still improper. Overdone. Confusing.

Pardon me if I don't particularly fall to pieces at the sight of a man's forearms doing basic muscle stuff when they pick anything up.

"Are you not looking at me because I'm scary with my low-end weights, pudding?"

"Stop it," I breathe. "I'm alone with you in your

apartment. You shouldn't be teasing me like that."

"I'll stop if you really want me to."

The scary thing is that I don't. I don't want him to. And I think he knows. I haven't *really* wanted him to stop all night. It's just a lot of effort for me to sort through feelings I don't completely understand. I'm alone with him in his apartment. I am alone with a man who lifts four hundred pounds for sport. And he's flirting with me. And the most unease I'm facing is because my noodle arms are starting to burn.

"I think that's your five hundred. Why don't you take a moment before the next set?" Hayes says, lowering his own weights to the ground on either side of him. I know I haven't done five hundred. I probably haven't even done fifty. I think he has, however, and I'm happy to take the excuse for a break.

My arms are trained purely for steadying my hands as I speed type through editing novels. Nothing else. My "exercise" often consists purely of walking or jogging in place while listening to audiobooks. Stamina-focused cardio for heart-beating-too-fast management. Up until this moment, my only "weight-training" has been the feat of getting my groceries up the stairs.

I am not ashamed to say I have given myself complete POTS crashes on account of *only one trip!* mindset. It's a toxic mentality, honestly, yet we humans can be insufferably attracted to whatever we find a bit threatening.

"Do you honestly see yourself marrying me some day?" I ask before I register that the question is insanely off-topic, embarrassing, and probably not the sort you ask a man during the first week of actually dating.

Hayes doesn't flinch. He also doesn't so much as give my question thought. "It's rare a day passes that I'm not imagining that very thing."

A weight slips from my hand, rolling off the couch, and Hayes lunges, catching it before it hits the floor, or my foot. The sudden motion shakes me, and I blurt, "Sorry. I'm sorry."

"For the record, it's not anything you need to worry about or concern yourself with." He places my weight beside his while I clutch my remaining one tight against my chest. "I'm serious about wanting to be with you. That's all."

That's all? Everything I've always wanted from *anyone* is a *that's all* to him? Like it's effortless to want to be with me? I fight to sort through my thoughts, then I say, "Please don't take this the wrong way…but is something…wrong with you?"

His brows knit, and he mumbles, "I'm not entirely sure how I'm supposed to take that a right way?"

"Yesterday, a lot of the questions you answered centered around whatever would make me comfortable. The entire time I've known you, you've been perfect. Gentle. Kind. To an extreme. The only times you've broken from completely focusing on me and my needs were when you were having panic attacks." I grip the weight I still have until the hatch-mark pattern of the metal indents my skin. "I've never met anyone like that. Not even my parents are that selfless."

"Ah."

"Marit said you're easy to take advantage of."

Hayes's voice hardens. "Pudding, I know you have an inflated sense of moral justice, but don't worry about it. Yes, something's…wrong with me. But, no, it's not a problem you have to feel guilty about. I'm not stupid. I've picked you for a reason."

"I don't understand."

"I like you for a reason. Many, actually, and one of

them is because of conversations like this."

I still don't understand, and he must see it on my face.

He sighs. "You don't take advantage of people. For the first time in my life, I wish someone would be a little more selfish with me. I want to give you everything you want. The sky, the stars, the breath from my lungs. And you? The most you shyly, timidly, adorably ask for is a moment of my time and whatever attention I'm willing to spare. Your gentle spirit is like coming home, Ellen. I'm safe with you." His eyes roll off me, and he mutters, "So, yes, I am a people pleaser, and I have a *problem*, but, no." He curses. "—no. You do not get to twist that into any kind of excuse that belittles all of the wonderful things you are. I have picked you. It was intentional. You do not get to use my issues as fodder for yours."

I flinch at the blow, and I wonder if it may have hurt less had he hit me.

A people pleaser.

That makes so much sense.

Oh, goodness.

I have to be careful with him. Very, very careful. I understand people pleasing. I used to be infamous for it. It was awful. And who knows if I overcame it or if I just got rid of the *people* part. Determined, I set my weight down. "I will protect you."

A dry chuckle leaves him. "I know. Like I said. I'm not stupid, and I'm not unaware. I'm picky when it comes to choosing what deserves my energy."

"You're not picky. You're precise."

His gaze heats. "Very precise. I don't want less than perfect."

"No pressure, right?"

"Why would there be pressure to be exactly what you are, pudding?" Stretching his neck, he offers me my weights again before bracing his hands around his. "Five hundred more. Then we'll move on to something else."

With the way he's making me feel—wanted, desired, lovable, *perfect*—I'm up for anything at all.

CHAPTER 22

> ♥ Love is scary and strange and *a lot*. But, you know what? So is exercise.

I'm either a masochist or an idiot.

I have not excluded the possibility that I am both.

The reasoning behind this speculation is simple: I have been exercising with Hayes at roughly *past midnight hours* for the past four days. My body hates me. It's been long enough that he's rotated me through every muscle group, and even my toes are sore. But...well...

"You did such a good job," Hayes breathes into my hair, cradling me against his chest on his couch.

Yeah...that's what I'm living for. Soft words from this man, who I might hate because while I am actively *dying* during warm ups, he doesn't break a sweat until he's either squatting with an extra two hundred strapped to him or dead lifting over five hundred.

The pinnacle of masculinity is my willing chair. And he's warm. And he smells good. And the sweat isn't as off-putting as I think it should be. And his gentle praise is absolutely, shamelessly addicting.

I *love* feeling like I'm made of good, correct things.

I love being with him.

It's harder and harder to leave each night, and not because my muscles give up a little more of their will to live with each session.

If Mouse didn't need his hugs, I'm almost sure I'd have submitted to the rom-com gods and "only one bedded" this thing up. In a sweet and clean sense. We're looking more toward Prince's YA limits than Blaire's…ahem. Anyway.

Velcro peels as Hayes removes his gloves, and I smile foolishly, gripping my hands against my chest. I didn't even need to show up two nights in a row. By the time I was asking to join him the second night, he was handing me my own pair of little pink workout gloves and saying he picked them up that morning. Just in case I felt like giving the barbell a shot.

I did.

After he took approximately eighty-seven percent of the weight off.

He spotted me like the fifty pounds were going to crash down on top of my chest and murder me.

I've spent most of my life afraid of being hurt. Now, I think I'm with someone who refuses the very idea that anyone or anything might have the audacity.

Hayes combs his fingers through my hair and adjusts my weight in his lap, angling me so I'm cozy. His heartbeat is my new favorite sound. Including tonight, this is the third time I've been in his lap. And the fact I snuggled up so naturally after he sat down makes me feel like whatever this magic between us is, it's getting stronger.

A breath stutters through his chest, and he shifts his hips beneath me, breaking me out of the trance enough to look up at him.

"I know I'm not too heavy."

His molten gaze roams my face. "Yeah. You aren't too heavy."

My eyes widen at the barely-restrained sound of his voice.

"Your birthday's next week," he murmurs, lifting a hand to my face, drawing the shape of my cheek into his fingertip.

"It is."

"What's the plan?" His gaze drops to my mouth. "And on the off chance my family knows it's your birthday soon and they want to do something to celebrate…"

"What?"

He takes a deep breath. "I may have needed Liv's help with…something…and…yeah." He wets his lips. His finger stills against my cheek. "Liv wants to make you a cake. *Mamma* wants to exchange gifts. They adore you. I think they're just happy for an excuse to have you over again." The almost drowsy look he's giving me hardens, and he pulls his gaze back up to my eyes. "I know your parents probably have a big party planned, so we can work around that, or space out our gathering so it's not so much all at once."

His family adores me? Really? "I'm just meeting my parents for dinner and to talk about my cottage. There's no one to invite to a party."

His thumb smooths across my cheek. "My sisters. The other one."

"Paisley?"

"Is that her name?" He makes a deep sound. "My mother would love to celebrate as well. Liv's pretty determined about making a cake. But what's wrong with extra cake?"

Absolutely nothing. I suck in a breath. "Are you sure they'd want to come? I haven't been able to figure out how to talk to any of the girls since our slumber party, and they haven't contacted me either."

"Marit's told me in no small way that if I hurt you, she's going to beat me with a lead pole, so…" His gaze drifts back down. "I think it's safe to say she likes you almost as much as I do. And I barely got *Ellen's* and *Birthday* out before Liv was asking if you liked chocolate or if she needed to look at other cake recipes."

"I like cake."

"She will make you literally anything you want. Trust me. I know. I've been her little brother my whole life."

It's hard to picture Hayes as a *little* anything.

"Is it?" he asks.

Did I say that out loud? Oops. Relaxing, I melt back against his chest. "I don't need anything special. Just their attendance would be enough. I can ask my mom if it would be all right to have your family and Paisley over. If Paisley wants to come. I don't want to exclude her, but I don't know if she likes me."

"She has also threatened me."

I look at him again. "What?"

"I have been threatened several times since the slumber party. *Mamma* says I better be a gentleman. Marit says *or else*. Liv has warned me about coming on too strong, and Paisley has suggested I learn how to flirt." His eyes close, and he sighs. "Which was not at all uncomfortable to hear at a family breakfast I didn't know she was joining us for."

"I was told they'd been trying to set you up so you'd be taken care of. Shouldn't they be threatening me?"

He murmurs, "Have you seen yourself? You're the little mouse, and I'm the big bad snake."

I don't know how I feel about that. All the same, I let my attention fall to his tattoos. I trace the body of one snake full of stars. "You know how to flirt just fine."

"Thank you. Surprising that I'm not half-bad when I actually want to flirt with someone, right?"

"It's not surprising at all." I let my fingertip follow the head of his galaxy snake, and I wish I were less like a mouse. At the very least, I want to be a snake, too. I lace my fingers with his. "Hayes?"

His lips tremble, and I missed when he rested his head

back. Harsh, he whispers, "Yeah?"

"Are you all right?"

"Yeah. Just...slowly losing my mind. I'm tired. And you...you're..." He wets his lips, lets his grip on my hand squeeze. Prayerfully, he says, "*Everything*."

My heartbeat, which only just settled, kicks back up. "I want to take care of you," I say. Sitting up, I kneel around his hips, and he hisses a curse. I cup his face with my free hand. "I'm not a mouse."

He swears, sharply, several times. "I know that, pudding."

"Do you?"

"Yes." His eyes open, pained. "Appearances are deceiving. And you're very guarded, keeping up a façade to protect yourself. You're bright as a star, twinkling gently in the distance. So frail and lovely. It's easy to think you'll wink out of existence if I don't cup my hands around you and keep you safe. It's easy to forget that you are larger than life and made of raging gas. *Elskan mín*, you are elemental. Soothing as a stream of crystalline water. But the very atoms that make up water and bring life can also be repurposed into a bomb."

I squeeze his hand as tight as I can, thankful I'm still wearing my heavy-duty gloves, and I'm exhausted. My body aches. And he's too wonderful, sitting here, comparing me to stars and bombs and streams of life. I touch my lips to the corner of his mouth in a timid kiss.

His hand flexes, too tight for a second, then forced lax. "Ellen," he exhales.

"Am I misreading this moment?"

"No." He curses. "No."

"I know Paisley—"

Breath hisses past his teeth. "I never want to think about that experience again."

I wince. "Sorry. You're tense, so I don't know if I have consent. I should have asked first. I just...I don't want to put you in another situation like that."

"*You* can't. And...I'm tense because I don't want to hurt you. I don't know how well I'll be able to control myself if this continues."

"It's okay. I'm on top, so I'm in control."

Hayes's eyes close, and he covers his heating cheeks with his free hand. "You are the most frightening mixture of innocence and awareness. If I lose control, you will not be *on top* for very long. I cool down with weights heavier than you."

I know that. I've seen it.

I can't stop my delirious giggle. Lifting his hand from his cheeks, I smile at him. "My gentle giant."

His chest fills, and he grips my wrist, slipping his fingers into my glove, against my palm. The velcro tears open. "Yes," he growls. "*Yours*." Forcing my glove off, he pulls my wrist to his mouth and kisses, nips. He breathes me in, one great big shuddering inhale at a time.

It leaves me trembling, but I'm shockingly calm. "I will have to go back home tonight," I tell him as he dots kisses against my forearm. "Mouse will be sad if I abandon him all night."

Hayes grunts, releases my still-gloved hand, and braces his palm under my butt. While I'm still computing that shift, he stands, and I jerk, throwing my arms around his neck, potentially strangling him, if it's possible to strangle a tree. His hands fit at my thighs. "Lock your ankles," he grumbles, and I do, so he mutters, "Good girl."

I might exhale a curse into his hair, but who can be sure?

Bracing me with a hand at my back, he sweeps my purse off the ground where I left it when I came over. As though I'm not clinging to him, he walks me across the balcony to my apartment, unlocks the door, and ducks us both inside. "Hi, Mouse," he murmurs as my cat coos, darting over to Hayes's feet. "Couch or bed?" he asks, and it takes me several heart-pounding moments to realize he's not asking my cat that.

"I…"

"I'm not talking about sex."

I clutch him, whisper, "Bed."

He obliges and has my other glove stripped off before he's caging me to the mattress and undoing my legs from around his waist. His touch grazes reverently up my thigh before he meets my eyes, and I…

He…

"I don't know what I'm doing," he whispers.

My head shakes, and I clutch my hands against my chest. "Neither do I." My voice is all breathy, and it's stupid. What a cliché.

"Scared?" he asks.

My head shakes again. "I'm most disturbed by my lack of concern. You're…massive."

Humor glitters through his eyes. "Yeah. You keep reminding me." Bracing his weight on one arm, he caresses my cheek, lets the pad of his thumb graze my warm skin. "Do I kiss you now?"

"You won't be able to."

"No?" He arches a brow.

"The second you lower your head, Mouse will jump up here and interrupt. I know my rom-coms. He's the lovable animal companion. He serves as comic relief in moments like these. The catalyst of frustration. Rom-com gods are sadists."

Hayes angles a look off me, toward the floor, and he makes a low sound in his chest. "Look at that. He's poised and everything."

In the next moment, Mouse leaps up and flops against my shoulder, nuzzling himself against my cheek.

Hayes scoops him up and falls onto his back beside me. "It's probably for the best."

"Wait. What?"

"I should cool down before I eat you or something."

I sit up, look at him. "Why? I bet I'm delicious."

Hayes's laugh jostles Mouse, and my kitty mews. "That's not in question, pudding."

"Is that why you call me 'pudding'? Have you thought I looked yummy this entire time?"

"My secret's out," he murmurs.

My nose scrunches. I get hives any time I read about this stuff, those words—*delicious*, *yummy*, yuck. No thanks. They make no sense in reference to a person. Unless you're a cannibal. Maybe I've never understood it before. Thinking about it literally, whenever a character *just wants to bite* another, neon question marks appear in my brain. Now that the feeling of Hayes nibbling my wrist is in my head, however, it's like a quiet, italicized *oh* has taken the question marks' place.

Yeah, that was nice.

Maybe I'm a bit edible.

Hm.

No.

Still weird to think. Maybe I just don't like that word. Some people riot against *moist*. I hate *ooze* and *edible*.

Lying back down on my side, I face Hayes.

Mouse purrs, slinking between our bodies, and I pet him, fixing his little raccoon hood atop his head.

"It's supposed to happen in the rain anyway, isn't it?" Hayes asks, voice still roughened by whatever we were about to do, whatever I think I still want to do.

"I hope not. That sounds uncomfortable."

He rolls to his side. "How would you like it to happen?"

Closing my eyes, I murmur, "Suddenly. Breathlessly. Incomprehensibly."

"Shouldn't you have a vendetta against adverbs, Miss Editor?"

"Only when they weaken their lines. Don't say *walk quickly* when you can say *run*. Try not to overuse *really* or *very*. Adverbs have their place. Sometimes you need them for clarity, and not all of them end in *ly*." Mouse's motor hums, constant and comforting. "Sometimes I've felt like an adverb. Or a conjunction at the beginning of a sentence. I'm not actually incorrect, but people decided I was overused, improper, or wrong without ever giving me a chance to prove I serve a purpose."

"Serving a purpose is overrated."

I smile. "If we really believed that, I don't think we'd try so hard."

"And we'd probably be happier."

Slowly, I open my eyes. "If you had nothing to fear, what would you do right now?"

"Lock Mouse out of this room and kiss you senseless." He doesn't need a moment to consider the question, but once he's responded, he tenses, like he needs a moment to recover. "I am doing a poor job of cooling down."

"I doubt it helps that we're about three accidental seconds of drowsiness away from turning this into *only one bed*." Without even brushing our teeth for the night. Disgraceful. I wonder if Hayes tastes like the pre-workout fruit we had for our snack. You'd think ranch would be the taste that sticks, but it's always more palatable and romantic in rom-coms. Inexplicably minty. For some reason strawberry, peaches, or honey. Even if the guy's been drinking alcohol, it's never putrid unless it's not *the* guy. What foolish rules of reality we break in fiction.

And some readers have the audacity to suggest some books aren't realistic enough. Like. Go read a biography.

"It's still 'only one bed' if I have a bed across the hall?" he murmurs.

"It's *only one bed* if there's another in the same hotel room, but *oops* we're in the same one."

His brows knit. "Interesting. So it's not so much about the bed. It's about the sleeping together."

"Tangling limbs and pressing bodies. Heartbeats you can hear. Breaths you can count. Delicate or timid touches turning achingly familiar. It's trust. Sleeping around someone, near someone, with someone is trusting them with your vulnerability, whether it turns sexual or not."

He's watching me, intent on my every babbling word, half-lidded eyes, half a sleepy smile on his lips. On his side like he is, he's a wall. Formidable and dangerous, towering over me, ready to consume me. And I'd let him.

"Do you trust me, Ellen?" he murmurs.

"Yes." I don't hesitate. And I realize it's the first time I've trusted since the last time I dared to so much as try.

Hayes reaches for my face, pools his fingers into my hair, threading his sturdy touch to the nape of my neck. Ignoring Mouse between us, he leans for my mouth and claims my lips with his.

Breath leaves me.

And…I thought I'd be worse at this for my first time. But I don't think I am? It's definitely rom-com magic. The way my mouth fits to his, the way my actions match. The way it's not sloppy. The way it starts slow. The way it turns desperate.

It's familiar.

I don't know why.

Maybe it's just that he's familiar.

I forget that Mouse is between us and reach for Hayes's shirt, clenching my fists in the fabric. A whimper escapes me, and I'm half-certain Mouse has fled when Hayes rolls over me, lifts my face, tugs my hair.

Gasping, I rock my head back to his demand, and he kisses the base of my throat.

A shudder crashes into me. My short breaths battle for some kind of purchase. I'm trembling and crashing and soaring. Nonsense spills from my mouth. Curses shatter from his, breaking apart on my skin as he trails his kisses across my collarbones.

It's a lot of pleading and reassurance and heat. Heaving breaths. Warm.

Warm.

His mouth tastes *warm*. Not like fruit or ranch.

"Hayes…"

He curses, kisses me quick, forces himself to say, "Yes? Yes, Ellen?"

"Are you okay?"

He exhales a chuckle and sweeps his hand into my hair. His fingers are shaking. "Yes, *elskan mín*. Yes."

"What does that mean?"

"Mine." The word is a growl. Possessive. Overflowing with straining heat. He nuzzles his lips against my throat, teasing and tasting, whispering sweet words I don't know the meanings of. For someone who doesn't know what he's doing, he sure seems to. He's branding my flesh with his mouth, searing the sensation of his touch deep into my memory. His fingers tease the hem of my shirt, then his palm spreads warm and solid against the bare skin of my stomach.

My abs clench, painfully, because we killed them two days ago, and I reach up around his big body to brace myself. A guttural noise pours into the crook of my neck when I grip his back.

Then his hand leaves my waist, and he plants his palms on either side of me, pushing up over me, panting.

My back lifts off the bed because I'm hanging onto him, and it makes me laugh. "What's wrong, big guy?"

"Nothing." He fights to get the word out past what I assume is an inexplicable amount of gravel hiding in his throat. He heaves a deep, forceful breath. "If I don't stop now, I won't." Squeezing his eyes shut, he forces more deep breaths into his chest. "What's the least sexy thing you can think of?"

"Celery."

He nods, repeating the word quietly.

"Especially when they're stringy." I gasp. "Not to mention that whoever made up ants on a log should be in prison."

"Ants on…" His brow furrows, and he opens his eyes, and his gaze slides down my body. "What's that?" he murmurs, and I'm suspicious that he's once again doing a poor job of cooling down.

"It's peanut butter and raisins on celery. Which you'd probably like. Because you are a lunatic and eat blueberries covered in ranch."

His gaze snaps back up to my eyes. "It all goes to the same place."

"Spoken like a true psychopath."

Planting a palm against my back, he touches our foreheads together. "The only thing I'm crazy about is you, pudding."

"And space."

"Hush. I'm *flirting*."

I bite my lip to do as I'm told.

Taking a shaking breath, Hayes moves onto his knees, clasps my wrists, and frees my hands from his back. Tense moments pass where he struggles to compose himself and I struggle with the beauty of it.

In a very real way, I think Hayes is everything I've always wanted and never been able to find.

I shift a little uncomfortably as I realize he's not the only hot and bothered one right at the moment. I'm flushed to the core of my being, and I've never experienced anything like this before. Attraction before him was a mystery, something I was *supposed* to feel at some point for someone. Probably a movie star or singer was my assumption based off the people around me. Being attracted to a stranger based on their shirt coming off in a show or some move they did in a music video felt strange, uncomfortable in a way that made me a bit nauseous.

This discomfort is because I think I want to crawl inside Hayes, tuck myself near his heart, and live inside his warmth for the rest of my life. I want to play with his big fingers, experiment with whatever makes him lose his mind. I want to kiss trails up his arms along the rivers of ink staining his skin and feel more of his stubble scratching my jaw.

Hayes is a sensory playground.

And he's so beautiful.

In contrast, I don't like my skin right now.

I don't like that it's on me. Touching me. It's being very inconsiderate. Flexing my fingers, I bundle my shirt in my hands and try not to jitter. The compulsion to throw myself in his arms is unkind, so I'll not humor it.

"Can we get married tomorrow?" I ask, then I gasp and clap my hands to my mouth. Breathless, I say, "Sorry. That was weird."

Every muscle in Hayes's body has gone still. He stares at me, lips parted.

I force myself out of bed, away from him, and start

pacing, letting the energy out as I tap my hands against my thighs. To think I was exhausted nearly to passing out just a few minutes ago. Now, I need something colorful, loud. "I don't mean whatever you think I mean. It was just a silly thought that should have stayed in my head." I turn on my heel, swallow, wet my dry lips. "You know what it is? I know what it is. I'm way too comfortable around you now. I've hit *the* point. I trust you. I like you. I think you can handle me. And then I get *real* weird. And you wonder what the hell you're doing wasting your time on me."

Hayes catches me in his arms, stilling my movement, and hoo boy. That is *not* good.

I shove out of his hold, and this might collapse into a panic attack if I'm not careful. All I can do is point at him and say, "*No*," with some kind of authority. Backing away, I grip my fists, tap them against one another in front of my chest. "I'm…doing a thing. Don't stop the thing, or I won't be able to think anymore."

"What are you thinking about?" he asks, and the tension in his tone hasn't gone fully away yet.

I open my mouth. Close it. Giving him a stern look, I shake my head and tut. "Almost tricked me there. No, these are secret thoughts. They're as disturbing as ants on a log."

"The food that you think I'd probably like?"

He makes a very good point. I might hate him.

Except I know I don't.

Rather, I might love him.

I might be inconsolably in love with him.

Fantastic that I stumble into *that* idea while I'm having a mini freak out.

It's nothing definite yet, which means I absolutely shouldn't blurt it. It's just a probability. Based on…

What just happened? The fact I think a couple kisses reprogrammed my body as *his*?

No.

Love like that is shallow. The worst kind. The stupid kind. The kind that makes me roll my eyes and stop reading.

I love the way he's looking at me like I'm not crazy, like he still wants me, like it's physically painful that I pushed him away, like it's physically painful that I won't recite every insane thought in my head. I love all his words. The things he says when the murmurs seem to overflow. The way he looks at me and calls me *adorable* only to suggest I terrify him a moment later. I love when he grumbles about math yet rattles off the exact number of moons each planet in our solar system has.

I love his family.

The people who care about me because I care about him. The people he cares about.

He is care.

Hayes is *care*.

And I want to destroy whoever has ever taken advantage of his massive giving soul.

Taking a deep breath, Hayes drops his unwavering attention off me. "Should I ask for your father's blessing at your birthday party?"

My ability to connect with my body shuts off. I don't know how I remain upright. I can no longer feel my legs. It takes me a couple tries to figure out how to use my mouth, but I finally manage a weak, "W-what?"

His gaze lifts, pinning, severe, every bit the terrifying person he appears to be. "Even if we elope and skip the loud mess that is a wedding, you probably still want your parents' approval, right?"

"Yes, of course." They care about me. They'll know if I'm being insane before I do.

"So I'll ask them when we see them at your birthday

party Wednesday."

"You'll ask them to…"

"Let me marry you."

I blink. Dropping my hands to my sides, I take a step toward him. "I am not following."

Tenderly, Hayes combs his fingers through my hair, and I might have no connection with my body, but I *feel* the heat of his hand as it skims through the strands. "I want to marry you."

My head shakes. "No. We're being weird. Because of the kisses."

"We're being weird 'cause we're weird, pudding."

A purely logical statement. I am skeptical. "If we were married, we'd still be kissing. Therefore, of course we want to get married. Our brains are lagging. From the kisses."

He tilts his head. "If we were married, we would not still be kissing. We'd be…doing other things."

My face turns crimson. "Indecent."

"Yes, indecent things. Most likely very indecent things."

"Hayes!" My numb flesh tingles, and it occurs to me I definitely need to sit down, so I march to the foot of my bed. With a huff, I drop and fold my hands in my lap. "There's no way you want to marry me. We haven't known each other very long."

He sits beside me. "Five years isn't long enough?"

I scoff. "I don't remember five years ago."

"Probably for the best. You'd be horrified if you knew."

"If I knew what?"

He grunts. "How cute you were in front of a perfect stranger."

My eyes roll.

"I'm going to ask your father either way."

I laugh. "You won't want to by Wednesday. You'll have

had time to really cool off by then."

"Debatable."

"We are presently debating," I state.

He loosens my fingers from my other hand and starts tracing the lines of my palm. It tickles. I hate how much I love it, how much my crazy body almost seems to need it. Drawing my palm to his lips, he catches my eye and kisses with tedious, thought-melting precision. "You are perfect."

My mouth goes dry.

"I want to find every secret freckle and praise them for existing. I will cherish you until you forget every reason…" His eyes spark, heated, furious. "…*every lie* that suggested you were not precious. I will spoil you until you can exist without shame. Don't you dare think for even a moment that I only want to marry you so I can touch you until you're screaming my name. Am I understood?"

"Y-yes."

Wrapping an arm around me, he presses his lips to my forehead and whispers, "Good."

CHAPTER 23

♥ All's fair in love and birthday parties.

Hayes: March 21. I still want to marry you.

I chew my lip and shake my head as I fix my hair in the mirror, smooth my hands down the green dress Hayes refused to let me buy for myself when we went to the mall. He said *one of us would get it*, but then he pointed behind me right before it was time to pay and said *is that a moth dress?*

Cruel, devious man.

The dress is still pretty outside the dressing room. That's nice.

Hayes's morning texts ever since we nearly only-one-bedded ourselves into R ratings have been…nice, too. Very nice. All *Good morning, beautiful future wife* and *Shocking, I know, but I just took a cold shower and still want to marry you* and *Ellen Sallow or Hayes Little? I can't decide if I like you better with my last name or if I prefer the irony. Should we hyphenate?*

A chill goes down my spine. Hayes is going to ask my father if he can marry me today. I'm going to have a birthday party for the first time in years. I'll obviously have met my parents' terms and be able to move into my cottage soon.

Everything is coming together.

Only one problem…

Sagging onto my bed, I draw Mouse into my arms and hug him like it's the end of the world.

When everything comes together, that's a mere few pages before everything falls apart.

Get ready for the plot twists. The long-lost cousins and evil twins. The mysteriously unmentioned exes. The unexpected and uncharacteristic parental rejection. The sudden, inexplicable fire.

Maybe Hayes's bar will explode, and we'll have to rush back from the party to assess the damage. Then he'll only be able to get a job out of state, thus leaving me behind until ten years later when he returns with a full beard to claim he never stopped loving me. I'll be widowed, obviously, and struggling emotionally to raise a child. Or three. Usually not more than three.

An overwhelmed breath whistles past my lips, and I set a hand on my stomach, hoping all three children are cats. I can't even imagine having children with someone who isn't Hayes. Mouse wiggles into my hand, and I snuggle him another moment.

Then a cop knocks on my door, so I know Hayes is here.

"Be a good boy," I tell Mouse before I grab my phone and my purse and slip from the room to meet him.

He's in his usual clothes, probably because no dress shirt can hold him. He'd comically pop a button into my father's eye right as he asks for my hand. He's freshly-shaven; I can smell the aftershave. It won't last long. He'll be prickly again before we get home.

I am anxious.

I think I want to go back to bed.

The moment I begin debating whether or not it's an option, since it *is* my birthday, Hayes reaches for my hand, draws my fingers to his lips, and closes his eyes. "Happy birthday, *elskan mín*."

The second I figure out Norwegian pronunciation, it's

all over for this man. *Mine*, as it turns out, is only that second part. I have no idea what the first means, and when I try to look it up, I get a dissociative hallucinogen. *Esketamine* treats depression and is used in anesthesia. I know that now. That is a thing that I know. "Thank you, *eskamin*."

"*Elskan mín*," he repeats against my knuckles, holding my eyes, hopelessly amused. "*Jeg elsker deg*."

I do my darnedest to repeat him, but he just chuckles and kisses my fingers again before murmuring, "Very good."

"Are you making me say weird things?"

"I'm not *making* you do anything."

Fair enough. I lock my door and gather my dress so I can descend the stairs. I'm a moth princess. In sneakers. Because heels are an affront to nature and more often than not a catalyst for ending up in precarious situations.

Threat of heel breaking in real life? Mild.

Threat of heel breaking in a rom-com? Spicy. We're talking multiple chili peppers.

"What does 'yai eske die' mean?"

"I have absolutely no idea." He opens the car door for me, sweeping my skirts up inside.

I lift my head, regal. "I am going to ask your sisters."

"Good luck."

"My pronunciation isn't *that* bad."

He watches me for long, teasing moments, eyes glittering. Cupping my face, he kisses me—sweet, gentle, quick. It's like every brief kiss that has come since the night we were falling to pieces in my bed, yet it still leaves me breathlessly desperate for more. He murmurs, "Your pronunciation is very good. I just don't think they'd betray me my fun. They're neat like that. Must be on account of my frog in top hat pictures."

I want frog in top hat pictures.

Waiting until Hayes has reached the driver seat, I say, "Are you teaching me dirty words?"

He looks at me, blinks once, then murmurs a line *very gently*, before indicating that it's my turn.

Even though I have no idea what he said and none of the words sounded like anything I do know, I blush, narrow my eyes, and mimic.

He coughs, pulls out of the parking space, then hoarsely pleads, "Don't say that to my sisters. Especially not in front of my *mamma*. Maybe…maybe never again."

"Will you get in trouble?"

"Extreme trouble."

"Tell me what it means, and I promise I won't."

"Pudding, that's blackmail. We agreed to have a healthy relationship. In writing."

I pet Spotz's little tuft. "You're the one teaching me crass statements. In front of my giraffe no less."

He grumbles, "I'm not going to tell you, and you're not going to mention it again."

"How can you be so sure?" I challenge.

"Because you're a good girl."

I squirm in my seat. "You've got to stop with that. That whole section of the relationship form wasn't meant to be used until after we were married."

"That would explain why you still forget to eat several times a week." At a red light, he cuts a glance my way. "I expect eight glasses of water, twenty minutes of sun, and three full meals a day once we're married."

I repeat the line I shouldn't repeat at him.

His cheeks turn red. "I mean it. Don't say that to anyone else. Ever."

I giggle. "*Fine*. I am going to ask about the *eskamin* though."

Again, he says, "Good luck."

❖

Our housekeeper opens the front door for Hayes and me, and Mom—as though poised for this moment—flutters down the stairs in an elegant spiral of pale blue gown. Her heels click across the floor as she opens her arms and welcomes me into a hug. "Happy birthday, Ellen."

"Thank you, Mom."

She kisses my cheek and turns to Hayes. Her eyes warm, and she spreads her arms wider. Clearing his throat, he accepts the hug, startling still when my mother pecks his cheek. "Welcome back, Hayes. It's so good to see you again."

Eyes slicing toward me, Hayes murmurs, "Thanks. Happy to be here."

Mom spins, clicking toward the hall. "Come along, come along. Oh, Ellen. I hope you like everything. We haven't had a party for you in so long."

Preparing for whatever it is I'm about to see, which literally was once a live animal in the dining room—yes, that's how I got my pony when I turned eight—I link my hand in Hayes's and follow my mother.

The back hall opens up into our pool lounge, for billiards, not the *pool* which is a different room, and butterfly decorations flutter over a thousand flowers while moths hung on thin strings cluster near the lights. Food covers the bar counter, a several-tier cake pouring luna moths cascades into a sea of butterfly cupcakes.

A squeal rips out of my mouth before I remember I'm an adult and not alone with my parents. I think I'm vibrating. I'm absolutely vibrating. It's the most beautiful thing I've ever seen, second to Hayes.

Dad grins by a table stacked high with gifts wrapped in pale green paper and adorned with more silk moths and butterflies. My mind trips through naming every last one, because they aren't cheap echoes of colorful sort-of moths and butterflies; they are mimics of real ones.

"Do you like it?" Dad asks as he tweaks a package for *aesthetic* purposes.

I nod, violently, and tap my free fist against my leg. "I love it," I squeak.

He opens his arms, and I pull away from Hayes's side to throw myself into his hug. His starchy suit is annoying, but I'm surrounded by *moths* and *butterflies*, and they are all so amazing, and I'm going to save every last one and decorate my cottage with them after I move in. "Thank you, thank you, thank you."

Dad laughs, squeezing me tight. "Only the best for my little girl."

When I release him, it's so I can take my time perusing the room like a lepidopterist on a mission to identify each new fluffy friend. Vaguely, I register my father greeting Hayes, Hayes mumbling a joke about how he hopes he's not under-dressed, Dad missing the joke and assuring him our family is just a bit *over the top*.

High energy. High maintenance.

By the time Liv, Marit, Paisley, and Hayes's mother get here, I've managed to contain my excitement—purely by having sneakily defaced a present in order to thread the thin wire stand of a luna moth decoration into my hair. I'm a moth princess now.

The first thing out of Marit's wide mouth after our housekeeper drops everyone off in the party lounge is a curse followed by, "*Since when are you* royalty?"

Her mother smacks her, snaps something in Norwegian, then greets my parents. They hit it off immediately, bonding over *what a sweet girl I am*, which is…awkward, but I ignore it in order to focus my energy on greeting my friends.

Liv stares at the three-tier moth cake, a plastic-covered cake plate in her hands. Her blue eyes remain shocked when they skim toward me, then she gathers a smile. "Happy birthday, Ellen."

"Thank you."

"I made a cake," she says. "Hayes said you like chocolate."

"I do. I'm very excited to try it."

Marit marches past me, sets a bag and a package down with the other gifts, and returns, grabbing my arms. She shakes me. "Why didn't you tell us you lived in a *castle*?"

"It's not a castle. Mom just likes the style of towers."

Paisley clasps an oddly wrapped bundle to her chest and blinks blankly ahead. "I am ashamed to have made royalty sleep upon my living room floor. My puny apartment is a disgrace. I apologize, Your Highness."

The smile I've held in place falters. "I don't understand. Your apartment is nicer than mine."

Marit shakes me again. "You didn't think to mention that you were *rich* somewhere amidst the moth facts?"

My brows knit. I've never been in a situation like this before. My friends up until now have either known who my parents are and what they have or have never met them. I obviously don't talk about my own financial situation, because I've learned that's often inappropriate.

From across the room with our parents Hayes barks something in Norwegian, and Marit releases me in order to snap back at him. It's surprising to hear how her flawless accent shifts perfectly between the languages.

Lifting her cake while her siblings bicker, Liv asks, "Where should I put this?"

"Over here," I smile, because at least I know where the food goes. I rearrange some of the platters of my favorite snacks to make room, and when she pops the lid off, it reveals a puff of frosting fashioned into a moth centerpiece. It's the most adorable thing I have ever seen, and I squeal again. "I love him! He looks like a *Bombyx mori*! Those are the moths that primarily produce silk. They're little and white, and I love them."

Liv grins. "Marit helped with the topping, since she's the artist."

I look at Marit when she trails away from the argument with her brother. She sniffs and folds her arms. "It's hard to draw with a piping bag, but, yes, I am that incredible."

"Thank you so much."

After the initial shock of where I live wears off, Marit and I team up against Paisley and Liv for a game of pool. They laugh and talk, and everything melts into the tired familiar calm of late-night slumber party.

It wasn't a fluke.

I do have friends.

And we're all here laughing together again.

That might just be the best birthday gift I've ever received.

"Is Hayes still treating you right?" Marit asks, sneaking me another deviled egg, for strength against our enemies.

Liv gasps as she narrowly misses sinking the eight ball.

"Do we have to castrate him yet?" Paisley asks, relaxing after Liv's error. The spark in her hazel eyes says *I can and will take down a mountain for you*, and it's enough to make me blush in my seat by the table.

It is not enough to make me skip sinking the next stripe for Team Marit x Ellen with a whole deviled egg in my mouth.

"He's as pleasant as always," I note once I've swallowed, glancing toward where he's seated with his mother and my parents on the couches at the other end of the room. Dad has a tumbler of brandy in his hand. Our mothers seem to have fruity margaritas. My Hayes has something red and bubbly. I bet it's a cherry soda.

"As pleasant as always?" Paisley wiggles her brows.

Marit nudges her in the stomach with the butt of her pool cue. "Nope. Not going there. Brother. Remember?" She doesn't sink the next ball and groans.

I wonder if Hayes has brought up asking for my hand yet. Is that the kind of thing Dad would get overenthusiastic about and announce to the entire room? He is the same man who interrupted a business gathering in order to announce to the room of men in suits that *his little girl had just lost her first tooth*.

Mercy…

I can still hear the chime of his spoon against his glass as he asked for everyone's attention then pulled me up into his arms so I could grin stupidly.

Yeah, Dad's dramatic.

I love him so much.

I thought that girls fell in love with guys who reminded them of their fathers, but even the way the men are sitting over there is starkly different. Anyone can tell Hayes is reserved while Dad's leading the entire conversation like the CEO he is. I can hear his laughter every so often. I haven't even heard Hayes speak since he chastised Marit earlier.

He probably hasn't asked yet.

That makes the most sense.

Steadily, the party moves toward cake, and I head straight for Liv's, holding my plate, grinning, eyes sparkling.

She laughs as she cuts through the dense chocolate with a long string of floss. "I'm honored you're tasting my cake first."

Mom's chiming laugh trickles into the conversation, and she braces a gentle hand against Liv's shoulder. "Darling, our Ellen has had a hundred cakes ordered special from our favorite bakeries. What she has never had is a friend willing to make her one at home." Holding her own plate out, Mom beams. "I'll take a slice as well."

It is the best cake I have ever had, and I whisper at Hayes that I'm stealing his sister, to which he replies that I can't steal what's already mine.

Cake time begins and ends without any notion of Hayes having asked for my hand. By the time I'm sitting in a mountain of gifts, I wonder if maybe I've missed the joke. If Hayes asks to marry me after barely one month of really dating, it would be somewhat fast. Who cares if he feels like another piece of my soul? It probably doesn't matter that we already know all the details that might be problems in the future. Just being perfectly compatible on paper doesn't translate into real life, right?

Oh, what am I saying?

That's stupid.

Of course it does.

Suggesting that honest answers and discussions don't translate perfectly into real life is like saying there's no truth to be found in stories. Stories *are* truth.

When I blurted my question about getting married, my head was foggy and wanting, but seated here, surrounded by a love I never would have found without him, I know I want him for the rest of my life.

I want to marry him.

I want to love him.

I think I already do.

I shriek.

Thoughts forgotten, I clap my hand to my mouth and stare at the plush in my lap. I'm shaking. I can't. It's…I…

How?

He's perfect. Absolutely perfect.

"I love him. I love him." I can hardly take a breath. I look at Liv, tears welling in my eyes, and shakily hold my new little moth child against my chest. Plush red wings. A striped body. I absolutely have no words. It's a cecropia. It's a perfect cecropia.

Liv laughs. "It was a challenge, but I think I'm addicted to making stuffed animals now. Expect a new moth plush for every holiday."

I scream, "*You made him?*"

She sticks her nose in the air. "Obviously. Nothing but the best for my *lillesøster.*"

"Mine next!" Marit says, and I die again as I lift a painting out of the bag she hands me. I'm dreadfully predictable, it seems.

Trembling, I hold the painting and stare at the moth princess surrounded by a hundred perfect wings. A tear traces down my cheek, and I can hardly think. It's perfect. This is perfect. I'm going to keep it forever. It shall be a central fixture in my cottage. I shall admire it daily while I hug my cecropia plushie.

"Show offs," Paisley mutters before handing me her lump of a gift. It's hard to peel the tape off without tearing the paper, since my hands are still shaking, but I do my best and freeze as the tiara presents itself. "It's not handmade or anything. And I'm pretty sure those are butterflies…but I hope you like it. And don't have a better one somewhere in this castle."

My lashes flutter, damp, and this is the best birthday I have ever had.

When I get the email stating Blaire's moth book has not only published but has also been dedicated to me, it may be the best day of my life. Which means, according to all the rom-com rules I know…it is about to become the worst.

CHAPTER 24

♥ May the rom-com gods have mercy on your weird little soul.

It's *the moment*. The one where everything crashes and burns, sending everything hurtling apart.

I really do know better than to leave the safety of the crowd on a day like today…but…well. I had a lot of cake and soda and snacks, and I had to go to the bathroom. Foolish. I know better. Bathrooms are not mentioned in stories unless they are used to lead a character into a precarious situation, whereby they overhear or witness something occurring away from the safety of the collective.

My mind reminds me of the rules too late. I've already heard Hayes ask if he can marry me, and now I'm stuck even though I know this storyline. I know I shouldn't listen any longer. It's predictable and silly, and I'll get hurt somewhere in the middle.

The flow is simple, leading in and out of misunderstanding.

Hayes asks my father if he can marry me. Something *bad* happens. Then it shifts into something *good*. But silly main characters never wait around for that shift. No, they hear the *bad* and run off crying.

Because *drama*. Because *dramatic irony*. Because *insufficient brain cells*.

So, anyway, I've heard Hayes ask. And now my insufficient brain cells and I are stuck pressed against the wall outside the parlor door in the resulting silence.

I don't know why Dad hasn't replied yet.

Are we really going for the whole *unexpected and uncharacteristic parental rejection*? Dad's supposed to be the one who's a little ditzy and overly adoring. He's supposed to pop a bottle of champagne and cheer about how amazing I am, because he does that without someone asking to marry me, and I really assumed his blind love would be the response now. Unconcerned affection. Of *course* my first boyfriend wants to marry me after only a month. I'm incredible. His dearly beloved Ellen.

Eerie silence is wrong. It makes my stomach tight and my legs weak as my heart pounds. I've already done a lot of activity today. I need to keep my physical limitations in mind.

I sit on the cold floor, forcing myself to wait throughout the *entire* conversation, no matter what happens in the middle. I'm smarter than leaving at the misunderstanding. Honestly, I'd like to believe I'm smarter than sitting here now, but *emotions*. Emotions are stupid. And they don't behave or listen to outlines.

"Are you sure you want to marry Ellen?" Dad asks at last, and my brain collapses on itself. The tone of his voice isn't *him*. I don't know how to decode it, and especially not without other clues, but I do know that it's wrong. It's almost stern. Distant.

Hayes's emotion comes a bit stronger in his voice, in a growl. "Yes, sir. I've never been more sure about anything else in my life."

Dad's sigh drifts, full-bodied.

It breaks my heart.

"Son, have a seat," Dad murmurs, and it's severe, and I'm crumbling into dust. A moment passes. Dad begins speaking. Silent tears cascade down my cheeks. "Ellen is… special. I'm sure you've already gathered that. She's innocent and full of light, and I wouldn't have her any other way, but you have to understand what you're getting into. Pieces of her refuse to grow up."

My eyes widen, and I don't know what's going on. I just know I can't breathe, and I'm shaking. This is cruel. Rom-com magic is cruel.

Dad continues, oblivious, "She needs someone who will take care of her and protect her, who will be patient with her immaturity—her meltdowns, if you will. She has a hundred little quirks I doubt she's grown comfortable enough with you to show you yet. She's very good at mirroring the people she's around, and her mother and I have seen her shift into a hundred different people depending on who she's with. Even just today, she's occasionally picked up on your sister Liv's accent. She doesn't realize she's doing it most of the time, and I will admit that you and your family are among the firsts kind enough to let her be."

Hayes grumbles, "She sometimes picks up on touches of my accent, too. It's adorable."

I shatter. How could I not know I do that? Why wouldn't anyone have told me?

"It's not adorable," Dad says, firm but kind, proving that he is still my father and not some endgame rom-com boss sent to break everything.

Because drama.

"It's concerning for us as her parents. We were horrified when she decided to move out, and it took some work to make sure the apartments she picked were safe for her. We approached the situation after she got her kitty poorly, made her think she'd done something wrong, and pushed her away before we could encourage her to make the cottage cat proof in a way this place isn't."

Hayes grunts.

"We never expected her to find a partner."

Huh?

Hayes mutters, "I don't understand. Why did you make it a requirement for her to get her cottage if you didn't expect her to succeed."

"She wasn't coming home. We know how she is, and we knew if we connected a deadline to her cottage, she'd begin planning to move back home, all while *finding a stable relationship* would be too big for her to act upon."

"You used her executive dysfunction as a weapon against her?" Hayes asks.

"To keep her safe. If we gave her this 'requirement,' she would end up talking to us when she was unable to succeed. At that point, we had prepared to invite her back home to her cottage with her cat and work together on finding someone who would treat her right. Despite how she is."

Despite. Despite. Despite. Despite. Despite. My head clouds with that word, and I can't see anything past the silent tears clouding my eyes. I don't have the energy to drag myself away from this conversation. And that's good, I think, because it's supposed to turn around before the end. If I run away now, I'll never hear the conclusion that makes everything all better.

Hayes mutters, "You don't trust that Ellen is mature enough to find her own partner, but you trusted her to live by herself for these past years? She's built her own career and taken care of herself and Mouse on her own. For years."

Right. Yes. Hayes will reason all of this away. This is the character growth moment.

Dad sighs again. "No. We haven't trusted anything. We've kept a close eye on where she lives. Before you moved in, we went so far as to clear her building of neighbors. We can only assume you intimidated our connections when you were adamant about moving in, and it was only recently we gained information of that oversight. As far as her career is concerned, her mother and I pulled strings in order to get her started when we first noticed her interest. There is nothing in this world we love more than our Ellen, but she needs a lot of help. And, son, if you do want to be the person to help her, we are happy to discuss this relationship, but you must understand that she can't manage without assistance, people protecting her, her mother and I messaging to make sure she's okay every other day."

"I don't care what it takes or what assistance she needs. I want her."

My chest aches. He's not denying any of it. He's not even questioning that I can't do my career by myself. He's just accepting that I'm immature and dysfunctional and… wrong?

"She likely won't ever be interested in the things that lovers do, Hayes," a thread of harsh tension tightens my father's tone. "She's never mentioned crushes or shown any interest in intimacy. She turns away when cartoon characters kiss."

Because it's indecent. Private. I don't know. Help. *Help me, Hayes*. Please. You know better, don't you? Maybe I pulled away too frantically when we got carried away, but he's seen my romance form. We've discussed these details. He knows that I see intimacy in my future. He knows that *I'm not a useless broken child.*

Hayes grunts, clears his throat, says nothing to contradict. All he says is, "I'll do anything for her, whatever she needs, whatever she wants. Anything she asks for that I can grant is hers. *I* am hers. I have been for a while now."

I hate those words. Those perfect, kind, self-diminishing words. It's not all about *me*, and I don't want Hayes to enter into a lifetime of thinking he has to treat me like glass at the expense of himself. I don't want to be his burden. I want to love him.

I want so desperately to love him, to be loved, to share something wonderful with a person.

Do people like me not get to have that?

"She is precious to me. From the moment I met her, she was the most adorable person I'd ever seen. I couldn't get her out of my head, and now I don't know what I'd do without her in my life."

He told me *adorable* wasn't patronizing. But maybe I've been confused. I *am* weird. I might not agree with my father completely when it comes to the ways I'm weird, but I do misunderstand situations and get lost. What if Hayes isn't contradicting Dad because, on some level, he sees my father's reasoning?

I don't eat when I should. I get too wrapped up in the things I love. My joy is hyper and eager and childish. I forget to drink enough water, go outside, take care of myself. I can be oblivious.

"Even physically, she needs help," Dad says.

"The POTS," Hayes grunts. "I've looked into it. We've begun exercising each day to help manage it better."

I thought we were exercising each day to spend time together, to laugh when he makes me blush, to be normal people doing a normal thing without some ulterior motive behind it.

A touch of surprise infiltrates my father's tone. "Really? When we first found out, we tried to encourage her to exercise more, but she struggles to put energy into anything that doesn't actively interest her."

"Is her case more severe than she lets on, or has it been

made more severe by the fact her lifestyle isn't entirely consistent or healthy?"

"It is a mild case, all things considered, but she was offered a low dose of medication to help manage it. She just doesn't like the idea of taking something every day." Dad's tone turns pensive as he discusses my medical history with my boyfriend, not wedding plans. "She was supposed to be on medication for the depression and anxiety as well, but she's adapted to refusing to acknowledge her depression as a real problem and claims her anxiety isn't bad as long as she stays away from her triggers. Which is everything."

"Hm." Hayes murmurs, "I've witnessed both anxiety attacks and depressive lows. I know how to handle them."

Hesitation suffuses through my father's voice. "Are you sure you want this, son? Ellen is a great many beautiful things, but in the regard you're asking for, she's a lot of work. And I will not tolerate you ever changing your mind in the future and breaking her heart. She's been hurt by the people she loves far too many times. In spite of everything, she believes herself to be independent, and her mother and I haven't wanted to bruise that spirit, so we've failed to protect her far too much."

"Relationships are a lot of work. I can handle it."

Dad makes a low, considering sound. "Very well. This has happened much too quickly for comfort, however. You'll forgive me for understanding my position and hers as heiress to everything I own."

"I'll sign whatever I need to that says I have no right to a penny. I don't care about any of that. I just want her."

"I still ask that you prove to me your dedication and sincerity with more time than you have. I'll have a talk with Ellen later on and make certain nothing troubling has happened." Dad's tone hardens. "I am nowhere near as trusting as her, and there will be problems if I discover that you've done anything less than kind."

Hayes mutters, "Whatever sets your mind at ease," and that's it. That's the conversation. It's over.

It's over, and there wasn't a resolution, and now I have to get away, or I'll be caught, and then I'll face all the lies attempting to placate me and make one.

Forcing myself onto shaky limbs, I run. I run, unsure where I'm going, uncertain what I'm doing, where I'm supposed to end up, where the storyline demands I go in order to reach the happily ever after at the end.

I can't breathe. I'm shaking. My heart's beating too fast. One way or another, my trembling limbs take me out into the darkness of night, and I run across the property until I reach the moth path that leads to my cottage. Every tree and bush and plant I hand-picked for the moths based on their dietary needs. I did all the research, arranged all the lights. It's not as simple as a butterfly garden, which I also planned and plotted around the house in a kaleidoscope of colorful flowers.

Moths need trees. Butterflies need flowers.

One is easier to attract. The other is a lot of *work*.

Maybe I've always been the moth—more work, less appreciated.

No matter how calmly I'll sit on your finger when a butterfly will immediately fly away, I can't change the fact no one wants me there.

I can hardly see the strings of fairy lights through my tears. I can hardly make out the handful of moths lingering around them. It's a little early yet for peak moth mating season, but that never stopped me from waiting out at the first sign of warm weather before. I've been distracted with a new fixation. And now I might be heartbroken.

Sobbing, I pull the door to my cottage open and throw

myself into the darkness split only by moonlight streaking in through the large living room windows. It's spotless and clean, furnished exactly how I remember when I played here, pretending to be grown up.

My future home.

I never suspected it was the place my parents assumed they'd be able to situate keeping an eye on me even after they'd passed. I never thought it was the location they'd planned to coddle me in bubble wrap because I don't know how to function.

It was *home*.

Home.

My home.

Not the palace that always felt like their home.

Mine.

By *my* choice. Because I loved it. Because I'm not too stupid or immature to know what I like, what I have to do to function, even though I'm fighting uphill when others *less weird* don't have to. I have it so much harder, battling my brain every single day just to do the "easiest" tasks. I am *so much stronger* than the adults who look like adults because they don't express themselves in ways dictated as socially unacceptable for their age.

I thought Hayes understood stuff like that.

I thought we were both…

Heart cracking, I curl up on the couch, pull my fuzzy white throw blanket down off the back cushions, and burrow into my sobs. Maybe if I didn't feel emotions so harshly I could have collected myself and stood up to my father on my own, maturely, proved him wrong. But it hurts too much for me to think clearly right now.

I don't know what to do.

I don't know how to communicate the chaos in my skull.

I don't know how to be with someone who thinks I'm *work*, a *burden*, someone who thinks they need to sacrifice everything in order to take care of me. Even if I won't intentionally abuse Hayes, that doesn't mean I can stop him from forfeiting himself for my sake all the same.

Cursing into the damp fabric in front of me, I wonder what I'm supposed to do when I *promised* I wouldn't but this feels an awful lot like the prelude to the third-act break.

CHAPTER 25

♥ Above all else, trust that you're not the only weird one.

I'm still sniffly by the time the front door eases open, but I've mostly composed myself. Either that or I've dissociated into a depressive low. I've been staring out the window at the gardens bursting from the yard, remembering what they look like during the day in peak butterfly season. It's beautiful. Life is good. I am not depressed just because I'm sad and don't want to exist.

Everything is fine.

And the world is beautiful.

And there are reasons to live in this place that I've plotted and planned and longed for—even if it was always meant to be a padded cell in order to spare me from a life I can't handle.

"Pudding?" Hayes murmurs into the dark, entering and making his body the biggest shadow in the room.

The endearment pierces my chest, and I tuck a little tighter into my blanket, into the couch.

His weight settles on the cushion behind me, drawing my body into his center of gravity. I fight it until my core muscles burn from the strain, but I don't give in. "What are you doing out here?" he asks. "Everyone's been looking for you."

"I bet Mom sighed and mentioned how I've done this before, too. Didn't she?"

Hayes mutters, "There was a mention of how you'd left other birthday parties as a child and hidden from the guests…yes."

"I guess nothing has changed since I was eight."

"You don't really grow out of needing to decompress from sensory overload, no. You just find better ways to hide it usually. Like dissociating. Which, judging by the sound of your voice, seems to be what's going on here. Along with the hiding in a cute fluffy blanket."

There he goes again. Acting like he understands everything. Acting like all of it makes sense and he's on my side and it's all so normal.

My stomach hurts, so I move in order to avoid the gravity of him. "I built my own career."

"Hm?"

"I built my own career. My parents tried to help give me my starting clients, but I guess those idiots *knew* there was something *wrong* with me, and they proved more than ever why I have to hide the fact I'm different." I don't know why I'm starting here. Maybe because it's the easiest place I know to defend myself. My career is the proudest part of what I am capable of. "They didn't trust anything I told them. They rejected my suggestions and changes. They didn't even believe I knew how to use commas. I dropped them after our first book contracts were over, and they still haven't so much as managed to find any agents because they've got their heads so far up their asses they didn't believe me when I said if they wanted to publish, they'd have to go independent." I rake in a seething breath. "They got upset with me and started patronizing me when I'd spent *hours* agonizing over the email, *knowing* there's a stigma and they'd think I was insulting them. Some books just aren't written to the traditional market, and that doesn't mean they're *bad*. It means agents and publishing houses are unlikely to pick them up." Furious, I whip my blanket off my head and turn, pinning Hayes's gleaming blue eyes in the dark. "To be honest though? Those books *were* bad. Completely trash. I wanted to die while I was working on them. They were written by self-righteous pricks, and I *could* have fixed them, but they didn't let me. I never told my parents that I shifted my sights, and sought out my own clients, and put together coaching programs, and studied deeper than editing, and figured out how to make publishing *work*. I never told them that I selected my own people and said that if they wanted to be authors, I'd make it happen. I'd make them successful, and they wouldn't have to pay a penny until they were. People rely on me, Hayes. I get emails from clients on the brink of panic because something's gone wrong. I get emails from people who have only heard about me from my clients and need help because their books weren't edited well by companies with three times my experience." I plant a hand against my chest. "I told you I wasn't useless. I told you. You said you knew that."

He arches a brow at me.

"I'm also not an infant just because I get shocked when cartoon characters kiss. Do you even *want* to know what I've *edited*?"

Hayes lowers his brow. "Ah. I see."

"Do you?" I demand.

"Yeah. This was on the outline, pudding."

I blink.

"Overhearing a conversation you aren't supposed to. Or something."

My fists clench. Right. Yeah. *I outlined this*. Yet more crap I've been right about. Because I'm smart and capable in my own ways, even if those ways aren't always eating every day. "I listened to the entire conversation, and you didn't defend me. Not even a little. You started talking about my mental health and medical history, and *I can't do this*. I cannot be with someone whose reaction to being told I'm a burden isn't *no, she's not* and is instead *I can handle it, no matter what, no matter how heavy*. I know you can handle anything, Hayes! But I don't want to be something you have to *handle*. I just…" The rest of my words shrivel up on my tongue, because they are *I just want to love you, take care of you, make you mine*. I can't say that before ending it.

"Are you breaking up with me?" Hayes grumbles.

I close my eyes. "Yes."

He sighs. "Is there no sacredness to the pinkie swear anymore?"

My damp lashes flutter open, and while obviously irritated, Hayes seems entirely unconcerned. He's relaxed more into the couch, bracing his chin against his fist, elbow resting atop the back cushion.

Frowning, he glares at me—intimidating. "Did you ask what *elskan mín* means?"

My brow knits. "No. I didn't get a chance to." What, with all the crying and all.

"What about *jeg elsker deg*?"

"Do they mean 'this is all one big cruel storybook joke'? Because *drama*?"

His eyes roll. He pulls his phone out of his pocket and turns the brightness all the way down. Still squinting at the light, he types something in, turns it around, and shows me.

"There's no way that's how those words are spelled."

"I promise you I am actually literate in two languages. More so since I met you and got a little obsessed with learning English grammar for a couple months. Have you spared the translation a glance?"

I do, and…I scoff.

"Wow. That hurt my feelings," he mutters.

"*My* feelings are hurt. This information is irrelevant,

and I don't believe you."

"I mean. It is Google Translate, so I understand not having the utmost faith in it, but—"

"No," I growl, and will you look at that? Now *I'm* growling. Great. "The first time you said those words to me, we barely knew each other. I don't believe love is so fickle."

"*Fickle?*" he growls back, and he does it way better than I do. "Fickle." It's a hiss the second time, and I fear I have made a mistake.

I cower before I can remind myself I'm not supposed to. I'm supposed to be fighting for my title as a *strong, independent woman* with a couple brain malfunctions that have switched my central processor from *normal* to *fancy, but with some less-than-ideal side effects*.

It occurs to me I have never seen Hayes truly and utterly pissed before. As in angry. Not drunk.

His eyes narrow, and I'm scared.

He sneers. "I have loved you for five years, ever since you were too drunk to remember how to behave yourself and be whatever the—" He swears. "—this crappy world has taught you is appropriate. You were sunshine in the middle of the night, rambling on about things you adored and pissing love all over the—" He curses again. "—street. I would *kill* for that girl. And I know she's capable, mature, and brilliant. I also know that parents are—" Another curse pierces me. "—difficult to change. They have opinions about their kids, and those opinions aren't up for debate. If you try, bad things happen. My *far*, for example, liked hitting me and locking me in my closet whenever I questioned his authority."

I pale. All the blood rushes out of my face, and I stare, shocked to the center of my being that anyone even *could* lift a hand against Hayes, force him to do anything he doesn't want to. Even though I know at one point he wasn't this big. Nowhere close. At one point, he was a child. And the person who gave him his *big* was so much bigger than him.

"I want to marry you, so I don't want to argue with someone who is more likely to keep me away from you than accept that the truth they've believed for years is wrong. If you refuse to ever leave my side, I'll go curse your father into the ground in your defense. I was furious, but you aren't the only one who knows how to keep big emotions hidden, Ellen."

Very softly, I whisper, "But…you asked about my medical record."

"I'm—" Curse. "—concerned about you and wondering if we need to get a follow-up. You're literally—" Curse. "—disabled and pretending everything is normal because you've been taught that all the weird beautiful stuff about you is bad."

"Nearly passing out at the grocery store because I've been standing for too long *is* bad, Hayes."

"Yeah, and not handling it so you can pretend you're *fine* is worse, Ellen." He takes a deep breath, letting it past his lips. More tame, he mutters, "I love you. I want to take care of you because that's what love does. I'm struggling with my own crap, but I already told you that you do not get to use it as a weapon against yourself. We each have our own strengths and weaknesses, our places where maybe we could be a little more mature. Who doesn't? I'm scared of a lot of things, and making you hate me is at the top of the list. I know what I am, what I look like. I've done my part in working to accept myself, protect my energy. You're it for me, but I'm not delusional enough to think I'm it for you when you're this—" Curse. "—skittish when you aren't inebriated. I'm not going to let myself be selfish with you until I know it won't scare you. You have no idea what I want from you. All I know is that it *would* terrify you to find out." A self-deprecating laugh pours out in a brief exhale. He scrapes his fingers through his hair and tears his gaze off me. "Come on, Ellen. Your dirtiest wishes involve being told you're doing things right. You just want to be *right*, and what I want—in harrowing contrast—is incredibly wrong."

My face warms. "Well, why didn't you say so? Were you babying me?"

"Get that crap out of your head, Ellen. I have never and I will never *baby* you. I'm just smart enough to know you're timid and wary. It took me one night to think of you as my wife. I never recovered from the heartbreak of not seeing you again, of thinking I'd made a horrible mistake and made you despise me. I spent *five years* watching the door of Temptations, waiting for you. When I saw you again and discovered you didn't remember me at all, I thought I had a fresh chance for us to connect again like we did that first night. When you didn't pick me, I wanted to die." He rocks his jaw. "I moved into the apartment building where you lived before just so I could exist near the memory of you, whether you still lived there or not. Do you honestly think you wouldn't be scared if I were selfish with you too soon? Do you honestly expect me not to assume I'd overwhelm you and push you away? Do you sincerely believe I'd survive losing you based on something I could have done differently? I'd never forgive myself. And I don't think I'd be able to climb out of the grief."

Biting my lip, I drop my attention to the bare slice of dim cushion between us, separating us. "You said I could handle you."

"I did. Because you told me you could the night we met. Clearly, it's going to take time for you to realize it again."

"I don't need any more time. All my life I've fallen hard and fast into my relationships, then I get hurt because *normal people don't*, and I'm too much for them. But you aren't like them. You're like *me*." Clenching my fists, I look at him. "I love you. I want you. I want to know everything about you. I want to hear every detail that scares you and every detail that makes you happy. I want to protect you as fiercely as you're determined to take care of me. I want to marry you and be with you and tell my father off for getting me so wrong. I want to move in here with you. I want to make this place *our* home. Do you like it?"

Hayes stares at me, lips parted, eyes wide.

I lean against him, bridging the gap, and shove his chest. "Do you like it? We'll redecorate, of course. But it's nice, isn't it? It's big enough for you. Even the doorways. You won't have to duck anymore."

His brow furrows, and he mustn't like it. Well, that's fine. I have money. We'll…we'll find somewhere else, plan somewhere else as *home*. He's home.

Him.

So it'll be fine.

So long as it's with him.

"You…" His eyes close, and he drags one hand up to clasp mine against his chest. "What was that first thing you said?"

"I don't need any more time?"

His head shakes. "Following that."

I try to remember. And oh. Yeah. I think I know. "*Jeg elsker deg*."

His nostrils flare with an inhale, and when his eyes snap open, they're molten. His grip on my hand tightens. He mutters the thing I'm not supposed to say, then he wrestles me completely out of my blanket and throws me over his shoulder.

I blink down at the floor as he rises. "What are you... What *does* that mean?"

"I'll tell you after we're married," he mutters.

"Dad's planning on putting you through some kind of *prove you can handle my problematic daughter* gauntlet. So it could be years before we get married."

"Gonna be tomorrow."

"What?"

"There's no waiting period after applying for a marriage license in Georgia. I've been obsessively plotting this for five years, pudding." Careful of my head, he totes me out the front door, closing it behind him before adjusting my weight, like I'm a sack of potatoes.

"What happened to carrying me like a moth princess?" I protest. I'm in the dress for it and everything. I have a *crown* now, too. Even though I'm not wearing it. Thank goodness I'm not wearing it. It would have fallen off. What I am wearing is the little luna moth decoration. And my hair is probably all stuck in the wings.

"Moth princess carry is not conducive to punishment."

I grasp for a hold, try to turn myself and find his face, but I only get two fistfuls of his shirt and nothing else. "Why am I being punished? What did I do wrong?"

"You tried to break up with me after you promised you wouldn't. You assumed I could ever think anything bad about you. You ran off to cry alone instead of in my arms. You've made my family worry about you. You've made *me* worry about you."

With every accusation, my stomach knots, and I lose a little bit of my soul.

Hayes spanks me, and I gasp, forgetting the spiral. I writhe, grasping for his hair, anything. "What was that for!"

"To stop you from punishing yourself."

"What is *wrong* with you?"

He just shrugs, jostling me on his broad shoulder. "Listen, pudding. When we get back, everyone's going to be worried about you, ask what's wrong, make you feel awful that you've inconvenienced them. I'm skipping straight to dealing with the resulting guilt. Be a good girl and accept your fate."

"My fate?" I squeak.

"Yep." He slides me down onto his forearm and pauses a moment to fix the disarray of my hair around my luna moth. Once it's combed back neatly, he murmurs, "I'm going to take care of you, so don't spiral on me. I haven't even been able to give you your birthday present yet."

I search his eyes. "You got me a birthday present?"

"Of course I did."

"Why didn't you bring it?"

"Because, contrary to what you seem to believe, I am actually a little selfish." Gathering my fingers against his mouth, he kisses—then he throws me back over his shoulder and marches. With a huff, I brace my chin in my palm and accept my fate.

Like he said, the moment we're back, the energy that floods toward me—full of worry and *are you okay*s—is overwhelming, threatening to drag me down into wondering why in the world I overreacted when I know better.

Somehow, being a sack of potatoes makes the situation easier.

Sacks of potatoes can't respond. Sack of potato carriers can.

"She got overwhelmed and went to calm down. We overreacted by launching a witch hunt for her," Hayes mutters.

His mother snaps, "Why are you carrying her like

that?"

"Because she's not wearing shoes, and we just walked through the woods."

"There are nicer ways to carry a woman," Paisley protests and Liv agrees, right before my mother, my father, and Marit join us.

Mom shrieks, pinning me with wide eyes as she floats out of a side room and finds me in my true potato form.

I blink at her, and the smallest ache settles in my chest. She's believed all the things I've feared most about myself, just like Dad.

Speaking of Dad... His face turns red, and he demands, "You put my little girl down! What do you think you're doing?"

Hayes swings toward my parents and Marit, who seems the calmest person here. In response to what my father said, Hayes slides me down onto his forearm, and I close my eyes against the electric sensation of being moved directly against him for the second time in so many minutes. He does not, however, put me down, so I'm left sitting on his arm, a little flushed, bracing my hands against his shoulders, and breathing into his hair.

"What is the meaning of this?" my father demands.

"We're getting married tomorrow," Hayes says.

Hayes's mother gasps. Marit adds a curse to a shocked *really?* Liv and Paisley squeal.

My mother pales so violently, she teeters against my father for support. Fury twists into Dad's eyes, a distinct *we just talked about this* coming out in the way a vein in his forehead pops. Taking a deep breath, he makes sure my mother is all right before leaving her splayed against the archway that leads toward the kitchen. He marches up to Hayes.

"What is the meaning of *that*?"

"I fail to see how there are any hidden meanings to it. Ellen proposed to me a week ago. I said I'd talk to you first, today, and seeing as that's completed, we're getting married tomorrow."

A hundred things my father has never said to my face stream through his eyes. His gaze flashes between me and Hayes, sheer worry eating away at his usually bright demeanor.

I have calmed down.

I have processed.

It still hurts.

But I'm not illogical anymore. I am also not alone.

"I want to marry him, Dad."

He presses his lips together, slowly shaking his head. "Honey, you…you don't fully understand what that means."

"I do. Actually." Taking a breath, I ask, "Have you looked into any of the clients I've mentioned I edit for?"

His brow knits. "Of course."

"Not the ones you led to me. The ones I found after that. On my own."

"I don't understand, sweetheart."

"I'm not a child even if some of my mannerisms might seem childish. I can make my own decisions. I may not always be able to perfectly take care of myself, but I'm almost certain that applies to everyone." I turn back to Hayes, kiss his cheek, and move to slip from his arms. He lets me down, gently, pressed to his every muscle, and when my feet hit the floor, I feel short again, looking all the way up at him…but I do not feel small. Forcing a smile, I turn to my guests. "Thank you so much for coming to my birthday party. Please help yourselves to some leftovers and see yourselves out."

"Ellen," Mom whispers. "That's rude."

Is it? In that case… I add, "I am not intending to be rude. I have just suffered a stressful plot point in my life, and I would like to go home now, but before I can go home, I must account for my friends, whom I am very grateful for. I am exhausted, but it's not your fault. It's my father's. But maybe I shouldn't have said that."

"Ho—" Dad begins, but Hayes's grunt cuts him off, like a big bodyguard. I love him.

Marit hums. "Well, something happened. Can I take the top of the moth cake home, Ellen?"

"Absolutely. I wish there were leftovers of Liv's cake for me to take home."

Liv smiles, moving to swallow me in a hug. "I'll bake you a cake whenever you ask, and you've still got something sweet waiting for you, so don't be too disappointed." She winks at Hayes after she pulls away, and I guess that's one of those things I don't understand, but it doesn't matter. It doesn't matter. No one can be perfectly understood. The only thing the matters is the fact I *know* these are my people. They care about me. They worry about me. They accept me.

That's enough. That's more than enough.

That might be everything.

"Hayes, I'm ready to go home. Just let me get my purse and my presents."

He nods. "Do you need help? Everything should fit in the bed of my truck."

I shake my head. "I don't need everything tonight. Do you like my cottage?"

His gaze drifts toward the ceiling. "Yes."

"Do you want to live there?"

"In the middle of a forest on the edge of a field without light pollution where the doors are big enough I don't have to duck? Yeah."

I glance at my father. "Send me the paperwork and price."

His mouth drops open. "Ellen…what are you talking about? It's yours."

"It will be. I want the field, too. Hayes likes it."

Hayes nods. "Yeah, I do."

Dad shoots him a scowl, then clasps his hands together. "Honey, there's no way you can afford that. I understand that *apparently* a conversation I thought was private got back to you, but you have nothing to prove."

I face him, square my shoulders, and pretend I'm seen as a snake rather than a mouse. "You're right and wrong. I don't *have* to prove anything to you and Mom. I could ignore all of this. I could ignore it and take the cottage since I know you both love me and mean well and would give it to me. I could ignore it and house hunt elsewhere with my husband. I could ignore it and stay in my apartment for a while longer."

Marit, who is lingering, gasps and says, "*Oooh*," until her mother pinches her ear and drags her away while muttering in Norwegian.

I continue, "Ignoring things doesn't fix them. I want my cottage. Hayes likes it. You need to know that I am capable of standing on my own two feet, even if I can't for longer than ten minutes at a time. I will sit down for a while and get back up when I'm ready. I will manage the best I can."

"Baby, that property is worth close to a million dollars."

"And?" I ask.

Hayes curses, pins me with wide eyes. "Seriously?"

"My clients like me a lot. I picked them." My eyes narrow. "Then I made them fill out a *form*." I always knew form friendships were the way to go. *Always*. From now on, I'm trusting myself over the rest of this idiotic planet. "Lord Prince is a multi-millionaire. And he's not the only one who is adamant about paying me fairly in accordance with what he earns."

"Lord...what?" my father whispers, swiping his hand across his mouth.

"He writes fantasy romance," Hayes answers. "He started his career on a fanfiction-dominated site and became known for his username, so he kept it after a company picked him up."

I hum, eyeing Hayes curiously.

He lifts a shoulder. "I like research. And it's not exactly like your bookcases are locked."

True.

I need to get my things before I fall over. "It was my company that picked him up."

"Your company?" Mom asks, moving closer.

"I couldn't have lived here and not know how to start or run a business, right? I mostly use my company as a conduit in order to get the authors I want to edit for because I'm picky about who I want to work with and what stories interest me. I have other people running it. And some of my clients do prefer to go independent, but they are mine." I head toward the lounge so I can get my things, or the things I want to bring back with me for now. I return with my butterfly crown, my moth stuffed animal, and my painting. Also a bag of my favorite snacks, which my parents got me. I'm not trying to make them feel excluded. I'm upset with them, but I'm not trying to scorn them.

"Ready?" Hayes asks.

I nod, but Mom interrupts, "Wait. You're really getting married tomorrow?"

"Yes."

"No wedding?" She sets a hand against her chest. "We have friends who have wanted to see our little girl get married."

"They aren't my friends, but you're welcome to have a party on account of my nuptials. I'm happy to make a brief appearance and say my thank yous."

Mom's eyes get weepy.

I frown. "Don't look at me like that. You are an adult."

She sniffs, and a tear runs down her cheek. In the next moment, she throws her arms around Dad. "My baby's getting married!"

Dad soothes, patting her back, and I sway a little, beginning to rock my weight as a lightheaded sensation crawls up the back of my neck.

"Okay," Hayes murmurs. "That's it." Marching, he sweeps me up like a princess and turns to my parents. "Thank you for having me. I'm sorry about…this. Uh." He clears his throat. "I love Ellen, and I'll take good care of her, and we'll talk more later when she's not so exhausted." With that, he says, "Bye," and strides out the door.

EPILOGUE

♥ It's weird that I keep doing this, but it's not bad. Right?

Thirty minutes later

I don't say much the entire trip home. Mentally and physically, I've hit limits that leave me empty. I just want to think about diagramming sentences, so that's what I picture in my head as I sit curled up in the front seat, my left pinkie locked around Hayes's.

He's not said anything either, outside of when he captured my finger and told me my punishment for even thinking I was allowed to break my promise was to sit here, trapped.

It's very fitting, and very stupid, and I'm grateful for it, because now I don't have to berate myself about my panic response so much. If Hayes was holding back enjoying power plays, cool. Oddly calm about that. All things considered. And the main thing to consider is the fact he's a dominant built like a tank, of course.

Eh. I'm up for anything if it's with him.

"You good?" he asks, driving down our street and into our complex.

"Meh," I offer, intellectually.

"Are you too tired for my gift tonight? We can plan something tomorrow once you've had time to rest."

"Want."

"Speaking in fragments at me? That's not very Miss Editor of you."

I bury my face a little deeper into my fuzzy moth stuffed animal. "What is this? A high school paper?"

"Explain?"

I sigh, droning, "In school you're taught to maintain a level of literary professionalism. Young writers end up burdened by *rules* that have been decreed as standard, despite some of them lacking any real basis. Don't start lines with coordinating conjunctions. Don't use first or second person. Don't have fragments. In almost all other formats outside of scholastic assignment, there are numerous valid reasons to break these rules. And, sometimes, even in scholastic assignments you'll have a cool teacher who understands that good writing consists of a flow that requires that such menial obligations end up broken. Knowing actual rules is important because only then can you break them successfully. Knowing what 'rules' aren't actually rules but why they seem to be is also important in order to utilize the reasoning in your favor." I puff into my moth. "In the end, using *furthermore* instead of *and* to start a line just makes you sound like a pretentious nerd trying to meet their page count. Clarity and effectiveness will always trump insipid propriety." Glancing over my shoulder at his profile as he parks beside my car, I narrow my eyes. "Was my response unclear or ineffective?"

The smallest smile tips his lips. "No. I just wanted to hear your voice."

My cheeks heat well before he pulls my hand to his mouth and kisses my pinkie. Leaving me flushed, he exits, rounding to open the door for me. I do not get a choice on whether or not I am going to leave the car.

He unstraps my belt and drags me into his arms, shutting the door with his fine posterior, which—if this is the resolution to our rom-com—I have gone an entire book without mooning over.

Score.

Taking me up the stairs, he sets me in front of his door, unlocks it, then settles me neatly onto the couch. He takes everything except my stuffed moth away, setting my other gifts off in the corner by his weights. "Sit tight a second." He kisses my forehead.

"I love you," I say before he can pull away.

A breath sticks in his lungs, and he roughly murmurs, "Sit tight a second, *and* behave." After chastising me, he moves into the kitchen, and I hear his fridge open.

"Am I allowed to look? You know I don't like surprises."

"It's not really a surprise. You told me you wanted it." Glasses make pretty chiming noises.

I can't think of a single thing I have asked him for. I can buy whatever I want myself. Also, the fact he opened the fridge means it's either food or he got creative with hiding my gift, right? I've never asked him for food. Okay. I'm going to look.

I turn in time to see Hayes moving from the kitchen with a tray of elegant green-tinted flute glasses. My mouth falls open at the sight. As he moves closer, I see that the contents are layered, rows of cream broken up by pudding. There are five. Chocolate, vanilla, pistachio, something pink I'm betting my life is cherry, and butterscotch. The rims of each glass glitter with sugar. Laying at the base of all five is a slender silver spoon.

Snapping my mouth shut, I attempt to regain the moisture against my tongue. I've wanted this forever, distinctly, but I have never told anyone. Never.

Hayes sits beside me, setting the tray on the table that is his lap. Lifting the perfect spoon, he eyes me and rests it against his lips. "What?" he murmurs, knowing *what*.

I assemble the pieces and squish my moth stuffed animal. "I told you my secret when I was drunk."

"It was the most adorable and innocent little desire in the entire—" He curses. "—world." His attention falls on the assortment. "I asked Liv to teach me how to make them."

My mouth drops open again. "You made them? From *scratch*?"

"Obviously. Instant pudding mixes are like fifty cents. That's pathetic. I had to put at least a modicum of effort into this." His voice gets all grumbly, almost angry, laced in vendetta. "It's literally the easiest request on the planet. I don't think you understand how *painfully and agonizingly* simple you are to please."

I don't think he understands how much I might be on the verge of tears. How will I ever love him enough to compare to his memorizing every moment of a night I don't even remember? If I know anything about myself, I was babbling non-stop, probably nervous because he's so scary. But he listened. To everything.

He listened.

If he let on that he was listening to me that night, I probably fell in love with him right then and there.

"Which first?" he asks, and his breath fogs the spoon, making me think that I want his lips first. Him first and last. He eyes me for a long moment, then he says, "Cherry? My favorite."

I'm glad I know that. I want to know everything.

He scoops a bite of the cherry and holds it out for me.

I look between it and his heated eyes, blushing harder with every second that passes. "You're going to feed me?"

"Find out."

That's not cryptic at all. I open my mouth all the same, and he lets me take the bite. It's a blast of sweetness, tartness, cherry red. It's so good I think I start crying. No other reason.

Hayes prepares another bite and wipes my cheek with his thumb as he lines it up with my lips.

"Do you want some? I don't think I'll be able to have it all tonight."

"Mhm," he rumbles.

I accept the bite, and he grips my chin, drawing my face toward him. Before I have a chance to understand what's happening or even *swallow*, he steals a taste, pulls back, licks his lips.

I die.

I just die.

What was that? Can I have another? Forever?

My breaths get a little panicked, as though they're trying to match the hammering beat of my heart.

"Scared yet, pudding?" he murmurs as he preps another bite.

"No," I whisper, enraptured. "I can handle you."

He takes a bite, the small smile on his lips everything I have ever wanted, everything I had no idea how to find. Moving the tray to the floor beside the armrest, he pats his lap and murmurs, "That's right. You can."

Setting my moth aside, I climb on top of him and frame his cheeks with my fingers. They're rough with stubble. I knew they would be. Kissing his forehead, I say, "Always."

"I love you, Ellen."

"*Jeg elsker deg*, Hayes."

EXTENDED EPILOGUE

♥ Any guy can be a baby girl. It takes a real man to be a wife.

One year and a few months later

My wife terrifies me.

I have never met another person who puts fear into my bones like her. I have no idea what to say. *I love you* comes to mind. Other choice phrases I translated for her on our wedding night…also come to mind. I'm literally never going to recover from the fact *that* phrase turned into our *I want to go home and ravish you* code. It wouldn't be so bad. Except she sometimes forgets it's an actual language with an actual meaning.

So she may have said it to me when she was tired of being with my family one day.

Out loud.

Across the living room.

In front of my *mamma*.

Hayes, jeg vil k—

"You hate it," Ellen says insincerely as she puts another moth on me—this time an imperial, on my shoulder. I think there's a luna on my head. I hope they don't lay eggs in my hair.

Flexing my fingers, I murmur, "I am…processing…it." Because *it*?

Faen.

It is an observatory. In the backyard. Our backyard. Our

field.

What kind of crazy beautiful girl constructs an observatory for her husband in their backyard for his birthday? At least now I know why she told me I wasn't allowed to stargaze in the field these past few months on account of her "constructing a moth garden." Cheeky. The *moth garden* behind her is a collection of young trees littered throughout with flowers. Screens and lights are set up to attract the creatures she keeps retrieving and covering me with.

I accepted her request and—foolishly—took my stargazing to her parents' front yard instead. Her father can almost point out five constellations on his own now. And he's almost completely forgiven me for stealing his daughter away with the intent to, well, ravish her instead of just babysit her.

It would be nice if he got over himself.

Ellen deserves to be ravished.

Constantly.

She flutters back to her moths as soon as another imperial shows up, and I really should thank Liv for making whatever this lacy goddess sheer silk *mess* floating around her is. She's ethereal, made more beautiful with every smile and fearless action as she learns—more and more each day—to just *be herself.*

Another moth joins the party in my hair, and I sigh. "You're frightening, pudding."

"Thank you." She gets that luna off my head and puts it like a barrette above her ear.

"And adorable." An actual moth princess. No question about it. She walked out of one of the fantasy stories she edits. She's fact checking those things from experience.

Faen, I love her.

She smiles, stealing my breath, and her cheeks heat

beneath the light of the moon, Draco, Corona Borealis, Hercules, and Serpens. Notably. There are other constellations as well, of course. Every star in the sky no doubt vies for this girl's attention.

"Do you want to see inside?" she asks.

I very much want to see inside my observatory; however, the chances are high I'll want to spend all night out here. I can't do that. Releasing a heavy sigh, I mutter, "I need to feed you first."

"You take your career very seriously."

My *career*. Right. That's what she likes to call the fact I became a house husband shortly after we got married, we moved to our cottage, and I was grumpy on account of having to commute to Temptations for math.

This precious creature looked me in the eye and asked why I didn't just let her support us.

We argued—in accordance with procedure, which dictates that we fill out a very detailed little form of our grievances and the motivations behind our grievances, then assess the results together.

It boiled down to *I'm the man, manly, man, man, man* and she countered all that nonsense with *I hate gender roles, they're stupid, don't be stupid, make me dinner and play outside and let Liv and Marit have the bar already.*

Once I got my head out of the toxic masculinity, I talked to my sisters, and they gladly dropped their minimum wage jobs in favor of taking over. Together, they evolved Temptations Lounge into a pub, which means it serves alcohol alongside Liv's food while displaying Marit's art and playing her music.

Also.

Vince and Marit enemied-to-lovered themselves. Which was...weird to watch. Weirder still when Ellen dictated out the course of events nearly to the day they'd happen.

Classic enemies to lovers, brother's best friend romance, she said, casually, while typing away on her work and nibbling on the snack I brought her. *Sorry, Hayes. With that attitude, your role is the antagonist. Play it well, please. I need to finish this now, so be gone.*

Yes, they got trapped in a closet.

Yes, I experienced…*character growth*.

I don't know what my life is anymore.

Bliss, probably.

Bliss.

Ellen grabs my arm and steps up on her toes, which are thankfully cloaked in new shoes. I bought her new shoes. And I fought to get her out of the old ones before they melted off her feet. My job is to do the shopping and the cleaning and the feeding. Her job is to make the money, not build me an observatory. But she spoils me in every way she can find.

I bend myself so she can reach my face, mumbling, "Hm?"

"I ordered pizza," she whispers. "It's inside."

Have I mentioned that Ellen Little-Sallow scares me to my core yet? Because. Yeah. Her outlines are so precise they're practically written in the stars.

I whisper *I love you* in Norwegian, and she giggles, sunshine and stardust and raging, lovely things. Grasping my hand, she tugs me along to the door and flicks on a string of dim fairy lights she strung around. I really shouldn't have assumed this place would be an empty chasm with a central stand for the telescope. That's not Ellen's style.

It's tiered. Up the steps in front of me, the area plateaus into wooden floors scattered with desks of solar models and star charts. The deck with a telescope bigger than me centers that area, but down the steps, carpet washes in front of a cozy sectional sofa. A pizza box, bottle of fake wine, and a basket of cherries sit on the small glass table in front.

Faen. I really am spoiled rotten.

Ellen takes tedious care in freeing all the moths she covered me with before she closes the door behind us and starts down the steps.

She slips.

But of course she does.

Panic wells in her eyes as though rom-com magic doesn't assault us every other day. With a sigh, I tug her back to safety in my arms and brace a hold on the railing. "You're okay," I murmur.

Taking a breath, she nods, hands planted against my chest. "The rom-com gods are angry that we still haven't third-act broken up. We must remain vigilant."

Alternatively, she could accept the fact that she might be the smallest bit clumsy and have a tiny bit of bad luck. There's a reason I keep lock-picking sets available. The universe is determined to trap me in small spaces with her. *Still.* It's happened almost once a month like some kind of cosmic exposure behavioral therapy. I'm almost over my claustrophobia. I'm almost grateful the rom-com gods are benevolent enough to never get me locked anywhere without the literal sun to walk me through the situation like magical, crazy, weird things are just par for the course in life.

Composing herself, Ellen tries to pull away and move down the stairs, but I don't let her. I whisper that I love her in her ear again, and she melts a little.

"I love you, too," she says, beautiful hazel eyes fixed on mine, unafraid, entire galaxies of color.

I smile, stroke a finger down her cheek, across her most prominent freckle. She's beautiful. Her body is beautiful. Her every little mark is a new constellation for me to explore. And I could spend decades studying each. I plan to.

"What kind of a wife gives her husband a building for his birthday?"

"A weird one?" she queries, and there's no self-deprecation in her claim. Not anymore. I've gotten her to own up to it, bit by bit.

"That's right. The weirdest." I kiss her nose, and her eyes close. She turns liquid in my arms. I love this. All of this. I don't even know how to wrap my mind around it. But, then again, I never have.

I've been trying to catch my breath long enough to process *her* from the first moment this perfect, precious girl let me take her home, nuzzled herself into my heart, and refused to let go.

Prying myself out of her arms was the hardest thing I ever did, once.

Now, I don't ever have to again.

I found what I wasn't looking for, and it's been an unending story from the moment seeing her turned the first page. No matter how weird, I wouldn't change a chapter.

Or a line.

Or a word.

After all, people are like books. Editing the ones that aren't right for you is a waste of time. Loving the ones that speak to your soul…well…those make all the difference in —

The End.

But Wait… There's More.

You are hereby invited to join Moth Club and receive a fuzzy friend sticker each month!

P.S. Message Laurel to let her know you're coming from *How to Find Love When You're Weird*, and she'll send you an exclusive Moth Princess sticker for your first month.

And Even...More?

Keep reading for an unedited sneak peek of *How to Make Your Enemy Fall for You*!

Melanie, yes *The* Melanie Richards, has an awful case of rom-com-itis. Her self-help books are a coping mechanism for the real life experiences she faces constantly.

Her checkered past has turned her off to two things—love and men. Unfortunately, her editor is a man she has more history with than she wants to admit. And his interest goes well past professional.

Desmond is constantly looming; correcting her, which is his job; teasing her, which isn't his job; and satisfying his vampiric thirst for amusement with that lazy smirk of his, which should be no one's job. Melanie's rom-com experience tells her that the way to make her enemy go away is simple—cast him as the lead in her life.

Once she falls, he'll disappear.

So maybe this time she'll work on making *him fall first* then take her sweet revenge as *the one who leaves*. Or maybe Desmond will do what he's infuriatingly best at and edit that ending, too.

Reader Expectations

Heat Level: Fade-to-black, innuendos, one double hockey stick curse and one beaver needed a house and—it is unfortunate—but a bull had to go to the bathroom, sensual description, mentions of sex, non-sexual immodesty also known as "why can't male leads keep a hold of their shirts?"

Notable Tropes: Enemies to lovers, academic rivals, forced proximity, office romance, flashbacks, guy falls first, touch her and may the ancients have mercy on your pathetic worm-eaten soul

Triggers: Physically and mentally abusive ex-relationship, flashbacks, on-page righteous violence (with blood), men

Style: First person present, single POV (with guest speaker)

Stress Level: Potentially high, read that author's note

Ending: HEA

PROLOGUE

♥ Desmond Micheal(s) is a stupid butt.

When I wake up, there is a notification on my phone that indicates I have an email. Reluctantly, and fully aware of the breath I'm holding, I check it.

Today, 5:26 a.m.
FROM: desmond.micheal@iap.com
TO: watermelanieon@gmail.com
SUBJECT: Deadline

Gentle reminder that if you ignore this, I know where you live, and have known, for twenty years. ♥

I can't keep pushing back the deadline for your next draft. If you need more time to finish, send me whatever you currently have, and we'll work from there.

That is, of course, if you currently have anything. I'll, personally, understand if you don't. But Ink&Paper Publishing might not. So some drastic measures may need to be taken.

This is your final warning, bunny. U•w•U
DM

My eye twitches as I comb my fingers back through the tangled mass of black curls haloing my pale cheeks. I've not even left the warm safety of my bed yet. Is this harassment? Abuse?

Probably.

Definitely.

Great. I thought that chapter of my life ended when I got divorced.

Huffing, I collapse against my pillow, prop my phone on my stomach, and stamp out a reply.

Today, 9:48 a.m.
FROM: watermelanieon@gmail.com
TO: desmond.micheal@iap.com
SUBJECT: Re: Deadline

Micheals.
First of all, who wakes up at five in the morning? Second of all, it's rude to use my personal email for business-related inquires (so unprofesional, you should be ashamed of yourself). Third of all, have you ever seen a miniature dachshund sitting while all stretched out? Their legs are so short it barely looks like their little bums are on the ground.

Stop calling me "bunny."
Melanie

P.S. What in the name of all things good in this world is "U•w•U"?

CutestThingI'veEverSeenAndDesmondMichealsIsAStupidButt.png Attached

I barely get a moment to contemplate going back to sleep when my phone buzzes with Desmond's reply.

Today, 9:50 a.m.
FROM: desmond.micheal@iap.com

TO: watermelanieon@gmail.com
SUBJECT: Re: Deadline

It's a lop-eared bunny, bunny. Now it's winking at you.
UvwU

1) Productive people wake up early. 2) I imagine you've logged out of your business email, considering silence has met my last five inquires. (You lost an "s" in "unprofessional," and I think it ended up at the end of my last name. Again. Silly mistake. No hard feelings.) 3) I have been wondering for a while now... Do you have a collection of animal pictures titled with insults? Genuinely curious about where your energy has gone these past months.

Since it hasn't gone to writing.

Which is a pity.

You know you're my favorite author.
DM

I *have* logged out of my business email. I do not appreciate his calling me out on that fact.

Today, 10:03 a.m.
FROM: watermelanieon@gmail.com
TO: desmond.micheal@iap.com
SUBJECT: Re: Deadline

Calling me "bunny" and winking at me is sexual harassment. I'm taking screenshots. Expect HR to be in touch with you soon.

Melanie

TinyCatAndDesmondMichealsIsDumb.png Attached
YawningPuppyAndDesmondMichealsIsANarcissist.png Attached
BabyBirdAndDesmondMichealsShouldGoBackToJupiter.png Attached

Today, 10:05 a.m.
FROM: desmond.micheal@iap.com
TO: watermelanieon@gmail.com
SUBJECT: Re: Deadline

Wyatt and I were planning to get drinks tonight. I guess a harassment claim will give us something interesting to talk about.

Mention of my extensive space travel aside, I take it there's no draft?
DM

Today, 10:06 a.m.
FROM: watermelanieon@gmail.com
TO: desmond.micheal@iap.com
SUBJECT: Re: Deadline

IttyBittyPigWhoIsRelatedToDesmondMicheals.png Attached

Today, 10:07 a.m.
FROM: desmond.micheal@iap.com
TO: watermelanieon@gmail.com
SUBJECT: Re: Deadline

Come into the office with your laptop. I have a cubicle prepared just for you.
DM

Blinking at the email, I stare until the words cease to be recognizable, then I jerk out of the app and go to my contacts. The phone rings a singular time as I cross my arms against my chest and burrow deeper into my nice warm bed, where—mind you—*all* of my writing is accomplished. Not even all of my *best* writing. Just, *all* of it. Period. No exceptions.

If it does not occur here, it does not occur.

"You've reached Desmond Micheal, editor at Ink&Paper Publishing. How can I help you today?"

"I called your personal number, idiot."

"So you did. My mistake, Richards. I've been so consumed with work this morning." He sighs, despondent. "If only you could say the same." Humor taints Desmond's silky smooth voice, and I picture him reclining in a corner office's obnoxiously large leather chair. Not that I've ever seen his office. Even though I&P is based fifteen minutes away, I avoid the office on account of Desmond's existence.

My teeth grit. "What do you mean *bring my laptop to the office*?"

"Hm?" Sheer bewildered innocence saturates his tone. "It's been months since your original deadline for the next book in your series. I assumed you needed a babysitter."

"A babysitter?" I hiss, fiddling aggressively with a persistent knot in my hair.

"Someone who can motivate you to sit down and meet your word counts. It appears you're much too distracted by baby animals at home. Hence, I've created a space for you here. You're welcome."

"They are my emotional support baby animals, and I cannot thrive in an environment without them," I snap.

"Heh."

The sound makes me flinch, and I swallow hard.

"Listen," he murmurs, conversationally lethal, "this

company pays you to write. You're under contract to complete one more book in this series. Failing to do so prior to your agreed-upon deadline could have gotten messy, but I pulled some strings. And now? Now I'm pulling a few more. You know the repercussions as well as I do."

I chill through. I've already been paid my advance. Even attempting to break the contract now would mean having to pay it back. *All* of it. The double-edged sword to being popular is the fact my advance was a *very hefty sum*.

Dropping the severity, Desmond says, "I don't mean to pressure you, but it comes with the territory. What's the problem, Richards? All through school, the teachers could barely drag you away from your notebooks. You submitted novels for short story assignments. Research papers in lieu of essays. Writing has never been a problem before."

Before.

Before is exactly the thing. Writing wasn't a problem *before* I learned the terrible truth about my life.

Before grumpy bosses, and fake dating, and childhood crushes, and *getting married* to the single dad next door…

Softer, Desmond says, "Does this have anything to do wi—"

"It has nothing to do with anything you could possibly begin to understand, Micheals."

"Then…"

I suck in a breath. "I can't come into the office. I do not go outside anymore. It is…*dangerous*."

A touch of whimsy lightens his voice. "Oh?"

"*Oh?*" I mock, eyes rolling as I slouch flat under my covers. "I could spend hours explaining it to you, but you wouldn't get it if you haven't already picked up on it in my books."

"Why don't you spend hours explaining it in text? Then I'll edit those words. And we'll be out of the woods."

He sounds just so *pleasant*. But I know better. I have

always known better with Desmond Micheal.

Some guys are the friends, the kind strangers, the sunshiney idiots, the heroes and princes; other guys are the bullies, the rivals, the *enemies and villains*. Desmond—despite his blond hair and moss green eyes—falls squarely within the latter group.

I've done my rodeos with the former, so I can confirm that *neither side* contains the *good guys*. Simply put, *good guys* exist solely in fiction.

I mutter, "Are you *sure* you want to welcome *me* into your place of employment?"

"It's basically high school. It'll be just like old times."

"You teased me. Every day."

He sighs, merry. "Did I? Lovely memories."

Someone else starts talking to him, and his response comes in complete deadpan, void of character and humor. The moment the other person is gone, teasing reenters the chat, and he says, "Anywho. You have two hours to get here. Or I'm coming to pick you up."

"I don't live with my mother anymore, Micheals. I have a gate. And a security guard."

He rattles off my gate pin before noting, fondly, "How is Oliver?"

Oliver, my neighborhood's security guard, is doing *great*. His youngest just graduated kindergarten. And he only *occasionally* makes me want to punch him in the face when he mentions how he'd retire if he wouldn't be *stuck at home with his wife all day*, ha ha ha. Like it's a joke. To spend time with the person he married. The person he claimed to love more than anyone else in the world.

Men are filth.

All of them.

No exceptions.

"If you keep your face like that, you'll get wrinkles," Desmond remarks, which makes me scowl harder.

"I am allowed to get wrinkles if I want."

"And yet you're so much prettier when you smile."

I'm going to castrate him. For sport.

"Well, I have work to do, so I'll see you in a few hours, one way or another. Hopefully by then you'll have gotten imagining my disembowelment out of your system."

"Don't count on it," I snip.

He chuckles. "Bye, bunny."

"Don't call m—" The line cuts off.

CHAPTER 1

> ♥ Men are worse than pond scum, because even pond scum serves a purpose.

Two hours later

By some miracle, I survive my commute to the Ink&Paper Publishing House without running into any plot points. Or, rather, without running into any *majorly apparent* plot points. One can never be too careful. Sometimes a commute is the literal vehicle *to* an *event*, thus it becomes an element of plot. Even though I hate Bearston City, North Carolina traffic, I drove, so at least there were no opportunities for the bus to stop suddenly and send me into the lap of some secret prince.

Again.

That was almost an interesting summer.

I park in the lot outside the three-story mid-century modern office building that sits on the only swathe of lush grass this side of a four-lane highway. The slanted, sleek white roofs complement the vertical rust-orange panels that frame entire walls of windows, and the building stands out in stark contrast to its gray, blocky neighbors. Taking in a deep breath, I pull my laptop case onto my lap, scan the vacant sidewalk, and take my chances with *the outside*.

Cool air combats summer heat when I push into the lustrous white lobby. Shelves displaying company work—from women's fiction through to women's self-help—serve as the sole decorations in the minimalistic space. The brightest covers are the only splashes of color against ashen floors, white walls, and pearly furniture.

The receptionist—a woman whose fire orange pantsuit is also doing its duty of drawing color into the sterile environment—bounces up in her seat, grinning hopelessly at me as I pathfind toward her. My short heels click, leaving ominous echos in my wake.

Blue eyes flash above bright white teeth, and serious dimples peek out when I stop in front of her desk. "Ms. Richards?" She stands and offers me a manicured hand. "It's such an honor to meet you. My name's Sienna. I read *How to Not Be Alone on Christmas* first last year because I was horribly depressed. It changed my life, and then I couldn't put the others down. Huge fan."

"Lovely to meet you." Taking her hand, I try not to wince at the fact this woman has read *all* of my books. The descent into madness comes clear—*if* you read them in the order I wrote them. Thankfully, seeing as they were not published in order, I pretend it's harder to tell.

Lifting her left hand, Sienna points at an engagement ring, and her eyes sparkle. "Never be alone on Christmas again, right?" Crystal laughter spills out of her slight frame. "Don't worry. He's an absolute book boyfriend, too."

My stomach knots, filling with dread, but I let my smile remain plastered across my face. Inside, I want to scream that *there's no such thing* as a *book boyfriend* in real life. I want to warn her to run, if she still can. If it's not too late.

But I don't.

I can't.

It's not very *on brand* of me.

Honestly, it's thanks to the miracle of an amazing PR team and a gang of supporting readers that my divorce didn't ruin my budding career two years ago.

Who knows what people would think if they knew that my divorce wasn't the first of my failures, if they knew that *every* book came from a disastrous experience. Happily-ever-after author Melanie Richards failed in attaining her own. Again. And again. And again. And when she finally managed to get married?

Well.

That relationship was worse than all the rest.

Women deserve better than what reality can offer.

And...yet...I can't stop myself from wanting the best for this stranger.

Bracing my arm against the desk and slinging my laptop bag over my shoulder, I ask, "He has a stable job?"

Sienna straightens to attention, tiny and blindingly optimistic. "Yes'm."

"He's nice to his mother and sisters and other women without being *too* nice to them, of course?"

"He's a devoted *angel*." She swoons.

"He opens doors for you, stands on the traffic-side whenever you're walking together, refrains from crass language directed at you or about you, never raises his voice, never shuts off communication, never gaslights or isolates you from your friends or family?"

She bobbles along, nodding.

Jutting a lip, I hum and pinch my chin.

"I made him read *How to Turn Your Husband into Your Book Boyfriend* in preparation for our wedding, so he knows my expectations completely as well as what will happen if he doesn't live up to them. Mr. Darcy is, and always will be, waiting. Like you say—" She lifts a finger and recites, "'Never let your husband forget that you've settled. Should they fail to live up to your favorite archetype, there are entire shelves ready to replace him.'"

A slight bout of nausea hits me, but I swallow it down. I'm not supposed to feel *bad* when the lesser gender witnesses the *men suck* fest that is the second to last book I was able to write, the first published book in my series, the one that spurred my career into motion even while my personal life fell apart. Men deserve to be called out on their BS. It's not like they have *feelings*. If they did, maybe they'd take better care of ours.

Tossing my dark curls, I sniff. "Very good."

Sienna's blue eyes shine, and she clasps her hands together. Before she can get another word in, however, I point at her and say, "*Never* accept anything less than you deserve. No matter what." Love is a weapon. The sharpest one. And its cuts don't go away, because it injures and scars the very soul.

Sienna salutes me. "Absolutely." Plopping back into her seat, orange pantsuit squeaking, she scoots into her desk and looks at the computer. "Gah. Look at me, fangirling away. You probably have an appointment of some sort, right? It must be important. To my knowledge, you never come by the office."

I open my mouth, but I don't get the luxury of speaking a word.

"Richards." The *reason* I shun the office like the plague calls my name from the second floor.

My gaze follows the glass steps up, up, up to the clear-panel balustrade above the receptionist bay. None other than *the* Desmond Micheal leans against the ash gray railing and looks down on me. A glint of strange interest ignites his pale green eyes as ours meet.

I had *so* enjoyed avoiding him.

A quiet gasp fills Sienna's lungs, and heat slashes across her cheeks after she's turned to look up at the prowling creature.

Nausea might be a lingering affliction related to my presence here, now that I think about it. If I manage to make it through this *event* without vomiting, the comedy deities that run my life will have been merciful.

The comedy deities that run my life are *never* merciful. In fact, they're cruel.

My expression hardens, and the corner of Desmond's mouth curls in what could almost be a tender smile—if malevolent *teasing* didn't so thoroughly saturate it.

Sienna practically swoons again.

Warning drums pound in my skull.

Rolling back my shoulders, I stride to the steps and let the reverberation of my heels mark in time with the thunder. Clichés fill my mind. *So, we meet again*s and the like prepare me for the encounter as though I'm the suave, femme fatale lead in a serious documentary about breaking glass ceilings and demanding equal rights.

Sadly, I made a rookie mistake in my efforts to dress like I haven't been eating ice cream and chocolate, sleeping in, and watching *Pride and Prejudice* twice a day ever since the aftermath of my divorce calmed down.

First rule of being me—never wear anything that can facilitate a malfunction of *any* kind. This includes: skirts without shorts, low-cut shirts, bathing suits, dresses with zippers, and, yes, *half-inch heels*.

On the final step, I trip, suck in a hard breath, and launch toward the rough carpeting that lines the upper hall. A slew of curses streak through my head as I squeeze my eyes shut and brace for impact.

Falling over nothing.

Getting hurt.

Some people call it *bad luck*. I know better.

Pain is comedy. This is *comedy*. And now that I know better than to think I'm living in a *romantic* comedy, I understand that sometimes—when you fall—nobody catches you. But everyone still laughs.

Moments before I'm certainly about to face the worst rug burn my face has ever seen, hands brace my shoulders, steady me, and I land solidly against a firm chest.

Dragging my attention up, I locate…*Desmond's stupid face*.

Lips rolled into his mouth, he looks down at me. Laughter vibrates in him, contained, until the first explosion leaves in a single burst. "You haven't changed a bit, Richards."

"Shut up!" I swat.

He twists our bodies, so when I push him and jerk back, I don't go tumbling down the stairs. Unfairly, neither does he. Grinning, he cocks his hip against the corner railing and folds his arms as though he'd planned the motion entirely on his own and my shoving him had nothing to do with it.

He takes me in, all cool regard and devilishly attractive smiles. Against my will, my heart rate picks up.

Desmond Micheal goes beyond attractive. Everyone knows it—even Sienna who's engaged but hasn't been able to yank her wide-eyed gaze off him for even a moment since he made his presence known. Mouth hanging open, she lifts her phone and snaps a picture, squeaking when the shutter sound draws Desmond's attention.

Her soul leaves her body as she plops into her seat and pretends she didn't just photograph him.

He hardly pays it another second of mind, like having his picture taken without advance notice happens to him constantly.

I bet it does. Arrogant prick.

My jaw locks.

Desmond's brows draw together, the picture of despondent offense. "Richards, this is our place of employment. You shouldn't contemplate pushing me down the stairs."

"For your information, I am *past* contemplation. I already tried to." I clench my free fist in front of my chest and let my eyes narrow. "I just need to succeed."

Cool beauty seeps from every last one of his perfectly chiseled man pores as he cocks his head and smiles fondly. "Still upset I made valedictorian over you?"

My eyes twitches.

Expression unchanging, he pushes off the railing and leans into my personal bubble. "Or are you still upset that I turned down the position so you could have it?"

I cannot stop myself, and my fist is already clenched, so I swing.

He dodges back, letting his lips form a perfectly irritating O. Sincerely, he says, "That's not ladylike."

Unfettered rage boils in the pit of my stomach. "I'm leaving!" I shout and march past him.

But.

Again.

Heels. Stairs. *Me*.

My foot skids on the first glass step, and it takes about five slow-motion seconds for disaster to emanate. Chest going light, I watch my entire, pitiful life flash before my eyes. Then, in a horrific twist of fate, Desmond grabs my fist and twirls me away from danger, into his arms, like this is some foolish dance I never learned the steps to. He knows them perfectly.

Clamped to his body, I want to hit him again.

Pure delight glimmers in his eyes and in the calm smile resting on his lips. Sensually, he leans ever closer and whispers, "You are a hazard to society, bunny."

Heat erupts in my cheeks, but he's already relinquished his hold on everything but my hand as he tugs me—tripping—down the hall and toward the office space where he and the rest of the team works.

"Your office is right next to mine," he notes, plowing into the room. Ignoring the inexplicable onslaught of cheers, Desmond pulls me past a slew of desks and work spaces spread across the vast tile floor. Glass offices frame the central room, any open blinds presenting neat, sanctioned-off areas with important people in suits not unlike the one Desmond is wearing.

Now that I think about it. Desmond is in a suit. And not heels. He gets to look nice *without* heels. My deep-seated hatred for him kindles hotter, and I'm scowling by the time he's drawn me into a vacant office. The big windows dead ahead look over the city, letting sunshine pour onto full shelves of books and an empty desk. In a single smooth motion, he's taken my laptop bag, sat me down, and set it in front of me. "Now then," he comments, hands relaxing on my shoulders, "work."

I fold my arms and glare up at him. "You said *cubicle*."

"Did I?"

My gaze cuts toward the slew of desks beyond this *whole dang office*, and there's not a cubicle in sight. There are, however, a dozen pairs of eyes.

I'm an exhibit. In a zoo.

At least they've stopped clapping? Do they all know I'm here because I need to be *babysat*? What kinds of publishing companies even accommodate this sort of thing? I know I make good money for Ink&Paper, but one more book seriously can't be worth this much effort. Wouldn't it be easier for them to demand their advance back? Scandal sells just as well as anything else. I learned that several years ago.

Exactly how much pull does Desmond have here?

And why didn't I challenge him to go through with his threat by staying home? It's not like he could have honestly picked me and my computer up and dragged me here against my will.

"Hey. Bunny."

I flinch, and the tempering disdain reignites as I toss a frown at the man who thinks he's allowed to sit me down and tell me what to do.

He leans forward, blocking my view of the rest of the office. A lock of blond hair slips across his forehead, and his needless handsomeness compels me to fix it.

I don't.

"You can do this," he says.

"Don't patronize me." Scooting in, away from him, I tug my laptop out of the bag and set up my computer. "The sooner I finish the book, the sooner I can go back home, right?"

"That's the spirit."

I growl at him like I'm the male lead in a

grumpy/sunshine.

He tuts. "Careful. You still have an image to uphold."

Sitting very straight, I open my laptop and cross my ankles. "I'm well aware of my image, Micheals. It has no patience for men who are not worth a woman's time. I suggest you concern yourself more with how my attitude toward you will affect *your* image. If this is like high school, we're at the same cafeteria lunch table now."

"If memory serves, we both normally ate lunch in the English classroom with Reagan."

Humming, I ignore that tidbit, open a fresh document, and create my first chapter headline. "'Entitled men should stay in their lane.' Chapter one…making the jerks in your life mind their beeswax."

Shaking his head, Desmond slips his hands into his pockets and sighs. "I don't know what I'll do if you write me another love letter, Richards."

"For the last time. *How to Destroy Your Lifelong Bully* was *not* a love letter, and you need some serious therapy. As was stated in that book. *Several* times."

"Your books are my therapy."

My lips pinch, and I type an amendment to my disclaimer.

Warning: the following content is not a substitute for mental health care. The author strongly urges you to seek profesional help.

Desmond's fingers skim my shoulder-length curls, and he murmurs, "You missed the second 's' in 'professional' again."

"*Can it, Micheals.*"

With a laugh, he leaves me in something akin to strained peace.

Available Now

Also by Camilla Evergreen

Historical Romance
Untempered

Contemporary Romance
Unspoken
When Summer Flowers Bloom

Could Have Been Sweet Rom-com Series
Could Have Been Us
Could Have Been Closer
Could Have Been Romantic
Could Have Been Real

How to Rom-com Series
How to Turn Your Husband into Your Book Boyfriend
How to Fake Date Your Grumpy Boss
How to Not Be Alone on Christmas
How to Marry Your Single Dad Neighbor
How to Destroy Your Lifelong Bully
How to Confess to Your Childhood Best Friend
How to Find Love When You're Weird
How to Make Your Enemy Fall for You

Printed in Great Britain
by Amazon